INFESTATION

AILEEN ERIN

INK MONSTER
AUSTIN, TX

INK MONSTER

First Published by Ink Monster LLC in 2024

Ink Monster LLC
100 Commons Road, Suite 7-303
Dripping Springs, TX 78620
www.aileenerin.com

ISBN 9781955974233

Cover by Cheri @ Ink Monster

Also by Aileen Erin

The Complete Alpha Girls Series

Becoming Alpha

Avoiding Alpha

Alpha Divided

Bruja

Alpha Unleashed

Shattered Pack

Being Alpha

Lunar Court

Alpha Erased

The Days of Iron and Clay

Invocation

Infestation

The Aunare Chronicles

Off Planet

Off Balance

In Command

On Mission

On Destiny

The Shadow Ravens Series

Cipher

For anyone needing a little light in the dark.

2 Cor 4:6

CHAPTER ONE

PHOENIX

THE NIGHT WAS calm and quiet. There was no more screaming. Or demons. Or danger. And yet, I couldn't get my body to relax.

Samantha was fine—a sleeping-like-the-dead kind of fine. I'd checked on her thirty minutes ago, and she was definitely okay. Her room? That was a mess. Destroyed by an invisible monster—also known as her father. I wasn't sure how it was possible a demon was her father, but I wanted the chance to find out her whole story.

And I would get that chance. Because if Sam was okay, then I should be okay, too. But I wasn't.

I wasn't fucking okay *at all.*

My heart was still pounding in my chest, and it felt as if my ears were still ringing from the scramble to save Sam.

I was sitting on Sam and Ana's porch in Sam's bright red Adirondack chair. It was late—so late that it was almost morning. But my mind just kept spinning. I'd had one insane experience with Sam six years ago, and only reconnected with her yesterday. Today had been…

I didn't have words for it.

What the hell just happened?

A cold breeze brushed against my face, and I zipped up my hoodie, popping the hood over my head. The Adirondack chair was stiff against my back, and the winter night had a bit of a chill to it, but I wasn't ready to go inside. Not yet. I needed room to breathe, and I had a feeling Ana—Sam's mom—needed the same. She was moving around in the kitchen. I could hear pans rattling and soft noises as she made something, but I couldn't make myself get up to ask if she needed any help. I needed *this* more. I needed to sit here in the dark for a second listening to the cicadas' song—with an occasional wolf howl—while sipping on my *café con leche*.

I wasn't sure how everything today had shifted so fast from having lunch to crisis mode to severely scary shit. Between demon-dead spirits, Samantha leaving her body to go on a suicidal rescue mission in Hell, and a monster terrorizing her and destroying her room, somehow, I'd ended up saving Sam. I had no idea how any of what happened last night was possible, and that terrified me. I was so out of my depth on this.

And then it hit me. I knew why my thoughts were spiraling so much.

I'd done something that I couldn't take back—that I didn't *want* to take back—but once Sam knew about it, she might wish we'd found another way to save her.

Anxiety knotted in my stomach, and I set my mug down, raking my fingers down my face.

Shit. Yeah. That was why I couldn't settle.

Eli—Sam's guardian angel—had been so convincing in the moment. He really made me think that she'd want this bond—for me to anchor her to this world—but man…she'd been unconscious. If anyone did that to one of my sisters without their permission, I would fucking end them.

Had I taken advantage of her somehow?

I rubbed my eyes. What the hell was I going to do now?

I wasn't taking it back. I couldn't, even if I wanted to. Which no, it just wasn't going to happen.

What if I ruined my chance with her, and she hated me? And now, she'd be what? Stuck with me? Or worse, what if she was too polite to tell me to get lost?

Oh shit. I might've just fucked up my shot with her entirely.

The knot in my stomach twisted, and the milky coffee suddenly wasn't sitting well.

I got up from the chair and rested my arms on the porch railing so I could stare up at the moon.

Sam's friends had left a couple hours ago, and so had all the wolves that had come by to watch me sitting on the porch. I knew other supernaturals lived in the neighborhood, but only the wolves had come to visit. At least as far as I could tell. Around thirty or so had stopped by in wolf form, sometimes alone, sometimes in small groups or pairs, but some of those could've been repeats. Telling them apart was tricky, so there was no way to be sure. But it seemed like the whole neighborhood had stopped by to check me out. They'd watched me, howled, and I swore some of them were smiling.

Did werewolves smile?

I huffed at the thought. It was absurd. Maybe they could, but my whole train of thought was nuts. She didn't have a werewolf boyfriend, so why would they all come check me out? But that was what it seemed like to me. And they honestly should be checking me out. I had tied myself to Samantha...without her permission.

My phone buzzed, and I looked down at it. My agent was calling me. Again.

I sent her to voicemail. She was the last person I wanted to talk to right now, and from the way she kept calling, she knew I'd been lying to her.

I'd been lying to everyone. Her, my coach and teammates, my family.

I kept telling them my knee needed more time, but it was

mostly fine. I could go back to playing soccer, but a voice inside my head kept telling me not to go.

I thought back to what Eli had said earlier—the three voices in your head—God's, mine, and the Enemy's. Man, I'd never heard anyone say that before, but God had laid out some crazy dominoes in my life with so many twists and turns that all led me right here, right now. When I looked back at it, it blew my mind.

That had to be a sign that this anchor bond thing would be okay. That she'd be okay with it—with *me.* If I was wrong, I wasn't sure anything in my life would make sense again because this felt exactly, perfectly right.

I had no idea how long I'd been out on that porch—minutes, hours, I wasn't sure—but eventually, the sound of a car on the dirt road rose above the other quiet sounds of the night. I could see the shine of headlights entering the small rural neighborhood. The car turned, the brights flicked off, and it eventually slowed down to park next to my car.

The front door creaked, and Ana stepped onto the porch. She looked so much like Samantha. Either Ana had Sam when she was a baby, or the Lopez genes were excellent. Ana looked like she was in her early thirties with no wrinkles in sight, but Sam was twenty-three. So, there was no way that was possible.

Ana wore an oversized, flowing shirt with the front tucked into wide-legged jeans. Her hair was up in a messy bun, and she wiped her hands on the dishtowel that hung over her shoulder as she came to stand by my chair.

"It's past midnight. Who is that—" Ana broke off, and I figured she must've recognized the car.

A second later, I realized who it was. Frank.

"Did you call him?" Ana asked.

"No." The thought never even crossed my mind.

Samantha said Frank was her mentor, but I wasn't sure that was true. From how they interacted yesterday, they were more than coworkers or friends. They treated each other like family.

"I didn't call him either." She blew out a breath. "And I really should've. He's going to be so pissed."

I didn't know Frank well enough to guess, but I knew I would've been pissed if no one had called me, even though I had no right, no stake, no claim on her life.

Except, I did now. That was something I'd need to get used to.

"Yep." Ana wrung the towel in her hands as she stared at him through his windshield. "Really pissed."

Everything had happened so fast, I wasn't sure how anyone would've been able to think of calling Frank. One second, we'd been eating. The next, Gabe—Sam's demon-dead friend—was back. Everyone scrambled to get that other fey guy back from Hell. No one stopped long enough to think it through or talk about what might happen. At least not in any way that I understood.

Frank got out of the car. His priest collar was unbuttoned and hanging open. His short, dark hair had small flecks of gray peeking through, as did his beard, but he hadn't seemed old to me when I met him yesterday. Tonight, he did. From the way his shoulders hunched and how he moved slowly toward the porch steps, Frank must've had a bad night, too.

"What are you doing here?" Ana said. "You know the deer on the road get bad after dark and—"

"Stop. Ana. *Please*. Everything has gone wrong tonight." Frank held a prayer rope in his hand, his fingers moving over the knots as he spoke. "It's been a long night…and I'm exhausted. I got in the car, driving on autopilot, and I was already halfway here when I realized where I was going. I swear I meant to drive home, but God had other plans for me tonight." Suddenly, everything shifted in his demeanor. His shoulders straightened, and some of the exhaustion faded away before my eyes. "Why are you still here?" he asked me. "And where's Samantha?" His voice was calm, clear, and had just a hint of an edge to it.

"Sleeping." Ana looked about as exhausted as I felt. "She's fine now."

"But she wasn't fine?" His voice rose—in fear, panic, anger, or maybe all three.

The front door opened, and Eli stepped out. "Don't wake her, priest." The angel looked more California bro than anything I considered angelic. His wavy blond hair brushed his shoulders, and he wore faded, torn jeans, a white button-down, and his feet were bare. But I'd seen his other form—the one with the wings, glowing armor, and a sword made of fire. That version was as far from a California bro as someone could get.

I didn't ever want to get on Eli's bad side.

Eli turned to me. "That's for the best."

And he could read my mind. Why did I keep forgetting that?

"I don't know. You'd think it would be memorable."

"Agreed." I shook my head. "But it's been a long couple of days."

Eli grunted and sat in one of the Adirondak chairs. Ana met Frank on the porch steps and quietly filled him in on our day that had bled into the night. About how Sam had left her body to go to Hell. How she'd saved Van, a fey warrior, but then got trapped there. How I had somehow pulled her back to her body, linking myself to her forever.

"Potentially forever," Eli said.

I should've been afraid, but I didn't think he'd kill me.

I hoped he wouldn't.

Actually, I should be clear with him. "I'd rather you not kill me." He'd said that anchoring her to me—some kind of supernatural bond that I sealed with a kiss—was permanent. But then he said he'd find a way to break it if she didn't want it or if I changed my mind. He wasn't lying when he said it was permanent, but both couldn't be true.

Eli's grin sent chills down my spine. "See," he said. "You're not just a pretty face."

I huffed a soft laugh. He said that as if killing me wasn't a big deal to him, and maybe it wouldn't be. "So, am I right?"

"I've spent a long time bending rules, and I've found that there are many ways around things, even ones that seem a hard and fast law. I wouldn't punish you for the choice you made—so, no. I won't kill you. But if you choose to go back on your word, I'd question my judgement for a while." Eli shrugged. "It will work out."

That was why I wasn't afraid of Eli. Even if he did test me, deep down, I knew he was on my side.

And yet, he sounded completely sure that everything would work out while I'd been sitting out here stewing. "How do you know?"

He looked at me if he could see right through me. With his eyes bright blue and a hint of a glowing aura around him, it was as if he really could *see* me, my past, my future, and all the time in between.

"Not exactly, but close," Eli said. "It helps when you can see a person's soul and glance inside their head. I've also lived long enough enough to make accurate predictions. I don't have any form of precognition, but I guess you could call it divine intuition."

"Alright." I was glad he was so sure. Not because I was rethinking things—I wasn't going back on my decision—but because I wasn't sure how Sam would feel.

I wanted Sam. I wanted to be there for her, to fight with and for her, and nothing was going to change my mind. But Sam might need some convincing.

My phone buzzed in my pocket, and I pulled it out. My agent was calling. *Again.* If I kept sending her to voicemail, she'd just keep calling.

I opened up our text chain. *I'll get back to you when I can, but something's come up. I'll be a little MIA for the next few days.*

The three dots telling me that she was typing back popped up almost instantly, but I didn't have it in me to text with her right now. I was money for her, which meant she could be aggressive and pushy. In her mind, you could never make enough money. But at this point, my money was making money. I would have to try really hard to spend it all. So, I didn't *need* to do anything else in terms of work. Years of endless workouts and practices and games had given me what I always wanted. *Freedom*.

Frank and Ana came up the porch stairs. "I hear a thank you is in order," Frank said to me.

"It's not." I didn't want a thank you. Helping Sam was something that I'd wanted to do. "But I want a chance to tell her what happened. Everyone agreed not to tell her about it until I talk to her. Which I will do soon. I just…" I let out a breath to think through what I was going to say. "So, if you could keep it to yourself…"

For years, I'd daydreamed about what I'd do if I ever ran into Sam again, but I never planned on moving this fast with her. I hadn't even gotten to take her out on a date, and I had a feeling she was dye for a good version of one of those. It sounded like she'd had enough bad ones to last a lifetime.

Maybe if I took her out on a *good* first date. Get her in a good mood. Something to help ease the potential sting of—

"Potential sting? If you're thinking that way, then she's definitely going to freak out," Eli said.

Not having my thoughts to myself was extremely unpleasant.

"Well, then, I guess I won't help you."

"I didn't ask for help," I muttered.

Frank studied me for a second. "I won't say anything, but I won't keep anything from her either. I won't lie to cover anything up."

"I'm not asking for that. She just needs some rest, and then I'll tell her."

Frank pressed his lips together as he studied me. I had a moment of panic that he was going to go straight to Sam and spill everything, but then, he nodded. "Alright. I'll warn you not to take too long. Honesty is—"

A scream broke through the night, and suddenly, Eli was gone.

"Sam," I whispered before I took off running.

I raced into the house, up the stairs, and found her writhing in her bed, tangled in the sheets, screaming as fire encircled her body.

Holy shit.

Eli was beside her, wings out and glowing, watching but not touching her. "Don't worry. She's okay. It's not hurting her. The screaming is from the nightmare, not physical pain," he said to me without looking away from her. "The fire won't hurt you, either. It's part of her subconscious defense—a supernatural fire that she keeps contained. She never lets it out, even when in a fight. She sees it as too much of a link to her father and thinks that if she were to use the fire inside her, it would be a slippery slope to becoming like him."

"Is that true?" I didn't see how it could be. Samantha was *good*. She wouldn't turn into the thing that ripped apart her room.

Eli shrugged. "Maybe. Maybe not. It would be up to her."

That was one hell of a non-answer. "But I can see the fire?" That didn't make sense, unless there was something I was missing.

"Everyone can when she presents it this way, but she only does this when she's really and truly exhausted." The angel actually looked sad as he watched Sam. "It's the lingering nightmares that really do her in." His voice was soft and filled with pain, as if watching her suffer like this broke his heart. From his tone and what he'd said, this wasn't his first time seeing her like this.

Once was enough for me. I'd do anything I could to keep her from nightmares that consumed her like this.

Frank and Ana came through the door looking worried but not panicked. They stayed back. Even her mom, which surprised me, but I was grateful for it. I was feeling territorial, which was new. I wasn't usually a jealous person, and being jealous of Sam's mom or Frank was excessive, but I was. I was even jealous of Eli, which yeah, okay, that made more sense. He was powerful and knew everything about Sam and the world she fought in, and I was new. So new. But I wanted to be the one to help her. It was a deep-seated need in my soul that I couldn't explain and didn't have the bandwidth to figure out right now.

I forced myself to stay calm and study her. She was still screaming and writhing in the fire that engulfed her, yet somehow Eli was right. It wasn't hurting her. Her skin and clothes were fine, as was the bed.

"Samantha. Wake up." Ana's voice was firm, loud, but Sam didn't rouse. I wasn't even sure Sam could hear anything other than the screams and whatever nightmare she was living in.

Eli stood guard over Sam, watching her while Frank and Ana discussed what had worked in the past and how to safely wake her so she didn't attack whoever woke her.

Sam kept screaming, her body thrashing under the sheets, and I knew I had to do something. My hands itched to shake her awake, but I wasn't sure if that was a good idea. I had no clue what to do. She needed help. That much I could see for myself.

"Exactly. She needs to wake up." Eli looked at me then. His blue eyes had flames in them. "So, wake her up."

He'd said it so plainly that I knew it had to be a trick. I hadn't been around the angel very much, but I knew enough to figure that out. "How do you mean?" For a normal person, I would just go shake her awake. But from the emphasis Eli had put on his words, I had a feeling he meant something entirely different. "I can't wake her up by shaking her, can I?"

"No. She won't wake like a normal mortal would right now. She's in too deep, but in this case, it'll be helpful for you."

"This is helpful?" How could he say that? She was suffering.

"Because it gives you a chance to practice being her anchor. Call her to you."

Call her to me? Great. Easy. No problem. "How the hell do I do that?" Fire covered every inch of her body. I knew it wasn't real and wouldn't burn me because it wasn't burning the bed. But two feet away from the edge of the bed, it was *hot*.

"Call her. Use the anchor bond. Do it. Do it *right now*." From the way he said it, I knew this was a prove-it moment.

Okay. Fine. I'd figure it out.

I stepped toward the bed and prayed I was doing the right thing.

CHAPTER TWO

SAMANTHA

THIS WAS IT. I was trapped.

Dead.

Done.

There was no way I was getting out of this.

Astaroth—my father, the fallen angel—had chased me here.

I was huddled in a ball in one of the rooms in my father's castle, hiding, trying not to cry or scream even as the heat of Hell beat against every inch of my skin.

How had this happened?

How had I ended up trapped in Hell again?

I'd saved Van. I knew that much. But everything after that had been a blur.

I'd fought hordes of demons. Ran through tortured souls. And I thought—I'd *stupidly* thought—that I'd been fighting my way out, but my father always won.

My demon-dead friend, Gabe, and I had been cornered in one of the caverns. Demons were everywhere, and suddenly, they were gone. And my father was there. And...

And Gabe told me to run. He yelled that he'd buy me some time.

So, I ran, but his tortured screams followed me as I'd raced through Hell.

But I wouldn't waste his sacrifice, so I'd ran and ran and ran until I'd seen my father's the castle carved from the lava rock inside his gigantic cavern. I'd thought about all the rooms inside it. All the places I could hide. I thought it would give me options.

So, I sprinted for it and raced through the castle, looking for a place to hide, until peeked in here.

The tall armoire inside this room had just enough space for me to fit between it and the corner of the wall. The armoire was along the same wall as the door, so if my father peeked in here, there was a chance—a small chance—that the door would block me from view. If I tucked myself tight enough into the corner, he might not even come all the way inside the room. I stupidly thought this would be the perfect hiding spot.

But as the rough rock dug into my spine, I knew I'd made a mistake.

Because I hadn't noticed the table filling the center of the room with thick metal legs and a slab of more lava rock on top.

Or the chains draped across the tabletop, dripping down to the floor.

And I definitely hadn't seen the blood and bits of gore on the table, the chains, the floor, and—oh God.

Oh God.

Were those knives?

Was that a *saw*?

I tried not to look at it, but now it was all I could see.

Lord, help me. Why had I found this room of all rooms?

A manic laugh almost slipped free, and I slapped my hands over my mouth to stop it. Tears rolled down my cheeks, but they never hit my chin because they evaporated. It was so hot—not as hot as out in the caverns of Hell—but still so impossibly hot in my father's version of a palace.

I pressed myself harder into the corner, trying to become as small as I could be, hoping the armoire hid me from view, but I knew this was a trap.

My father had tricked me into coming here. There was no way I ended up in this torture chamber on my own. He'd whispered in my mind where to go, when to turn, what door to open. It'd sounded like my own voice, but I was wrong. It was him the whole time.

The walls rumbled, and I knew he was coming for me.

I had to stay alive. I had to find a way—

The walls suddenly stopped rumbling and the castle grew quiet.

No more screams.

No more tortured souls.

Only the sound of my heartbeat and my gasping breath.

I kept both of my hands over my mouth, trying to stifle the sound as I scanned the room for another way out.

A door.

A chute.

Something.

God, please. I don't want to die in here. I don't want to be stuck here for the rest of my life—the rest of my afterlife.

The door flung open, slamming against the lava rock walls, and my father laughed—deep, long, rumbling in the way that sent fear like fire rushing through my veins.

I tensed, ready to jump up and run again, but I had nowhere to go. I'd backed myself into a literal corner.

I tried to flatten myself against the wall a little more.

Stupid. This was a stupid place to hide.

Stupidstupidstupid.

I was so tired, so hot, so thirsty, but I shoved it all down. Shoved it as far and as fast as I could.

His footsteps were soft—nearly silent—and I tried to hold my breath, but without air, I felt like I was drowning. My heart was beating too fast to—

A hand gripped my shoulder, talons ripped my flesh, hot blood splattered against my face as I screamed.

I panicked for a second, but there was a voice in my head telling me to stay calm. To breathe. To fight.

So, I fought.

I wrapped my arm around my father's hand, pivoting, breaking his grasp, and I saw my opening.

I slid between his legs and threw myself toward the door.

Please let me get away.

Pleasepleasepl—

An arm hooked around my waist, and my father lifted me up and hurled me across the room. My back slammed into the stone wall as I screamed from the pain, from the terror, from the fact that I knew he had me and I wasn't getting away. Not this time.

He was on me before I hit the ground, slamming me into the floor, and I couldn't breathe.

His red eyes stared into mine. His long, black hair fell around my face, hiding everything from view but his face. He laughed at me—at the fear I knew had to be rolling off me in great, big waves—then he rose up just enough so I could see his body.

He was beautiful in his fallen angel form. His body was so perfect that it could've been carved marble with every muscle defined. His massive black wings spread out on either side of him.

"You will submit." His voice was dark as he shoved the command down the tie that bound me to him. The tie from father to daughter. The one I'd tried to cut, burn, break, but it always came back.

I fought against the command, willing myself to stay strong just a little longer.

"No." I forced the word out.

He leaned down again. "You are *mine*."

"No. I'm a daughter of my Lord and King, Jesus Christ—"

He roared at the name, and I heard it echo through the house, the caverns, and into the depths of Hell.

Answering screams from the suffering rose up, and I knew I couldn't back down now.

"—and I will *not submit* to any but *Him!*" I screamed the last as loud as I could, my throat burning with the force of my words.

Even if I was afraid, even if I got stuck here for eternity, I would never *submit* to this monster.

"*He* cannot save you here."

Was he right? I didn't know. I wasn't sure if God could reach me here or not. God didn't obey rules—He made them—but I knew that Eli couldn't get me in this part of Hell.

God. Please. Help me.

My panic spiked until it was suffocating me, but I heard a voice in my head telling me I wasn't alone. And it felt true. Because I wasn't. Not really. Somewhere back in Texas, in my house, in my room, I wasn't alone.

One word came through, as clear as if someone else was in this room with me. Someone other than Astaroth. *Breathe.*

I wasn't sure where the voice came from, but it sounded good. Kind. So, I took in a gasping breath.

One small breath cleared my mind enough, and I knew I could fight.

I could do this. Just like Chris taught me.

Another small breath. In and out.

Right. Okay. Fast.

I had to move fast.

Speed and surprise were my strengths.

My father was saying something, but I ignored it. His threats were always the same. It didn't matter. His words didn't matter. My actions were the only things that mattered.

I waited. I didn't want to. It took everything in me to wait. But I did.

And then, I slowly—so, so slowly—tucked my knees into my chest as if I was curling into a ball, but I wasn't. I was getting ready. And waiting.

I waited for another breath. And five more. Until he relaxed his grip on me just a little and glanced away.

I hit his wrists, breaking his grip on me, and then kicked my feet into his stomach with everything I had.

Astaroth flew across the room, and I didn't wait around to watch him crash into the wall. I didn't want to see if or how fast he'd recover. I ran.

Through corridors.

Down hallways.

Past his rooms.

Down.

Down.

Down into his dungeon.

I raced down the winding staircase, taking the stairs two at a time, ignoring the stench and the screams and the heat that grew even hotter with every step.

This was the safest place for me in Hell. It had to be. There were other people down there. Others screaming and crying and begging for mercy that would never come.

I could hide here among the condemned. Even if I freaked out, my screams would be covered by theirs. I could—

"Samantha." I heard the voice—the same one that told me to breathe—but it wasn't my father.

This was a good voice. Familiar, but not so familiar that I knew who it was.

"Samantha!" It came again. Not from here. Not from Hell. From the other side. And with it came a tug, an urgency to move, to leave this place and go home.

"Samantha! Wake up! You're dreaming. You have to wake up now."

I froze. Wait. What?

No. I was here. This was real. This was—

I closed my eyes. Sometimes—especially after a fight with my father—it was hard to know what was a nightmare, what was relived trauma, and what was real.

"You're having a nightmare. Wake." The tug came again, stronger this time. *"Up."*

The tug came again, and I looked down, searching for the source.

And there it was.The silver cord that tied my body to my mind. I hadn't been able to find it before, but it was here now. And it was stronger. Thicker.

It wasn't just one strand now. There was another one twisting around it. I held them in my hand, and everything in the room froze instantly—the sounds, the heat, the feeling that my father was just around the corner. It all went quiet, still, cool.

Oh shit. This wasn't real?

I looked around the dungeon, and I pushed it away.

Hell disappeared, and I was floating in space, a black abyss of nothing.

Home. I needed to go home.

I closed my eyes and focused on my body.

I woke up gasping. I felt people in the room, but my body was in a ball, and my face was pressed into the mattress.

"Hey." That voice again.

I turned my head toward it and saw hazel-green eyes.

Phoenix.

Phoenix was still here?

Yes. He really was. He was kneeling beside the bed, looking at me with concerned eyes.

Slowly, as if coming out of a fog, I remembered that I'd woken up before.

After I saved Van, after I fought off my father, after I came to in the ice bath—Phoenix had been here. He'd carried me into bed. He said he'd stay, and he had.

First came the floating feeling of happiness that he was still here.

But it was quickly followed by horror.

He'd seen me having a full-on nightmare. Only Mom, Eli, and Frank had ever seen me like that. I knew what happened when I had nightmares. The fire. The screams. It made me feel incredibly vulnerable that he'd been here for that.

And yet, he hadn't gotten scared. He hadn't run away. And from the look on his face, he was truly worried about me.

Huh. That wasn't what I'd expected, but I was learning that Phoenix usually did the opposite of what I expected.

"Hi." My voice sounded hoarse, like I'd been yelling for a while. Which meant I probably had been.

I took another breath and cleared my throat. "Sorry."

"You wouldn't wake up," Eli said from behind me. I didn't need to look to know it was him. He'd been a part of my life since before I could remember. "Where were you?"

"Trapped in his domain." I closed my eyes, pressing my face into the mattress again. Being curled up in a ball somehow made me feel safer. "Man. Just when I thought the whole having nightmares thing was over…" I swallowed. "I haven't had one like that in so long. I couldn't tell it was a dream. I thought I was back there. That I hadn't gotten free. And…" And I couldn't linger on it. I didn't want to live through it when I was asleep, and I definitely didn't want to relive it when I was awake.

I took another breath, letting it out so, so slowly, and my heartbeat slowed with it. "I did the thing, did I?"

"The thing?" Phoenix asked. I knew his voice now. I hadn't while I was asleep, but I wouldn't forget it again. Nothing had ever been so soothing in my whole life.

"Yep," Mom said from somewhere behind me. "You did the thing, but you're fine. Everything's okay."

Yeah. Maybe *some* things were okay, but not everything. Everything was far from fine.

Gabe.

What was I going to do? I couldn't go back there. I just couldn't. The idea of it—

A whimper slipped free before I could stop it.

"Don't you dare."

I sat up at the threat in Eli's tone. I turned toward my guardian angel, who stood on the other side of my bed.

Wait. This wasn't my bed. This was a pull-out couch.

Right. My father had destroyed my room. Nothing was were it should've been.

Whatever. I didn't need to deal with that right now. I focused back on Eli. "I'll do what I want. When I want."

His eyes flared, and his wings appeared.

I started to slide from the bed to confront him, but Mom cleared her throat, stopping me. "Samantha."

I looked at her in the doorway, and she motioned down.

Shit. I was in a sports bra and boy shorts.

Just when I thought I couldn't be more embarrassed.

I grabbed up the flat sheet from the bed, wrapping it around my body while I struggled to hold onto some of my dignity. "I'm a grown woman, Eli. I make my own choices."

"Fine." Eli's wings rippled before they disappeared, and I knew he wanted to get in my face with some snippy comment.

Sure enough, he leaned down until we were almost nose-to-nose. "Don't do anything *stupid*."

"What?" Mom charged into the room with Frank—when had he gotten here?—not two steps behind her. They stopped at the foot of my bed. "What stupid thing do you think she's going to do?"

Eli answered her before I could. "She's thinking about how to save Gabe." He couldn't read my mind, but he knew me well enough that he didn't need to. "She only just got back in one piece, and she's already thinking about going back." Eli was still in my face as he spoke to Mom. "I don't know. Why. You. *Trust. That demon.*"

Eli was pissed. I got it. I did. On the surface, Gabe sounded like someone I should absolutely not trust, but he'd proven himself over and over and over again.

"Wasn't tonight a good enough example? He's in a cage. For *me*. He *sacrificed* himself *for me*." Why was this so hard to understand? "Gabe was like me. We could be the same. Sure, he made terrible choices when he was alive, but we all make mistakes. *Everyone does*. That doesn't mean he's fully evil now that he's dead. He wants to do good, and that means he's good. Doesn't it? Don't his actions prove that?"

Eli rose, stepping away from me, and it was like a mask slid over his face. All of the emotion he'd been raging with was snuffed out. "Agree to disagree," he said too softly.

I hated it when Eli got like this. I needed this conversation to end, not just fester below the surface. I needed everyone out of my room, and some space, and to put on real clothes before I forgot I wasn't wearing any again.

Wait. I could fix this with two words. "I'm hungry," I said. That set everyone off like I wanted. My mom said something, but I wasn't paying attention. Phoenix said he'd give me room to change—I did pay attention to him. He was kind of impossible for me to ignore. And Frank went down with both of them, but Eli stayed.

Of course, food wouldn't get him moving. He could eat food, but he didn't need it. He didn't understand our obsession with it either. Eli wanted to take care of me—which sometimes meant food—but more importantly, that included saving me from myself.

"Please, angel. Don't do anything now. Not when you're tired and weak. You only got back a couple of hours ago. Rebuild your strength before you attempt anything."

"I wasn't going to go now." I wasn't sure about tomorrow, but definitely not right now.

"Promise me you'll wait a few weeks. It took you nearly a year to recover last time, including all those months of physical therapy."

My sheets slid off as I sat up, and I tugged at them until they covered me. I wanted to get dressed, but I wasn't going to do that with Eli in the room. "No. I can't promise you I'll wait that long.

And it won't be like last time. I'd been in a coma for a year. I had to rebuild all my strength from scratch."

He crossed his arms. "You could take time to recover if you wanted to, but you *won't*."

I blew out a breath. That was fair. "Right. I could, but I won't. And I refuse to give you a promise that I might end up breaking."

Eli shook his head, and from how his eyes flared and the way he pressed his lips together, I knew he was disappointed in me. It wasn't the first time I'd seen that look from him—and I knew it wouldn't be the last—but that didn't mean I liked it.

He stood there like a statue beside my bed. The only thing that moved was his shoulder-length, blond hair as if it were being blown by some supernatural breeze. "Do you remember what it was like after you were trapped in Hell last time?"

"As I just said, that was different. My body had been in a coma *for a year*. All my muscles had withered to basically nothing. I had to go slowly. But I was only there for a few hours this time. Am I tired? Yes. Am I down some energy? Sure. But do I need to sit around twiddling my thumbs for weeks? No. I don't." It would be different this time. It had to be.

"You're right that it won't be as bad, but your recovery will take at least a few weeks. You rush into anything right now, you'll be putting your life in danger. Your powers come from the spiritual realm, so they won't need time to recover. But your body and your soul do. This night has weakened and traumatized you. And you know what that means."

It meant that I wouldn't be able to help anyone who needed me if I made myself weaker, sick, or worse—dead.

I hated this. I didn't want to fight with Eli, but I wasn't going to stay in bed for weeks. That just wasn't happening. I refused. I was older now. I'd been in Hell for a fraction of the time. And that meant I'd recover faster.

If someone needed help, I would help them. And if that someone was Gabe, then there was no way I would say no. Zero chance. None.

Gabe had helped me get away. I *owed* it to him to try with every bit of me that I had left.

"If you go after that demon, you will regret it. Forever."

A chill settled over my soul. "What do you know that I don't?"

Eli didn't say anything. He didn't move. He just focused his powerful, angelic stare on me.

For better or worse, we were at a stalemate.

"I can't tell you all the things I know and see," he said after what seemed like forever. "Just like I can't force you to rest for a few weeks before you consider what—if anything—you need to do for that *demon*. But I caution you to take a moment to remember that Gabriel is a *demon* for a reason. He was a very, very bad guy when he was alive, and despite what you think you know, he didn't get better after he died."

I opened my mouth to defend Gabe again, but Eli shook his head.

"I know that he's helped you in the past, but how much of that was genuine and how much was laying the groundwork for a bigger manipulation? That's something you haven't even considered."

He was right that I hadn't thought about that because I was pretty sure that Gabe was good.

But was I willing to risk being trapped in Hell again for *pretty sure*?

Suddenly, I didn't know.

Eli's eyes flared brighter as if he knew exactly where my mind had gone. "I can't read Gabe—just like I can't read you—but I've been alive long enough to understand him. You cannot trust Gabe, angel. You *cannot*. Putting yourself in danger for him would be idiotic at best. At worst, it could mean your nightmares becoming true."

I knew he was right, but it didn't feel right in my heart. "Gabe is hurting because of me. He—"

"I'm going to remind you once again that Gabe is used to being down there. You might hate it, but Hell is his *home*. If you think he's not used to getting out of those cages, then I don't know what to say to you."

I dropped my chin just a little. There was a chance that Eli was right, but Gabe had never ended up in a cage because of me. At least, not that I knew of.

"Taking the blame for his circumstances isn't right, angel. With time and rest, I hope you'll accept that you are both exactly where you belong." His tone softened. "So, I'll leave you to think on it, but I'm not leaving here. Not truly."

I met his gaze again. "You're not?"

"No." He let his shoulders slouch a little as he met my gaze, a small smile on his face.

The fight was over. Thank God. I hated fighting with Eli.

"Don't worry, angel. I have some things to see to, but I'm staying close unless I'm called away again."

"Okay. Thank you." Even if I was annoyed at Eli, even when I disagreed with him, I always felt better when he was close by. "I won't do anything without trying to tell you first."

"That's at least something." He gave me a smile and a wink before disappearing.

I let out a long sigh, then swung my feet over the edge of the mattress.

I took a second to look at my destroyed room. Someone must've cleaned it up, but there were still shards of wood and paper and what had to be pillow fluff on the carpet.

Man. This was much worse than I'd realized.

Where were my bookshelves, my chair, *all of my things*?

Son of a goat herder.

CHAPTER THREE

SAMANTHA

I HADN'T NOTICED how torn up my room was when I first woke up, but something bad definitely happened here. Was that a person-sized dent in the drywall?

I shook my head. Whatever. It was just stuff. The important thing was that I was here, home, alive.

Van was alive, too. I knew that much. I'd at least accomplished something.

And Gabe…

I thought about what Eli had said. He was right. Gabe was home. Just not in the kind of home I'd wish on anyone. Gabe was dead, but even the souls in Hell could bleed and suffer. No matter what Eli thought, I still felt like it was my fault Gabe was in trouble.

I rose from the pullout couch, and the room began to swim a little, and yeah. Okay. Eli was right. I was going to need to rest for a while. Just standing for a few seconds was wearing me out, which meant I was no good to Gabe. Not yet.

But I still wasn't promising Eli anything. If Gabe didn't get himself out of that cage and come find me soon, I'd have to figure out a way to help him.

How? I had no freaking idea. I wasn't sure I could go back and get him. I didn't have it in me. It would take years before I'd do something that stupid again, but—

I took a step and almost face planted but caught myself against my closet door.

I couldn't think about Gabe. Not right now. I actually did need to eat.

I opened my closet and thanked God that everything was still there.

Getting dressed took much longer than normal, and by the time I managed to tug on a long sweater and some shorts, I was sweating. I hit the bathroom before heading downstairs, and it was a mess in there, too. I glanced in the mirror.

Holy shit. Even *I* was a mess. My skin was pale, shadows under my eyes, and I felt hollow. Even if I had the energy to put on makeup, I wasn't sure makeup could fix this.

My vision grayed, and I knew I needed to move before I passed out.

I flicked the cover down over the toilet and sat. I hadn't been this weak in a long time, and from how this kind of thing usually went, it would take me a while to recover.

That was beyond frustrating. I couldn't afford weeks of downtime. Not with how things were trending, but that was where I was.

I had to remind myself that saving Van was worth it. That if this was the price I had to pay, that was fine. I would pay it and be grateful I'd been able to help a friend.

Aside from that, I needed to eat. Food would fix this. Maybe. It had to.

I rose slowly, making sure I wouldn't pass out before leaving the bathroom.

My legs were weak as I padded downstairs, but I refused to

ask for help. Stubborn. I was being stubborn, and I knew it. But I wasn't backing down.

It took until I was nearly at the bottom of the stairway for the scent to register. I paused for a second. Churro chip cookies. Like snickerdoodle but better because chocolate made everything better.

Churro chip cookies were a tradition for Mom, who told me she'd been making them since she was a kid. Whenever she hit hard times growing up, she made churro chip cookies to tell herself that life wasn't all bad.

Now, Mom made them for me anytime I was struggling or when I needed to celebrate a win.

Today was a win.

Smelling the cookies made me remember that no matter how I was feeling about Gabe, I'd done something good. I'd saved Van, and I was alive, safe, home. No matter what else happened, that was worth celebrating.

I met her gaze across the open-concept kitchen-dining room. "We did it."

"No, baby. *You* did it." She handed me a cookie like I'd won an award. "You brought Van back safely, and you're home." She closed the distance between us, and I leaned into her, taking some of her strength.

She squeezed me tight and gave my back a little up-and-down pat. "It's going to be okay. You're safe now, but it'll take you a bit before you settle into that. It always does. We've been here before, and we'll get through the rest. Whatever it is. Okay?"

How did she always know exactly what to say? My eyes burned, and before I could stop it, a tear slid free. "Okay." I wasn't saying it to anyone or about anything in particular. Just like—*Okay. I'll try.*

"Do you want to talk about it?" she whispered as she pulled away.

Oh, yeah. No. "No, please." I was still dizzy and covered in a memory-driven cold sweat, and I could feel the nightmare still coating my skin with its oily, evil residue.

Mom was right. It would take me time before I shook this feeling off. The feeling of Hell.

Mom gripped my hand and walked me over to the island stools. Frank sat on one, so I took the one next to him.

I glanced over at Phoenix, who was leaning against the counter on the other side of the island, watching me.

He wore the standard T-shirt and sweatpants that the pack always had lying around. His tattoos were showing on his arm, and I wanted to get a better look, but I was caught by the look in his eyes.

Something in those hazel-green eyes...

I was missing something. Forgetting something. What?

Man, I felt like I was going crazy, and I didn't know what to say to him. I didn't know why he'd stayed. Not that I wanted him to go, but I just…

Why would he want to stay? I was a mess right now. I knew I looked as bad as I felt, and I wasn't great company. I wouldn't be for a while.

I didn't have any answers, so I moved on to the easier thing. "When did you get here?" I asked Frank, and then took a bite of the cookie Mom had handed me.

The cinnamon and chocolate coated my tongue, and I knew I was home again. Everything would be okay. It might take some time, but I'd be okay.

"Just before you woke up," Frank said. "I started to drive home after a particularly bad exorcism but ended up here. Funny how that happens."

"Yeah. Funny." But it wasn't a coincidence. I didn't believe in those, so I wondered what had happened during his exorcism and why he was really here.

I was too tired to think too hard about that, though. So, instead, I took another bit of cookie, like it would fix everything.

I could feel everyone watching me, but at least Tessa, Dastien, and the rest of the gang had left. If it was truly *everyone,* I might've gone back upstairs and hid for a while. Or forever. Or at least long enough for them to leave.

But Mom knew that. I knew she must've convinced my friends to go—that I would sleep fine, that I would be okay, that all was well—when she knew that none of those things were true.

The microwave dinged. "Let me get your food," Mom said, snagging a plate from the microwave. She slid it across the island, handed me a fork, and then stood next to Phoenix.

Great. Now, they were both watching me. Feeling way too exposed, I stared down at the plate and grabbed the fork.

"How are you feeling?" Phoenix asked.

"Tired." My stomach rumbled, and I started ate. I didn't even look at what she'd made me. I didn't taste it. And if someone told me to name what I'd eaten or die, well then, I guess I'd just die.

The only thing that registered was that it was warm. So, I moved on autopilot, shoveling in the food until I was done.

When my plate was clean, I dropped my fork and swayed on the stool.

"Whoa," Frank said. "Careful."

"Hmm." I blinked, but with my stomach full, the exhaustion was coming back. I was sitting here mostly asleep.

Except, my stomach was rumbling again, and there was the scratchy sound of the plate sliding across the counter.

So, I ate.

And when that one was gone, another one came.

And another.

I didn't know how much time had passed or how many plates I'd eaten, and I really didn't care.

My eyes grew droopy. I pushed whatever was in front of me away and put my head on the counter.

A second later, I was weightless. Safe. Warm.

"Thank you," I muttered to whatever was making me feel this way.

"You're welcome." Something warm pressed against my forehead. "Sleep." The word was sweet and soft and full of a kind of hope that I'd never felt before. There was peace to it. A peace that washed away the evil, oily feeling on my skin. When the warmth was leaving, I reached out, grabbing onto something. Someone.

"Stay. Please."

"I'm not going anywhere. I promise."

The world tipped and tilted, and then the warmth was back. So, I surrendered to sleep, trusting that everything would be okay when I woke up.

Please, don't let me be wrong.

CHAPTER FOUR

SAMANTHA

I WOKE up feeling surprisingly good. The last time this had happened…well, I'd ended up in the hospital for a while, and then moved to an in-patient psychiatric facility for even longer. Right now, I had a wicked headache and was a little weak, but that wasn't bad, considering how it could've been.

I could see the light in my room through my closed eyes. I didn't open them. Not yet. I took stock of my body first. Head to toe. My legs ached a little, and I had a few sore spots, but aside from the headache, nothing hurt enough to make me want medicine for it.

That was a relief.

Time to wake up, Sam. Face the day.

I blinked my eyes open slowly because there was just enough light in the room to hurt my eyes. The blackout curtains darkened the room, but a little bit of light bled out from the edges, making my head hurt even worse. I breathed into the pain, and eventually, it let up enough that I could look around.

Mom sat in one of our living room chairs beside my bed. She had her feet tucked under her and her phone in her hand. She looked up suddenly and froze as she studied me. Her eyes were rimmed in red and had dark circles under them, like she'd been up a lot of the night crying.

I smiled, trying to reassure her.

She smiled back, despite her visible exhaustion, and dropped her phone. She caught it right before it flipped out of her hands, then quietly laughed.

Mom seemed okay, but man, I hated how tired she looked. That was my fault. The tears she'd cried were also very likely my fault.

Her long, dark hair was pulled back in a knot at the nape of her neck, and she was wearing her most comfortable sweatshirt—the one that said, "blessed be the peacekeepers" and had a hole along the neck. She wore it whenever she was upset.

Yeah. All of this was definitely my fault.

I started to say something, but she put her finger over her mouth and pointed at something.

I looked down.

Someone was lying at the foot of my bed.

Wait. Not just someone. *Phoenix* was sleeping curled up at my feet.

So, he really had been here last night. He'd stayed.

I was confused. And excited. And thankful. Then, confused, again. Truly. I couldn't believe he actually stayed.

When I thought about it, I barely knew him. That was the logical part of me. But the rest of me—the emotional, spiritual, soul part—felt like this was right. That I *knew* him and that of course he should be here. Because where else would he be?

But that made exactly zero sense. And yet, here he was.

I glanced at Mom in question, but she just shrugged. As if that explained everything, but it really didn't explain anything at all. I needed actual words. A hand gesture. Something. *Anything.*

Phoenix was still in the pack's standard joggers and T-shirt, which triggered more of the memory from last night. He'd been here when I had woken up earlier from the nightmare. I'd gotten dressed, and he'd been in the kitchen. He'd cooked for me. Fed me.

I didn't have any memory of how or when I'd ended up back here in this bed. The last thing I remembered was someone handing me a plate, so I must've been carried back upstairs. Mom couldn't have done that. Or Frank. One of the werewolves could've, but they'd been gone. I didn't remember Eli being in the kitchen, either.

That left Phoenix.

He'd carried me?

Oh, man. A foggy memory hit me, and I cringed. He totally had carried me up here, and I'd grabbed him and begged him to stay like some massive clinger.

Way to just show him all the ugly bits in one go, Samantha.

Of course, he stayed. I'd guilted him into it. What a nightmare.

His long legs were tucked in tight as he slept, but his feet still hung off the edge. It was almost as if he didn't want to risk touching me and waking me up. And yet, he had one arm reaching out to me, lightly gripping my ankle.

He looked younger when he was asleep, but no less fierce or handsome. The short sleeves of his shirt had ridden up on one side, displaying more of his tattoos. They took up more of his arms than I'd thought, and I wanted to get a closer look, to run my fingers over them, to ask what they meant, but that could wait. I didn't want to wake him up.

I glanced at Mom, and she gave me a barely-there smile. It was as if she were holding back whatever she was thinking about him.

That was a first. Mom was never shy about her feelings. She had to be hiding something, but from the way her smile quirked up as I stared at her, I knew she wasn't going to spill anytime soon.

Fine. I guessed I had enough to think about already.

The last two days had been intense. I hadn't been expecting to see Phoenix in Frank's office, and when he said his sister needed help, I certainly hadn't expected to find her possessed by my father.

Then, barely recovered, I'd had to face my father again to rescue Van. Two attacks in as many days? This had never happened.

Yes, my father sometimes tracked me down. He had a few times over the course of my life, wreaking all kinds of havoc. Then, he'd go quiet. Sometimes for years.

He'd spent so much power the day before that I had no idea how he'd been able to do what he'd done yesterday. Although, to be fair, I'd gone into his domain. Maybe that was the difference? But he'd wrecked my room. How?

And was it over now? Would he come back again with something awful and new?

I didn't know what to expect anymore, but I hoped he was done for a while. I officially had nothing left in me.

Mom bunched her fingers together and tapped them to her mouth. *Hungry?*

Was I? I knew I should be, but I'd eaten a ton last night. That had to have been enough, even after a trip to Hell.

I shrugged. I was still too sleepy to feel hungry, but maybe.

She nodded and got up, tiptoeing to the door.

I was going to have to get up. I knew that much. But how did I do that and not wake up Phoenix?

The embarrassment made my face flame with heat as I realized I had no idea what I'd said to him last night. I remembered eating, but I hoped I hadn't made an idiot of myself.

And then I realized something.

He must've seen me puke up blood after I woke up.

I covered my face with my hands. *Dang it.* I didn't remember it, but that always happened. With how much he was hovering now, there was no way he missed it.

And when I woke up last night, I was in my underwear. Which meant he'd seen that, too.

Way to really impress the guy, Samantha. I can't believe I puked in front of him.

I tugged up the sheets, barely restraining myself from pulling them over my head. I felt so...*exposed*.

I wasn't humiliated—not exactly—because I hadn't done anything wrong. I'd been doing what I had to, and I didn't regret saving the fey warrior. Not even a little bit. And yet...this fluttering feeling in me had to be somehow related to humiliation or embarrassment or...I didn't even have a word for it. All I knew was that I was nervous. I really, really wanted this to work out.

I dared myself to look at him again.

His eyes were open, his gaze searing me from the inside out.

This heat was good. It wasn't the shame of embarrassment anymore, but it was scary. Maybe even a good kind of scary.

"Hi," I said.

"Hi." His voice was a deep rumble, still waking from sleep.

"You're still here?"

"I didn't want to leave. You slept better once dawn broke. It's not quite lunchtime, but close to it." He moved to sit in a fluid, graceful motion that I didn't dare try to replicate. "I'm..." He closed his eyes and bowed his head. He was quiet for a second, then shook his head as if coming to some decision.

Then, he looked at me, and I knew I was right. "You know, yesterday you told me I could stay. All that craziness happened, and I'm really glad I took you up on the offer. Some things happened while you were asleep."

"Yeah. I can tell."

"You can?" He seemed surprised.

"I mean—my room is trashed, and I'm sleeping in a pull-out couch. I'm pretty sure that's a sign not everything went as planned."

"It did get trashed, and yeah, I don't know enough about how something like that usually goes, but it didn't feel like it went as planned."

"Are you really glad you stayed?

The look in his eyes made my heart race. "Yes. One hundred percent. There's something I can't explain exactly that happened, but by the time you were back and safe, I felt like I'd found home. I didn't even realize I'd been looking for it."

I wasn't sure what he meant. My trashed bedroom made him feel like home? The attack from my father? Fighting demons? I was so confused. "I'm sorry, but you found home? I don't think I understand what you mean."

"I mean…" He was quiet for a second. "I don't even know where to start. Or how to start." He took a breath and let it out slowly, nodding to himself. I liked how he thought things through before he said them. It meant a lot that he took care with his words.

"Okay," he said, finally. "Maybe I should start with something you know. I'd been playing soccer for forever. It was my life. I made a lot of money, which helped to make sure my family was taken care of. But I spent a lot of time flying from one place to another for matches. I had a home base in a condo I shared with a teammate. We could both afford our own places, but neither of us liked to live alone. I dated and hung out with friends, but…" His voice trailed off, and he covered his face with his hands. "I'm rambling because I'm nervous. I did something last night." He dropped his hands away from his face, and he looked…sheepish was the only way to describe it. "I did something *big*, and I'm completely freaked by what you might say once I tell you."

Something *big*? Now, I was dying to know what he'd done.

I had a million questions in my mind, but sometimes being quiet was the best option. People would say what they wanted, and then I could react or ask questions. I could go off whatever they revealed. But trying to get something out of someone who didn't want to say it? That was hard. I didn't have it in me for hard today. Patience would have to win.

I sat up and pushed against the couch's stiff back, waiting for whatever he was going to say next.

"I guess I'll start with the smallest part from last night. I'm moving in next door."

A surprised laugh slipped free. *"What?"* I didn't mean to yell, but that was insanity. Was he for real? "Why would you do that? You have an *amazing, brand new* house that's not in the middle of nowhere. It's close to all the things the city can offer—restaurants, stores, life. Why would you possibly want to stay at the Sanctuary?" We were extremely secluded here because the supernaturals that lived here needed that. It was a sanctuary for them from all the things of the world—both mortal and supernatural.

"I want to be closer to you." He said it as if it was the most obvious thing in the world.

"What?" It was like waking up and finding out that you'd slept through winning the lottery. I couldn't quite wrap my head around it.

Wait. Before my mind went racing off and imagining all kinds of happily-ever-afters, I needed to know exactly what he meant. "Why do you want to be closer to me?" I slapped my hands over my mouth as I realized one more thing. "Your mom already hates me for essentially no reason. If you move out, she's going to murder me." I dropped my hands. "You can't move in next door. She'll never forgive me for taking you away from her." There was no way that lady wouldn't blame me for this, even if he'd decided it while I'd been passed out. I wasn't sure I cared what she thought of me, but it was his mother. If they were tight enough to still live together—like me and my mom did—then this would be a problem. A potentially relationship-ending problem.

He made a pained face, then rolled his eyes. "I already told her, and you're right." He gave me a crooked, half-smile. "She's not happy."

"Great. Fantastic. Just *perfect*. Phoenix... What is even *happening* right now?" It felt like this wasn't my world, my life, my reality. I'd woken up in some other dimension where nothing made sense.

He smiled like he thought my freak out was cute, and my heart raced.

Why did he have to be so freaking hot?

His smile widened, and it was almost as if he could read my mind. Or maybe I gave it away because my cheeks were on fire.

Whatever. I was a mess.

"Look, Sam. You're going to have to let me handle my mom. I'm a grown adult, and I can do what I want. Yes, my mom is freaking out, but that's really not my concern. I…I feel like such a stalker just moving in without talking to you first, but that's what I'm doing. As long as you're cool with it."

Him? *My* stalker? That was rich. Back when we were neighbors, I used to call myself *his* stalker. I'd watch for him out my bedroom window when he'd return from his night runs. He'd be all sweaty, with his T-shirt tucked into the back of his shorts, and I had been completely obsessed with him.

It wasn't just his looks or how incredibly fit he was. It was his soul that shone like nothing I'd ever seen before. So bright and pure. I couldn't help but be drawn to him.

The idea that him stalking me was even a thing made me laugh.

"I'm glad you think this is funny, but I don't want to leave you."

I stopped laughing.

He was serious, and I had no clue what to say.

"After what I saw all those years ago, after what I saw with my sister and what happened last night…I'm sticking close until you tell me to get lost." He leaned over his legs, reaching out for my hand.

I never let myself want things. Not real things. I mean—I wanted a house and a job and food and all those basic things. And in theory, I wanted a boyfriend, but it never worked out. But Phoenix? He was a stretch. Like a really big reach. Like a want that was too dangerous to indulge in.

But I couldn't help myself. If he was reaching out to me, I

couldn't ignore it. Being with him was automatic, natural, magnetic. So, I gave in and grabbed his hand.

Warmth spread up my body as he linked his fingers with mine. "Please don't tell me to get lost."

Yeah. That wasn't even in the realm of the possible.

So, no. I wasn't going to send him away. I *couldn't*. "Don't get lost. Stay. Move in next door." I couldn't believe I'd just said that.

His chin dropped, and he let out a soft laugh. "Is this weird?"

He looked at me with his hazel eyes and little hint of a dimple and my stomach somersaulted.

"This is kind of weird, right?" he asked again. "Going from zero to a hundred in a day?"

"It's completely weird." That didn't mean I was going to push it away. "But you have to remember that nothing about my life has ever been normal."

"So, this isn't freaking you out? Like I'm moving way too fast." He stared intently into my eyes as if willing me to be honest.

He didn't know me well enough yet, but I didn't lie. Lying went against everything I wanted to be. "Honestly?"

"Yes. Always, please."

I rubbed my thumb along the back of his hand. "It's been two days, so yeah, logically, this is way too fast. But it doesn't feel wrong for you to be here. At least not to me. So, I'm not going to kick you out. But if you need to go, if you change your mind, I won't beg you to stay either. I get it. My life is a lot for most people." I gave him a smile, hoping to ease any pity he might feel for me. I hated pity more than anything. "Plus, I have to maintain some form of dignity."

He chuckled, just like I'd wanted him to. But his laughter faded, and that serious look was in his eyes again. "It's been two days, and I already feel like I just want to be around you as much as possible. I've never felt this way about anyone else, but at the same time, it doesn't surprise me. Because I felt the same way six years ago. When I tried to leave you on the stairs—after we talked —I couldn't do it. It was so hard that I had to force myself to go.

And then with the cops…" He ran his free hand over his short hair, making it stick out crazily, yet it was adorable. "So, yeah, please, say something. Tell me something that will make this not feel so insane."

Oh, man. I got it. I did. "Look, I'd be an idiot not to be afraid." I gave his hand a squeeze. "Not of you, but of something going wrong. Of getting my heart broken." That was the biggest risk—my heart. "But I have too many other things to be afraid of that are real, legitimate, life-or-death fears. I'm going to do my best not to overthink this. So, yeah. Move in next door. It'll be easier for us to find out how serious this really is if we're not constantly trekking back and forth into the city. We'll take it one day at a time."

"Okay."

"Okay." He moved to sit next to me with his back against the couch, legs stretching long over the thin mattress.

I studied his profile as he grew quiet. "There's something else I need to tell you," he said without looking at me. "—but I can't yet. I have to work up some courage."

I raised my brows. "You really are stringing me along, huh?"

"Not on purpose. I'm an open, honest person, but…" He gave me a hopeful look. "Do you trust me?"

"I do." It was the truth. I totally did. "But I'm not the kind of person that will freak out either."

"You might freak out about this. It would be totally fair if you did." He winced. "I just…"

He wasn't saying anything, and honestly, whatever it was, as long as it wasn't something awful, I was sure it would be fine. "You don't have to tell me yet," I said. "But know I will do my best not to get upset. I can't make any promises, but I'll do my best. Okay?"

"Yeah. Okay." He said the words, but something in his tone made me think he didn't actually believe it.

Without knowing more, there wasn't anything else I could do to reassure him. So, I just had to do the next thing. "I'm going to get up and shower. I'll be down in a bit." I slid my hand from his, and it immediately felt like I was missing something. The feeling was so strong it was almost like a physical hurt.

He slid off the fold-out, and the whole mattress bounced with the movement. "I'll be downstairs."

"Okay." When he was gone, and the door clicked shut, I leaned my head back and groaned. "What is even happening right now?" Now that he was gone, I knew that I was missing something. Something *huge*. But I didn't have a clue what it was.

What on Earth happened while I'd been in Hell?

CHAPTER FIVE

SAMANTHA

I LAY in my bed for a minute, trying to think of what Phoenix might have to tell me, but nothing came to mind.

And he was moving in next door?

For someone used to traveling between realms, it wasn't every day that I felt like I was in a different universe. But apparently, today was that day.

It was almost too much to process, especially when I didn't even know what I was supposed to be processing. So, I did the next thing on my to-do list.

I got up.

I showered and got ready for the day. Normally, I'd train. Rain, shine, no matter what. But not today. Not after a night like last night. My limbs still felt heavy and maybe a bit like Jell-O. It was a weird combo, but I wasn't about to try working out. I'd break something for sure.

Instead, I put on a little bit of makeup because it made me feel normal. Today, I needed that. Getting ready like I did every day made me think that this was going to be okay, even if I wasn't exactly one hundred percent okay right now.

I threw on my comfiest pair of leggings and a super soft, oversized, flowy V-neck. Comfort was king today. I slid my feet into my cushiest slippers and loosely braided my wet hair as I walked down the stairs.

Mom and Frank were seated at the island, drinking coffee. Phoenix paused whatever he was doing at the stove to turn to me. He'd showered, too. Changed. Shaved. He gave a small smile, and the single dimple on the left side of his face deepened, making my heart rate speed up and *holy shit*, he was way out of my league.

Maybe I should've put on more makeup.

There was an ache in my chest, and I pressed my fist to it, trying to rub it away as I went down the last few stairs.

Frank pulled out the stool next to him, drawing my attention away from Phoenix. "*Gurl.*" He drew the word out as he motioned to the stool.

"Don't say that. And definitely, really, don't say it like that. You're not a tween girl." I made my way to the island and took the offered stool. I was kind of glad that Frank was there to distract me. I wasn't sure what to do with or say to Phoenix now that I was fully awake.

"Why can't I say it like that? I can pull off anything," said the forty-something Orthodox priest. He was wearing the usual pack T-shirt-sweatpants combo, too. He must've slept here. It almost never happened, but nothing about last night had been usual.

"No, you can't pull off *everything*," Mom said from the other side of him. "That's absurd."

"You really can't," I said, and I heard Phoenix laugh but I stayed focused on Frank because Phoenix made me feel too many things.

"Fine. I won't say that again." He rolled his eyes, and I swear I saw his fourteen-year-old daughter in that expression. "How *do* you *do* today?" He said primly, then took a sip from his mug with his pinky sticking out.

I rolled my eyes at him. "Good. Fine. I think?" I spotted the churro chip cookies on the counter and reached for one, but Mom slapped my hand away. "Ow." I shook it. "Come on. Don't be like that. It's *tradition*."

"A tradition you partook in last night," Mom said.

Right. I remembered that. Sort of.

"And even if you hadn't, you can't have a cookie for breakfast." Phoenix was leaning against the counter. He had a pot of boiling water on the stove, a bowl of something he'd been mixing, and a bunch of other ingredients on the counter. "You have to have real food first."

I met his gaze, and everything in me heated. We were both quiet for a second.

I was missing something. I could feel it, but I didn't know what it was. So, I cleared my throat and went back to something easier. "A cookie is real food. There's eggs in there. Butter. Flour. All the basics in one tasty little treat."

Phoenix crossed his arms, showing me more of his tattoos, and man, I wanted to ask so many questions. Especially about the one with some kind of script woven through flowers. He tilted his head, drawing my eyes up, telling me he'd noticed where I was looking without saying it.

Get yourself under control, Samantha.

He raised a brow as if to see if I'd ask about it, but when I didn't, he went back to the easier stuff. "Sure, it's got eggs, butter, and flour, but it also has a lot of sugar. Chocolate chips. Protein is what you need. I texted Chris, and he confirmed it."

Wait. What? He'd texted Chris?

Since when were they texting? When did they exchange numbers?

How much did I miss while I was out of it?

I guessed I'd missed more than I thought. But in all honesty, I wasn't sure if I minded. This—Phoenix being here, cooking—it was kind of nice. I'd been wanting a relationship like Chris had with Cosette or Tessa had with Dastien, but I hadn't thought about how much the men in their lives tried to take care of them.

Was this that?

And did I mind?

I thought about it for exactly half a second, then smiled. No, I didn't mind. It actually felt good. "It's going to be like that, is it?"

"What?" His smile spread into a grin that made my stomach somersault. "Me making sure you get what you need? Yeah. It's going to be exactly like that."

I looked at Frank, wondering what he thought.

He shrugged, but there was something in his eyes, a kind of giddy excitement that I'd never seen before, and I wasn't sure what to make of it. "I'm not telling you anything. They already let me have a cookie, and I can't risk losing the second one."

"Traitor." Sold out for cookies. To be fair, they were seriously amazing cookies, but still…

I looked at Mom. "Can I at least have a coffee?"

"Sure."

Whoa. I didn't expect her to agree. "Great." This day wasn't going to be so—

"After you finish a glass of water."

This was bull, but a glass of ice water slid in front of me. I looked up, and Phoenix gave me a wink.

"Fine." I took a sip, tasted the electrolytes in it, and glanced at Mom. This had to be her doing. I didn't mind them every once in a while, but she had been pumping me full of them recently. It was getting old. "Mom. Come on. Is this really necessary?"

"I didn't give you another IV like I wanted to. You were sleeping so hard, and—"

"Fine." I didn't like the edge of fear in her voice. If my drinking electrolytes made her feel better, then I would drink the dang electrolytes. "But I actually feel okay. I swear." Maybe I was a little worn down, but I should've felt a lot worse. I wasn't sure why I felt so good.

"Good. You ate a ton last night." She sounded happy about it.

"I did?" I often didn't remember it, but that was my usual MO.

"Yes." Phoenix shook his head. "I've never seen someone eat so much. I think for most of it, you were half-asleep. But we just kept sliding food in front of you, and you kept eating until you pushed away a plate, put your head down, and went to sleep on the island."

Huh. "I vaguely remember that last part, but not the eating. What did I eat?"

"Lots of things."

Weird. "Okay. Well, I'm hungry again. And I'm guessing the *real food* from last night doesn't count for today since you're still not giving me the cookie."

Phoenix gave me a small shake of his head. "No. It doesn't count."

"Fine." I wanted to argue, but it seemed like the odds were against me if even Frank was backing them. "What are you making?" I tried to look around him but couldn't figure it out.

"Eggs Benedict. Your mom said it was her favorite."

Mom leaned against the island and raised a brow. She was enjoying Phoenix cooking for me, maybe a little too much, but she was right. It was pretty fantastic.

Eggs Benedict wasn't just Mom's favorite. It was one of mine, too. We just didn't have it often, and never at home. "With hollandaise?"

"Yes. Just finished making it."

"Shut up." Who was this guy? No one made hollandaise from scratch. Did they?

"Right," Mom said, but the way she said it, there was an implied *can you believe how awesome he is?* And yeah, she had a point.

He snagged a bowl from the counter and tipped it. "It's a lot easier than it seems."

"If you say so." I glanced from him to the bowl and back again. "How do you know how to make that?"

He shrugged. "I told you. I like to cook." He put the bowl back on the counter behind him.

"But it's a big difference between liking to cook and making your own hollandaise." I *liked to cook*, but not like that. Mom was super great at following any recipe, but she didn't make sauces like that. At least not as far as I knew.

"It's really not that hard. You just—"

"That's what she said." Frank blurted out the words, then laughed at his own lame joke.

I hung my head. "Frank." I was going to murder him.

When I looked up, Phoenix was silently laughing, chin to his chest, eyes closed, whole body shaking.

Mom was holding back her laughter. Barely.

I looked back at the graying priest, who was rubbing his hand along his beard and smiling his I-made-a-joke smile. What an idiot. "I apologize for that moron."

A loud laugh burst from Phoenix. "For a priest, you don't exactly act like one."

"I'm still a human, and there's joy in laughter," Frank said. "Tell me that you're not enjoying that laugh. I dare you."

The laugh did feel good.

"If I can find time to make someone laugh, to bring them a bit of happiness, then I feel like it's my duty to make that happen," Frank said. "I don't get the chance to do it often. For the most part, I deal with people going through the hardest of times, so I lighten it up when I can. My kids find me hilarious."

That was factually incorrect. "No, they don't."

Frank crossed his arms as he looked at me, then back at Phoenix. "Well, my wife, Rachel, she definitely does."

I rolled my eyes. "She married you. Clearly, she has questionable taste."

Frank bumped his arm against mine. "Well, then, why are we friends?"

"You tell me, buddy. I met you one time in a mental hospital, and I've *never* been able to get rid of you. I even moved across the country, and look where you found yourself."

Frank sat up straight with a haughty look on his face. "That was divine intervention. God wanted us to work together. An opening came up, and the church asked me if I would come. I took the sign that I was supposed to continue mentoring you. You're welcome."

"Did I say thank you?"

"No, but you were definitely thinking it. You frequently do. I can tell. Especially in moments like these."

I leaned my head on his shoulder. "I sure do." I might tease Frank, but I'd been really glad when he moved his whole family from LA to Austin. I hadn't realized how much I'd leaned on him until I moved away. It'd been a long three months before they arrived.

Mom and Phoenix shared a look. "They've always been like this," she said. "Since the day they met."

Phoenix gave her a nod, then turned to me. The smile faded away, and I knew what he was going to ask. "Mental hospital? That's where you met Frank?"

It felt like forever ago, and to me, maybe it was. "Yeah." I sat up straight in my chair. "Seven years ago?" I looked at Frank for confirmation.

He nodded. "Roundabout."

"I want to hear this story," Phoenix said from where he leaned against the counter.

"No, you don't. It's not an interesting story." At least I didn't think it was, but if he wanted to know, I didn't mind telling it. The whole thing was just a little sad and depressing, and I never wanted anyone to pity me. I hated that. It was the worst.

Getting pity from this man who was here, cooking me food, being basically perfect, would suck, but I wasn't going to let that stop me. I wasn't ashamed of my past.

"Please. I want to know more about you." He didn't smile when he asked, but he was kind. Always kind.

"It was a few months before we met," I said. "Before that night on the stairs."

"I remember when you came home." He crossed his arms. "Your mom let us know. Asked me to keep an eye out for you when she was working."

"Yeah." People sometimes treated me differently once they knew my past, but not Phoenix. That gave me some hope that this wouldn't go as badly as it had before. "That wasn't my best time. I'd been a bit of a mess, trying to adjust to normal life and mostly failing."

"You weren't failing at anything." Mom hated it when I talked badly about myself. It was a pet peeve. One of them, anyway. "You're too hard on yourself."

"Maybe," I said, mostly to appease her. But this was so far off track. And so not the way to get Phoenix to stick around. "So yeah, back to meeting Frank." *Ugh.* Why did this always feel so awkward to talk about?

Probably because it wasn't something I talked about. There was such a stigma with being in a facility, but he already knew this about me. So, I shouldn't have felt weird about it. And yet…

Screw it. "Frank and I met at the in-patient pediatric mental facility. Baycroft."

"As in, he came in as a priest to counsel you?"

I laughed but couldn't meet his gaze. Not while talking about this. "Him? No. I'm not sure why anyone would listen to him. He's a real ding-dong."

Frank let out a fake-insulted gasp. "I'll show you a ding-dong."

I shoved Frank. "Ew. Gross. Please don't."

Frank started laughing, and I couldn't help but join in.

"Are they really always like this?" Phoenix said to Mom over our laughing. His slanted smile told me he was at least amused by our shenanigans.

"Usually," Mom said. "Unless they're working. Then, they behave. The rest of the time? You get this nonsense. They're ridiculous. Supposedly, they're two grown-ups, one of them with teenage children of his own, but you wouldn't know it when they're like this."

Something about that made me laugh harder. "Sorry." I tried

to smother the laughter. "It's a coping mechanism for all the dark stuff we see."

Frank bumped my shoulder. "For the record, lots of people come to talk to me and love getting my advice."

"Sure, they do." I laughed again at the offended look on Frank's face, and this time, Mom's rich laugh echoed mine.

"But no, I didn't counsel her at Baycroft," Frank said, turning to Phoenix. "I didn't work there."

"Thank God." I swallowed down the next wave of laughter at the face Frank made—tongue out and everything.

I finally looked up at Phoenix. He was standing there, still leaning against the counter, arms crossed, no judgment on his face. He looked genuinely curious and interested in the story.

Right. I guessed I should stop goofing off with Frank and actually tell it. "The thing about mental health is that sometimes there's a spiritual component that people ignore or don't have the capacity to recognize. Sometimes people get admitted that maybe shouldn't be. A lot of patients had various sorts of demonic problems, and I tried to help those cases when I could." It didn't always work out right away, but eventually, I was able to help anyone who came in with a spiritual problem.

"One day, there was this girl…I knew right away that she needed my help. So, I went to help her." I thought back on that night. The tolling of a spiritual bell that woke me from a dead sleep. The chill in the air. The way the lights flickered in the hallway.

For some reason, I didn't exactly mind my time at Baycroft. I mean—it wasn't a resort, but it wasn't horrible, either. It was the only time I'd ever been safe from my father.

In some ways, I wished I could go back to a place like that. My room upstairs was torn up. The only way that could've happened was if he'd made his presence known. I wasn't sure what that meant for staying at the Sanctuary, and—

Mom cleared her throat, drawing me back to the present.

Right. I'd deal with whatever came next later. "Sorry. Got lost in my memories for a second. Anyway…I went down to help this new patient out, and there was this guy in the chair." Oh, boy. I was slow this morning. I just realized that this story was going to turn into a can of worms. I suddenly wished I'd never started telling it.

"Frank," Phoenix asked. "He was the one in the chair? That's how you met him?"

"No," Frank said. "That's how she met *Hunter*."

"Who is Hunter?" Phoenix asked.

"Her ex," Frank said before I could stop him.

"Frank!" I shoved him off his stool.

He caught himself on the edge of the island. "Excuse me. It's the truth."

"Yeah. Maybe. But you didn't have to bring that part of it up." And now, the can of worms was officially open. "We could've left him as a vague shadow of a guy." That was how I always wanted to remember him. A person who was only a part of my life for a little bit but had left a lingering shadow.

"Okay. Now, I really want to hear this story. The full version." Phoenix pointed to me. "You're not getting out of this." He turned to the stove and shut off the pot of boiling water. Then, he snagged the bowl of hollandaise and put it in the fridge.

Frank's phone vibrated on the counter.

Saved by the phone. I looked up at the ceiling. *Thank you.*

"Um. Samantha…" Frank's voice had an apology in it, and I didn't like it.

I took a second because I knew what that meant, and when I finally looked at him, all the humor was gone from his face. He was in full priest mode.

"No." I knew what that meant. He was going to need my help with something. "I *can't*."

"Okay. Just…wait. It could be nothing." He slid off the stool and went outside to make a call.

I closed my eyes and took a breath. "I have this feeling that

Astaroth is up to something. Whatever last night was, it's not over yet."

"What makes you think that?" Phoenix sounded close.

I opened my eyes to find him on the stool that Frank had left. "Something he said to me. His tone. I don't know…" I glanced at Mom. "He might have been taunting me."

"You'd know better than me." My mother didn't really know Astaroth at all, other than the attack that made me. She pressed her lips together, and there was a question in her eyes.

I didn't know how to answer it, but I could try. "I don't have any proof that says he's up to something—no evidence or anything he explicitly said he was going to do—just this growing knot in my stomach and his open-ended threat…" I rubbed a hand down my face. "Or maybe I'm just tired. Maybe he was trying to rattle me." That wasn't quite right. "Wait. No. He's always trying to rattle me, but this time…" I wasn't making sense, and I knew it. I just couldn't find the right words. It was all a jumble because I needed time to sort through everything that had happened. Which would take more time than I had right now.

"The psychological toll and the warfare will be bad for a while, Samantha. You can't go all end times on me," Mom said.

"Right, but—"

Frank came back into the house. He tapped his phone into the palm of his hand as he studied me. "How tired are you?" He slid the phone into his pocket.

Was he kidding right now? "Very."

He loosened the *komboskoini*—a knotted prayer rope that he kept wrapped around his wrist—and moved his thumb over it. "I don't think this involves your father, and if I'm right, then you could get a boost from it."

Frank was right. Sometimes, I got a boost from doing what I did. And with how drained I was, it felt like a fair risk to take. But there was always a chance my father would show up. "What are we talking about? Give me the details."

"I'll cook while he talks. You're going to need the fuel."

Phoenix got up, gesturing for Frank to take the stool again, and went around to the stove.

I watched him move around our kitchen as if he lived here. He didn't, but somehow, he felt like he fit. He made an iced coffee and snagged two cookies from the plate, and then turned to me with them.

Wait? Those were for me?

"Phoenix." Mom drew out his name. "She hasn't finished her water or had breakfast."

"She's going to have it soon, and it sounds like she's going to need the sugar-caffeine boost." He walked around the island and set them in front of me. "For you," he said it like he was offering me more than what was on the counter.

The way he said it—the way he placed them there while looking into my eyes—made me feel like he was giving me so much more than some food and drink.

"Thank you." My words meant more, too. It wasn't just a thank you for what he was giving me. It was for sticking around, for cooking for me, for just being here, but I couldn't seem to voice all of that. Not here. Not right now.

He looked into my eyes, and it was as if he understood everything I'd left unsaid. "My pleasure." He brushed a kiss on the top of my head and went back to cooking.

I sat there, staring at the offering he'd just given me, still feeling the warmth of the kiss and remembering the understanding in his eyes. I would remember this moment for the rest of my life.

It wasn't much. On the outside, it was pretty much nothing. But it felt like more.

It felt like the start of something big.

I took a sip of the iced coffee.

Dang it. He'd made it just how I liked it. I looked up at him as he moved around the kitchen, following him with my gaze.

"I watched your mom make it yesterday. Did I do it right?" he asked over his shoulder.

"Yeah." Phoenix needed a flaw. Something. Anything. Otherwise, he just didn't feel real. "It's perfect."

Frank put his head on my shoulder. "It's just *so romantic.*"

I jerked my shoulder. "Stop it." I waved a cookie at him. "Spill. What's going on? I need all the details." I took a bite of the cookie and groaned. Mom had made them just right. As always.

"Enjoying the cookie?" Frank teased.

I rolled my eyes. "Shut up."

"Can't. Not when I'm having so much fun." He glanced down at the prayer rope, and when he looked back at me again, he was all business. "The exorcism I did last night involved a teen boy. Not a religious house. No wards. From the chat I had with the parents, there's likely some generational things happening, which is tricky for me, but I know you can fix that."

I made a cutting motion with my hand as I chewed the last of the cookie. "Snip, snip. That's no problem." I could cut demon ties pretty easily.

"It was the usual at first—bad friends, bad words, bad actions. It grew, and the parents seemed to be a little out of their league with it. They're busy—both work—and they just let some things slide."

That was understandable, even if it was a bad decision. "Easier to do that than face your problems."

"Hey. Being a parent is hard. Things slip sometimes."

"You're lucky you had it so easy," I said to Mom. I put my hand under my chin and fluttered my lashes at her.

"Sure. Easy. That's what we'd all call your life." The sarcasm was thick with that one, which was earned. I didn't think easy was even in my vocabulary at this point.

I laughed, then turned to Frank. "Right. So, the kid is messing up. Sounds like normal rebellion. Busy parents and an attention-hungry teen."

"Sure, until they started hearing things in the hallway. Voices. In a language they didn't understand."

Now, he was getting somewhere. "Demonic?"

"Confirmed. I heard them myself."

Okay. This was getting interesting. "Right. So, generational, plus some dabbling?"

"Exactly. The son didn't think it was real at first."

I snorted a laugh. "Right. Best trick the devil plays." The scent of ham cooking wafted through the kitchen, and my stomach grumbled. Loud.

"Holy shit." Phoenix turned to look at me. "Was that your stomach?"

My face was burning, and I desperately wanted to hide under the counter in embarrassment, but I refrained. Barely. Because I was a grown-up. "I guess I'm hungry." I gave him a smile that was more grimace-less smile.

He turned back to the stove and finished plating something. "Good thing this is ready." He slid a plate to me, then got to work making more for everyone else.

I took a bite and moaned. "You gotta be kidding me."

Phoenix turned back to me, brow raised. By the slow grin on his face, he knew how good it was. "What?"

"I need a flaw." I held up a hand as Frank listed off some of my flaws. "Stop. No. I have plenty. I think everyone is well aware of my baggage." I looked at Phoenix. "I need to know one of *your* flaws. It'll help humanize you."

"Do I look stupid? Why on earth would I tell you my flaws? You think I'm fabulous right now. I'm not ruining that." He gave me a smile. "No way. You're going to have to figure them out for yourself."

I rolled my eyes. "Fine," I said, then pointed my fork at Frank. "The call you just got was from the parents of the boy."

"Yes. It was a mess last night, and I knew it would take several sessions, but everything went wrong."

"What happened?"

"The demon…" He tugged his *komboskoini* fully off his wrist and started praying silently, working his thumb over each knot. "It just wouldn't go. I did everything I was supposed to, but you know, for mere mortals like me, it can take time. It felt like I'd make some headway only to have the demon come back stronger. I eventually grew so tired that I had to call it a night. I meant to drive home, but ended up here." He rolled the *komboskoini* between his fingers. "This one seems like it's going to take a very long time, unless..."

"Right."

"Unless what?" Phoenix asked.

I met his gaze. "Unless I take care of it."

Mom made a noise.

I started to say something, but Frank touched my arm to stop me. "I can't imagine how hard this must be for you," Frank said to Mom. "I have two girls of my own, and I would destroy anyone who tried to my weaken child—because even if Samantha is fully grown now, she will always be your child. And yet, I have a teen who tried to kill himself this morning. He's in the hospital, recovering and under a mandatory hold."

Mom let out a gasp. "Lord, help him."

"The warfare in that house...I had to force myself to walk in there. It felt thick and heavy. And the battle last night...well, you saw me when I arrived. I thought I'd come here at first because I was weary, and my spirit knew I needed Sam's help. And then I learned what happened to her, and I thought it was so I could help her this morning. So, I stayed. But now, I'm wondering if I ended up here for an entirely different reason—I needed to be here to ask you to help this child."

There wasn't really a choice. I couldn't say no. "Let's eat, and then we'll go." I looked at Mom. "I'll do an IV or whatever else you need, but this kid needs help. I won't say no."

"Do you ever say no?" Phoenix had a little wrinkle between his brows, and I wished I could say something to ease the worry. But lying had never been my thing.

"No. I've delayed before, and I've learned that it only makes things worse. With this stuff, sooner is always better. And it sounds like it's already pretty bad for this kid. So, let's eat, IV or whatever, and let's go."

"Alright." Mom crossed the kitchen, heading down to the basement. "But I'm giving you a vitamin dose in your IV," she yelled up to me.

I held up my hands. "Totally fine," I yelled back. I wasn't about to argue with her.

"I'd like to come with," Phoenix said. "Is that okay? Will the family be okay with it?" His hands were shoved in his pockets. His gaze kept darting between me and Frank, as if he wasn't sure which one of us—or both—would object to it.

"I'll make it conditional." Frank looked at me and winced. "But I might have to say that you're weakened and need him with you." His voice was a little too high, like he thought I'd be upset with that.

I wasn't upset about something that was true. "I am weakened, and if he wants to come with me, then I need him. It's not a lie."

"Okay. Great. I'll make the call." Frank went back outside.

Phoenix motioned to the plate. "Eat."

I would absolutely eat this and enjoy it. "Thank you. This is amazing."

"You don't have to thank me. I like doing it."

"Well, I still think saying thank you is nice no matter what." I ate a few more bites, and he went back to cooking. "You sure you'll be okay with this?"

"I told you I wanted to stick close, so yes. This is what you do, and I'm excited to see what your typical work life is like."

He plated up another batch and set it on the counter for Frank. Watching him in my kitchen was a little surreal. Having him in my life was surreal. Actually, everything that was happening was surreal. I *still* felt like I was in some alternate universe.

And something was going on with Phoenix. Was it normal for the guy you've just reconnected with to want to hang out twenty-four-seven?

But I didn't want him to leave. At all.

So, I'd just enjoy it while it lasted and hope he'd be around for a while.

And really, the best way to find out if he'd stick around would be to show him my world.

If he'd been any other guy, he'd already be gone—long gone. I went through the facts in my mind. He'd stuck around through one of the worst nights I'd had in years, and he even carried me upstairs and slept curled at the foot of my bed. He was moving in next door and had somehow learned exactly how I liked my coffee. He even stood up to my mom, giving me the coffee and cookie before breakfast. No one ever went against her. Not even Dastien.

This was a good day.

Honestly, any day that started with Phoenix felt pretty amazing.

I took a sip of iced coffee.

Okay. Yeah. I could do this.

CHAPTER SIX

PHOENIX

SAM and I had talked a little bit on the way into Austin, but after a few minutes, her words slowed and slurred. So, I'd turned on soft music. I told her to get some rest, and that I'd wake her when we go there.

I'd attempted to tail Frank the whole way into the city but failed miserably. The man drove like a maniac. Which didn't make sense for a priest, but what the hell did I know about priests? Frank was the first one I'd really talked to for any length of time, and he was odd. Sometimes, he acted like one of my sisters, using awful slang. Although, it was much worse when he used it. Sometimes, Frank went heavy on the dad jokes. Sometimes, he was a mature priest—serious, deep, Godly. I'd only seen that for a little while in our consult in his office, but I knew he had that side to him. But for some reason, no matter how he was acting, the man was growing on me.

I parked in the emergency room lot at the hospital, and a minute later, Frank was tapping on my window.

When he'd been sitting at the counter making jokes and teasing Sam, he'd been the silly, teenager version. But the man at my window was Frank the Priest. The one I'd met in the office a few days ago.

I rolled down the window. "She's asleep," I whispered to him.

"I can see that." He studied her with a parental-like eye. "I don't know about this. I have a bad feeling. Not for this kid, but for Samantha. I'm asking too much."

I thought so, too, but I knew Sam felt differently. "You said she'd gain energy from this?"

"She usually does, except when she doesn't."

"When doesn't she?"

"When it's her father. Otherwise, she's fine. Or better than fine —annoyingly peppy."

I glanced at Sam. She'd somehow managed to fold herself up in a tight ball in the seat. Her chest rose and fell steadily. "I don't know how she's sleeping with the sun on her face. I need it pitch black."

"The sun makes her feel safe. The veil between the realms is thickest during the day, making it the best time for her to fully relax. Which works out, since she keeps unusual hours. Afternoons tend to be when she gets the most sleep, but usually, she sleeps with blackout curtains. Which is why I have a bad feeling. She must be really exhausted. Especially if our whispering hasn't woken her up."

"But with the sun up, she can't get hurt? With the veil thick?"

Frank waggled his hand back and forth in a so-so motion. "Depends." He nudged my shoulder. "Wake her up."

I reached out to her, but he hit my shoulder. Hard. "*What*?" I whisper-shouted at him.

"Not that way. The other way. Like you did last night. Practice," he whispered back.

I understood what he meant but didn't know *how* to do that.

"Follow your gut."

That was always such a helpful piece of advice.

But maybe not totally wrong in this case.

I closed my eyes and focused on the feeling of her—the way

she made me feel, her laugh, her smile. The same way I had focused on her when I'd kissed her in the ice bath. It worked then. And it worked when she was having a nightmare. But was this the best way to do it? Was there another better way? I didn't know.

I honestly had no idea what I was doing at all, but I did it anyway.

Wake up. I thought the words and tried to shove them at that feeling. At her.

"No," she mumbled.

My eyes flew open, and I looked at Frank. I couldn't believe that had worked.

He gave me a thumbs-up and motioned for me to do it again.

Okay.

Come on, Samantha. I imagined my thoughts reaching out to her. *We're here. Time to wake up.*

She stirred in the seat. "Tired." The word was more whimper than anything else, and I couldn't help but reach out and brush her hair away from her face.

I felt bad for waking her up, especially with how hard she was sleeping. *We're at the hospital. The boy needs your help. Will you wake up, please?*

She jolted up out of her seat. "What?" She looked around. "We're here?"

"Sorry to wake you. I wish I could've let you sleep longer, but Frank says it's time to go inside." I motioned to where Frank stood beside the SUV.

She wiped her hands down her face. "Right. Sure. I got this." She looked around, then sighed. "I wish I'd brought a coffee with me."

"Actually…" I'd filled a water bottle with her iced coffee concoction while she was getting ready. When Ana saw what I was doing, she pulled out a soft cooler and said we might as well add some food. By the time Sam had come downstairs, I'd already put the bag in the car.

I reached behind my seat, snagged the cooler, and unzipped it. I handed her the bottle.

She unscrewed the top, peeked inside, then gave me a sleepy grin. "My hero." She closed her eyes as she took a long drink. "Thank you. What else you got in there?"

I tipped the bag so she could peek inside.

She raised a brow. "Wow. Mom went all out." She snagged a bag of homemade protein balls, then grabbed her belt bag from the floorboard. She dug into her belt bag and pulled out a pair of headphones. She plugged them in, turned on some music, and then shoved the earbuds into her ears.

I looked at Frank for some sort of answer.

"It helps her concentrate. Hospitals are her least favorite place—lots of pain, sadness, fear, and anguish. Which attracts lots of demonic activity."

"Got it." That made a lot of sense.

Sam closed her eyes and when she opened them, I swear I saw a flicker of flame in them. "Ready."

"Alright." If she was ready, I was ready. "Let's go."

The hospital was busy, but we didn't have to wait long to get visitor tags. There was a little concern about how many of us were going to the room, but Sam whispered to let Frank handle it, and he did.

It took a few minutes, but a nurse came to lead us through the hospital.

I tried to keep track of the turns so that we could find our way out while listening to the nurse's rules.

"Be prepared for the restraints. We've given him enough sedatives to knock him out, but they're not working. We can't give him more for the next three hours, so be ready for him to shout some really awful things at you." The nurse laughed. "I've heard some messed up stuff from all kinds of druggies, but this kid takes the cake. Some of the shit he's said..."

"He's not himself," Frank said.

"Sure. I bet." The nurse slowed. "This is it. Room thirty-three.

If something goes wrong, we'll hear it." She motioned to the nurse's station down the hall and knocked on the door. "Visitors are here." She waved us in. "Good luck," she whispered as I walked into the room.

Even with the warning, I was not prepared for what was inside.

The teenager was writhing on the bed. Restrained. His parents sat in chairs against the wall, as far from the kid as they could possibly get. I didn't blame them. He was yelling some pretty vile things—about their love life, about their past, about things that no kid should ever know about their parents.

Everything non-essential had been removed from the room. The bed was pushed away from the wall, and all the various cords and instruments had been either removed or taped to the wall. They were making sure this kid couldn't get to anything in the room.

Frank moved straight to the parents. Sam pulled out her earbuds, shoved them in her pocket with her phone, and walked right up to the kid.

I stayed hovering in the doorway, unable to make my feet move. Even if I hadn't known that there was something spiritual going on, I would've guessed it by the way this kid looked.

His face was yellow. Sickly. Pale. His brown hair stuck out in all directions. The tips had been dyed red at some point, but the dye was fading, leaving them a pinkish color. Spit flew from his mouth as he yelled, and then he turned to me and smiled. There was something dead in his eyes—evil—and I took a step back before I could stop myself.

"Fucking Marissa wasn't enough for you?"

I froze. "How…?"

"Don't listen to him," Samantha said. "That's not him. That's something *other*."

He started speaking in a language I'd never heard before and never wanted to hear again. It made everything in me rebel and want to run away. But I stayed in the doorway, and as I looked at the teenager, I was beginning to understand what Samantha really did and who she really was.

Brave.

Confident.

Powerful.

Last night wasn't a lone example of her bravery. Neither was that night six years ago. This was her normal, and I was in awe.

"Full name, please," Samantha said without looking away from the kid.

"Zane Michael Anders," Frank answered. "Let me know when you're starting."

"Will do." And then I almost had a heart attack when she climbed on the bed and straddled the kid, who was fighting with all his might to get free.

She turned to me and gave me a small smile. "I hate restraints, but I'm glad he has them today. I really hate it when they try to rip out my throat or strangle me. Sucks. Big time." She gave me a wink.

A surprised laugh slipped free before I could stop it. Was she joking with me? Right now?

Then, she turned to the parents on the other side of the room. "Sit tight. This might get ugly, but be patient with me. I'm going to fix this."

Zane yelled again in that awful language, and the sounds of the words, the way they echoed in the room, something about them made everything inside me rebel.

Sam leaned down closer to get in his face. "No, thanks. I like my face how it is."

I didn't know why it surprised me, but clearly, Sam understood whatever language Zane was speaking.

Sam looked at something off to the side of the kid. "But you have got to go." Her gaze narrowed. "Wait. You're familiar. I can feel it in your tie."

Something about the way she said it worried me.

She sat back, still staring at something only she could see.

"You're the one that had Jennifer. You were gone by the time I got to her, but you're not gone this time. Too bad for you."

"Wait. Who is Jennifer?" Frank asked.

"You know, *Jennifer*. Hunter's Jennifer." She sighed. "I can't remember her last name. It's been too long, but it's weird that I was just thinking about her today and how I met Hunter. We were just talking about that, and now the demon is back? With the same boy you were trying to help last night? It's almost as if something wants me to remember Hunter."

"That's a pretty strange coincidence," Frank said.

The parents were looking back and forth between Frank and Samantha. Their faces were a mix of confusion, horror, and hope. It was the hope that made it more painful.

"You know what I think about coincidences?" Samantha looked to the side of Zane's head, to where I imagined she saw the demon. "They're not a thing. It's always some machination." She shrugged. "Whatever. I'm too tired to think about that right now. Let's do this."

My gaze met Frank's, and he raised a brow and nodded toward Samantha.

I wasn't sure what he meant by the look. I wasn't following what she was saying or doing, and I had no clue how to help her.

I was trying to figure out what I should do when the boy turned to me. His eyes glowed red. "You thought you could take her from me, but you can't. She's *mine*."

Everything in me froze.

I hadn't taken any girl from anyone except Samantha from her father.

I suddenly had a terrible feeling that coming here was a huge mistake.

CHAPTER SEVEN

SAMATHA

THE ROOM WAS QUIET—WELL, quiet aside from the constant yelling of the demon, but I was pretty good at ignoring it. I twisted to talk to Frank and spotted Phoenix. His face had gone pale.

Wait. That wasn't right. What did I miss? "Are you okay?"

He didn't look away from the demon.

"Nix!" I shouted his name, and he finally looked at me. "What's wrong?" Was this it? Had he finally reached his weird limit? I kept waiting for him to panic about everything I did, but this was the first time something had actually gotten to him.

"It said…" He swallowed. "Could it be your father?"

Oh. That wasn't what I'd been expecting him to say. At all.

I looked down at the boy. Why was he asking that? The demon had been saying all kinds of things, but as a general rule, I tuned out as much as I could. I'd learned to do that the hard way.

When I was a kid, the things they'd say would get me all worked up. But now I knew that I couldn't control what anyone—including demons—said, did, or how they felt. I could only control what I said, did, and how I felt. Once I truly understood that, nothing could hurt me unless I let it.

So, I shut down whatever garbage any demons said and let it float right over my head. It was usually all lies anyway. Demons wanted me angry or afraid or anything other than focused on sending it to Hell. It would literally say anything to save itself.

If this demon was somehow connected to my father, I felt like I would've noticed, but there was no harm in making sure. "Let me check." I relaxed my vision fully to go into the spiritual realm.

The boy's soul wasn't there. It was just like what this demon had done to Jennifer. Man, this was going to be more work than I thought it would be.

That night at Baycroft, I'd pulled her from the Lake of Fire. I'd have to do the same thing here. Except with Jennifer, the demon had been gone by the time I got there. I hadn't been able to hunt it down, but every demon had a unique feel. I never forgot a tie that I burned.

And that was exactly where I'd start. The demon ties had to go, but I kept searching for any sign of my father just in case I was wrong. I needed to be sure I wasn't getting in over my head.

When I found nothing, I reached forward, ignoring the demon's snarling, and held the tie. I shoved my power at it, burning it to ash.

As soon as it was gone, two more popped into place.

"Hmm." I didn't like that. "Frank?"

"Yes, dear?"

I didn't look away from the boy while I motioned with my pointer finger in a circle. "Let's get praying." I spared a look for the parents. "Specifically to Jesus. I know you don't have a religion, but this is your very literal come to Jesus moment. Demons are real. Satan is real. There's a war going on for souls, and right now, your son's soul is the one on the line. Frank is going to pray—he can give you handouts to follow along—and I'm going to get to work."

I glanced back at Phoenix. "It's not *him*. At least not yet."

Phoenix let out a relieved breath. "You're sure?"

"Mostly. But it could change. So, I'm going to do this fast."

He rolled his shoulders, and his color came back a little more.

"You okay?" I asked him.

"Yeah. As long as you're okay, I'm okay."

"I'm five by five. That coffee was the key." I gave him what I hoped was a reassuring smile. "Take anything it says with a grain of salt. Demons can't read your mind exactly. They're not omniscient. Not omnipresent. But a lot of them are old enough to know human nature and fears, and your thoughts have a frequency. They can tell if what they're saying is upsetting you—they'll feel your fear and anger—and they can prey on that. And if it was about me, well..." It would be good if he could ignore what the demon said, but that was easier said than done. "Just don't let me fall through any portals."

"I won't let you fall."

"Thanks." I glanced at the demon's face. Its eyes glowed a bright red. Its arms were too long for its body, and its fingers were too long for its hands. Its legs were wrapped around the boy's waist, arms around his neck, and I could already tell from the way it looked at me and tightened its grip that I was going to have a heck of a time getting it to let go.

"It's *you*," it said.

Great. I'd wasted too much time. "This one knows who I am now, but my father doesn't know where I am." Yet.

The demon started to say my father's name, but I grabbed its face, pushing a little power into it.

The demon screeched in pain, but I didn't care. Maybe that would seem cold to someone who didn't understand what a demon truly was, but they were pure evil. They lived to torture mortals and belonged in Hell. It could take a little pain, and I didn't feel even a little bit bad about it. "Don't you dare say *his* name."

Pushing my power at the demon should, theoretically, drain me, but instead, I felt power pouring into my veins.

I usually hated that feeling. I always associated it with my father, even though it wasn't oily or ick-filled, which meant it wasn't that bad. But it felt very gray area to me.

Today, I could use the extra juice.

The power that flowed into me felt good, vital, life-giving. My mind began to clear, and I didn't feel like I needed to drink ten more coffees to get this done.

Frank had been right. This was helping me.

I focused back on Zane. "Leave me some room there." I pointed to a spot on the floor that was away from everyone in the room. "I'm going to open a portal *right there.* No one go near that corner of the room." I paused—hoping everyone heard and understood—then said the word. "*Aperta!*"

The screams came immediately. The smells. The terror.

My breath grew faster and faster as I remembered where I'd been just hours before. I felt the heat. The pain. The—

No. I couldn't do this.

I didn't want to do this. Not again.

My heart raced and my vision tunneled and I wanted to go home.

I didn't want to do this anymore.

I didn't want to be this anymore.

I heard myself whimper, but it felt like it came from somewhere else.

Then, a warm hand pressed against my back and stroked up and down, soothing me.

"Samantha." Phoenix's voice cut through the panic. "Take a breath. Just one."

I closed my eyes, shutting out everything. Instead, I focused on the pressure of his hand as it went up my back, then down.

Up, then down.

Up, then down.

I timed my breathing with the feel of his hand, and when I blinked my eyes open, he lowered his face, pressing his forehead against mine.

His eyes widened for a second, and I knew he could *see* again.

"Shit. Sorry."

"For a panic attack? Don't be sorry."

"No." I let out a helpless little noise. "I meant for making you *see*."

He pressed a soft kiss on my forehead. "I'm not sorry, so why should you be?" He rose up a little more. "Better?"

"Yeah. I just…" I took another breath. "It's too soon."

He motioned with his head toward the portal. "I can hear it now. Smell it. Feel it. I can't imagine how you must feel, but I'm here. So hurry up and get this done, and I'll take you for a milkshake after."

"A milkshake?"

He studied me for a moment. "Don't you ever treat yourself after a job well done?"

I was quiet. Did I?

No. I guessed I didn't.

His hand ran up and down my back again. "Now seems a good time to start treating yourself. Get this done so we can go do something fun."

"Right. Fun." I had fun, didn't I? Just maybe not often.

Was I a workaholic?

Whatever. I didn't need to think about this right now.

I focused on Zane. Then, the demon.

First things first.

Moving quickly, I grabbed the demon ties in one hand and burned them, and as I did that, I switched my focus to the demon. I grabbed its hands and wrenched them away from the boy. I slid toward the floor, twisting my wrists as I dropped to the ground, using my whole body to pull the demon away, then tossing him into the portal.

The demon's screams alerted the hordes below. I glanced down into the portal just long enough to see them swarm like hornets coming after an intruder. Except these weren't hornets. They were demons that could do more harm than any insect.

Demons devoured souls.

But not mine.

Not today.

"*Claudere*!" The portal slammed shut.

Okay. That was done. Zane was free of all demonic ties, but his soul still wasn't there. I had to get him back.

Only one way to do it.

I didn't want to do it. I really, *really* didn't want to do it. But life was filled with so many things that I didn't want to do. This was just one of them, and I'd do it anyway. Because doing the right thing, even when it was hard, was important.

Zane was lying there, completely still, eyes closed. Frank was still whispering his prayers, but the parents stared at me wide-eyed.

"Almost done." I climbed back on the bed, putting one knee on either side of his hips and then my hands on his shoulders. I put my nose just above his and closed my eyes and released my hold on this world. That was all it took for me to leave my body.

I focused on Zane, on the link between his body and his soul. This was going to be super not fun.

I glanced at Phoenix for a second. "Milkshakes?"

He crossed his arms and nodded. "Yup. My treat."

"Okay. I can do this." I looked at Zane and found his silver soul cord. I wrapped it around my hand.

The portal needed to be small this time. Just enough for me to bring his soul back from wherever the demon had hidden it. Tiny. The size of a quarter would do, which would make it impossible for my body to fall through it.

"*Aperta*," I whispered.

I could pull his soul cord and tug him home. But depending on where he was, it might do some damage to him—mental and spiritual damage. If I could avoid that, I would.

I let my soul follow his cord, leading my soul away from the mortal realm.

Zane's screams grew louder. So loud that I wanted to cover my ears and run, but I waited. I waited until I could feel the heat from the pits. And then I wanted to scream, too.

Zane was in the Lake of Fire.

It was soon—too soon—to be back in Hell. But if I thought about it too much, I'd leave before bringing Zane's soul back to his body.

My body was safe. I was going to get a milkshake with Phoenix soon. That was enough to keep me going.

Milkshakes and Phoenix.

Phoenix and milkshakes.

All around me were fires. They weren't faded or misty. They looked real. They felt real. The heat made my skin hot, and it felt like it was burning me. But it wasn't.

Because the part of me that was here didn't have skin. I couldn't burn. But it was hard to think with the heat and the screaming.

It was so loud.

So incredibly loud.

Souls thrashed, screamed, begged for mercy, but no mercy would be found here. Everything that was sent to the Lake burned.

"Zane Michael Anders. Reveal yourself."

Instantly, I was drawn to Zane. He was in front of me, bathed in flame, screaming, tortured, unaware of anything but his pain. His soul was brighter than the rest because it wasn't supposed to be here. This wasn't his time. Which meant that he wasn't truly here. He could leave the Lake, just like I could.

"Zane!" I yelled. *"Zane Michael Anders!"* But he didn't respond, didn't glance my way, didn't do anything but stay in the lake, consumed by fire and pain and fear.

He couldn't hear me, which was fair. I couldn't even really hear me anymore. It was so unbelievably loud. And hot.

Oh God, I was burning.

I slapped a hand over my mouth to stifle the scream because no. No, I wasn't burning. It felt like it, but I wasn't.

I shoved that feeling, that pain, into a box in my mind and locked it away. It wasn't gone, but it was better.

Then, I forced myself to take a step closer.

Tears streaked down my face, and I tried not to think of the flickering flames that licked my skin. It wasn't real.

The pain wasn't real.

I wasn't really here.

It would be over soon, and I'd found that I could suffer through a lot as long as it was temporary.

I could leave any second.

I took a big breath, stuck my fingers in my mouth, and blew a piercing whistle. As I forced the air out, I pushed it through Hell. Zane's eyes widened, and he twisted toward me.

"Zane Michael Anders! Take my hand!" I reached for him, and I knew my body wasn't reaching out a hand. It was my soul. My soul reached for his, and I saw hope in his eyes.

That's right, Zane. This is your way out.

"Zane Michael Anders. Come here. Right now!" It was time. I tugged on his cord.

His eyes widened as if he were seeing me for the first time, and he flung himself at me.

His soul raced to me, and I caught him.

I squeezed my eyes shut again and let the pull of my body take us back.

The heat vanished, we stopped moving, and I'd barely settled into my body when I said, *"Claudere!"*

I opened my eyes, and I was kneeling above Zane again. Because I hadn't moved. My body had been here like this the whole time. Except now Zane was crying. Soft sobs. I looked down at him. "You're fine now."

I moved to get off the bed, but my foot got caught under Zane's leg, and I fell.

"Whoa." Phoenix caught me and set me on my feet.

I looked up into his hazel eyes. "Thanks."

A flash of something bright caught my eye, and I looked

down. Between us were our soul cords—mine and Phoenix's—and they were twisted so tightly together that I didn't think I could ever untangle them.

What the heck was that?

Why were our souls linked?

How did that happen?

When—

Wait. It had to have been last night, but—

A sob—Zane's sob—cut through my thoughts.

I had to deal with Zane first, and then I had questions. Lots of questions.

Zane's parents stood up, looking from me to their son and back again. "He's fine. No more demonic ties. No more demon. I don't know how long you've been having trouble, but you shouldn't have any problems. But Frank should bless your house, just in case."

The dad nodded. "How can we thank you?"

"You don't need to. Just be good." I turned to look at Phoenix. "*Let's go,*" I mouthed to him.

He gave me a barely-there nod and tucked me to his side. "We're going to head out," he said to Zane's parents. "We have another appointment. Frank, are you okay with finishing up here?"

"Absolutely. I'll call you later, Sam." He gave me a look of concern. He wanted to know if I was alright, and I was. In some ways, I was better than I had been before I walked into this room. But something was shifting in my world, something I hadn't noticed, and it was throwing me off.

What the heck had happened with our soul ties? I'd never seen anything like it before.

I couldn't talk to Frank right now. Even if we had privacy to talk through what I'd seen, I had too many questions.

But Phoenix had the answers. So, I gave Frank a nod to reassure him and reached for Phoenix.

I wasn't worried about it or upset. Just confused. Really, truly confused.

Phoenix took my hand and pulled me toward the door, then paused as he looked into the hallway.

"Everything okay?" I whispered to him.

"Everything is fine," he said as we left the room. "I guess I only touched your clothes before. There's a lot happening in the spiritual realm here. I can see why you'd want the headphones."

I looked around the hallway. Nurses were milling about, patients, a doctor going into a room down the hall, but around all that, there were demons. So many demons. Hanging on people. Lurking in corners and doorways. Hiding in every shadow they could find.

"Yeah. It's noisy. I'm sure my headphones are tangled in my pocket now, but—"

"Let's get you out of here. The exit isn't that far."

"Thanks," I said, and he glanced down at me.

"You don't have to keep thanking me. I'm happy to do it." He looked down at me as we moved through the hallway. I hoped he had paid attention because I had no idea how to get out of here. "How are you feeling? Tired at all?"

"No. Actually, I'm much better now." I spotted the exit and sped up. I wanted out of here.

As we stepped out into the sunshine, I closed my eyes and lifted my face into the warmth. "Still a little tired, but not as completely exhausted as I was when I walked in here."

"Still want that milkshake?"

"Yes," I said it so quickly that he laughed.

"How about a burger, too?"

That actually sounded perfect. "Yeah. I could definitely go for that."

"Cool. I know a place close by that I think you'll like." He walked to the car and opened the door for me.

I started to say thank you again, but he raised a brow, stopping my words.

"Sorry." I slid into the seat, and he stepped in, leaning down.

"Don't apologize." He brushed his lips against mine. Just hard enough, just long enough, that my heart skittered.

He closed the door, and I leaned back in the seat.

That hadn't gone so badly.

Demon vanquished. Soul saved. No mortal freakouts.

It had actually been pretty easy.

Everything with Phoenix seemed easy.

I just hoped it stayed that way. Especially after I asked him why the heck our souls were linked.

CHAPTER EIGHT

PHOENIX

THE SPOT I wanted to take Sam wasn't far from the hospital. This time of day—between the lunch and dinner rushes—it was usually quiet, too. Which I was sure Sam would appreciate. It wasn't anything fancy, but the beef was grass-fed and the fries were fried in tallow. So, it was way above any fast food, which I knew Sam was against.

She texted her mom on the way to the restaurant, and I didn't mind the silence.

"Sorry," she said after a few minutes. "I need to check one more thing."

"No worries."

She went back to her phone, and I kept driving.

Driving while being able to see the spiritual realm was an adventure. I knew that Sam had a way to separate the two, but I couldn't. Or at least for now, I had no idea how to do something like that. I'd seen the spiritual realm multiple times now, and so far, it wasn't something I'd been able to get used to. Demons hid in every shadow. There were things that looked like strings all over the place so that it looked like I was driving through spaghetti, but I knew I wasn't. So, I just kept following the road and ignoring what I hoped wasn't on this realm.

"Okay. Sorry. My mom wanted advice on a couple of the consult forms we got, and now, that's done."

"Do you get a lot of those?"

"So many." She shook her head like she didn't quite believe it. "It seems like every day I get more than the day before. That's why my mom quit nursing. I needed help, and she wanted to be with me. So, win-win. But I'm honestly thinking we should hire another person. Or a few more people. As it is, she's working pretty much around the clock. There's only so much we can do, but we don't like turning people away."

"Wow." That was impressive. "And you built that from just social media?"

"Yep, but it's not fair to say that it's all me. Yes, it's my social media that takes in the inquiries, but I've been building a network of priests, pastors, and believers with deliverance ministries. So, a lot of the work my mom does is passing along inquiries to the right people." She pulled on her necklace as she spoke, tugging her cross back and forth along the chain. "And the social media stuff really took off because of the pack. I got a lot of recognition with Tessa and Dastien and my work with the Sanctuary. I never did any news interviews or anything like that. I just—"

"Wait. Have people asked?"

She shrugged, as if it was no big deal. "Sure. But that's not what this is about. That's not why I do what I do. Having a big following is great because I help more people, but I don't want to be famous or anything. I don't post about myself at all, and I didn't set out to be known. Honestly, I don't get recognized or anything. I'm not like you."

I huffed. "Hey. Is that an insult?" I asked to tease her.

"No. I…that's not…" She froze for a second, and I knew she didn't get my joke.

"Kidding." I shot her a quick smile before focusing back on the road. "I'm kidding. I didn't start playing soccer to get famous, but the interviews were part of the gig. Why won't you do any interviews? It might help you reach more people."

"I don't know." She continued to play with her necklace as she thought quietly for a moment. "I just don't like being exposed like that. This isn't about me. It's about reaching everyone else. Spreading awareness about the spiritual realm."

"From what I can tell, you're doing a phenomenal job."

"Thanks." She dropped her necklace and shifted anxiously in her seat.

Interesting. She wasn't good with compliments, which meant I was going to have to give her more until she started to realize how amazing she truly was.

I pulled into the tiny parking lot beside the burger joint. Sam peeked up at the sign. It was a big neon planet with a guy's name under it. The small red and white building was charming. It looked like it hadn't been touched since it was built in the fifties, and I knew from all the times I'd been here before that the inside was the same.

I really hoped this place was okay with Sam. I'd made a decision without really asking, but the milkshakes were so good here and I'd promised her a milkshake. Not all sweets were breaking my training diet, but theirs were.

"I've never been here before." She smiled over at me. "I honestly don't come into town unless I have a meeting or it's my weekly lunch with Frank."

"You two are pretty tight." I was stating the obvious, but I hoped she'd fill in a little more. I wanted to know everything about her, but also, didn't want to pressure her into sharing more than she was ready.

"I know it's weird to be friends with a middle-aged priest, but he's not exactly the cliched priest-type. He's...Frank." Her stomach growled, and she rolled her eyes. "Sorry. I'm not as tired, but apparently, still hungry."

"Let's get you some food." I got out of the car and motioned her to follow me.

When we got inside, there were a few people at the counter, and another couple in a booth across the room, but other than that, it was empty. We'd missed the lunch rush, which was good. I might not know everything about Sam yet, but I knew she didn't like crowds.

The waitress led us to a table next to the other couple, but I wanted more privacy. I had a feeling Sam would close up if she thought the couple was listening in. "Can we get one in the back over there? That booth?" It was far away from everyone else, which would give us a lot more privacy.

"Sure thing." The hostess changed direction.

"Thank you."

As soon as we were seated, Sam looked at the menu. "Holy moly. There are so many options."

I laughed. "Excuse me. Did you just say *holy moly?*"

Pink flushed Sam's cheeks. "Sorry. I have this thing about cussing. I'm not always great about not doing it, but I try—*try* being the operative word—not curse as much as possible." The pink darkened even more. "Sometimes I get a little creative with them. So, yeah. That's kind of embarrassing."

She didn't need to be embarrassed. The more I learned about her, the more I liked her.

Sam cleared her throat. "So, what's good here?"

"Everything." It was all good. I'd tried a bunch of the things, but now I'd found my perfect order. Double Cheeseburger with bacon, jalapeños, grilled onions and peppers, fries, and a mocha shake.

I watched her chew on her bottom lip as she scanned the offerings. This was nice. Time with just us—no demons or parents or werewolves or anything else.

"Okay. I think I know what I want," Sam said.

I looked over for the waitress, and she was coming back with waters.

Even though Sam said she knew what she wanted, she asked the waitress what her favorite milkshakes were. It was nice watching her go back and forth, laughing with the waitress. She finally settled on a shake the waitress recommended.

As soon as she was gone, Sam straightened her back. "So, do you have any questions about what just happened?"

I leaned forward. "I have other questions."

"Okay. Shoot."

"Is your life normally this busy? This dangerous?"

She thought for a second, tugging on the necklace again. "I want to say no. But I don't know if that's true. Usually, it comes in waves. And yes, there's always some danger with what I do. Things like what happened with your sister—that's only every few years or so. But last night was next level. He's never created a trap like that for me. That sucked." She gave a little shrug. "But that doesn't mean I give up. This isn't a job I can quit. It's who I am. So, even when there are bad days or rough times, I know that this is what I'm meant to do. It makes all the bad things somehow…not so bad."

She had to be incredibly brave to do what she did. I would've been done after a night like last night, but here we were. Having a meal after she just did yet another exorcism. "I know you get scared. I've seen it. So, why do you keep going?"

"I'd have to be a robot not to be scared." She gave me a small smile and shrugged. "But that doesn't mean I let the bad guys win. Just because something is hard or scary doesn't mean I shouldn't do it. It's just a sign to be careful. So, I'm careful. Even when it might seem reckless."

Reckless was a good word for it. "Saving Van seemed a little reckless."

"Maybe." The waitress came back with our milkshakes, and Samantha looked her in the eye and said a very clear *thank you* that sounded like she truly meant it.

I really liked that about her. I'd noticed that she treated all her friends well, but you learned a lot about a person by how they treated waitstaff. She'd been really nice when the waitress took our order, and now, again, she was kind.

That was something that bugged me about my ex, Melissa. She'd always been so rude to people she thought were beneath her. Looking back, it had to have been one of the subconscious reasons I was holding back with her.

Samantha took a sip of her churro shake. "Oh my gosh. This is the *best thing ever*." She turned to look over her shoulder. "This is so good!"

"Right?!" The waitress laughed. "I told you I wouldn't lead you astray!"

"Like seriously good!"

"Awesome. You enjoy it."

"I'm gonna." She turned back to me, and then her smile dimmed a bit. "Sorry. Was I—"

"Don't apologize. I'm glad you like it."

"How's yours?"

I took a sip of my mocha shake. "Amazing." I slid it across to her. "Try it."

She took a sip. Then another bigger one. "This is my new favorite place. I'm not sure which I like better."

"I told you—you really can't go wrong here. We can trade if you want."

"That's sweet, but I'm happy with mine. Thanks." She slid my shake back across the table. "I have a question for you."

"Go for it." I played with the straw, waiting for whatever she was going to ask. I was pretty open and definitely not shy. So, whatever she wanted to know, I'd tell her.

"I was hoping you'd say something, but I'm just not a person who beats around the bush. I'm pretty direct. Probably to a fault, seeing as how it's gotten me into major trouble. So, fair warning here." She sighed. "But I have to ask, what's this?"

She pointed to something, but I wasn't sure what it was. There were so many things I could see right now. I'd been trying not to pay attention to the spiritual realm while we talked, but now that she'd pointed it out, that was all I could see—the man in the corner. The demon on the ceiling. The one hanging off the cook in the back.

I blinked a few times, trying to focus. "What's what exactly?"

She hooked her finger and pulled it toward her, and I gasped and slammed into the table.

I looked up at Sam. "What did you just do?" For a second, it felt like my soul was leaving my body, then snapped back in place. It was uncomfortable to say the least.

She shrugged, looking like nothing huge had just happened, and took a sip of her milkshake. "Dunno for sure, but it looks like your soul's tie to your body is wrapped around mine."

My eyes widened. "Oh, shit. *That*." She must've seen the bond when she was doing the exorcism. Because of course she saw it. How could I expect her not to?

She gave me a grin that was a little mischievous. "Yeah. *That*." She pushed her milkshake away a little bit so that she could lean forward. "What the heck happened last night? Why is my soul suddenly tied to yours? Because it definitely wasn't like that when I went to save Van."

Right. "I thought I'd have more time."

"Time?" Her brows rose. "For *what*?"

My heart started to race. I had to get the words right. She had to understand what happened, and that I wanted this, and more than that, I wanted her to want this.

Sam tapped her hand on the table softly, bringing me out of my panicked thoughts. "Phoenix. Time for what exactly?"

"To figure out how to tell you. To explain in a way that wouldn't piss you off." I looked down at the table because staring at her felt scary right now. "Although, I guess I'm not sure what pisses you off. Yet." I braced myself for whatever she might say next and looked her in the eyes. "I want that shot though. I want a chance to find out, and I want you to not be mad about this."

"For the record, I try not to get mad. That's not who I am." She paused. "I just…I feel like whatever you did was done under duress. Clearly it was a bad night. So, I'm just not sure if I should be yelling at Eli right now." She closed her eyes and shook her head, and I knew she wasn't understanding what I meant. "I probably should be yelling at him, but first—" She looked at me, but now there was sadness in her eyes. "Let's talk."

"Thank you."

A little crease formed between her brows. "For what?"

"For giving me a chance to explain."

"I've gotten through life by taking things as they come. It's not always easy to do, and I've had some pretty dark times, but I like to think they made me stronger. I probably would've noticed this tie sooner, but I was really wiped. The exorcism helped with that, so, now we deal with it."

"Deal with it." I wasn't sure I liked the sound of that.

"What happened to make *this*—" She gestured between us. "—happen?"

So, I told her about how we'd waited for her to wake up. How hours passed. Then more hours. About how her temp went up, her heart rate went up, and how Claudia tried a few spells to bring her back. But no matter what we did, she didn't wake up. Not even after Van came back.

I told her about how things got worse once he was back.

I told her about the ice bath and the panic and that we'd come so close to losing her.

And I told her about the kiss. About what I'd done to bring her home, knowing exactly what it meant. Wanting exactly what it meant.

"Anchor?" She sat back in the booth, slowly taking in what I'd said. "Eli called you my anchor? Specifically?"

"Yes."

The waitress chose that moment to bring the food. She noticed the change in mood. "You okay?" she asked Sam.

Sam gave her a shaky smile. "I will be. Yeah. Thank you so much for this."

"You enjoy, honey." She patted Sam on the shoulder. "Let me

know if you need anything else." She gave Sam a look and walked away.

Sam sat there staring at her food, and I wished I had Eli's power for just a little bit so that I could know what she was thinking and say the right thing to fix this.

"The waitress thinks I'm breaking your heart." I really hoped I wasn't. That was the opposite of what I wanted. "She thinks I'm a jerk." And I truly didn't want Sam to think of me as a jerk. That would suck. "You better smile when we leave or else I won't be able to come back here, and I'm pretty much a regular at this point."

Sam let out a little laugh. "It is breaking in a way." When she looked up at me, there was hurt in her eyes, and I hated that. Even worse—I hated that I was the cause of it. I wanted to redo the morning. Start over again. Try telling her a different way or…

I didn't know that anything would've made it easier. "Sam, *please*."

She shook her head. "Don't worry. I'll find a way to fix this. I'm so sorry this happened to you."

All the air went out of my lungs. She'd done exactly what I didn't want—she'd assumed the worst.

Wait. She thought *she* was something horrible that happened *to* me? "No." I made my voice very clear, firm, leaving no room for misinterpretation. "I don't want you to do a thing. Don't undo this. *Please*."

"Why?" She shoved her untouched food away from her. "From everything you said, it sounds like you were pressured—"

"No. I wasn't. There were other options available." She had to understand that. "For a second, I thought being a normal human meant I couldn't do it. And the idea of it—that I would forever be in the friend zone—made me sick. I wanted to throw up. It felt like I was losing everything I'd ever dreamed of."

She let out a laugh that held no humor. "I'm not a dream, Nix. My life is kind of a nightmare."

I shoved my food away. "Don't say that. *Ever*. Because I

dreamed about you for *years*. The smart, kind, funny girl who was so brave and confident and faced monsters like they were nothing. I know in some parts of the world I'm a big catch. I know that. But really, I'm just a guy who got paid a lot of money to play soccer. You're so much more than that. What you do…it's amazing."

"It's not…I'm not…" She blew out a hard breath. "How do you know you're not feeling like you want to be with me because you tied your soul to mine? There's a chance that the tie could cloud your judgment. It could make you drawn to me just because our souls are tied, but you might end up hating me for it."

"That's never going to happen. I can't hate you, and I know this is real because I felt this way about you *before* I did it. Nothing has changed. Not for me. Except that now I have a good excuse to stick around and not come off as a total stalker weirdo."

Sam grew quiet, and I gave her time to let that sink in. I wanted to be with her period. But I knew she'd been burned so badly, and she'd had a really rough night, which had to leave her feeling exposed.

This was why we needed to come share a meal together. Have a milkshake. Just talk. She needed time to build trust in a way that made sense, which I got.

But I didn't need that time. It hadn't taken me very long to realize that Sam was everything.

So, I waited and watched her as she thought. Sam hadn't put on a ton of makeup, but she was the most naturally beautiful person. Her eyes were large and gray. Her nose small and straight. Her lips full and red. And all of it combined into something that drew me in, body and soul.

I'd never felt this drawn to someone. Not since that night on the stairs. Never had I ever felt so completely all-in for someone.

Over the years, I'd dated. I was what my sisters called a serial monogamist, but after a little while, I always ended up breaking it off. My longest relationship had been two years, but I'd known it wasn't right early on, and yet, I didn't break up with Melissa until right before I moved here. She'd seemed like everything I wanted—all the boxes were checked—but there was something missing, off, not fully clicking like it should have. On the outside, it seemed like we made sense together, so I stayed with her, but the relationship felt like work—hard, endless, slogging work to keep it functioning. In the end, I realized that kind of hard relationship wasn't what I wanted for myself or my future.

I wanted more. I wanted an easier, natural relationship. I wanted someone who would push me to be better. Someone who I could take care of and support and truly be myself without any judgement.

I'd glimpsed all of that once, and I wasn't going to stop searching until I found it again.

But deep down, the one that I'd been searching for was Sam.

I'd had a relationship that made all the sense in the world, and I couldn't make it work.

Holding out so that one day I might run into Sam again and have a shot made no sense, but I always thought that if it was meant to be, she'd somehow show up in my life again.

And that was exactly what had happened.

Sam was always the more I'd been looking for.

So, no, I wasn't upset about what happened last night, but I had no idea how to convince Samantha that everything was okay. That as long as she was okay with this, I was more than fine with it.

Unless she wasn't fine with it? Was she looking for a way out for me? Or for herself?

Shit.

"Did anyone explain the implications to you?" She put her arms on the table and leaned forward. "Was more said that you didn't tell me? Because from what you just said, you went into this a little blind."

I could already tell she wasn't going to like what I had to say about that. They had told me some things, but they hadn't told me everything. I had no idea what I was doing with this anchor bond. Could I honestly say I knew all the implications?

No. I couldn't.

When I didn't say anything, she dropped her head, chin to her chest, and closed her eyes as she breathed. I wasn't sure if I should say something or let her figure it out, but over the last few days, I'd noticed that she liked to pause to think things through. Then, she'd go into action, doing whatever needed to be done. Which made sense. Sometimes I needed a second to think, too. And right now, I could use a little time to figure out how to make her see what Eli wanted.

She finally looked at me, and pain wove through my heart at the sorrow in her eyes. "I'm so, *so* sorry," she said. "You shouldn't have to be stuck with me and my mess, and—"

Wait. No. I was done being across the table from her. I slid out of the booth and went next to her. "Please don't say that. I'm not *stuck* with you."

Her eyes widened, and she turned to put her back to the wall, putting a little space between us. "I understand that you felt like you had to save me, and Eli must've talked you through how to make this bond, but—"

"You can tell me a lot of things, but you can't tell me how I felt about you the night I met you or how much I thought about you since that night or how even how I felt last night when we were losing you. And you definitely can't tell me how I feel right now." I hoped I could get through to her. "I want you. That night all those years ago changed me. Not just what happened in the apartment—because that blew my mind—but the talk on the stairs. And even if it was wrong, the flirting through your window. I noticed you before, and I have a feeling that this was always where we'd end up. Because otherwise, it makes no sense why we ran into each other again or why it feels vital that I stick close by you. And that's not because of the tie. That was there before. I showed up on your porch yesterday morning and refused to leave. That had nothing to do with the tie."

"I'm messing this up." She took a breath and let it out, and as she did, her shoulders slouched. It was as if she was crumbling under the weight of her disappointment. "I just..." She closed her eyes. "I wanted this, too. I wanted to go on a date with you."

Okay. Now, this was something I could work with. "Great. You got it. We're on one right now."

"*What*?" Her eyes flew open. "No." Her eyes widened, and she let out a surprised laugh. "This is so not a date. I just did an exorcism."

I couldn't have stopped the smile from spreading across my face even if I tried. "So, you had to work before our date. No problem. I was happy to tag along." I could work with this. "But we've got milkshakes. Burgers. Salty fries. We're sharing a meal with no one else around. This is definitely a date."

"Stop." She let out a helpless whimper that was kind of cute. "Don't you want a normal date? Like without all this stuff." She motioned to the air around us, and I knew what she meant. She didn't need to explain.

Without all the *spiritual realm* stuff.

"I don't even know what normal is, and I don't think I need it. If I'm being honest, normal sounds a little boring." She laughed at that, and it felt like I was winning something big. "I want you. Full stop. I'm old enough to know what I want, and you are it. And I don't mind repeating that you that until you believe me."

She groaned. "Do you have to be so charming?" She crossed her arms and glared at me. "Stop it with that smile."

I couldn't help but cheese up the smile. "Better?"

She kicked my foot with hers. "No. Super not helpful." She let out a little moan and *thunked* her head into the wall behind her.

I laughed because I couldn't help it. Her little groans and helpless faces that she made me want to hold her and never let her go. "Look. I get it. You feel like I was roped into doing something I didn't want."

"*Exactly*. It's impossible to make a good choice when a life is on the line. Any decent person would make the same choice."

"That might be right, but here's the important part. I saw my shot to save you *and* have a life with you, and I took it. I didn't hesitate *at all.* I jumped in that ice bath with you, and I would've destroyed anyone that tried to take that spot from me." There was no softening that blow if she didn't want this. "If you need time away from me or you don't want me around…" Man, I hoped she didn't want that. "I'll give you some space if that's what you need. You have to tell me if I'm coming on too strong, and we can see if we can ease into this. But you don't get to say I didn't want it or that the way I feel is because of the tie. That's flat-out not true." I wasn't backing down on that.

She started playing with her necklace again, then added in the lip chewing, and I knew I had her. She was going to give me a shot. I just had to finish strong.

Good thing I was fantastic at finishing strong.

"And you don't get to say you're some kind of burden. Or any of the other terrible things going through your mind. None of those are true. I knew what I was getting into—that it was going to be forever—and I'll say it over and over until it sinks in—I'm all-in on this. You and me. I don't want an out. I'm here because I want to be. Because it's where I feel like I'm *supposed* to be. We'll figure this anchor bond part out as we go, and I'll need help and patience with that. Because it's new to me, and I'm human. I'll mess it up at some point. But I'm not leaving you unless *you* want me to go."

I forced myself to ask the hard question. "Be honest with me right now. Please. Don't worry about hurting my feelings because I really need to know this."

"What?" Her voice was so soft and quiet.

"Do you want me to go?" *Please, God, let her say no.* Walking away from her now would be impossibly hard. I didn't think I'd ever get over her. I'd die sad and lonely and dreaming of what could have been.

She was quiet but shook her head. "No," she said, finally. "I really don't want you to go."

Fuck yes.

This felt better than scoring a goal in the World Cup.

I wanted to get up and shout and celebrate, but I forced myself to sit still, take a breath, and not scare her away with any of the insanity going on in my head.

Instead, I smiled a stupid, goofy, happy smile. "This works out perfectly. Because I don't want to go either." I gave her hand a gentle tug, pulling her toward me, and then brushed my hand on her cheek. "This okay?"

She looked up at me, her gray eyes wide. "Is what okay?"

She was adorable. I leaned down and brushed my lips lightly against hers. "This."

When she didn't pull away, I took that as a yes.

So, I closed my eyes and truly kissed her, pouring all the feelings I had into it, just like I had last night.

After a second, I felt her let go and her fingers threaded through my hair, and *yes*. This was it. This was what I had been waiting for my whole life. *Her*.

I pulled back, resting my forehead against hers. "That would've happened yesterday before all the other stuff, but we were interrupted."

She blinked at me. "Yeah. I remember, but—"

"No. There is no other explanation. You ever had a better kiss than that? Because I haven't."

She let out a soft laugh. "I mean, no. But it's not like I've gone around making out with a ton of guys." She closed her eyes. "I need to think or breathe or maybe both."

That was totally okay. I knew she wanted this. I could tell when we kissed, but she needed time to trust me. I would give her that time.

"Let's eat. Our burgers are getting cold, and if your stomach growls one more time, I'm going to lose it." I went back to my side of the booth.

Samantha stared at her burger for a second. "Thanks."

"For what?"

She looked at me. "For saving my life. For being here. For talking me through this and being patient."

"All of it was my pleasure." I nudged her foot with mine. "Eat."

Man, my *abuela* was so right. *When you know, you know.*

And I definitely knew.

Every second I spent with her cemented that fact in my mind and in my heart.

Samatha was my forever person, and I'd never been happier.

CHAPTER NINE

PHOENIX

AFTER OUR HONEST conversation about our relationship, we had a few really amazing days. Quiet. The kind of quiet and normal that Sam had been asking for. She'd started training again, but from what Chris said, she was low on energy. Was it crazy to ask her to do another exorcism?

Yes. It was. That was a shit idea.

And yet, was it? She was so much better after the exorcism at the hospital, but the effects faded. She was having trouble sleeping at night, but tonight after dinner, she'd wanted to watch a movie. So, we were in her room—newly fixed up by Cosette. The TV came up from a chest at the foot of her bed, which made lounging here really nice. I was propped up against the pillows and headboard, and she was curled up in a ball with her head on my lap. With the blankets and soft mattress, I wasn't surprised she'd fallen asleep so quickly.

I hadn't been paying attention to the movie at all, so I turned the volume down once I knew she was asleep and continued reading my latest pick—a book about the spiritual realm. I was pretty sure that was going to be my life now, and I wanted to understand and be helpful to her.

I flicked away a drop-down notification. They'd been nonstop all evening.

The latest one was from my agent. She'd get the hint eventually. I tilted my head back, melting into the mountain of pillows on Sam's new bed.

The second day after becoming Sam's anchor to this world, Chris and Cosette showed up with a delivery truck. Cosette said it was a gift from Van. What they unloaded was basically Samantha's dream bedroom—at least according to her. Not long after that, another car pulled up. This time it was a designer who came with all the trimmings and details to make her room feel like something out of a magazine.

It was weird to me that the fey warrior dude—Van—had never shown back up, but no one else seemed surprised by that. Still, it was solid of him that he'd refurnished her room and then some.

The bed was much bigger than her old one—a massive king-sized, cream-colored, tufted linen head and footboard, beast of a bed. The mattress was the top-of-the-line memory foam with crisp white sheets and a cushy white duvet. There was a brightly patterned quilt filled with rich colors depicting a forest sunset at the end of the bed. The throw pillows pulled colors from the quilt, and that seemed to really, truly make Samantha happy. The smile on her face…it had been the best.

The walls were now painted a rich, dark forest green. They'd put up patterned blackout shades. The bed tables were light wood with drawers, and glowing lamps that looked like clear, iridescent bubbles. They'd even put down a new geometrically-patterned rug that was soft on my feet.

The sitting area was completely redone, too. The shelves were now built-in along one wall, complete with little gallery lights at the top and a sliding ladder. There were two chairs instead of one, plus a loveseat.

When I'd asked how Cosette found the designer who could

get all this done so quickly, she said not to worry about it. I felt like that was code for fey stuff because when I furnished my house, it had taken a while. I'd paid to expedite shipping on everything, looked for things in stock, but in the end, it was only *just* finished. It took me months, but they got hers done in forty-eight hours.

In a weird way, the room made me realize how different her life was from mine. From normal. From anything I knew. I was pretty sure the fey guy had somehow made the room bigger because it *felt* bigger, but I wasn't going to ask. My mind had been blown so many times the last few days, I honestly didn't need to go looking for more things to make me feel like I didn't belong.

Because I did. With her, I knew I did.

Samantha stirred in her sleep, and I ran my hand along her spine, easing whatever dream she was having, then went back to reading my book.

I didn't get past one line before another notification popped up. This time from my mother.

Were my agent and my mother tag-teaming me on purpose? It wouldn't be the first time. They both wanted something from me, but this time I didn't feel like giving them anything. Right here was exactly where I wanted to be, and I wasn't going to be swayed by what either of them said. Not to come home. Not to go back to play next season. None of it.

It buzzed again, and I opened my texts. Mom. There was nothing I could say to make her understand. She'd never liked Samantha. She knew about the time Sam had spent in an institution and assumed some pretty awful things, and that was before that night with the cops. I'd never seen her more upset.

Wait. That wasn't true. She was really pissed for a long time after my father left us.

But aside from my father leaving, I'd never seen her rant about anything like she had after that night. She blamed Samantha entirely for my near-arrest and refused to hear anything I said.

After Samantha saved my sister from Astaroth, she ranted that whole lecture to me again. It felt like it was almost word-for-word. I knew it probably wasn't, but the gist was the same. It was all fear-based. The first time, she was afraid I'd get thrown in jail and that she wouldn't have the money to get me out. My budding career would've been ruined, and I wouldn't have played professional soccer.

With Rain, well…Mom was just helpless with what had happened to my sister. She couldn't make sense out of it and really didn't like it when she couldn't control something. But the spiritual realm wasn't something to be controlled.

Even if I knew her reasoning, I didn't think it was fair to take any of that out on Samantha. None of what happened was Sam's fault, but Mom disagreed. The truth was—she and I didn't agree on much. Hadn't for a while. Abuela had been the only one that held us together.

I thought moving here and us all being together would fix things, but now, I was pretty sure the only thing that moving here did was put me back on my path with Samatha.

I glanced at the text, but it was still Mom being upset with me. Wanting me to come home. Hating on Sam. It wasn't even worth the time to read it, especially when it made me angry. I put my phone down. I'd deal with that later.

The sound of the garage door opening told me that Ana was home. She'd gone to help someone. Thankfully, everyone was giving Sam a break. There hadn't been any demonic activity that required her help.

I grabbed my phone, checking the time again. 2:30 AM. I'd be shocked if Sam made it another thirty minutes before waking up.

I opened my text chain with Ana. *We're in Sam's room. She fell asleep two minutes into the movie. Sleeping soundly so far.*

Good. I'll be up in a few.

I looked down at Samantha. Her face was so relaxed as she slept, and she looked at peace. I was really thankful she wasn't having a nightmare and was truly resting. She'd been so restless all night. But this was good. She'd feel much better when she woke up.

I heard some rustling in the kitchen below, then footsteps coming up the stairs.

Sam's bedroom door opened, and Ana stepped through. She tiptoed to the bed and looked down at Sam. She reached out like she wanted to touch her but pulled her hand away.

That movement reminded me so much of Sam. I wondered if they knew how much they were alike.

Ana gave me a smile, one that looked just like her daughter's, and pulled out her phone. She motioned to mine, so I opened up our text thread.

She doing okay?

I gave her a nod, then typed back. *Yes. Ate some dinner. We went for a walk around the development, but she fell asleep really fast once the movie was on. Hoping that she makes it through the night.*

Ana let out a soft *hmm. I don't know. I want that for her, but I have a feeling tonight will be rough.*

My stomach dropped. I glanced up at her quickly. I didn't like that at all. *Did something happen while you were out?*

Ana gave me a sad smile and started to type again. *Not exactly. I mean—this lady is going to need a lot more help than what we could do in one night, but she'll be okay. I think.*

You think?

Unfortunately. We've seen that sometimes demonic ties are like an addiction. Once formed, you have to continually work to not go down that path again.

Interesting.

Ana motioned to Sam, then texted. *She'll be okay. She's been through a lot, but she always bounces back.*

I nodded. From everything I knew—everything I could see about her—that was true. But I wasn't sure what I would do if something happened to her.

The idea had my heart racing, and I honestly thought I might throw up. I wanted to be here—there wasn't a chance that I'd leave—but watching her suffer like that again…

Sam suddenly stirred in her sleep. Her eyes didn't open, but her hand found mine—the one that was resting on her shoulder. She wove her fingers through mine and muttered softly. "Everything's okay, Nix."

"Shhhh," I said and rubbed my free hand down her back. After a second, she settled back down.

I'd been noticing things like that the last few days. One of us would be thinking something, and the other would respond in some way. I wasn't sure if Sam had noticed it. I wasn't sure what to think about it, but I had a feeling this was something to do with the anchor bond we shared. It was like we were hyper attuned to each other's emotions.

My phone lit up again.

You okay?

I looked up, nodded. I couldn't explain what I was feeling to myself, let alone to someone else. Maybe that was why I was avoiding my mother's texts. I had no idea what to say to her or how to explain it in a way she'd accept.

I'd told her I was visiting a friend, and that I was twenty-eight, almost twenty-nine. I'd be back in a couple of days to get some more of my things, officially putting her off for a little while longer.

I wasn't outright lying to her. She knew the friend was Samantha, but I wasn't elaborating it for her. Especially with how awful she was in her latest text, saying that I'd abandoned my sister in her time of need. Which I hadn't. I'd found someone to truly help Rain when no one else could, and now Rain had the support she needed. And I was needed *here* for now.

I knew that for certain because I'd texted with Rain, and she was fine. She told me to stay with Samantha. That Sky was keeping an eye on her, and she'd call me if she needed me. Then, I confirmed that was true in a separate text with Sky. My sister told me that if Rain got in trouble again, I'd be her first call. Which made me feel much better. If that happened, I would go home. No problem. I'd probably bring Samantha with me, but I'd deal with Mom if it happened. There was no way I'd let my mother insult Samantha again.

My phone lit up. *You okay?*

She'd asked again, which meant I should probably answer. *I don't know what I'm going to do with my mom. She really doesn't like Samantha.* I hit send before I could stop myself, and then winced. It probably wasn't the smartest thing to send to the person-in-question's mother. Ana was just so kind and easy to talk to. Nothing like my mother.

Ana sat on the foot of the bed, studying me for a second, before typing on her phone. *Part of growing up means deciding who you are, who you want to be, and who you want to spend your life with. Unfortunately for your mother, you seem to have answers to a lot of those questions, that she just doesn't agree with. But it is your life. You can only walk the path that God sets before you, which I think you are doing. Your mother has always been extremely opinionated. You might want to think about drawing boundaries for how much you let her into your life.*

I read the text, but I was confused. *What do you mean by boundaries?*

Ana bit her lip as she typed, and again, it reminded me of Sam. A minute later, my phone lit up.

Drawing boundaries became essential for me when I got pregnant with Samantha. If my mother had her way, I'd have either aborted or gotten rid of her. But my mom helped me for a little while so that I could finish my nursing degree while Sam was a baby, but I left as soon as I could. I haven't looked back. Letting her in even a little bit was toxic for all of us. I'm not saying that you have to cut your mother out of your life, but sometimes you have to evaluate who you let into your life and how much access they have to you. Regardless of your relationship with them.

Deciding how much access someone had to me. That made sense, and it made me feel like I was on the right path. Some of the guilt I had for telling my mom what she was allowed to demand from me and what I wouldn't tolerate faded away.

Thank you. That's actually helpful. I sent it and realized that I hadn't seen or even heard any mention of Samantha's grandparents. *I bet it was hard when you left.*

Ana gave me a small smile before texting me back. *Life is hard, but worth it. She was worth it to me.* She immediately sent another text. *Not that you have to choose between Sam and your mom. Your mom never liked us. She thought Sam was trouble, that I was a bad mother, and our religious beliefs bothered her. I don't think your mom will come around to liking Sam, but I could be wrong. It's something that you're going to have to work out with her. I just ask that you not pit my daughter against your mother. It would only hurt Sam. Maybe your life with Sam is something that's off-limits for your mother? Maybe you decide when you talk to her or how she's allowed to talk to you? I don't know, but it's something to think about.*

I nodded. *I won't let her hurt Samantha. For sure. I want to protect Sam against anything and everything. Even my mother.*

Thank you.

She didn't have to thank me. Not for that. My mom and I…we had a difficult relationship. She was harsh, brash, rude, condescending…but she could be kind. When it suited her.

That didn't sound good even in my head.

My phone lit up, and thankfully, it was my agent. She was likely overseas and not expecting me to answer in the middle of the night, but she must've seen me checking the text—those three dots screwed me over—so she decided to call me.

Not right now. I sent her to voicemail.

She called again. I sent her to voicemail again, then texted her. *One second.* And then I pulled up the text chain with Sam's mom. *Will you take a picture of us?*

She smiled, and slid her phone into her pocket, taking mine.

She stood up and angled the phone a little to get both of us. I looked down at Sam, who was still fast asleep. Still beautiful. Still blowing my mind at the depth of my feelings for her.

Maybe they didn't make sense, but they were there all the same.

Ana handed my phone back to me, and I smiled at the picture of us. I was definitely framing that one. I sent my agent the picture. *I can't talk right now. My girl is asleep, and I'm not waking her up.*

Who is that? What the hell is going on?

Samantha. The One. I'd gotten embarrassingly drunk once and told my agent the whole story of that night. I wasn't sure she believed me, but in the end, I told her Sam was the one. The one that got away. The one I dreamed about more often than I ever dared to admit. The one I wanted and would never let go of now that I had her.

Wait. That's her? That's the Samantha you were talking about? The demon girl?

What the hell. *She's not a demon girl.*

Ana waved at me, motioned to the door, and then quietly tiptoed out of the room, closing Sam's door gently. I was glad that Ana had stayed and texted with me. Her advice about my mom and boundaries really hit home. Samantha was lucky to have the mom she did.

My phone lit up again.

No. That's her. I've seen her on the news. She works with the pack in Texas, right? That's who that is, right? She's the girl that kills demons.

Wait. Was this a known thing? I know Sam said she'd turned down interviews, but if that was true, how could my agent know about her? Sam never posted pictures on social media of herself. I checked. *How do you know that?*

Shit. Nix. Do you ever watch the news? They got a picture of her once, and Tessa—the pack spokesperson or whatever—talked about who she was and what she did for the pack. She's been incredibly hard to pin down, but there's whole online communities trying to track her down and find out more info about her.

I couldn't believe I didn't know this. *You know I only watch sports news. Just soccer stuff though. Aside from a match, I hardly watch any live TV. The rest of the news is fear mongering and lies.*

I'm not going to respond to that, but okay. Call me when you can talk. I have amazing news for you.

News? I knew what that meant. My agent wanted me to keep playing, and if not that, she wanted me to be a sports commentator.

No, thanks. I was done with that part of my life.

And it wasn't because of Sam. I was done before I found her again. I used the injury as an excuse, but I didn't want to go back. I hadn't been lying to Sam on that stairwell. I didn't love soccer. It was never my dream.

As I'd lain on the stadium floor in Madrid, it had hit me.

I'm not upset.

I'd suffered what could've potentially been a career-ending injury, and aside from the pain, I didn't care. More than that, I was relieved.

And I knew I was done with the sport.

I never had a dream of my own, but as I sat there with Samantha lying across my lap in the dark of night, a movie playing softly in the background, I felt like whatever this was, it could be a pretty nice dream.

I had finally found my place. Doing something that I wanted to do. Being with the person that I never thought I'd get to be with.

And she was mine.

Maybe she didn't understand it yet, but I did. She was mine, and I was utterly and completely hers.

Samantha gasped suddenly—a sharp, scary sound. She shot up off the bed in one movement.

"Sam?" I asked, softly. "Are you okay?"

She spun around the room, searching for what, I didn't know.

There was a howl of a wolf.

Then another.

And one more.

Then a bunch all together.

"Shit," she said, then she raced out of the room.

It took me a second to realize that something was wrong. I wasn't sure why I was slow, but the 180-degree turn was hard to wrap my mind around. Other than the wolves going nuts, nothing seemed wrong.

I heard Ana call out for Samantha to stop, and I raced across the room, taking the stairs three at a time, jumping the last bit before racing out the front door after Samantha.

I wasn't sure what was happening, but I knew I had to get there. Fast. Something told me she was going to need me, and I wasn't about to let her down.

Not now.

Not ever.

CHAPTER TEN

SAMANTHA

THIS WAS MY FAULT.

All my fault.

I'd messed up, and now I had to fix it. I had no clue how, but I'd find a way.

I heard people calling out to me, but it all sounded so far away. I was focused. I had a goal. I knew what I needed to do.

I raced down the porch steps and into the middle of the dirt road. Tiny pebbles stabbed at my bare feet, but I tried not to pay attention to it. It was too quiet. Way too quiet. No owls. No frogs. No wind. No cicadas.

The spiritual realm was awake and overpowering the whole neighborhood. Maybe a normal human wouldn't feel it, but the supernaturals might. And me and the animal kingdom? Yeah, we felt it.

My breaths came in short pants as I ran. I didn't need to see a clock to know it was close to 3:00 AM. I could feel it around me. I could see it in the spiritual realm—it was brighter, stronger, weaving through, around, on top of our realm, nearly overpowering it. Pack bonds ran through the neighborhood this way and that—bright golden ropes. Some thin wisps. Some thick enough to hold a cable car. And every size in between.

And running through them were veins of red.

Blood red demon ties.

What had I done?

"Chris!" I yelled as I ran down the road because I was going to need help. But I didn't stop. I could feel the pack coming toward me, and I knew that energy. The red among the ties started to brighten, deepen, drip with blood.

That wasn't good.

It was seriously not good.

I'd never seen a possessed werewolf, and I never wanted to. Ever. I could wrestle a demon-ridden human. But a werewolf? No. Hard pass. They would kill me.

And yet, I was running toward them.

The Sanctuary wasn't supposed to have demonic ties like that. They shouldn't have been able to exist on this land. It had been sanctified by angels. The houses were literally formed by them. It was built to always be a safe place for traumatized supernaturals, but it wasn't. Not anymore.

I'd broken that covenant.

I'd desecrated the land.

Feral growls broke through the silence of the night, and I knew that I wasn't in control of what might happen next.

God, help me. Make me strong. Help me help them.

Then, I saw them racing down the street. I couldn't tell how many there were, but it felt like a lot. They were running faster than I could, which meant even if I turned now, they'd be on me before I got inside the house.

I wanted to laugh at that. They'd tear through the door like it was cheese. I had to hold my ground.

I took a breath and let go of the mental chain I kept wrapped around myself and my power. I felt the energy pull in, and then flow out of my body, encasing me in fire.

I didn't like to show this side of myself. It was something my father could do, and using it—being like *him*—felt wrong. But sometimes—every once in a while—I needed something a little more.

Fire wouldn't kill a werewolf. They healed so fast. I wasn't sure it'd be enough to stop them, but I needed it to be.

I didn't want to hurt any of the wolves here. This wasn't their fault.

This was my fault. Completely and totally my fault.

I'd broken my own rule, and now, I was going to pay for it.

I studied them as they approached. If I could cut any demonic ties before they reached me, then I might be able to—

Phoenix stopped beside me. "What's happening? Why do those wolves sound like that?

Oh no. I couldn't let him get hurt. They'd kill him. "Go inside. They've gone feral. Let me deal with them." I didn't dare look at him. Not with the wolves coming.

"Why are they feral? What's happened to them?"

"Because I opened a doorway to the spiritual realm. I wasn't supposed to do that. Not here." Stupid, *stupid* amateur move on my part.

"How do we stop them?"

I glanced at him—jeans, a hoodie with the sleeves pulled up, gaze on me.

It was in that moment I knew I wanted him to stick around. Probably forever. He'd seen me struggle, seen me fight evil, seen me pass out I don't know how many times, but he never left.

Standing there in the middle of the night with a pack of feral wolves racing toward me, I realized I was in love with this man.

Which seemed obvious, but I'd never loved someone. Not like this. Not even my ex.

"Samantha? You okay?"

I shook my head and forced my gaze away. "They need their Alpha." I didn't dare look behind me. *"Hurry up, Chris!"* I screamed as loud as I could. *"I need your help! Right now! The pack has gone feral!"*

They were coming. I had five seconds, and no clue what to do. I didn't want to die, but I didn't want to hurt any of them either.

"Go inside," I told Phoenix as I tried to step in front of him. "This could get—"

Cosette came out of nowhere, sprinting in front of me, holding out her hands. "*Stop!*" She yelled the command to the wolves, and they all slid, skidding out of control to follow her command. A few of the wolves flipped over their front legs. One hit her legs, and she pushed him away with her foot. "What in the world is your problem? You do *not* attack Samantha." She paused. "Wait. Is that Axel? What is happening?"

I took a breath, willing my heart to slow down. "It's not their fault." Not even a little bit. The wolves were all laying there, submitting to Cosette's will, but would it last? "How long can you hold them like that?" I needed to get closer to help them, but I couldn't help them if they ripped out my throat.

"Don't insult me. I'm a princess of the Lunar Court." Her voice was full and haughty. "They will stay where I command them to stay until I tell them they're allowed to get up." Cosette stood as if she were wearing a big gown and a crown, but she was in pajama pants with dragons on them and a black tank. Her long blonde hair was pulled into a knot on top of her head, and yet she looked fierce. Although, that might have something to do with the flaming sword pointed at the ground in her right hand.

Chris came strolling up behind her in a pair of black sweatpants and nothing else. His wavy blond hair stuck out at all angles, and I knew I'd for sure woken them up.

"You're not going to obey her?" Phoenix asked Chris.

"Me? No. I went through a lot to cut my lunar tie. I don't have to obey her."

Cosette cleared her throat. "Excuse me."

"But I love making her happy." He gave her a sweet smile and batted his eyelashes at her.

She barked out a laugh. "You do." Her shoulders relaxed, and she somehow turned from princess to the Cosette I was used to.

"What is going on with the fire?" Cosette asked, waving her non-sword hand at me. "Could you always do that?"

I sighed. I hadn't ever shown any of them this. "Yeah."

"Feels like you've been holding out on us, Sam," Chris said. "This could come in handy in a fight."

"I know." I hung my head. "I know. It's just…this side of me is complicated." I looked at Chris. "I didn't mean to hold out. I just like to pretend I'm not this much—" I held out my fire-coated hands. "—of my father's daughter. Usually, it's the kind of fire that only burns in the spiritual realm, but if I push it hard, it can be real fire." I took a breath and relaxed, letting go of the fire. "It's a last resort. The kind I only use if a pack of feral wolves comes running at me, and opening a portal seems overkill."

"I can get that, but we should talk about incorporating it if you need to. You can't hold back in a fight. Even if it means accessing a part of yourself you don't like." Chris moved to stand next to me, looking at the wolves in the middle of the Sanctuary's main road, just two houses down from mine. "Axel is in this group. He's too alpha and part *bruja*. He shouldn't have been susceptible to going feral. What the hell happened to my pack?"

Cosette had said Axel was in the group, but I'd hoped she was wrong. It was honestly really hard for me to tell the wolves apart. Especially when they were all in a group together. I didn't spend a ton of time with them in their wolf forms, and there were a few that were so identical they should've been twins in human form, too. But they looked nothing alike.

"Hey. Lucas heard you screaming and woke me up." Claudia came walking around the corner. "What's going on?" She was in sleep shorts and a sweatshirt. Lucas, her very taciturn mate, stalked behind her in sweatpants.

"Sorry, everyone. I made a mistake." I rubbed my hands down my face, trying to calm down. The adrenaline was pumping, and now that the wolves had settled, I had a second to sort this out.

"What's the mistake?" Phoenix asked.

"She left her body here," Mom called out to us from the porch.

"She usually wouldn't do anything in the spiritual realm in our home. We had to move a lot of times before we figured it out and made that rule."

"Actually, I remember that. That's why we met you in that crystal shop," Claudia said. "You wouldn't do stuff at your apartment."

"Wow. I honestly can't believe you remembered that."

"Steel trap," she said as she tapped her head. "So, you did something here, and now what?"

"And now my father can find me here, and he's clearly going to make life interesting if we can't find a way to fix it." And I had no clue how to even start fixing this. If I did, I wouldn't have moved so much as a kid. "I was in such a rush that I went for Van and left my body here. I broke my own rule. I was just so confident that the Sanctuary was safe, I didn't even think about it. But my father was able to destroy my room, which means I opened something here."

I knew better. Or I should've known better.

And now Phoenix was tied to me.

And my father was ruining the Sanctuary.

And I had no idea where to go from here.

"We need Eli. We need to—" Cosette cut off at the sound of a ring tone.

"Excuse me," Lucas said, pulling his phone from his pocket. *"Hola, qué—"*

I heard someone yelling on the other side in Spanish, but then another phone rang.

Cosette turned to her mate. "Answer it."

Chris sighed. "We're a little busy right now." But he did it anyways, pulling his phone from his pocket. "It's Dastien." He stepped away from the group. "What's up?"

I let them deal with whatever was going on and focused on the wolves. "Can I go near them?"

"Of course you can. They won't disobey me." Cosette gave them a look, and they whimpered and writhed on the ground.

"I'm in control of the wolves. Do what needs to be done." She'd gone full princess mode again, and usually, I'd tease her for it. She didn't do it often, but every once in a while, she would get it in her head that she was right about something, and that was it. She was Supreme Ruler Cosette.

But tonight was different. I needed her to be in control. I needed the princess of the Lunar Court to keep the werewolves in check. If she let them slip, even a little bit, I'd be as good as dead.

"What's wrong with them?" Phoenix asked.

"They've got demonic ties. I'm going to free them, and then I'll need to cleanse this whole place." But I wasn't sure I could. "The Sanctuary was sanctified by Eli?"

"No," Cosette said. "By my father." She paused. "Well, by a few of the archons—and Eli was present—but also my father."

"Can we get him here?"

She let out a small snort. "Sure. Let me get right on that."

"Alright, Princess Sarcasm." Whatever. I'd deal with that later. First, I had to fix the wolves.

I walked up to them, my hands still on fire. I'd use it before I put it away.

I knelt beside each wolf, reached for their demonic tie, and burned it before moving on to the next. I worked quickly, quietly.

I could hear Phoenix talking to Cosette, but I ignored them. Mom had joined them, and if I was younger, I'd probably be due for a lecture.

Actually, I was still probably due for a lecture.

Another thing for me to deal with later.

I had so many fun things to look forward to.

Focus, Sam.

One by one, I freed the wolves. They lay relaxed on the ground. A few of them shifted into their human skin and asked what had happened, but I asked them to wait. Mom brought them clothes to change into, and that was fine. I wasn't worried about anything but clearing everything from the wolves.

Axel was the last one. "Hey," I said as I knelt by his wolf form. "I'm sorry."

He whimpered.

"I know. I'm sorry." I shook my head and reached for the tie that was wrapped around his neck, strangling his soul. One touch, and it was gone.

At least the ties weren't strong. There hadn't been enough time for them to hook into their souls. It'd only been a few days since I saved Van, which meant that even if they got them the same night, they hadn't had them for long.

When it was finished, Axel hopped up on all four paws and ran his rough tongue along the side of my face. I tried to shove the three-hundred-pound wolf off of me—I didn't know why he weighed that much as a wolf when his human weight wasn't anything close to that—but there was no moving him. "Stop it. That's so gross." His tongue was rough and slimy. He did it again, and I started to laugh. "You jerk!" But then I looked at him, and he was sitting on his butt, tongue hanging from his mouth, and looking happy with himself.

"Fine. You made me laugh when I was feeling pretty down. Gold star for you." He let out a howl—this time, a happy one—and darted off into the neighborhood. I had a feeling he'd come back in human form, preferably with clothes.

I sat back on my heels, facing the wolves that hadn't run off yet. "I'm sorry this happened to you. As you know, I saved Van a few days ago, and I must've left a gateway open—not a full portal, but a spiritual path. You had demonic ties. None of you were possessed, which is good. You were just driven feral and out of control through the tie. They're gone now. You're fine. Get some rest, and if any of you feel the least bit antsy, come see me. I'll make sure it hasn't come back."

Once I was done, some of the wolves got up and left on their own. Some of them stayed in wolf form and went off together, probably to sleep in a big puddle like puppies. Whatever had happened clearly rattled them. But none of them had the spunk that they usually did. They all moved a little slower.

They were werewolves. They'd recover quickly. But that didn't make me feel that much better about the whole thing.

"What's next?" Mom asked from beside me.

I looked up from where I was kneeling and shrugged. "I don't know. Honestly. I don't want to move. I really, really like it here." I was feeling so…*defeated*.

"You're not moving." Chris's deep, raspy voice was firm, leaving no room for argument. "We'll fix what needs fixing. Between you and Claudia—"

"No, she should call for Eli," Phoenix said. "If I'm following correctly, then he needs to know. He could fix this."

He was right. I knew he was right, but I also knew Eli was busy. Still… *"Eli! I need help!"* I yelled through both realms. *"I need you now!"*

Please, let him be able to fix this.

CHAPTER ELEVEN

SAMANTHA

ELI WAS beside me in an instant, hovering just above the ground in the middle of the street, and I knew whatever I'd pulled him from was bad. Really, truly bad. He wasn't in his normal armor. This was his I'm-fighting-the-end-of-days-war gear. His whole body was enveloped in shining gold. He wore a full helmet that covered his whole head—eyes and all—and his wings weren't gray-tipped white anymore. They were made of fire.

"Yes, angel." His voice was booming and the kind of loud that was physically painful.

I tried to look at him, but he was way too bright. I shielded my eyes. "Can you tone it down a little? This is extremely uncomfortable."

"Fine." In an instant, he transformed back to normal Eli—ripped jeans, button-down, bare feet fully on the ground. "What is it?" He looked around, taking in the scene, trying to assess everything, likely reading everyone's minds to fill himself in.

I rose from where I'd been kneeling on the ground. "The pack here somehow suddenly had demonic ties tonight, and I realized that I shouldn't have crossed over to Hell from my house. I'm pretty sure my father sent some of his minions after me. Can you re-sanctify the Sanctuary or something so they can't come back?"

"I thought this might happen, but I hoped I'd have more time." He finally looked down at me. "Look, angel. This stuff isn't easy. It took more than one archon to do what we did here. And—as you can probably guess—we're busy."

Yeah. I caught that. "What's happening exactly? Should I be worried?"

"We're beating back evil. As always." He rolled his eyes, as if angels and demons fighting in an everlasting war for souls was no big deal. "As for being worried? No more than usual. Time is nearing the end, and dark times for Earth are ahead. I wonder if this is worth the effort." He motioned around the Sanctuary, and I knew what he meant.

Eli got all moody and emo when he was fighting big battles. Especially if I called him in the thick of it.

He grunted as if something occurred to him. "I can do a little protection that could help if you want, but again, if the end comes, maybe it's better if I didn't. Going out quicker might be a mercy if the hordes are loosed."

I hated it when he got like this. "Shut up and fix it."

"Patch it," he muttered softly.

"What?"

"I'm going to *patch it.*" He looked down at me as if I were being dense, and I wanted to kick him. "I can't fix it alone. You have to remind me to come back with at least two more archons."

I knew he had a lot going on, and I was trying to follow, but his tone was annoying me. Although, maybe that was because I was frustrated with myself. If I'd done it the right way in the first place, none of this would be happening. "Okay. When do I call on you?"

"You'll know when." His tone was flat and yet somehow flippant.

I couldn't even with this. "Eli! Stop being like that. Just tell me—"

"I can*not*." He said the words with such emphasis that I knew it was true. He didn't have to say that he would've done more if he could've. That part was implied in the look he gave me.

"Got it." This was going to be one of those times when Eli walked the fine line of what he could and couldn't do. What rules he would break and the ones he shouldn't. And apparently this was one of the times he would follow the rules, even if he didn't want to.

"I'm sorry, angel. I'm distracted right now but trust me on this. You'll know when the time comes, and we'll be ready. Okay?"

"Yes. Thanks for coming. I'm sorry I pulled you away from a fight."

"Being your guardian has been one of the true joys of my life. I will always come if I am able. Let me take care of what I can, and then I must go."

"Thank you. I appreciate it. I can't believe I messed up this badly."

The mate bonds lit up around me, and I was sure they were discussing how I was talking to Eli or how I messed up…or maybe they were just trying to figure out what Eli meant, and it had nothing to do with my mess up.

I'd get over it. I knew I would. It would just take some time.

"No one is perfect, angel. Everyone makes mistakes. It's how you deal with those mistakes that reveals your character, and you did the right thing to call me." The light around him started to brighten. "Close your eyes. This might hurt."

Instantly, Eli was back in his full gear—flaming wings, full armor, all of it. He held the sword above his head and said something in a language that hurt my ears.

I slapped my hands over them, trying to ease the pain, but I noticed no one else reacted to it. Only me.

Right. This might hurt *me*. He'd left that part out.

Which meant, it was going to knock me on my ass.

Dang it. I couldn't stop him. I needed this done, and if it hurt, well, then, I guessed it would just have to hurt.

There was a warmth and a pressure in the air as he spoke, and he flapped his wings to rise above the ground. He went higher and higher until he was a star in the sky.

And then all of a sudden, he was getting bigger. *Fast.*

"Oh shit!" I started running as far away from him as I could get.

I was going to murder Eli for this. I could hear my friends yelling at me and asking questions, but they didn't need to worry. They'd be fine. I, however, was screwed.

There was a roar so loud that I felt it through my soul, and I did a stupid thing. I turned to look right as Eli hit the ground.

He stabbed his flaming sword into the ground where I'd been standing. There was a flash of pure white light and a boom that knocked me off my feet.

My back hit the ground. Hard.

I couldn't see anything. "I'm blind."

My ears were ringing, and I couldn't feel anything. "Am I dead? Did you kill me, Eli?"

But then I heard his laugh. Not from my ears, but along the spiritual realm.

"I hate you," I said.

"No, you don't. Just breathe. I told you to close your eyes."

"No one ever listens when you say that. It's the stupidest thing to say *ever.*"

"And that's my fault? How?" He didn't leave me time to respond before he spoke again. *"I have to go, angel. You'll be fine in a few minutes. Call me if you need anything. Or before you do something stupid again."*

"Again?! I don't do stupid—" I felt a ripple along the spiritual realm, and I knew he was already gone. *Rude.*

Whatever Eli had done to fix the Sanctuary—even if it was a temporary fix—had really knocked me out. I was lying in a pool of black nothingness. I couldn't hear. Couldn't see. Couldn't feel anything.

Dang it. Eli was such a jerk.

"Hey." Phoenix's voice sounded far away, but it felt like an improvement.

"Hi." My answer echoed in my ears.

"You doing okay?" He sounded worried.

"Eli said I'll be fine. He just blasted my senses with his mojo."

I blinked my eyes a few times, and slowly everyone faded in, looking down at me. Something squeezed my arm, and I looked down to see Mom taking my blood pressure. "I'm fine."

"We'll see." She didn't even spare me a glance. Not because she was mad, but because she was worried. Which was fair. I'd given her more than a few scares this week.

I glanced around to see even Axel watching me. "Oh. Hey." This was a lot. I didn't want to be rude, but a little space would've been nice. Because whatever Eli had done really sucked.

"Dramatic, huh?" Axel said, teasing me.

Not really. If he'd felt what I had, he'd be on his tush, too. "Whatever he did was like setting off a nuclear weapon along the spiritual realm."

"Her vitals are good," Mom muttered. "Maybe another IV—"

"No!" I was done with those for a while. "You can't keep sticking needles in me, Mom. I'm fine." But I did need a little room. "Can everyone just back up a little?"

They immediately did, and I felt like a jerk. "Sorry." I closed my eyes and counted to ten. Everything was fine. "Sorry," I said again, and opened my eyes.

Phoenix reached out a hand, and I took it, letting him pull me into a sitting position. Not dizzy. No more muffled senses. Just tired and cold. Which was nice. Early December in Texas wasn't all that cold, but it was the middle of the night. Now that I was upright, I realized that the ground had been cold enough to chill me through my clothes. "Thanks."

"Well, that went well," Claudia said, and I felt every bit of her sarcasm.

"Nothing like a middle-of-the-night demonic visit." I was tired. Bone tired. But they all seemed to be waiting for me to say something. "What I did to save Van…how I did it…" I'd rushed. Nothing good ever came from rushing. Being busy, hurrying, weren't things of God. They were things that caused chaos. That was Satan's realm. I knew better, but in the moment, I'd forgotten. I'd been too worried about what might have been happening to Van to slow down and think of all the implications of what I was doing.

"It doesn't matter how or why this happened. The bottom line is it's my fault. I cost the Sanctuary its safety, and I accept full responsibility." I looked at Chris. "If you want me to move out, I can—"

He jerked back a step in surprise. "Shut up. You're not going anywhere. Eli said that you'll know when to call him back. And when you do, he'll bring a few archons to fix it. It's fine. We have a plan."

It actually wasn't as easy as Eli made it out to be. "I'm not sure how I'll know when it's time, but I trust Eli enough to at least go with him on that part. The tricky part is getting enough archons here to fix it. There's a solid chance that when the time comes, he'll tell me that he'll be right back with the gang, but take days, weeks, or even *years*. Archons are weird with time."

"That feels like borrowing trouble." Chris didn't seem bothered, but that was part of his calm nature. "I'm not worried about it. The Sanctuary has had a nice run so far. If we have a couple years where we have to deal with something here and there, it's not that big of a deal. We'll take it as it comes." He looked around, his gaze searching everyone. "Anyone else worried?"

I glanced at my friends. Lucas had his arm around Claudia. She looked worried. I wasn't sure if it was about this or something else. I was leaning toward the something else because of the look on Lucas's face. His eyes were glowing.

I didn't know Lucas super well—the man was quiet, except when it came to his mate—but I wasn't sure I'd ever seen his eyes glow with his wolf. He wasn't the kind of werewolf to hold back a change, but he was holding back now. Which meant he was upset about something, but there was no enemy to fight.

Phoenix sat next to me, and I was grateful to have someone to lean on. So, I leaned into his warm strength. "I have a feeling I missed something while I was out of it. What's going on?"

Everyone was quiet.

Okay. Now I knew I'd missed something. "Spill."

Chris cleared his throat. "I've got news." His blue eyes flashed wolf-bright.

"What happened?" I wasn't sure I was ready for another battle, but sometimes I didn't get to decide that. If I had to, I would find the strength and do what needed doing.

"We got calls right as everything was going down," Chris said.

That was right. I remembered the phone ringing. "Who called?"

"Dastien called Chris," Cosette said. "Three wayfarer wolves died tonight in South Carolina. In Charleston. That's why we were slow getting to you. We felt the deaths along the pack lines right as you started yelling. It woke us up from a dead sleep."

"What?!" Three was a lot of dead werewolves.

"Dastien and Tessa are headed to the airport as we speak," Cosette kept talking as if she hadn't said anything, but there was nothing normal about werewolves dying. Especially Wayfarers.

I'd been helping the Wayfarer Pack since I accepted the job as demonologist. Whenever they came up against a mystery bad guy, I flew in to help. Over the years, we'd been in some incredibly crazy situations. I'd seen some werewolves get hurt before, but I'd never seen a werewolf die.

Before I could even process that, Lucas spoke up. "I have news as well," Lucas said in his slightly accented English.

"You got a call." He was the one with his ringer on. "Who was it?"

"My second. There's a problem in my pack. My third is dead, and no one knows how. I've already texted my pilot. I have to get back to Peru. We're leaving in—"

"No." The word was out before I could stop it. I wasn't even sure why I said it.

"Why?" Claudia took a step toward me but stopped. Mostly because Lucas was gripping her hand, and I wondered if that was the only thing keeping him in control of his wolf. "What do you know?" she said softly.

I didn't have a good answer for her. The word just came out. "I don't know." I shook my head. "But things don't naturally happen like this—everything all at once. You were all supposed to stay here, and now we're splitting up. It feels wrong. That's too many attacks in too many places. My father is up to something, but…" I blew out a breath, and I knew I couldn't leave my friends to fight whatever was killing werewolves alone. "I should go with you or with Tessa."

I looked up at Chris. He trained me to fight. He was the one who hired me to be the demonologist. He decided what missions I went on. I could absolutely leave without his approval, but if this was pack business, he had to be the one to tell me which pack to go help. "Where do you want me?"

He squatted down beside me as his eyes flashed even brighter. "Nowhere."

I sat up straight. "What?!" That wasn't an option. "Have you lost your mind? Clearly, I'm needed somewhere, but I can't pick. Whoever I don't go with might very well be up shit creek." I hung my head. "Dang it. I just cussed." I took a breath to calm the anxiety that was rising in me. "I hate it when I do that." But I wasn't perfect—I couldn't even attempt to be—so I'd just do better.

No more cussing, Sam. "So, where do I go?"

"Nowhere." Chris's raspy rumble had a hint of his wolf in it.

He wasn't getting it. That wasn't an option. "Chris."

"Samantha. Absolutely not."

He couldn't be serious. This was ridiculous. "Why not?"

He reached out and gripped my hand, leveling his gaze in mine. "Because you're still recovering. Because we trained today, and you were slow. Because we don't know what they're up against, and I'm not sending you anywhere unless I absolutely have to. Do you hear me?"

"Yeah. I hear you." I hated that he made sense. That wasn't playing fair. "Dead wolves are a big deal."

"I know. Trust me, I'm aware." He let go of my hand. "But for now, you stick here."

He couldn't make me stay. "I could just leave."

"You could, but I'm asking you not to. Please. You know you're not at full strength, otherwise, you wouldn't still be sitting on the cold ground in the middle of the night."

He had a point. "Fine." I looked him straight in the eyes because I needed him to hear me. "But if more wolves die, I'm going. Even if you think I'm still out of shape."

"Even if *I think*?" He gave me a look.

"Don't be a jerk. I already cussed once tonight. I don't want to do it again."

"You're proving my point, sweetheart." His voice was softer, but his eyes were still bright. "Dastien is going to Charleston. No more will die there. And Lucas is heading home. His pack will be stronger with him there. So, fine. I'll take that deal because they're not going to need you." He rose and took a step back, leaning into Cosette.

I was going to punch him. He had no right to—

"I'd ask you not to hurt my mate," Cosette said. "But he might deserve it." She grinned at me.

The fight drained out of me. I didn't actually want to hurt Chris. I just hated being sidelined. "Okay. I won't hurt him tonight, but you owe me."

Cosette snapped her fingers, and something appeared in her hand. She tossed it at me. "Debt paid."

I looked down at the chocolate bar. It was my favorite, but still not as good as having a favor owed to me by the princess of the Lunar Court. But Cosette was too fey to ever let something like that stand.

Lucas started telling Claudia it was time to pack in Spanish, and I got up. The world spun a little, and strong hands steadied my shoulders.

I looked into Phoenix's eyes. "Thanks."

"No problem."

I felt the heat rush to my cheeks as I remembered what we'd been doing before all of this happened. "Sorry I fell asleep on you earlier. That's kind of embarrassing."

"It's not a problem. Or a hardship." He gave me the smile that I was pretty sure he did on purpose now. The dimple showed up, and it was too much. It made my cheeks burn even hotter, so I walked over to Claudia.

I gave her a hug. "Call me if you need me." I wasn't sure if the worry I felt was just a general worry for her safety or some kind of foreboding from the spiritual realm. Either way, if she called, I would be there.

"I'll call if anything comes up. I promise." She pulled away just enough to look in my eyes. "Be good to yourself."

"I will." I gave Lucas a nod, and they rushed off to the house they'd been crashing in the last few nights.

"I just came back to say thank you," Axel said. "I honestly don't know what happened, and I don't really want to know. The shit you do freaks me out. But thank you for doing whatever it was you did to fix it."

"I'm sorry it happened in the first place. If you start feeling off, call me."

"Will do." He turned and walked back into the night.

I opened myself up as far as I could without stepping into the spiritual realm and took a good look around the neighborhood. I walked slowly in a big circle, trying to see if there was anything left in the spiritual realm that I should take care of, but there wasn't. At least, nothing demonic. No ties that shouldn't have been there. It was like whatever had happened was truly done and over.

But I knew that wasn't true. "Well, that was not how I expected my night to go."

"It wasn't totally unexpected, though," Mom said.

Maybe it wasn't. Maybe it was. I had no idea anymore. But one thing was for sure, my father was ramping things up. He sent demons to turn the pack feral, and then had them come after me.

If Cosette hadn't stopped them, they would've killed me. He was betting that I'd end up in his domain when I died. That thought chilled me.

I wasn't sure where I'd end up, but I hoped it wasn't with him. I knew my father was evil, but I hoped that I could be redeemed beyond my heritage. That wasn't why I did what I did, though.

I fought evil because I had to. I could either choose to be like him, or choose to be like my mother. I'd choose her every time.

But it was clear to me now that my father was escalating his games, which meant everything was about to change.

"Hey," Phoenix said, gaining my attention. "Whatever happens, we can deal with it."

"Maybe." I wanted to believe him. I wanted to believe him so badly. "But I have a bad feeling about this."

"Me, too," Mom said. That she was agreeing with me made the knot in my stomach tighten.

I sighed. *Great. Just perfect.*

"Let's go inside and get some food," Phoenix said. "And then you need to sleep. If they need you, they'll call. And we'll go."

I looked at him at the last part. "*We'll* go?"

"Yes. *We.*" He looked in my eyes, and I could see how serious he was about this. If I fought him on it, we would have a real problem.

That actually made me feel a lot better. Every time he stuck around after something crazy happened, I felt more and more certain that everything would be alright with us. That being with him wasn't such a stretch, and like maybe, just maybe, this would end up with some sort of a happily ever after.

I never thought I'd get that, but with him, maybe I did.

"Do you feel drained from this?" Phoenix asked.

I was about to say no. Because I hadn't felt my father around here, and I would have noticed if he was close enough to drain me. But that wasn't true. That hollow feeling was back in my body, and I knew I was wrong.

"Yes."

Mom sucked in a breath.

Yep. Exactly. "I know. It's a bad sign."

"Why does your mom smell like fear, Samantha?" Chris's voice grew rougher, deeper.

I knew better than to meet his gaze when he was like this. He was a pretty calm Alpha, but not *that* calm.

I dropped my chin to my chest. "Because if I'm drained like this, then my father was close enough to hurt me. And that's never happened at the Sanctuary before." I blew out a breath, straightened my shoulders, and pushed all that worry away.

"I have to believe that Eli fixed it. He wouldn't have left if it wasn't patched like he said it was. I'm not *seeing* anything around here anymore. So, we should be fine, but my father knows where I am now."

"And that's bad." Cosette said it, but it wasn't a question. Not really.

"That's extremely bad." So much for having a safe haven.

"Food. Then, sleep." Phoenix put his hands on my shoulders, turning me toward the house, and then herded me home.

If anyone else had done that, I would've shoved them away.

But not Phoenix.

Never Phoenix.

CHAPTER TWELVE

SAMANTHA

TWO DAYS HAD PASSED since the night my father attacked me on Sanctuary grounds.

Two days of everyone watching me, waiting for me to fall apart.

Two days of me being told I needed more time to recover.

Two days of Phoenix hovering nonstop.

Okay, to be totally honest, that last one wasn't that bad at all. I seriously liked having him around so much.

I sat on my red Adirondack chair on my porch, attempting to read a book but failing. I'd read the last page no less than ten times and still had no idea what it said.

Giving up, I closed the book, setting it on the table, and stared out into the neighborhood and forest beyond it.

Mom was busy working on her laptop in the chair next to me, and Phoenix was working out with Chris and Cosette. They dared him to come along today, and he looked like he wanted to go. So, I said he should go and told Chris and Cosette not to break him.

Now, it was too quiet, and my mind was spiraling.

Phoenix and I hadn't been apart all week, and the doubts in my head were sliding their way into my heart.

One thing I knew for sure—the more I hung out with Phoenix, the more I realized I was falling completely in love with him. He was fun, kind, caring, attentive, and took things so damned easily that it made my head spin a little. Anything that popped up, he adjusted to it without any problem. He didn't need time to process. He just tackled every new thing with ease and grace and confidence.

Why did he feel too perfect?

And why did I keep waiting for him to leave?

Hunter. My ex. That was why.

I had no idea I was still so insecure after everything that had happened with Hunter. Everyone thought about their ex sometimes. That was normal. But when Hunter left, he said somethings that hit every soft spot in me.

He'd said I'd never find anyone to deal with what I was. That I was unlovable, unworthy, and would be utterly alone for the rest of my life. That my life was darkness and chaos and pain, and I'd bring that to whoever I spent any time with and—

Wait. I had to stop this spiral. Why was I letting what Hunter said years ago affect how I felt in my relationship with Phoenix?

I leaned back in the chair, tipping my chin up so the sun would hit my face. Spiritual warfare after dealing with my father was always horrific, and my thoughts these days…well, I was pretty sure that might be what I was dealing with.

"You okay over there?" Mom asked.

I let out a sigh. "Just thinking some messed up things. I'm doing it to myself."

"Want me to put on some music?"

I blinked my eyes open. "You don't think it'll bother the rest of the neighborhood?" The werewolves had phenomenal hearing.

"Do it!" someone yelled from across the way. "We don't mind!"

"Are you sure?" I said, not even really yelling.

"We're fine!" Another shout came from down the other way. "Play something upbeat. No whining singers. Just good stuff."

"Okay. Thanks." I turned to Mom, and she nodded.

I wasn't sure I'd ever get used to living at The Sanctuary, but I loved it. They might not be the same kind of weird as me, but I'd never felt more seen or connected than I had since moving here.

Mom tapped on her phone and then hit play on "Tread the Dawn" by The Gray Havens.

"Good choice!" someone else yelled, and I laughed.

"Thanks, Mom."

"Happy to do it."

I closed my eyes again, and this time, I focused on things I was thankful for.

Like my new room. It was amazing. It'd been so relaxing to cuddle with Phoenix and watch movies on my new bed or talk about all kinds of things in the reading nook. Even just sitting in the loveseat with him and reading had been nice. Getting to know him had been amazing, and since Phoenix was sticking close by, I was taking advantage of every second I could. I'd even taken a break from work while I recovered.

I was completely ignoring my inbox and my social media account. Mom was keeping an eye out on anyone that needed my help—she was currently referring out to other priests or pastors—but I knew if I looked, I'd get sucked in. I wasn't ready for that. Not yet.

Not while my friends were still in danger. I hadn't heard from Tessa today, which made me worried. Claudia swore that everything was under control, but she hadn't called me, just texted. I hadn't heard her voice, and I wasn't sure if that was because she was busy or because she knew I'd hear a lie in it.

"Is the music helping?" Mom asked.

"Yeah. It's helping me shift my thinking. I was feeling pretty down about myself."

"Remember not to treat my daughter terribly," she said.

I laughed. She used to tell me that all the time as a kid—not to treat her baby badly. At this point, it was an inside joke.

I sat up a little, reaching for my long-forgotten coffee, but the ice still clanged against the insulated metal. "I should've gone with them to workout. Too much sitting around isn't healthy."

Mom made a little *hmm* sound as she typed. "One more day of rest won't kill you," she muttered softly.

How would she know? "It's not helping me get back in shape," I muttered back.

"You can't get back in shape if you hurt yourself because you're exhausted." She shot me a look that told me not to argue or complain.

Sometimes it was lovely being an adult and living—as well as working—with my mom. Other times…

"If I want to workout tomorrow, I will." That was just going to have to be that.

She shrugged and sipped her coffee. We both knew she wanted me to stay healthy, and if she said no, I'd likely sit it out.

But every time I sat still and quiet for too long, I heard Gabe's screams. Not literally. Just from my memories. "I need to get my mind off everything—Gabe, my father, the Sanctuary, worrying about my friends… I need to do something before I really lose it."

Mom shut her laptop and set it on the table between us. "Be careful what you ask for, my love." She gave me her little know-it-all-mom smile and reached for her coffee.

She was right. Unfortunately. Whenever I said things like that, it always happened. Usually, pretty quickly. I knew that I should just enjoy the calm, but it made me feel nothing but restless. I wasn't good at relaxing.

"They should be back soon. I'm going to get some lunch ready." She rose from her chair. "You going to be okay out here by yourself?"

I picked up my book from the table. "Yeah. Of course."

She gave me a nod, went inside, and there I was. Still sitting. Still reading the same book. Still bored out of my gourd.

I checked my watch again, wondering when Phoenix would get back.

As if I'd drawn him back by thinking of him, Phoenix appeared down the road. The same path I usually took.

The group was talking as they jogged. Axel, Chris, and Phoenix were shirtless. Cosette was strolled along, looking as if she hadn't even broken a sweat, but I wasn't sure I'd ever seen her look messy. I couldn't make out what they were saying as they went from jogging to walking toward my house, but Phoenix laughed, and my heart picked up.

Oh man. No. This was bad. I was in so far over my head with him.

The four of them slowed to catch their breath, and while I'd admit both Chris and Axel were incredibly handsome, neither of them had anything on Phoenix.

This was the first time I'd seen Phoenix without his shirt on, which meant I could finally see more of his tattoos. Flames swept up his right side. There was an angel flying toward his heart. The angel was only visible from the profile, but the wings were beautiful. Except that I'd never seen a female angel, and the profile of the body couldn't be mistaken for anything but.

Axel yelled hello to me and mentioned work before he broke off toward his house. I gave him a wave, and then my eyes went back to Phoenix.

Wait. I was wrong about the flames. There was form to them. From far away, it just looked like fire, but as he got closer, I could see that the flames were actually a phoenix rising, chasing after the angel.

This whole tattoo was new. It hadn't been there when he did that magazine cover last year. I'd never admit it to anyone, not even Tessa, but I'd stared at the pictures of him for way too long.

When had he gotten it? Why an angel? I didn't want to read too much into it, but the phoenix felt obvious.

I stared at it before my gaze moved up his body to his face. He quirked a brow, daring me to ask as he walked up the porch steps, but now didn't feel like the right time.

I leaned back in my chair, closed the book I hadn't been reading on my lap and studied him. "Good workout?"

"Yeah. Actually. Chris nearly killed me."

Chris held up both hands in surrender. His blond hair was slicked back with sweat, which wasn't his normal, at least not when he worked out with me. His clear blue eyes brightened a little—not with his wolf, but with humor. "That's not true. He kept up well enough." He held out his fist to Phoenix, who bumped it with his. "Your guy can fight. Made me break a sweat, too. Which isn't easy."

"Really?" I looked at Phoenix. "Like street kind because we grew up in a rough area or something else?"

"I trained. When I was a kid, my mom put me in karate. Thought it was good for my aggression. I eventually dropped it because soccer took up all my time. But once I got to Europe, I started martial arts again."

"Really?"

"Yep. The coach would bring in sometime to do nontraditional workouts with us. Some of the guys liked to do Pilates. They said it helped them stay limber. I tried it once. It was fine, but I didn't enjoy it. But at the end of my first season, the coach brought in a Krav Maga Grand Master for anyone who wanted to try it. Two hours later, my roommate and I were hooked."

"Nice." I had no idea he could fight. That was somehow worse. How was I supposed to resist him now?

Who was I kidding? I couldn't. Not before and definitely not now. Everything I learned about him made him more appealing.

Phoenix reached for his water on the table beside me. He was sweaty, and his shirt was tucked into his shorts and man, I felt like I was a teen again, stalking him from my bedroom window.

Expect now he was here and I was older and he'd gotten so much hotter—which honestly, was that even fair?—and what the heck was happening?

"You've got drool," Cosette said.

I was going to murder her.

"Right here." She tapped beside her mouth.

I tossed my book at her, but Chris snagged it before it slammed into his mate's face.

She laughed, and it sounded musical, like bells in the wind. Her long, wavy, light-brown hair was pulled back in a ponytail. Having spent most of her life as her mother's assassin, Cosette was as fit as she was deadly. She turned to Chris, and their bond lit up as she said something silently through it to him.

When I first met them, it used to hurt me when they used the spiritual realm that way. Because that was where their mate bond lived—the spiritual realm. These days, it only hurt my head when I was exhausted. Like today. Which annoyingly meant I was still tired. "It's rude to talk about people when they can't hear what you're saying," I said, trying not to wince and failing.

Cosette grinned at me. "You don't want me to say this out loud." She looked from Phoenix to me again. "Trust me."

Perfect. She was making fun of how obvious I was being.

Phoenix leaned back against the porch railing, watching me as he drank his water.

"You working out with us tomorrow?" Chris asked.

"Yeah," I said. "I can't sit another one out, but I know I'm going to die." It'd been a week since I'd had a full workout.

"Never." Chris' voice had lost its usual teasing tone. "I would never do anything to hurt you." He sounded almost insulted. "We'll get in some movement later today and ease you in tomorrow."

I glanced at him, and he was staring me down. Gone was all his trademark casualness. This was Alpha Werewolf Chris. "We go slow. Just like last July."

Oh man. Last July. That string of exorcisms…

We chased demons around town for a week before finding the stupid portal. Man, I'd been a mess when I was done. So tired I'd slept for nearly two days. When Chris finally let me train again, he hadn't even let me jog for the first week. It took nearly a month to get back to my regular training regimen, and I hadn't been nearly as bad off as I was right now.

I groaned. "Come on, Chris. That's going to piss me off. I just want to get back to normal."

"No. We go slow. I know you get frustrated, but it's better than hurting you and needing more time off. You're way worse now than you were that July. And I caught your wince when Cosette and I were talking through our bond, so I know you're not better yet."

Fine. Chris had a point, and he always got me back to where I needed to be. Which I appreciated.

"Okay. We go slow, but it can't take a month this time. Seriously." I looked at him. "I have a feeling something is coming, and I can't afford to go slow. You promised to keep me able to fight, and I can't…" I swallowed.

"What do you know?" Cosette said.

I looked away. "Still nothing. I don't know anything, but I feel…" I closed my eyes. I'd been trying not to think about it, but ignoring the feeling that something big was brewing wasn't helping.

"What?" Phoenix's voice sounded worried.

I opened my eyes. "He's coming after me. Big time. Everything he's done before…he's been making plans since before I was born. I thought…" I huffed and looked away. "I stupidly thought he spaced things out because he was tired, but now I think I was wrong. I think he's been systematically testing me, and I'm pretty sure he thinks I'm ready for whatever he needs me for."

I looked up at Chris. "You have to let me train. Even if it hurts the first few days. You have to do it. You know why I asked you to do this for me."

"And I've always kept my word."

"You have, but now more than ever, I need you to help me. Please. I can't afford to be weak."

Chris was quiet for a moment. I wasn't sure when his eyes had brightened, but his wolf was very close. "Okay." The word was more growl than anything else.

Cosette put a hand on his shoulder, and he took a deep breath.

"I won't let anything happen to you," Chris said. "You might not be a werewolf, but you're more than part of the pack. You're family."

I looked down at my lap, not able to keep anyone's gaze. I hadn't mean to say all of that, but I hadn't been able to stop myself. But I knew one thing for sure. "No one can promise something like that, Chris," I whispered the words. "You can't feel responsible for me. If something happens to me…" When I looked up, I saw Chris was struggling with his wolf. As the Alpha, he felt the urge to protect his pack, which I wasn't technically a part of, but his wolf felt differently.

I didn't finish what I was saying because he knew.

Chris gave me a nod, then turned to Phoenix. "You coming with us tomorrow?"

"I go where she goes." Phoenix was still leaning against the porch railing right in front of me. His arms were crossed, and that crease was between his eyes—the one he got when he was trying to figure me out.

Chris said something and Phoenix turned to talk to him, but I was too busy thinking about what Phoenix said.

He goes where I go? I liked that. I liked it so much that it was kind of terrifying.

The guys were talking, and I wasn't really paying attention. I just watched Phoenix, enjoying seeing him with my friends, until he noticed me. He gave me a quick wink while he chatted with Chris.

The wink turned my mind to mush.

One look from him, and I'd totally forgotten what I'd been thinking about. Given how my thoughts had spiraled since he'd been gone, that was probably a good thing.

Mom cracked front door and poked her head out. "Is everyone staying for lunch?"

"No, ma'am," Chris said in his raspy drawl. "Not today. I have some things to see to, but we'll be back later."

"I am. I'm going to shower, but I'll be back over in a few." Phoenix stepped into me, leaning down with his arms on either side, caging me in, and he brushed his lips against mine.

My whole body heated, my heart raced, everything went into the feel of his lips against mine.

He rose just enough that he was looking straight into my eyes. "Don't go anywhere."

I blinked, trying to metaphorically claw my way back to reality. "Where would I go?" My voice came out softer than I'd wanted. "I've been ordered to stay put."

"Good." He rose fully and gave Chris and Cosette a wave as he went down the stairs, making his way to his rented house.

One day it would seem normal that Phoenix was in my life again, but today definitely wasn't that day. It still felt like a bit of a miracle that he'd come back into my life. I didn't know how it was possible that he felt the same way, but I was beyond grateful for it.

As I watched him disappear into his house, the image of his tattoo flashed in my mind, and there was something about it that felt familiar…

I'd have to remember to ask him later.

CHAPTER THIRTEEN

SAMANTHA

I WATCHED Phoenix until he was gone, and then sat there staring after him. For once in my life, I was truly happy and content, and that terrified me. I didn't want anything or anyone taking it away.

"How are you really doing?" Cosette asked as she slid into the chair next to me, drawing my attention away from Phoenix.

I twisted in my chair to face her. "I'm okay. Honestly. I'm not sleeping great—still waking in the middle of the night, which makes me tired—but other than that, I'm fine."

"And what about having that guy around?" Chris motioned with his head toward next door. "We haven't had a chance to talk without him physically present. I've tried to catch you, but..." Chris dropped to a squat between mine and Cosette's chairs. "Did I do the right thing by suggesting he stay in the house? A lot happened that night without you knowing it, and—"

"Cut that out." I didn't know Chris was taking on some sort of responsibility for what happened. "Yes. It's fine. I can't explain it, but—"

"Stop." Cosette cut in. "You truly don't have to explain a

strong connection to someone who has a mate, but we know what he did. We were there. And we know you both had an attraction happening before that, but that doesn't equate a mate bond. We're worried. Now that he's been around so much, any regrets?"

I took a second to think about it before answering. I wanted to be truthful and thoughtful with my response. "Honestly, I have no regrets. At all. I feel kind of like I won something that I didn't know was possible, but I keep waiting for him to feel chained to me or trapped." Who would want to be with a half-fallen angel like me? But maybe that was me still waiting for him to react how Hunter had.

Phoenix was *not* Hunter. I had to drill that into my brain.

"No way, Sam." Chris was staring at me like I'd lost my mind. "He's not going to feel that way. Ever. That guy is all about you."

He'd said it with such certainty. "How can you possibly know that? I've been sitting here while you were gone thinking about why on Earth this amazing guy wants to be stuck with the mess that is me. I mean…I'm a bad bet. Full stop."

"Shut up. And I know because I see him, and we've talked, and I can smell lies and hesitations." He tapped his nose. "Being a werewolf is good for a lot of reasons, but that scent thing comes in handy." He looked at Cosette for a second before focusing on me again. "I also know what it's like to meet someone, have them change your whole world, and then have them disappear for years. And I know what it's like to find them again in the most unlikely place."

Cosette smiled at her mate. "And I know what it's like to feel like your life is a dangerous mess and to worry about bringing someone else into it." She looked at me. "I think out of all of our friends, we understand the most. And—" she trailed off as Chris rose.

I ignored the ache in my head as their bond lit up, but before I could ask what was wrong, I heard it, too. A car was approaching.

I recognized it a second later, and Tessa and Dastien got out of their black SUV.

I rose from my chair. I was glad to see them, but they should've been gone for at least a few more days. "Hey. You're back?" Anxiety rolled through my bones, and I knew this was going to be bad news.

"Yeah." Tessa shared a look with Dastien as they rounded the car, and their bond lit up. This time, I didn't even notice the ache. When she looked at me again, all my internal alerts went off.

They hadn't said why they were here, but from the look on her face, I knew she was about to ask for help.

Man, I really did jinx myself. I'd said I was bored to Mom, and now, I had a feeling that boredom was about to end.

They walked up the stairs, and I sat back down to give them room on the porch.

Tessa gave me a thorough once over. "You didn't work out again today? Chris is a sweaty mess, but you're not. Are you okay?" Her voice was way too high-pitched and soft.

Yeah. I was right about this. Something was coming. My father wasn't done. I could *feel* it. I couldn't explain it. I just knew. "I'm fine. Mom told me I needed to rest one more day, and Chris is worried about pushing me too hard too fast. We're doing a light workout later. Why are you asking me this? What's going on?"

Dastien stood next to Tessa, studying me the same way she had. "You're physically okay, though? Totally?"

I started to nod, but then stopped myself. They were clearly worried about something and needed a firm answer. "For the most part, yes. I feel a little out of shape because I've been sitting on my butt for the last week, but I'm okay." I hoped that was enough for them to tell me what was going on.

"And emotionally?" Tessa reached for Dastien, linking their fingers together, and I could almost see the stress rolling off her. She was wound tighter than I'd seen her in a while. Maybe since the day she showed up on my doorstep asking for help breaking a demonic tie. "How are you sleeping?"

This was excessive. "Cut the crap, Tessa." We were too good of friends to do this now. "What do you need? What happened?"

Tessa and Dastien had a back and forth silently through their mate bond, and I wasn't sure how long they would've gone if Chris hadn't cut in. "You're right, Sam. That is really annoying." Chris gave me a half-smile before turning to them. "Spill it."

I wanted to laugh, but I was too busy focusing on Tessa. I didn't like how tentative she was being with me. That meant something bad had happened and they needed my help, but she was afraid to ask.

"We need your help."

Yeah. No kidding. "I got that much." But with what? I hadn't heard from her last night, and now I was wondering if something had gone really, truly wrong in Charleston. "What happened?"

"We don't know," Dastien said. "That's why we need your help. All I know is that we lost three wolves last night fighting a monster I couldn't see."

Chris let out a string of cuss words that I didn't ever want to repeat. "Man. I felt it, but I was asleep. I thought it was a bad dream, but I guess I didn't want to believe it. And you didn't call last night..."

"I'm sorry, man. They weren't very alpha, and it's not your pack. I didn't know if you'd notice their bonds break. I should've called."

Chris was quiet for a moment. "That's a lot for one night. And there were already three gone before you went. Plus one night before last—"

"No one told me about that." This was insane. If that many wolves were dying, then they clearly needed my help. How could they not tell me?

"We decided not to tell you," Dastien said. "We're worried about you, but I don't have a choice now. Seven wolves lost in total is a lot, and more injured. The only saving grace is that we heal so fast. Otherwise, it could've been so much worse."

I was sorry they hadn't come to me sooner, but I was glad they were coming to me now. "What's happened? Tell me from the beginning."

Dastien's eyes shifted from light brown to golden. "The Wayfarer pack has been there for two weeks. They went to investigate some rumors of supernatural happenings in the city, but it ramped up a few days ago. I guess they got close to figuring it out or something. But Tessa and I showed up and…" Dastien dropped his head, and from the way he was standing, he was taking the loss last night really hard.

"I couldn't find anything." Tessa leaned closer to him. "But I kept getting this feeling like I was being watched, and I know you said to—"

"Call me when you feel watched." Feeling watched when you couldn't find the specific source sometimes meant spiritual realm activity.

They really should've called me sooner, but I had to stop thinking that. My friends had been through something terrible, and I wasn't going to make them feel bad about it. "Sounds like you need my help."

"I think we really do," Tessa said. "And believe me, I'm kicking myself for waiting to come to you. So, I appreciate you not saying what you're likely thinking."

"Don't go there." I was letting it go, and she needed to as well.

"Thanks. I just…I kept feeling like something was hovering right behind me. It got worse when I went through doorways and down stairwells."

"Got it." Demons loved the *in-betweens.* In between one room and the next, one floor and the next. It's why they also liked corners in rooms—between one wall and the next. They also liked anything that could potentially become a portal—like mirrors or puddles or small bodies of water. And they really liked places where people had died—it left a rift in between this realm and theirs.

In an old city like Charleston, that could be everywhere and anywhere.

"And then last night, we were patrolling, and one minute everything was fine, and then the next, a headless wolf was tossed on the ground in front of me." Tessa swallowed audibly. "It was… it was awful. We fought something, but no one could see it. All we could do was run. Which has been truly humbling. I'm so sorry. I hate to ask you this so soon after everything, but will you help us?" Tessa sounded really unsure of even asking, but she didn't have to ask.

"It's literally my job. When do we leave?"

"Wait a second. No." Chris's voice was clear as he rose to stand. "Technically, I'm your boss. You're due a lot of time away from the job after what you did for Van. You don't have to do anything for a while. Besides that, your contract clearly stated that you can say no to any of us. For any job. It's your choice. Always."

That was nice of him to say, but I wasn't saying no. "I'm not going to let wolves die because I'm what? Traumatized by my father? Well, welcome to my life!" I was yelling, but I couldn't help it. I rose from the chair and spread my arms wide. "I'm *fine*! You guys need to stop worrying—"

A door closed, and I turned to see Phoenix coming back from his house. "Hey," he said as he came down and crossed over to my driveway. "You're back." He did a handshake, backslap thing with Dastien, and then gave a side-hug to Tessa. "Welcome, but also, why does everyone look upset? And why was Samantha yelling?"

"I'm not upset," I said to Phoenix, but I had been yelling. So, I couldn't refute that. "When do we leave?" I asked Tessa.

"Leave?" Phoenix asked, looking around at everyone, waiting for someone to fill him in. "What did I miss?"

We were all quiet for a second. Tessa and Dastien needed my help. Werewolves were beyond strong. They healed faster than anything I'd ever seen. So, to have multiple werewolves die so close together—and mysteriously—was a big deal. Clearly, Tessa hated asking me to do this, but I couldn't say no.

I wouldn't say no.

I glanced at Cosette, and she shook her head. *"Don't go."* She mouthed the words to me, and I knew on any other day—if the whole thing with Van hadn't happened—she wouldn't be saying this. She'd be helping me pack.

Chris turned to Dastien. "She's not ready, man. If something is killing werewolves, who's going to protect her?"

"Look. I know it's a lot to ask, but you weren't there. You didn't see the fight. It was like we were up against nothing. Body parts were flying, and we all had to run for our lives. I've never been in a fight where I didn't think I'd make it. Not like that. And you know we've been in some crazy situations," Dastien said to Chris. "She's the only one who might be able to figure it out. If she can see it, if she can give me that sight again, I will fight it. She IDs it, and we get her the hell out of there. No problem. But I *need* her."

For a moment, I wasn't sure if they were going to actually fight over this—which I didn't want—but then, Chris hung his head, submitting to Dastien who was just a touch more alpha than Chris. "I hear you. I just hate this, man."

"Me, too." He put his hand on Chris's shoulder and gave it a quick squeeze before dropping it.

Chris's eyes were wolf-bright, and I knew he was torn between duty to the pack and to me. But he didn't need to worry. I was a big girl. I could handle this, even if he didn't think I could.

"I'm so sorry to be asking more of you after what happened." Dastien moved to stand directly in front of me. "Chris and Cosette aren't wrong to try and stop you, but I have guys out there who are friends." His voice had a hint of a growl in it, and he cleared his throat. "I have more Wayfarers flying in, and if we need more, I can pull from other packs. We can decide how to kill whatever it is once you tell us what it is and how to do it. I don't want you hurt—"

I cut Dastien off with a hug, squeezing him tight. "Stop. I'm so sorry last night was awful. Everything is going to be okay. I'll always help you. You know that." No matter the cost, I would be there for them.

He let out a shuttering breath. "Thank you."

I stepped back from him. "This is what I do. You don't need to thank me."

"I know this is fast, but do you mind if we left soon? As in maybe pack a bag now, and we'll get back on a plane as soon as you're ready? It's already being refueled. I was going to have to go back no matter what you said."

"You didn't have to come in person. I could've just gotten on the plane. It would've saved time."

"No, we couldn't," Tessa said it like I was crazy for even mentioning that as a possibility. "I wanted to see you for myself and make sure you were okay. I didn't trust you to be honest on the phone. You would've just come."

"I don't lie. You know that." This was getting absurd. I didn't need everyone freaking out about my health. "You guys need to stop being so dramatic. I'm *fine*."

"She's not," Phoenix said, and I couldn't believe I'd almost forgotten that he was here. He'd been quietly leaning against the far railing, giving us all room as we discussed what was going on, but now he was standing straight, looking at me with his arms crossed.

This had to stop. I was officially done with it. *"I am fine.* I swear—"

"No. You're really not." He turned to Dastien. "She's low on energy. Still a little weaker than she was. She's been taking afternoon naps, and she wakes up during witching hour every night."

"Wait a second," Chris stepped in front of me. "You're still taking *naps* and you were trying to convince me that you're ready for a *full workout*. Are you kidding me right now?" He turned to Dastien. "She's not going. You're going to get her killed."

My mouth dropped open. Was this seriously happening? "Stop it." I stepped between Dastien and Chris. "This isn't helping anything. And it's definitely not changing a damned thing. I'm an adult, and I decide what I do. Not any of you." I'd had about enough of these alpha men. "I'm going."

They both turned to Phoenix.

"Are *you* serious right now?" I couldn't believe these two. "You're asking for Phoenix's permission?" I was going to lose my mind.

Phoenix reached out, pulled me from between them, and hugged me tight against his chest. "It's fine. You want to go, we'll go," he whispered in my ear.

That was nice, but I didn't need his permission.

I heard a throat clear softly, and I turned my head so I could see Tessa without letting go of Phoenix.

Tessa was watching me. She shrugged and jerked her chin at Phoenix, as if asking permission for him to come along.

Finally. Someone remembered that I was a grown woman who could make her own choices.

But yeah, I was fine with Phoenix coming. I gave her a tiny nod.

Tessa raised a brow, as if she were asking me to make sure I was sure.

She was sweet, but yeah. "It's fine."

"What's fine?" Phoenix's chest rumbled under my head.

"Tessa was making sure that it's okay for you to come with me."

He pushed away from me so that he could look at my face. His eyes widened just a little as he stared down at me. "You didn't want me to come with you?"

Oh man, he looked hurt. Dang it. I was already messing up, but could we not with the drama? "I said it was okay. And it's not that. It's…" I stepped away and looked at Tessa for help with this mess she just made for me, but she shrugged.

Great. That was so helpful.

Dastien grabbed Tessa's hand, and their bond lit up. "We'll leave you guys to it, but can you be ready soon? I know it's a quick turnaround, but I'd like to get you there and settled in a room that works for you before night falls. We don't have much time."

"That's a good idea." Finding a place that I could stay was sometimes tricky. "Give me forty-five minutes. I'll be ready."

"Great," Tessa said. "I need some stuff from my house. We'll be back in thirty in case you need help with anything."

"Perfect. I'll be ready." Or I'd be packed, but I needed to make sure that Phoenix was okay first. I didn't mean to hurt his feelings, and I needed everyone to hurry up and leave so that I could talk to him.

"Be careful." Chris pulled me in for a hug. "I'd go, but I can't right now. There are some things brewing, and…" He let go but grabbed my shoulders, lowering his face to mine. "But if you need me, call. I'll get on a plane. Screw everything else, okay?"

I wanted to ask what was brewing, but that felt like a can of worms I couldn't afford to open right now. "Okay. I promise."

"Thanks." Chris stepped away, seemingly reassured.

"Come on. I'm not a martyr. If I needed help, I'd ask for it."

"You better."

I would. Legitimately. Fighting a monster that was killing werewolves…yeah, no. That felt like a real hard pass, but I'd find out what it was. No problem. And then hopefully get far, far away.

Everyone left quietly, and I sat back in my chair. I stared at my lap until I heard Dastien's SUV pulling away. Then, I finally risked looking up at Phoenix, who had moved to stand right in front of me.

"Why don't you want me to go with you? I thought we were good."

"We were." I winced as I realized that I'd said that in past tense, and that wasn't what I wanted to imply at all. "We *are* good. Tessa was just making sure I was okay with it."

He crossed his arms. "Why wouldn't you be okay with it?"

How did I say this without being pathetic? "It's stupid." I hung my head and covered my face with my hands. I knew all the spiraling I'd done today was going to bite me in the butt. I just didn't realize it was going to happen so soon. "She just knows that I don't usually like a lot of people along when I'm working. And she knows me well enough to know that I might want to wait before I shove you even deeper into my world."

He nudged my foot with his. "But I'm asking to be there. So, you're not doing any shoving." When I said nothing, he nudged my foot again. "Spill."

"It's embarrassing, but the last boyfriend I had bailed—epically—after a really botched job. Like we're talking a portal-collapsed-a-building type of bad. There were cops, and it was awful. No one was hurt—the building had been condemned—but that's just one example. What I do…it can go really wrong, and I..." I dropped my hands. "I want this to work out for us. Really badly."

"Come on, Sam. It's not like this will be my first time seeing you do your thing." He ran his hand down my cheek. "This—you and me—isn't just going to be okay. It's going to be amazing."

I wanted to be that sure, but I didn't. "The last few days have been fun, but what I do, where we're going, what I'm going to have to do, that won't be fun. If werewolves are dying, it's going to be dangerous and scary and…"

"I'm okay with that." He studied me for a second. "What's the deal with the ex? Something tells me this is the root of it all."

Phoenix wasn't wrong about that. At all. "He just…" How did I even explain it? "He knew what I was from the start. We met at the psychiatric facility."

"Right. You started this story a few days ago, but we got distracted. What happened?"

A mess. That was what happened. "He was my friend for a year first, and he'd gone on exorcisms with me before. Lots of times. We started to date, and everything was great. I finally felt like I'd found my person." I couldn't believe I'd been so naive. "But then, one day, he asked to *see*. So, I showed him. And he flipped out. *Epically*. He said some truly awful things to me that I won't repeat right now because I have to pack and don't want to relive that trauma, but suffice it to say it would be awful if it happened twice in my life. And since it's you, I doubt I'd ever recover."

He leaned back against the porch railing again, arms still crossed. "That's not going to happen, but if it did, you'd recover." He paused. "I've *seen* you work before. It's been fine. I've pulled you out of portals. This can't be all it is."

I dropped my head again because I couldn't hold his gaze. I just couldn't. "I just…" Being honest sucked sometimes. "Hunter crushed me. Really bad. But you? You feel very out of my league. Like epically. I'm trying to get over that, but it doesn't feel quite real yet. And my feelings for you are…huge. I'm scared to shatter this nice bubble we have here at home, and I'm terrified of what happens when it does shatter."

"Come on, Samantha." He sounded exasperated, which was honestly fair. "I'm not out of your league. That's not a thing. I'm just a guy. I was your neighbor." He pointed next door. "I *am* your neighbor, and I'm still just that guy."

"Don't be dense. No, you're not. You're famous. You were on magazines covers. In your *chones*. You—"

He laughed suddenly, and my face flamed as I realized what I'd said.

"Sure, Sam. I let them put a picture of me on a magazine cover, but the underwear company is one of my sponsors. It was kind of a two-for-one deal. Do the interview and fulfill an obligation."

"That makes sense." He didn't have to explain it to me, but something about that cover intimidated me.

"Everything you said is true, but none of that is who I am. I'm the guy next door that you met on the stairs. I will always be *that guy*. Plus, my agent told me the other day that you're famous. She'd seen you on the news. She follows you on Instagram. So, don't give me that."

That wasn't the same thing. At all. "No one is stopping me on the street to ask for an autograph." I looked at him again. His smile…the dimple was showing, and I couldn't concentrate when it was there. "Can you stop with the smile? It really is distracting."

The smile grew. "Absolutely not."

"Why not?" I seriously couldn't think when he looked at me like that.

"No way." He looked at me like I was crazy, but the smile didn't go away. "Why would I give up an advantage when I'm in the middle of an argument?"

Wait. "Argument?" I didn't like that. It sounded bad.

"*Discussion.*" He picked up Mom's chair, placed it in front of me, and sat so close that our knees were touching. "Anything else I need to know before we go pack? Any other fears I can try to knock out? Anything I should know about how things work for you?"

I leaned closer to him. "You really want to know?"

"Yes. I want to be there for you. I can't do that if I don't know what to expect. Lay it on me, and maybe that will help some of those fears in your head."

He was right. I ran through a few things in my head and settled on a few key details. "Dastien wants me there early because I'm a different person when I travel. When I leave a known safe zone, it's hard for me. You likely didn't notice when I went into your house to help your sister, but I paused a few times. I take things in. I check things. And when I'm overloaded, I have a signal that it's time to go. Dastien wants me to hurry so that I can find that safe space to go to when I inevitably become overloaded before dark."

He leaned back in the chair, quietly thinking. "I already know about the signal. You pull on your ear. You did that at my house, and then everyone hustled you out of there."

I was surprised he noticed that. "Right. It's my sign that I'm done, overloaded, overwhelmed, and I have to leave as soon as possible." Oh no. That sounded bad. And super rude. *Wow, Samantha. Could you try to not put your foot in your mouth?* "It's not that I didn't like your house or your family. I just—"

"It's okay." He leaned forward again, reaching out for my hand. "I'm not offended. It had been intense, and you were tired. I get it. You needed to go home. So, I'll watch for you to pull on your ear. That's the signal. Anything else?"

I took his hand and instantly felt calmer. I just had to tell him the truth about what this would be like for me. "I might not be super with it. Or I might tune out at times. I'm not being rude. There's a lot that I take in around the world that normal people don't. A lot that I see that other people don't. I feel it, hear it, touch it like it's all in this realm, but I'm straddling two places. It gets to be a lot."

"I know. I've *seen* what you see. I know it's not the same, but it's similar, right?"

"Yeah. I think it's more intense for me because I'm giving you like a peek, but I don't know for sure. I can't see it through your eyes." I took a breath, trying to steady myself. "When I go with the pack, I can't shut it down. I have to be *on*. I'm searching for things. I never know what I'm walking into, and it's always different. The cost of what I do is sometimes really high, as you've seen. But I'm not giving up my job because it's not a job. It's a calling and a moral imperative and I would be going against my ordained purpose in this life if I backed down. Please don't ask me to."

He gave my hand a squeeze. "I'm not going to ask you to. I'm walking into this fully aware."

"But you *might* want to. No normal person would ever want to be messed up in this, and—"

"I want to be messed up in this. I've seen *everything* multiple times, and I'm telling you I'm staying. I need you to hear me."

"Why though?" I didn't get it.

"You tell me why someone like me would stay."

"I honestly don't know." If I could be anyone else, I would. "I have no clue. It's the thing that's messing with my mind the most right now. This goes back to the whole out-of-my-league thing." I winced. "I'm a mess. I'm sorry."

The pity in his gaze was something I didn't want. "I understand you're scared. You've had a lot of rejection and judgment. I get that you don't trust me yet, but give me a shot."

I chewed on my lip for a second. He was saying all the right things. "If you change your mind about this, it's going to destroy me."

"I'm not going to change my mind, but it might take you more than a week to believe that."

"I want to believe it." I knew it wasn't the same, but I was trying.

"I know you do, but I'm not in a rush. We have time for you to get to know me, trust me, all the things." He rose and put my mom's chair back. And then he reached a hand out to me. "Come on. Let's eat whatever your mom has been making real quick, and then we can pack."

"You're sure?"

"Yep. You go, I go. We're a team now."

"Because you were forced into it," I muttered under my breath.

"No." He bent in front of me, his hands on my knees, his face level with mine. "No way. Don't ever think that. I had a choice. I *wanted* this. I *want* you. You're not a burden or an obligation or anything that was forced. Fuck that, Sam. Don't say that about us again. I don't want you to even think it."

Oh man. "I'm sorry."

"I'm not. I'm not sorry that we're together or that I'm your anchor in this world. I'm *honored*." He rose, and this time, when he reached out his hand, I took it.

He pulled me to my feet and brushed a soft kiss against my lips. "I'm so thankful I'm here with you, and I'm hopeful that soon, you'll believe me. I am not your ex. I'm not leaving you, and I'm not going to turn on you. I take my role as your anchor very seriously, so I'm thankful to be going on this trip with you. Everything is going to be okay."

"In my head, I know that. But this fear…I'm just scared. You terrify me."

He rested his forehead against mine. "That's because you care about me. A lot. Don't worry, I think I probably care more about you than you do about me. So, I'm terrified, too. But we'll figure this out together. This is it. You and me. There's no quitting us. Okay?"

I wanted that to be true more than anything.

But I wasn't sure it would be.

He was right about one thing for sure—I needed time to settle into this relationship. I just hoped we had that time.

CHAPTER FOURTEEN

SAMANTHA

CONVINCING MOM—AND Frank via speakerphone—that I was going to be okay sucked up the most time I had for packing. They both wanted me to let Eli know that I was leaving, but he was watching me. I knew that much. If he was going to object, he would've shown up already. Wouldn't he?

I wasn't totally sure about that. It was possible that he was busy and not paying that close attention to me, but I decided if I needed him, I'd call for him as always.

But no matter what Mom or Frank thought, I wasn't going to let a little exhaustion stand in the way of fighting evil. I was too stubborn for that. So, I went upstairs to get everything I needed for the trip.

I had a special travel kit of my toiletries packed at all times. I gathered up some clothes in my carry-on roller bag, then loaded my backpack with essentials for fighting a spiritual battle, plus my belt bag with everything I needed on hand.

It took me a few minutes to gather everything, and then I changed out of my around-the-house leggings and baggy sweater into jeans, high tops, a black V-neck and a leather jacket with a hood attached for travel. The jacket made me feel a little badass and ready to fight, even if I might not *feel* ready on the inside.

When I got downstairs, Mom had boxed up the food she'd made for us and finished her chat with the Wayfarer pack's doc to make sure he had everything he needed to take care of me.

Tessa and Dastien were back, and Phoenix was waiting with them, wearing jeans, an army green hoodie, some killer kicks, and his backpack. A small roller bag was by his feet. He'd packed light. Which—as a light packer—I appreciated.

It didn't take long to get to the small, private airstrip the pack liked to use. It gave them more freedom than any of the other airports in the area.

The airport only had a few hangars, which were open with small planes inside. The jet that was on the runway was much nicer than this airport usually saw. A group of techs was giving the plane its final look-over. If the runway had been any shorter, the pack would've had to go land the plane somewhere else, but thankfully, this one was just long enough.

A couple of guys stood on the tarmac by the plane. They definitely had to be werewolves. I couldn't see their faces, but I felt like I could pick a werewolf out of a crowd now. They had this way of carrying themselves, plus their size—tall, lean, always massive males—made them easy to spot.

Dastien took my bag, leaving me with just my backpack and belt bag trailing behind him and Tessa.

Phoenix kept pace beside me. "So, you travel private a lot?" He looked down at me with a half-smile that made his dimple pop. From his tone, he was teasing me, but I couldn't help but be a little embarrassed.

"It's weird, right?"

He'd grown up with five people in a small, run-down, two-bedroom apartment. Across the breezeway from the apartment where Mom and I scrounged to make rent every month. And now I owned my own house, had a lucrative job doing my life's work, and flew around in private planes.

Okay, so the last bit was because the pack was loaded, not so much because of anything I did. A lot of the wolves were old—as in older than dirt—and had a lot of years to build up wealth. Wealth as in the massive, generational kind. But even with that, if someone had told me ten years ago that I'd be flying around private with a bunch of werewolves, I would've laughed and asked how many mushrooms they'd ingested. Because what?

I'd never even flown before I met the pack. Mom and I didn't have enough money for a weekend road trip, let alone to fly somewhere for vacation.

Except, this was my life. But this trip wasn't a vacation.

He nudged my shoulder with his. "It's not weird. I'm just giving you shit."

"I know it's a little excessive. But honestly, I only travel private when I'm with the pack." Wait. I should clarify. "I don't travel much at all unless it's for work, so I guess I mostly travel private. But only by default."

"That's not true. We took you to St. John," Tessa said. "That wasn't work."

Dang werewolf hearing. "Okay. She's right. I sometimes travel with them on vacation, but only when they're not going to cities."

"Except you did come to Paris..." Tessa's voice took on a sing-song, know-it-all tone that made me want to hit her. Or at least roll my eyes at her.

I liked that Tessa was perking up a little bit. This was a good distraction, so I was willing to go with it. "Fair." It wasn't that I'd meant to omit that trip, but it was a one-time deal. Never to be repeated or spoken of again. Except today, apparently, we were speaking of it. But for Tessa, I'd talk about whatever she wanted.

"What happened in Paris?" Phoenix asked, taking the bait.

I looked up at him and saw the stupid, dimpled half-smile that always got to me still there. Dang it. I guessed I was spilling my guts. Again. "Paris was...an *adventure*." I didn't even know where to start.

"Don't remind me." Dastien's words were more groan than

anything else. "She was tossing demons through portals constantly, causing scenes everywhere we went. The damage control was next level. And getting her settled in a hotel..." He trailed off. "I think we visited five or six before we found a room she was okay with."

"Wait. You're not saying the rest of it." He was making me sound like a prima donna. "They were all *haunted*. There was so much spiritual garbage in those hotels there was *no way* I was going to be able to sleep."

"That's true," Tessa said. "But then the club incident..."

I hung my head. I was going to murder her. "Do we have to go there again?"

"Yes," Phoenix said, with his dimpled grin. "We are definitely going there." He looked ahead to Tessa and Dastien. "What happened at the club?"

Tessa spun to walk backward so that she could see Phoenix. "So, we were there dancing. It was a fabulous place." Tessa motioned with her hands wide. "Really crowded. DJ was *epic*, lasers, fog machine, visuals on point—" She started half-dancing as she walked. "—and then all of a sudden, poof." She made an exploding gesture with her hands. "Sam is gone. Like gone-*gone*. We couldn't find her anywhere."

"I nearly had a heart attack," Dastien said. "Sam is tough, but she gets hurt like normal mortals. I've seen her in the hospital more than a few times and—"

Great. This was getting worse. "Can we not talk about *that*?"

Tessa covered her mouth with her hand, smothering a laugh, and then cleared her throat. "Back to the club thing." Tessa shot me a look like she thought she was saving my butt, when no. She was spilling about Paris. So, I wasn't going to thank her for this.

My thoughts must've shown on my face because she stifled another laugh. "So, we catch her trail and finally find her in a run-down masonic temple. Turns out there were some satanic rituals that happened in there. Demons lingering in the area. All kinds of haunts. We got there just as she closed the portal."

"I barely had time to catch her before her head slammed into the pavement," Dastien said, sounding as exasperated about it as the day it happened. "She passed out cold."

Phoenix raised a brow at me.

I winced. "Probably not my best move to leave without any warning."

"You think?" Tessa rolled her eyes. "Turns out she spotted a demon attached to some girl and followed them out the back exit of the club without telling us. Ended up in a battle with her father," she said to Phoenix. Then she looked at me. "We won't even get into the New Orleans trip."

Oh for the *love*… "*Please*. Let's *not* go there."

Tessa narrowed her gaze at me. "Fine. As long as you don't disappear on us *again*."

There was no way I'd make a promise that I knew I'd likely break. "I'll *try*." I looked at Phoenix. "I often get distracted by what I see in the spiritual realm. Sometimes, it's so subtle that if I look away, I'll lose the thread. But if I see something, I know it's because God wants me to take care of it. So, I can't look away. I have to *go*. If that makes sense?"

He nodded. "It does."

"So, while I'd love to give you a promise that it won't happen this trip—or ever—I can't. I try not to make promises if I think there's a chance I might break them." I looked at Tessa, who was still walking backward. "So, no promises."

"I take it I should keep a close eye on you?" Phoenix asked softly.

I gave him a small smile. "Might be a good idea."

"Good to know."

I let out a laugh, and Tessa gave me a little eyebrow wiggle before turning to walk forward again.

As we approached the plane, I realized I was right. The two guys waiting by the plane were werewolves. One of them was a friend—Max Molloney.

Max was the nicest of the Wayfarer Pack.

Wait. Maybe that wasn't fair. I didn't know all of the Wayfarers. Just some. And usually, if I was there, things were going very, very poorly for the pack. Which didn't leave a ton of time for chitchat.

The Wayfarers were the problem-solver werewolves, traveling wherever supernatural help was needed. Max was usually there whenever I went on missions with the Wayfarers. He was tall—well over six feet—and the kind of ripped only werewolves could be. He kept his white-blond hair cut short, and his eyes were a clear, glass blue.

"Hey, Max," I said. "How've you been?"

His gaze homeed in on Phoenix for a second before he looked at me. "Could be better, but I'm really thankful that you agreed to come along. I have a team on the ground, and I won't let you out of my sight. Whatever is getting my wolves won't have a chance to get near you. Okay?"

That was a nice sentiment, but he might not be able to control that. "Thanks."

"It'll be my pleasure."

Phoenix cleared his throat. "Hi. I'm Phoenix."

"Max Molloney. Second in the Wayfarer Pack."

I made a mental note to make sure Phoenix knew what a second in the pack was.

"Nice to meet you."

Max grunted, which wasn't his usual thing. He was always super friendly. Maybe he was just being grumpy. From what I knew so far, he'd had a no good, very bad week. But something about the way he was acting made me think it was something else.

"I'm Garret," the other werewolf said, drawing my attention away from Max. His skin was a deep, rich brown, his hair buzzed tightly to his head, and he had a clean-shaven face. A few tattoos ran down his arms—one of them made me think he might've been in the military at some point. I couldn't tell how old Garrett was, but I never could tell how old a werewolf was. They didn't really age much, if at all.

Garrett's smile was bright and white, and he had a little sparkle in his eye as he watched Max bristle. "It's nice to finally meet you, Samantha. Usually, I travel with another group of Wayfarers, but I'm with Max this time because I'm from Charleston originally. So, I'll be driving you around and am here for whatever you need."

A local was a great resource to have. "Awesome. Thanks, Garrett."

"It's my pleasure. Honestly, we just hope you'll be able to point us to whatever needs killing."

"I hope I can help." I wouldn't know until we got there, but I'd see what I could do.

Tessa started up the stairs to the jet. "Come on, Sam."

Max gestured to the stairs, keeping an eye on me.

I looked back at Phoenix, and he put his hand on the small of my back. "You go first. I'm right behind you."

Max's eyes flashed bright blue as his gaze lowered to the hand on my back.

Wait. What?

Was Max jealous? Because his eyes hadn't brightened until Phoenix put his hand on my back.

That was interesting and new. How had I missed that?

The inside of the jet sat fourteen people, and I usually liked to sit alone. But there were four seats—two on each side of a table—that I decided to take. That way Phoenix could sit next to me on the aisle. Tessa slid into the seat across the table from us.

"Sorry to bail, but I'm going to catch some more sleep," Garrett said. "I've been on night patrols all week. I'm wiped."

"We'll be quiet," I said. "Thanks, Garrett."

"No. Thank you. Really glad you're helping us out." He yawned as he moved past us.

Max followed Garrett to the back of the plane, where there were two more seats and a sofa.

Dastien snagged Phoenix's bag and stowed it wherever he'd stuck mine, then took the seat next to Tessa.

As we took off, I read a book on my Kindle, while Phoenix talked quietly with Dastien. He had about a million questions about werewolves, the pack structure—specifically what a second was, Wayfarers, and how things worked in the supernatural world. I'd heard it all before, so I let their chat act as background noise to my book.

The enemies in my book were becoming friendly when Max showed up, leaning along the banquette along the other wall of the plane from our table. "So, Phoenix, you're just a normal human, right?"

Oh, boy. I didn't love the tone Max was using.

Phoenix turned a little to face Max. "Yeah." Phoenix reached over and gripped my hand as if he knew that I was about to tell Max to back off.

Max tracked the movement, and his eyes grew werewolf bright again. I'd never seen him lose control of his wolf, and now, I felt incredibly dense for not having seen that Max was interested in me. How had I completely missed that?

Not that I would've been interested in dating him. Max's life was too hectic. His job was literally traveling, and I wouldn't be happy with that. I traveled when I had to, but otherwise, I liked being at home and sleeping in my own bed.

"And how do you know Samantha exactly?"

I gave Tessa a look, and she widened her eyes, as if to say—*this is going to go great.*

Right. Great.

I motioned with my head to Max, and she shrugged. But I wanted her to step in. I didn't want this to get awkward, but it kind of already was. Dastien might've said something, but he'd left to get some food.

"Sam and I were neighbors a long time ago, and we just recently reconnected." Phoenix looked at me and gave me a wink.

"And what do you do for a living?"

Phoenix's eyes widened as he stared at me, then he looked at Tessa before he gave a little shake of his head. I took that to mean he didn't want us saying what he really did. Fine. That was fine, but I didn't know why. Was he worried that Max would take that as a threat? I couldn't see how, but I also hadn't seen this coming. So, what the heck did I know?

Phoenix focused on Max again."Right now, I mostly manage my investments, which means I have time to hang with Sam as much as she'll let me."

"Got it." His tone was sharp, and I didn't like that at all. "You have a lot of tattoos."

One side of Phoenix's mouth tilted up in a smirk. "Yep. I do."

Wow. I'd never seen Max like this. It was none of his business what Phoenix did, how many tattoos he had, or anything else. "Are you okay?" I asked Max before he could ask any other questions.

He rubbed a hand on the side of his face. "Yeah. Tired. It's been a long, bad couple weeks, especially the last few days."

Right. Of course. It didn't excuse the rudeness, but I got it. "I'm so sorry."

Max gave me a soft smile. "Just thankful you're able to come. I heard you had a bad night last week. Tessa was worried you wouldn't be available."

Dastien came back with two plates of food and set them down. The bond between him and Tessa lit up for a minute, then quieted.

Max cleared his throat, and I remembered what he'd said.

Right. About me recovering from my trip to Hell. "I'm fine." I hated that I had to keep saying that, but I didn't want to talk about it. Not with anyone really, but definitely not with Max. Not right now.

"Hey, Max. Can I ask you something over here?" Dastien waved for Max to follow him and moved toward the front of the plane.

I leaned close to Phoenix. "Sorry."

He twisted in his seat to face me. "It's okay. If I were him, I'd be bummed if I suddenly found out you were dating someone else."

I looked up at him. "Same."

He touched his forehead to mine. "Good thing that's not happening."

"No," I whispered. "I mean—if you change your mind, I'm going to be crushed." I'd already told him that, but it was worth repeating.

"Not happening, babe. You're stuck with me."

Dastien came back, and Max mumbled something about finding food, striding past us to the galley kitchen behind our seats.

Tessa typed a bunch on her phone, then slid it across the table to me. The WiFi on the plane had been spotty, which meant we couldn't text, but she wanted to talk to me without being overheard. Which I appreciated.

The Notes app was, and Tessa had typed a question: *Did you know that Max liked you?*

I looked at her and shook my head, then I started typing. *No. He never said anything about it. Never asked me out. Never even flirted, at least not that I noticed. I know he's a lot older than me, so maybe he was waiting for me to grow up a little more?* I slid the phone back to her.

A moment later, she passed it back to me. *Yeah. He is older. I think he's twenty years older than Meredith, who is our age. Maybe he didn't want to push? Or maybe he wanted to get to know you when we weren't in crisis mode?*

I looked up to see Phoenix reading over my shoulder. "*Twenty years?*" he mouthed to me.

I nodded, and then typed on the screen. *Werewolf hearing is legit, so we're using this. But yeah, they age super slow once they reach adulthood. It's almost imperceptible. Lucas is so old that he refuses to tell anyone his age. But think hundreds of years old.*

"Holy shit. For real?" he asked.

I laughed and deleted that part before handing Tessa her phone.

She gave me a look, but I just shrugged.

This whole Max thing felt really weird to me, but that wasn't why we were here. I couldn't worry about Max's feelings when I had bigger things to worry about. "Do you have a file with you? Anything with more information on what we're up against?"

Tessa nodded. "Do you want to see it?"

"Yep."

"Are you sure?" Dastien asked. "There are pictures in there. It's a little gruesome."

"I'm sure. Knowledge is good. I know you don't have a ton, but I'm hoping I'll see something you won't."

"If you're sure…" Tessa rummaged in a bag at her feet and then passed back a folder.

I opened the folder on the table, letting Phoenix see. If he was coming along, I might as well give him all the info.

What I saw inside was worse than I'd imagined.

Reports. Pictures of dead, dismembered bodies—people and werewolves.

This was more than a distraction from my problems. This was going to be dangerous and deadly before I managed to fix whatever was going on. They had literally nothing. Just theories and dead bodies.

This was potentially one of the worst cases I'd ever worked.

Phoenix was going to get to see us on a very bad day.

I hoped he was as ready as he thought he was because this was going to be rough.

I flipped through the pictures and kept reading. When I was done, I flipped to the front again, and reached down into my backpack, pulling out a pen. "Is it okay if I write on this?"

"Yep. That's your copy," Tessa said.

"Cool." And then started looking at it again.

But as I read, I was sure of one thing—they should've called me days ago.

CHAPTER FIFTEEN

SAMANTHA

THE REPORT DIDN'T HAVE anything about what they were fighting exactly—which made sense since that was why I was coming to help them—but it explained why the Wayfarer pack got called to Charleston in the first place.

The FBI had alerted them to a series of suspicious murders. That surprised me. I knew the packs had been working with the authorities on supernatural things ever since supernaturals came out into the open six years ago, but I didn't realize how closely they worked together. The attached printed email exchange between the FBI and Max was pretty familiar, not as professional as I would have expected.

"It sounds like the wolves that were killed were isolated." I circled that little piece of information on the document in front of me. "They were attacked when they were patrolling alone, but you always stick in groups. Why the change?"

"It's been a rough week," Max said as he walked up from the back of the plane. He was chowing on a thick sandwich, piled high with roast beef. His eyes were back to his normal human blue, which I guessed meant he'd dealt with his disappointment or anger or whatever it was he'd been feeling that set him on edge. "But yeah, we are usually in groups of no less than three. When Garrett and I first got the call to come to Charleston, we only brought a few guys with us. The first night on patrol, we got split up almost immediately. There had been too many calls that were routed to us, and we decided while doing our initial patrols, it was okay to split up. But then Peter died." He set his sandwich down on the table and brushed his hands off. "It just got worse from there."

"From what I could tell last night, something is drawing the pack apart," Tessa said. "It's like something was isolating us."

I knew what that was. "That's oppression."

"What?" Phoenix asked.

"Oppression is a way demons manipulate mortals via the spiritual realm. Whatever is doing this is separating them to pick off wolves. Or humans. Whatever gives it the most power." I thought about it for a second as I flipped through the rest of the folder's contents. "With all the wolves around, the demon will be drawn to them, not the humans. Werewolves have way more juice than any human."

Tessa gave Dastien a look, and their bond lit up.

I ignored their silent conversation while I flipped through more pictures of bodies. Phoenix let out a little noise.

I immediately slapped the folder closed. His face had gone a little pale. "You okay?"

"What the hell happened to them? That last one was dismembered. I thought demons couldn't do that. They're not even on this realm."

This was about to get really tricky. "I wish that were true, but honestly, it depends on a lot of factors. Demons fall under a huge umbrella along with so many different things that could be of this realm."

Phoenix turned to Tessa and Dastien as he reached over and gripped my hand. "Is it always this dangerous for her?"

The plane's cabin went silent.

Dang it. He was worried for me, and I got that. I wanted to answer him, but I didn't want to lie either. I honestly didn't know what to say. If I said yes, that wouldn't be exactly true. But I couldn't say it wasn't true either.

"Not *always*," Tessa said before I could figure out what to say.

"That's not really answering the question." Phoenix threaded his fingers with mine. His hand was warm but rough, and I liked the feel of it probably a little too much.

"For the most part, what I do is not that big of a deal. As long as I don't run into my father, I can handle it. It's usually more along the lines of what you saw in that apartment six years ago."

He rubbed his thumb along the back of my hand. "Scary, dangerous, but not deadly."

"Right. I mean—if something goes badly, it could always end up deadly, but I've been doing this for a long time. It's second nature to me now. I also don't usually go into unknown situations like I did that night. I get asked to help so many people that I don't usually get the cops called on me anymore, let alone arrested."

"Arrested?" Max nearly shouted the word.

"Yeah. That sucked," I said and Phoenix laughed.

"It really did," he said to me softly.

"Wait." Max rose from where he'd been perched to get in Phoenix's face. "You let her get arrested?"

"Max!" I dropped Phoenix's hand and stood, shoving Max away.

Max was strong enough that he didn't have to back down, but he let me push him. Which was a good thing because I'd had enough of his attitude. "Phoenix didn't *let* anything happen. There were guns on us, and we were technically trespassing, and…" Why was I engaging in this? "You know what. The details don't matter." I didn't owe him—or anyone else—an explanation.

But I did owe Phoenix one, who currently looked like he was ready to punch Max.

To be honest, I felt the same way. I wanted to be patient with

Max because he'd lost pack members and he clearly wasn't acting like himself, but he was seriously pissing me off.

My body grew hot, and I knew I needed to calm down. So, I took a deep breath and sat again, focusing on Phoenix. "Back to what we were talking about." Where had I been…oh yeah. "Some of the stuff the pack brings me is a little more dangerous, but I've always got a group of werewolves—sometimes fey, sometimes witches—watching my back. So, it's not like I'm going in there alone like I did with you when I was a kid."

I looked at Max. "We were both a lot younger, and I didn't have the backing that I do now. You've seen me go into places where people get pissed. If you weren't there to help smooth things over, how do you think it would go?"

Max gave me a nod. "I have a pretty good idea. Sorry for overreacting. I'm a little on edge."

"Don't worry about it, man," Phoenix said. "I can see you've had a really bad time." He motioned to the pictures.

"Losing pack members is always hard. So many…"

"All good. How many are in the Wayfarer pack?" Phoenix asked Max.

"In general?" Max said from his perch on the buffet table. "Maybe fifty or so. But if you mean in Charleston right now, I originally came with four guys—so five in total—but after the first night, I called in fifteen more. Now, there are thirty Wayfarers there. We can call in the rest, but I'd rather not. They're busy at the moment. If we need more numbers, it might be better to draw from another pack of cazadores—that's what we call the elite werewolves. Wayfarer is just one of the packs of hunters, but there are others. The Wayfarer pack has some of the toughest fighters, though, and that's not me bragging. It's a fact. Think of the cazadores as highly trained military, but the Wayfarers are the SEALs of the werewolf world—the best of the best. We'll fight for her. No doubt about that, if that's what you're worried about."

I reached for Phoenix's hand. "I'll be fine. I always am."

He gave me a nod, but I saw doubt in his eyes.

I knew I had doubts of my own, but not for the same reason he did. I was terrified of him leaving or getting hurt or worse.

I closed the folder and shoved it in my backpack. I was glad to be done with the horrific pictures.

"You have any ideas?" Dastien asked, leaning forward with so much hope in his eyes.

I chewed on my lip for a second before letting out a big sigh. I hated to let him down. "No. Not really. There are just too many options to narrow it down, and Gabe is…" Gone.

Just gone.

And just like that, the piece of my heart that was missing him ached.

Usually, I'd ask him for some advice. Sometimes he had nothing. Other times, he'd know right away just by looking at the pictures. Usually, he'd go into the fight with me.

But not this time.

Tessa took a cookie from her plate, then nudged the plate across the table to me. "How are you doing with that?"

I took a cookie, but I couldn't bring myself to take a bite. "Drowning in guilt." I tried to smile, but I was sure it looked more pained than anything else. I put the cookie down on the table. "I'm getting through it, though. I'm trying to figure out a way to help him without killing myself in the process, but…" I shook my head and looked out the window at the clouds and the ground far below. "I just hope he's okay." Although, I couldn't imagine how he was.

Eli might've been right—that Hell was home for Gabe—but it still didn't feel right to leave him there. Who knew what my father was doing to him.

As we got closer to Charleston, I busied myself by getting my earbuds from my backpack and untangling the cord. I'd used them a few days ago in the hospital exorcism, but I'd just shoved them in my bag after. Not my best move.

"Why don't you have wireless headphones?" Phoenix asked.

I did. I had a few pairs, but I always went back to wired.

"They don't work as well, and honestly, they mess with the electromagnetic energy around me. I don't like the way that feels. There's enough other stuff I can't control—WiFi and whatnot—that interferes with what I do. Bluetooth is one of them. If I can eliminate even just one thing…" I kept working on untangling them. How in the world did they manage to get into such a knot? "My wired earbuds have never failed me." I looked at him. "Unless I'm in a car or actively looking for something, they're on when I travel."

Once they were untangled, I plugged them in and cued up some music that I had downloaded, pausing it so I could finish gathering my things. I put my phone and earbuds on the table in front of me and pulled a belt bag from my backpack. I needed to load it with a few things before I got off the plane.

I dug through my backpack and pulled out one of my most important tools—holy oil. I studied the vial, trying to discern how I wanted to use it today. I wanted to put some on for protection, but then I didn't because it might keep away the monster I was here to find.

"We putting that on?" Dastien asked.

I shook my head without looking up. I knew he hated it. The oil had a pretty strong smell, and werewolves were extremely sensitive to scent. "Not today. At least, not yet." I dropped vial of oil into the belt bag, along with a vial of salt, a spray bottle of holy water, and a bigger cross. I tossed in my ID, a credit card, and some cash in the front zipper compartment of the belt bag, just so it was handy.

Was I forgetting anything?

I did a final search of my bag and decided I was good to go. If I needed something else, I'd have to just deal with it in the moment.

I zipped up the belt bag and slung it across my body, and then zipped my backpack, leaving it at my feet.

"What was in the vial?" Phoenix asked softly.

"Oh." I looked up and realized he'd been watching me. "It's

holy oil. I was thinking about using it because unknown city and whatnot, but decided against it. I can't exactly find a big bad demon if I'm keeping them away."

"Got it," he said, taking it as fact without any questions.

I wondered if he had more questions and he was just not asking them. He'd had a chat with Dastien about wolves when we boarded so I knew he didn't have any trouble asking questions. So, I didn't think he was hesitant to ask, but Phoenix had been shoved in the deep end of my crazy life. It was probably a good idea to explain myself more than usual.

That started now. "I like having the belt bag for smaller items that I might need to keep handy in a fight. The last thing I want to be doing is wrestling with a demon-ridden human while trying to find holy water at the bottom of my backpack." I slipped the belt bag off again and opened it wide so he could see all the little pockets and compartments inside.

"I try to keep it packed really well, so I'm not digging for anything. I put the holy oil in there in case I change my mind. I also moved a few other supplies with it—some blessed salt. It neutralizes evil, but it's also what's used to make holy water." I pulled the salt from its compartment and held up the bag, then put it right back in its spot.

"Holy water." I held up the small, one-ounce spray bottle. "A little goes a long way. And this—" I pulled out the cross. "—isn't a regular cross. It's blessed with a holy relic stashed inside." I showed him how the bottom screw came out to reveal a compartment. "The relic isn't big, but size doesn't matter with—"

Dastien snorted.

I sent him a look. "Oh, grow up, moron," I whispered, knowing that the werewolf would hear me. "Anyway…the one I'm wearing should be enough." I tugged my cross necklace from under my shirt. "—but the other one makes a statement. Especially with whatever Frank put in it. It's something he was Spirit led to find in Jerusalem. Whatever it is, demons hate it. Big time."

"Got it. Do you ever use other things? You asked for a mirror once. A bucket of water."

"Sometimes, but I've learned to do without a lot of things that I needed when I was younger. Although mirrors are great because I can open a portal through the mirror. It's a one-way thing—nothing can climb out of it while I'm working—and it's much, much harder for me to fall through it. But it has to be a big one." I motioned with my hands, making a three-foot by three-foot square. "Big enough for the demon to fit through without me having to shove it. If that makes sense?"

"It does, actually."

"But that's not exactly practical to carry around. If it cracks, it won't work. It has to be a solid plane."

"Why did you need the water before? I've seen you do this a few times recently, and you never asked for water."

I didn't usually need it anymore, but I had a version of it as backup. I tapped my water bottle that I was about to hook onto my belt bag with a carabiner. "The water is for overheating. I used to ask for a bucket or a bin or something of water to stand in, but like with the mirror, I've found it to be not exactly practical and sometimes useless. I can't stay still with my feet in a tub of water *and* chase after a demon, but when I was younger, I overheated pretty quickly when I was close to an open portal. The water is my way of trying to combat heat exhaustion. I mostly grew out of it, but I have a backup on the off chance it's an issue. I don't want a redo on passing out and waking up in Hell. That was beyond *awful*."

Phoenix's eyes were wide. "I bet."

I tapped the bottle. "This is much easier and more effective. If I'm doing something and I'm getting too hot, I just toss it over my head so that I don't pass out and end up in a dangerous situation. I don't do it often, but there are times when it's come in handy. I usually just hand it off to someone."

"Great." Phoenix reached over and took the bottle, tucking it inside the front pocket of his hoodie. "I got this."

"You sure?" I knew he wanted to help, but I didn't want to put too much on his shoulders.

"Yep. Absolutely." There wasn't even a hint of hesitation in his voice. "You do what you need to do and know that I'm here in case you need me. Mostly I want to make sure you don't get stuck somewhere bad. I'm your backup. Right?"

"Right, but you have to be careful. We're going into something really dangerous, and you're human. I—"

"Samantha. I'm going to be okay. *We* are going to be okay."

I let out a shaky breath. Leaning on someone else was going to take some getting used to, especially since I'd been getting nervous about his reaction to whatever we were going to run into. But if something was killing wolves this easily, then there was a very real chance that both of us could get really hurt.

"I'm not great at explaining what I'm doing or why. I'm really, truly not great at asking for help. But know that I'll try to let you know what I'm doing and if I need help. I won't be great at it at first. So, it's a good thing you're pretty patient."

He gave me that smile. The one that made everything in me race. "Thank you," he said it as if he truly meant it. "I know it's hard for you to trust, but I'm not going to let you down."

Phoenix was something I'd never had before—a boyfriend that I could actually rely on.

Although boyfriend didn't exactly feel like the right label for whatever we were to each other. We actually hadn't talked about what we were supposed to call this. I should probably do that soon. Eventually.Whenever I had the guts to do it. I could only tackle so many things at once…

But regardless of what I called him, Phoenix wanted to be a part of my life, and even if I hadn't said the words out loud yet, I'd definitely fallen for him. So, I'd be stupid not to let him in all the way.

He gave me a nod, as if he'd read every single one of my thoughts, even though I knew that he couldn't have. "When we fly back home, I'll be with you, and the only thing that will have changed is that I'll be more all-in than I was when we got here."

The fear that he'd be running home early to get away from me was bigger, deeper, more terrifying than any portal I'd ever opened, but I wanted him to be right. "How sure are you?"

"Fully. Completely. One-hundred-percent sure."

My gaze caught Tessa's. She gave me a look—a head-tilt, eyebrow-raise, half-smile look—as if she were telling me to just chill and give it a chance.

I was. More than giving him a chance, I was borderline obsessed with this man. Tessa didn't get why I was worried, but I didn't have a mate. That wasn't what Phoenix and I were. We weren't like Tessa and Dastien, a fated match. Phoenix could leave.

It might be hard with the tie, but he could.

And yet, every time he reassured me, the fear that this would end up with me nursing the biggest heartbreak of my life went down just a little bit.

Phoenix snagged my phone and earbuds from the table. He wrapped the cable around the back of my neck and handed me my phone. "There. Now they'll be ready when you need them."

"Thanks."

He reached over and took my hand in his. "Don't worry. You'll figure out whatever is doing this, and then we'll go home."

If only it were that easy. I'd gone into battles before, and I'd seen wolves get injured. But I'd never seen one die. I had no idea how long it would take for me to figure out what this was, what the fight might look like, or how bad it would get before we got to go home. If we were lucky, we could be going home tomorrow. If we weren't, it could be weeks. Maybe even longer.

A few minutes later, the plane touched down. I took a breath as the plane taxied and then parked. The copilot came out, opened the door, and lowered the staircase. The werewolves all jumped up from their seats, moving to the exit. Phoenix and I were the only ones with bags, and I usually liked to take a minute to prep.

Dastien snagged my suitcase. "See you down there."

Tessa followed Dastien, pausing to give me a nod.

I gave one back to say *Yeah. I'm coming.* And I would. I just needed a second to prepare.

This was it.

It was time.

Time to get to work.

Phoenix rose. "You ready?"

No. Not at all. I was tired of fighting. I didn't want to admit it to anyone—even myself—that I wasn't fully recovered from my trip to Hell, but this wasn't something I could quit. It wasn't just my job. It was my personal mission. My calling. My destiny.

"Yep. Ready." And I would be.

So, I got up, tugged on my backpack, and then followed Phoenix to the door. I let him go down the stairs first, while I popped my earbuds in and hit play.

God, let me see whatever is doing this. Let me find it fast without more deaths. Please.

Alright. Time to do this.

I opened up my self, my sight, my senses to the spiritual realm and took a step out of the plane.

And froze.

Everyone else kept going down the stairs. I heard the clank of the shoes on the metal steps, felt the rattle on the bottoms of my feet, but I couldn't move.

All the air whooshed from my lungs. *"Motherfu—"*

CHAPTER SIXTEEN

SAMANTHA

FIRST THINGS FIRST.

I'd cussed. Or partially cussed. I almost never cussed, but that didn't make it excusable.

I closed my eyes, dropped my chin, and took a breath.

Sorry, God. I didn't mean to say that. It slipped out because I'm overwhelmed, but I'm going to try not to do it again. I'll probably fail, but I'm trying. Guide my steps. Show me how to take care of this evil that is surrounding the city. Lead me to where I would be most effective in getting rid of it. Thank you.

I blinked my eyes open and took another look.

Yep. Still bad.

Phoenix was already at the bottom of the stairs and hadn't heard me, but all the werewolves who were by the three SUVs lined-up on the tarmac to pick us up—not just the ones we flew with, but others were there, too—all looked up at me, frozen, waiting for me to let them in on what was killing their pack members.

"What is it, Sam?" Tessa called up to me.

I tugged out my earbuds so I could hear her better.

"What do you see?" she asked, a mix of nerves and hope in her voice.

The horizon shimmered with an iridescent red haze. There was a small bit that was darker, grayer, that gave me a nauseating feeling when I looked directly at it. But there was no mistaking what that was.

"The source of your problem is that way." I pointed to my right. "The mother of all portals to Hell is open." I was going to have to be careful. My head was full of fears and doubts right now, and they'd be stronger—much stronger, more overwhelming, so much heavier—in a place the enemy had control of. I had to get my head on right.

Phoenix was here. He wasn't leaving. I would do my job, and we'd go home.

I wasn't sure I could make myself believe in the happily-ever-after yet, but I had to let myself lean on him. No more fear. No more worrying.

He was one-hundred-percent sure, and he'd never given me any reason to doubt him. I had to trust him.

"The fact that I can see it from this far away is a really bad sign," I said. "Especially given how it's daylight and all."

"You can close it, right?" Dastien stepped toward the plane's stairs, and his eyes were bright. His features were a little more prominent, and I knew he was struggling with his wolf for control. "Would that take care of whatever is killing the wolves?"

I wiped a hand down my face. I wished I could tell him that I could close it and all our problems would be solved, but I was going to have a mess to fix first. And that might not take care of whatever came through the portal.

"I don't know yet. All I know is that some moron who didn't know what they were doing opened a really big, really powerful portal." Or maybe they knew exactly what they were doing but didn't care. Which was way worse. "I don't know what—or how many of whatever it is—came through. But yeah…the aura it's giving off isn't good. I'm going to have to deal with that first, and then we can figure out what to do next." I took a breath to center myself, and then I relaxed my vision, letting the spiritual realm rise up so I could see.

I wasn't sure I'd ever seen a portal that powerful before, but now it made sense that wolves were dying. Something really, truly evil must've come through.

"*Fudge.*" I'd been hoping it wouldn't be something so bad, but that had been a truly stupid, *stupid* hope.

Just looking at the portal exhausted me. I didn't want to admit it, but Phoenix had been right. I was still tired from the battle I'd had in Hell. It would take another week or two to get back to where I was before I saved Van—maybe longer—but evil didn't have sick days. Which meant I couldn't either.

Maybe it wasn't just one thing killing the wolves. Who knew how many things had come through at this point. And that didn't take into account all the bad things that would be drawn to it. Something that size—miles wide of evil—would attract evil from the surrounding states.

This was a *cluster*—

Wait. No. I wasn't going to panic.

One breath, one step, one thing at a time.

"Are you okay?" Phoenix called up to me from the bottom of the stairs. He had one foot on the stair, like he was ready to come back up and get me, but he didn't need to do that. I was coming.

I started down the stairs. "Yeah. I'm fine." It was a small lie for now, but it wouldn't be soon. I hoped. "We're going to start with the portal. Close it down." I was talking so that they knew the plan, but mostly, I was thinking aloud. "I can't go around kicking things back to Hell only to have them come through again with a mind bent on killing me." My feet hit the tarmac, and I was officially in Charleston.

"I need to sit shotgun." I walked up to the large SUV that was in front of all the others and opened the front passenger door. I took off my backpack, tossed it on the floor, and hopped in, letting the werewolves figure everything else out.

I wasn't trying to be rude, but I had to focus on what I needed to do.

A hand gripped my shoulder, and I jumped in my seat, spinning to see who'd touched me.

Phoenix's hazel-green eyes widened. "It's just me." He lifted his hand away.

I took a breath. "Sorry. The werwolves know not to touch me when I'm working. I don't want to pass along my sight to them accidentally. The last thing we need is a wolf losing it right now."

"All good, but you don't have to worry about that with me."

"I know." He was pretty perfect for me.

He studied my face. "Are you sure you're okay?" His deep voice held more than a hint of worry in it.

"I'll be fine. I promise." I left out the fact that he was right about me—that I wasn't ready for a big fight. If I told him that, I knew he'd insist we go back home, and I couldn't. Now that I'd seen the open portal, I had to close it.

It wasn't just the portal, though. The look on the werewolves' faces when I said I could see what was wrong, like I was their only hope, told me exactly how desperate they were for help. I couldn't abandon them.

The SUV doors opened, and Tessa and Dastien climbed into the way back. Max slid into the middle row with Phoenix. Garrett got into the driver's seat and turned to me. His eyes were dark but had a faint glow to them, telling me that his wolf was close. He'd slept most of the flight, but from the little he'd told me, he was ready for a fight he could win. "Tell me where to go, and I'll get you there."

Right. He was from Charleston. That was why he was driving. "I don't know exactly where we're going, but it's that way." I pointed. "I've never been here before, so I'll leave you to figure how to get to where I need to be. Just head in that direction, and I'll correct you if you end up going away from it. Just be patient with me. It'll be a little trial and error. I might not give you a ton of notice on turns, and we might do some backtracking."

"Copy that. I got you." Garret started the car and slowly made his way out of the small private airport. His grip was tight on the steering wheel.

"What's that way?" I pointed again just in case he'd lost track of where I wanted to go.

"Depends on how far that direction. There are some retail and business stuff that way. Lots of residential."

"Which way to the water?" I knew Charleston was on the coast, but I had zero clue about where I was.

"That way," Garrett said.

"That tracks," I said.

"Why?" Phoenix asked.

"Well, there's this thing where people think that salt water isn't great for demons. And it's not. It's been used as a clarifier since forever. Sometimes it can be used in witchcraft, but usually by people who call themselves white witches." This is where Claudia and I sometimes disagreed, so I quickly moved on. I wasn't saying this to spark a debate or anger anyone.

"Salt is a neutralizer. It clarifies things. Preserves things—keeping them from spoiling. Rotting. Putrefying. Both metaphorically and literally. And salt is how you make holy water—you add salt and prayer to regular water." There were some grunts in the car, as if I'd just revealed a fascinating bit of information. Which—given the company—it might be.

"So, all of that makes people think that demons can't be in salt water or water at all. But that's not true. Jesus cast the demons into pigs, and they ran into the water. The pigs died, but the demons…" I shrugged. "They were already dead. They stayed. And in Revelation, the demons that rise up come from the ocean. So, I tend to find more activity in older cities with more history and by water. But a portal can't be in the water." Wait. Was that right?

I thought for a second to make sure that was true. What would it take to open a portal on water?

A mortal would have to do some incantations, sacrifices,

usually done with a version of a written spell on the ground. Maybe if they did it on the ocean floor? Or if they had like a float that could be anchored to a spot. Leaving a boat for long wouldn't be practical, but a float could work.

Either way, someone would have to be truly determined to do open a portal in the water, but I never said never unless I wanted it to bite me in the butt. "Maybe it's not impossible for a portal to be in the water, but I haven't seen it yet. It can pull some power from it though, so being by the water tracks for me."

"It makes sense to me because most of the activity we've seen has been in that general direction," Max said. "We've been focusing our people there the last few nights, but…" There was sorrow in his words.

This was why I had to be fine. Because there was something bigger going on than my exhaustion and fears.

There was loss, anger, grief. "I'm sorry for all the wolves you've lost."

"Thank you," Garrett said impossibly softly. "We're really hoping for a miracle from you. I was with Jax when he died. What killed him was something big. Something terrifying. We couldn't see it, but it threw Jax around like he was nothing. It had to have claws because he was shredded, and there wasn't enough of him to heal. I don't know why it didn't attack the rest of us. God knows it wasn't anything we did. We all could've died, and…"

"I don't know what we're facing yet, but I'm going to do my best to find it and figure out how to stop it for good." I wished I had something more reassuring to tell him, but nothing I could say would help Garrett right now. Only figuring this out and ending it would help.

I leaned forward, closer to the windshield, and scanned the horizon.

After a few minutes, I pointed again. "No. This isn't exactly right. We're veering away. No. We need to go that way. More to the right." I spun in my seat, looking out all the windows. "Can you get off this?"

"Sure." He pulled off the freeway at the next exit. "Might be best to stick to surface streets. Gives us more freedom."

"Great. I'll try to give you warnings on turns, but just bear with me." I leaned over the dash, searching. The haze seemed lighter and the edges faded the closer we got to it, but I started to see more and more demons on the streets—hiding in the shadows, hovering in doorways, hanging from the trees.

Yeah. This was the right way. The demons were moving away from here, which meant these were fresh releases. They'd want as far away from the portal as they could get.

Something caught my eye. A flash of red and the burn of power along my skin. "There." I pointed. "Take the next right."

He did, and we turned into a neighborhood.

Man. Why did it have to be a neighborhood? Innocent people lived here. Innocent people that I was sure were having a string of "bad luck" since that portal opened.

"Slower, please."

Garrett slowed. He was really good at following directions, which I appreciated. "Thanks."

"Of course. Am I still going the right way?"

"One sec." I looked out the side window, then twisted to see the other side. It was hard to tell because the aural haze of the portal had lightened as we neared it, making it feel more ethereal.

"Hang on." I closed my eyes. The haze was tricking me. I couldn't rely on it. I couldn't tell where the center of it was. If I relied on my eyes, I would lead us in circles.

I breathed in. And out. And in again.

And then I felt it.

There was a pull along the spiritual realm.

"Left." I opened my eyes, and we drove another block.

Something caught the corner of my eye. Demons were running down a street, and demons didn't run. Not unless they were trying to get away from something. Something like a portal they'd just escaped through. "Turn right. *Here*." I pointed.

Garrett slammed on the breaks and made the turn.

"Sorry," I said, even though no one made a sound of complaint.

We went a few blocks, and then I knew we were close. But I couldn't feel things as much inside the car, and it was hard to see the epicenter of the haze from my seat. I needed out of the car. "Can you pull over?"

"Is it here?" Garrett moved in his seat, trying to see what I saw, but he couldn't. No one could. At least not unless they touched me. "Should we shift? I don't see anything, but—"

"We'll stay in our human forms," Dastien answered for me. "But be ready."

"It's not here, but it's close. It's hard to see the exact the center, but it'll be easier on foot." I just needed to be able to feel my way to the portal. "I'm going to put on my headphones. I might not be able to hear you. You'll have to snag my attention another way, but don't touch my skin unless you want to see some crazy stuff." I snagged the cord that was still hanging around my neck and shoved one of the earbuds in my ear.

"We won't touch you," Dastien said, and I turned to look at him. "You do what you gotta do. We know the routine." His eyes grew a little lighter, a little brighter, and I trusted him to know when—or if—he needed his wolf.

Tessa gave me a nod, and I knew she had the routine down. Maybe we'd never done it exactly like this, but we'd been through a lot. By now, it was normal to have the two of them along. But at the same time, whenever I thought something was old hat, that was when things went crazy.

Please don't go wrong today.

But nothing ever went smoothly or to plan. I'd just have to take it one thing at a time.

"Sounds good." I needed to focus, and I could let Tessa, Dastien, and Max coordinate how they followed me. "I'm just going to feel my way around to the portal. I'll let you know when I find the right house."

"I'll make sure my wolves who aren't familiar with you know the rules," Max said.

"Right." I'd forgotten there were two other SUVs of werewolves trailing behind us.

I twisted in my chair and looked at Phoenix. I didn't know what to say to him or what to explain. I wanted to let him all the way into my world, but how?

His eyes were really green today, taking over the hazel brown center. I wasn't sure if that meant something or if it was just the army green color of his hoodie, but I wanted the time to find out.

"Hey." He said the word with such calmness and peace that I ended up taking a big breath. I hadn't noticed I'd been holding it as I stared at him until I let go.

"Hey," I said back.

"I'm good. I promise. This isn't my first time doing something like this with you, and I promise. I'll be there as back up. The others might be ready to fight something, but I'm going to be watching *you*." He gave me a wink.

A laugh slipped free before I could stop it.

"I'm happy to keep reassuring you as much as you need, but I promise. I won't run. You don't need to check on me. Keep doing your thing, and I'll be with you."

"Okay." I faced forward again. *Here goes nothing.* I put in the earbuds, cranked my music, and took a breath.

God, help me find the source of this. Lead me to where I can help the most. Guide my steps.

I snagged my belt bag but left my backpack in the SUV and got out. It was full daylight, but there were lesser demons hiding in every shadow, peeking out of every window, infesting the whole area with evil.

Man, that was annoying. If I sent them through a portal now, they'd just find their way back to the open portal and through it again. I'd only have an hour or two before they recovered and came back to this side. But I needed to get the portal closed quickly, hopefully before dark. We had a couple hours before sunset. Maybe it could be done.

If I found and closed the portal, a lot of these demons would get sucked back into the vortex of the closing portal, but not all of them. I was going to have to ask Mom if there were any nearby priests in our network. If so, maybe they could handle any after-care issues.

Demonic whisperings seeped through the music in my earbuds, and I shoved them deeper into my ears. I hated when the demons whispered at me. It was distracting and disturbing, not to mention annoying.

I took a few steps, but the shadow-like demons seemed to take two steps toward me with every step. One grabbed the back of my neck, and I spun, reaching into my bag for the spray bottle. "*Back off,*" I yelled through the spiritual realm. I sprayed the demon, and it started to scream.

Other demons nearby drew in closer.

"Oh, *heavens to Betsy.*"

I was pretty sure I heard someone snicker, but I ignored it.

Holy water usually drove them off, but the portal had to have been open for a while. They were confident. Daring. And that made them dangerous.

Garrett stepped into my eye line. "Everything okay." I couldn't hear him exactly, but I read his lips.

I ignored him, and glanced back to Tessa, who motioned to her mate. Dastien would fill Garrett in.

I mouthed *thank you* to Tessa, and she mouthed back *you're welcome.* And then motioned me to keep going.

Okay. Back to work.

Where was I?

Right. If I got rid of the demons on the block now, they'd get angry. They'd come back through the portal and head straight for me.

But if I left them, then I'd have a ton of demons circling me while I tried to work. Demons that had gained power from feeding off mortals' anxieties, fears, anger. They'd get in the way, which would be counterproductive.

Okay. That settled it. I had to send them to Hell. Now. But then, I'd have to find the portal before they came back for me. Which would keep me motivated to move fast.

I didn't sense my father behind this, but that didn't mean he wasn't. Hopefully, I wasn't making a decision that would weaken me even more before I faced the portal that caused this whole mess.

Whatever. I had to deal with this. I'd just have to hurry once I did.

Done. Plan made.

Okay, Sam. Get it done.

I relaxed a little, then opened the door to the spiritual realm a little more, letting myself fill with power. They wouldn't be able to ignore the power. They'd be drawn to it, even if they didn't want to be. They couldn't help what they were.

I stared at my feet and counted my breaths. I just had to wait long enough for them to gather.

After a minute or so, I could feel the werewolves moving around me, getting restless. Maybe I should've explained what I was doing—I'm sure I looked like a doofus just hanging out here with my eyes closed while they'd been running around with their pack members getting picked off every night—but that wasn't how I worked. I just did what needed to be done. I couldn't worry about everyone else.

I shut the werewolves out, focusing only on the demons that were getting noisier by the second.

I felt them gathering closer, closer, closer.

And then I looked up. I scanned the area around me. Easily a hundred of them were here, surrounding me, so that all I could see was them.

Their dark, pointed faces shoved in close to mine. Eyes glowing bright red and dark ooze dripping from their sharp teeth. Some of them had more defined features, with reptilian-like skin and forked tongues. Those hissed at me loud enough that if I didn't have my music on, the sound would've been deafening. The smaller, spider-like ones with tiny heads and long spindly legs were there, too. I could hear some of them muttering in demonic—cursing me, telling me to kill myself, telling me that I was dumb, weak, worthless.

I listened and waited. I wanted to know if they knew who I was, what I was, or if my father was behind this, but after a few minutes, I had no new information, and I'd had enough.

I pointed to the ground in front of me.

"*Aperta*!" The portal opened, and the force of it sucked them in. There were the muffled screams and hisses and demonic cursing as they tried to get away, but I wasn't having that. "*Claudere*!"

The force of the portal closing pulled the rest of them into it.

I took a moment in the sudden silence to scan the block. I turned in a circle, looking everywhere before deciding this was good enough. There might be some that were hiding, but that was much better than having them acting boldly and yelling in my face. Plus, it gave me the tiniest boost of energy.

Yes. This was better. "Much better." But now I needed to *move* it or they'd be back with vengeance on their minds.

Tessa gave me a questioning look, but I didn't have it in me to answer her. I had to stay focused.

I lifted my hand in the air and pointed which way I was going before I started walking.

I wove through an alleyway between houses, down a block, but after a few steps, the demonic activity felt lighter this way.

Nope. I turned around, backtracking and bumping into Phoenix in the process. "Sorry," I said automatically, but I was already moving on. I spotted a garage with a few demons spilling from it.

I watched it for a moment, then went around to the front of the house.

I didn't want to just bust into a random person's house, but the longer I studied it, the more I knew this one had to be it.

It was a pale-yellow craftsman style house. It had white trim around the windows, and a darker wood door. On any other day, the house would be cute with its white picket fence and a swing in the massive tree in front of it. But not today. There were too many demons peeking out at me. Too many coming from the house out into the street. They'd stopped when they saw me—which was how I'd missed it when I walked by it the first time—but this was it. There was too much activity for it to be anything else.

I pulled out one earbud. "Sorry. I was still sorting it out. There are so many things floating around here that I was having trouble finding the exact source."

I caught Phoenix's gaze for a second. I wanted to explain to make it less weird, but then I spotted a demon behind him. Hanging on Garrett.

I turned a circle, scanning everyone again.

Damn it. He wasn't the only one.

I'd been so focused on finding the portal that I hadn't noticed that something was wrong with some of the werewolves. I'd been filtering them out of my vision, and now one guy had a fully-attached demon. That wasn't good.

That was super not good. How was I supposed to go into a fight with compromised back up?

I couldn't.

I really, truly couldn't.

Which meant, I had to deal with this first.

I met the eyes of the wolf that had a full attachment, and his eyes flashed bright.

One second he was standing there, the next he was a wolf, leaping right for me, teeth ready to rip my throat out.

I started to drop to the ground, but I knew I was going to be too late.

Son of a forking biscuit.

CHAPTER SEVENTEEN

SAMANTHA

I SCREAMED as something slammed into me hard, tackling me to the ground. I didn't feel pain—well, any more pain than the feeling of my body being slammed into the sidewalk—but my head didn't hit the pavement. Something was under it.

There was the sound of a fight next to us, and then a wave of power hit me with enough force that it made my teeth tingle.

"Submit!" Dastien yelled, and there was a wolfish whimper.

I took that to mean Dastien had control of the rogue wolf. The weight on me lightened, and I looked up to see Phoenix raising up on one of his forearms. His hand slid out from under my head.

He'd saved me from being attacked. I honestly couldn't believe it.

Phoenix tugged the other earbud from my ear. "Hi."

"Hey."

"You okay?" He studied my eyes, as if searching to see if I would tell the truth.

"I think so." I took stock, but nothing really hurt. I might be bruised, but I'd take that over having my throat ripped out. "Yeah. I'm fine. Is your hand okay?" It'd cushioned my head.

"Totally fine. Maybe a little scrape, but worth it. I just didn't want you to get a concussion."

"Let me see."

He held up the back of his hand. There was a small scrape, just a little blood. But it could've been so much worse. I gave it a kiss. "Better now?"

The dimple I loved so much peeked out at me. "For sure."

"Looks like you're good at more than just pulling me out of portals."

He huffed a little laugh, brushing my hair away from my forehead. "I didn't see that one coming though. Not from one of our group. Rookie move." He hopped up and reached a hand down to me, pulling me to stand.

I glanced at our joined hands, and my eyes widened. "Oh, no."

He shook his head. "It's totally fine. I'm okay. I got your sight as soon as I tackled you, but remember that this isn't my—"

"First time. I know." But why did I keep doing this to him? Although, to be fair, I didn't know he was going to tackle me.

And he never seemed to mind. So, maybe it was okay. Maybe this was one thing I didn't have to worry about anymore.

Tessa moved to stand in front of me. "Are you okay? I can smell a little blood, but—"

"It's mine," Phoenix said. "My hand got scratched. No big."

Tessa winced. "I'm sorry. That shouldn't have happened."

"We're okay." If I hadn't been so open to the spiritual realm, I would've given her a reassuring hug. Instead, I gave her a smile. "He didn't get me, and Phoenix is okay." I scanned the group around me. "But we have a problem."

"Yeah, no shit," Garrett said. "What the hell is happening?"

He was right to be freaked out and angry. I wasn't because I was used to dealing with evil things like this. But I had to fix this before I dealt with the portal.

"Who here is having negative thoughts?" I asked as I scanned the wolves. "Thinking I'm crazy or wasting your time or things like that? Anyone feel a heavy weight on their heart making it seem like this is useless or that you're useless or anything like that?"

"Come on, Sam." Tessa crossed her arms and shook her head at me as if I was crazy for mentioning it. "No one is thinking that. We know how this goes."

"I mean, maybe you're right? But if that's the case, then what do you make of him?" I pointed to the wolf that Dastien had pinned to the ground.

One of the werewolves cleared his throat. "I am feeling all those things. What the hell are we even doing right now? We've been wandering around in circles for hours. We're running out of daylight, and when that happens, we're going to start dying. And you're doing *nothing*. You have to hurry the fuck up." The last word was more of a growl than anything.

Tessa started to argue with him, but then a few more chimed in.

It turned into a total pile-on with everyone except Dastien, Tessa, and Phoenix angry at me.

It was a good thing I didn't get offended easily. I'd learned the hard way that people could only hurt you if you gave them that power. These wolves didn't make the cut for that, and I could see what was wrong with them.

This wasn't them. Being in an anxious rush? That was Satan's work.

In a second, they'd realize that these weren't their thoughts, and when they apologized later, I would accept and tell them to move on.

I pointed to the wolf on the floor. "He's demon ridden, and the rest of you have ones whispering in your ears, telling you things, guiding your thoughts and emotions. I wasn't wasting time. I was finding this place." I pointed to the house. "You track things with scent. I do it through the spiritual realm. It's trickier. But I'm here, and I'm helping you all. So, now you're going to line up, and I'm going to clear you of demons."

"You're not going to hurt any of my wolves, right?" Max

asked, and I wanted to be insulted. But I knew he'd lost wolves, so he was getting a pass.

"I'd never hurt anyone. You know that. We've worked together how many times?"

He started to say something and then stopped. His brow creased, and I knew that there was a war waging inside him—facts against emotions. Demons could twist things and lie, but they couldn't change the truth.

Max had been acting weird since I saw him, and I wished that I could blame it on a demon, but I couldn't. I had to assume he wasn't himself because he'd lost some of his people. As the most alpha wolf here—aside from Tessa and Dastien—he must've been taking the responsibility of the deaths on himself.

When I was sure he wasn't going to argue with me, I continued on. "Once I make sure all the wolves here are okay, I'm going to go knock on the door of that house." I pointed behind me.

"That's the house with the portal?" Dastien asked.

I turned back to make sure I hadn't imagined it, and no. I hadn't.

"Yeah." This was it. I knew it.

The house didn't have as many demons hanging around outside of it as some of the other ones in the neighborhood, but there were demons crawling out of the second story window over the garage. I'd seen demons coming from other houses in the area, but only a few here and there.

None of them were going into this house. All of them were leaving. All of them. Even if they were waiting for me to leave, they all wanted to get as far from that portal as possible. It fed them power, so it would be a source of fuel for newly released demons—and it could attract other entities that were waning in power for the same reason—but once they were ready, they'd leave. They wouldn't risk sticking around and getting sucked back through it whenever it closed. Because all portals would close eventually. Even this one.

The portal was in there. I didn't need to see it to know it.

"It's not in the middle of the zone we identified," one of the werewolves with a demon attached said. "You sure you have the right place?"

Yeah, I was pretty much absolutely sure. "I don't know anything about zones." It wasn't like they'd shown me any maps. "But there's an open portal in this house."

"I'm going to find out who lives here." Dastien stepped away, pulling out his phone to make a call.

"Great." I didn't care about that. It didn't matter who it was. I'd clear the house one way or another.

First things first. I couldn't have a bunch of werewolves affected by demons. That would work against me, as that other guy had shown. He was still in wolf form. Still on the ground. He snarled at me, but a wave of power came from Dastien, and he whimpered.

This wasn't ideal, but it was fixable.

I had to have a unified front when I went into that house. I could go in there alone—that wasn't the problem—but the werewolves wouldn't let me. Not Max. Definitely not Tessa or Dastien.

Phoenix wouldn't let me, either.

But I couldn't fight against a bunch of unknowns and have wolves working against me all while trying to close a strong portal. Anyone with an attachment was a danger in this kind of situation.

I unzipped my belt bag. Time to fix this.

The werewolves were going to hate this next part, but I wasn't messing around. Not when I wasn't fully back to one hundred percent. I pulled out the vial of holy oil. "Everyone line up here." I unscrewed the bottle.

"No way. That's going to fuck with my sense of smell," one of them said. "I can't hunt if I can't smell."

"Good thing everything we're hunting right now is on the spiritual realm, then. Right? Nothing for you to smell." I gave him a smile and didn't even care that I was meeting his gaze.

Werewolves had a thing with meeting gazes. Sometimes it started a challenge for dominance. I usually avoided it with any wolves that I didn't know really well.

"Hang on," Dastien said to whoever he was talking to on the phone, and he lowered it. "You want in on this, you do it her way. She came here to help us, and whether you know it or not, you're about to make her job harder. That's unacceptable." Dastien stood before me and bent down so that I could reach his forehead. "Do what I'm doing." I felt the power in his command to the other werewolves. He'd shoved it through the pack bonds that wove in and around all of the werewolves, tying them together. Some of them thicker, some thinner than spider silk, but all of them visible to me. And none of them immune to Dastien's power.

I hated that he had to do it, but I was thankful for his help. I needed to get this done. And fast. Because they were right. It was getting later, and I wanted the portal closed before sunset.

I used the tip of the dropper to draw a cross on Dastien's forehead. "For protection against all evil and spiritual guidance to lead them where they need to be. Let your Spirit speak to them, and send the enemy away. Amen." Tessa was next. Then, Phoenix. I went down the line, repeating the actions on the other nine werewolves with us. I hadn't studied all the werewolves that were there to pick me up, but I was pretty sure none of them had anything demonic around them until we started walking around, trying to find the portal.

The first six were easy—oil anointed and poof, the demon ran for the hills. The two that were being influenced fought harder, but an extra line of prayer had them running. But the one that was still on the ground, still in wolf form, was the one who had an attachment.

Garrett caught my eye, and I noticed he hadn't moved since I anointed him. "You okay?"

"Yeah. This is maybe one of the weirdest things to ever happen to me. I just kept getting this feeling as we were patrolling around that we were wasting time. It was getting worse, but I felt…low, drained, and kind of helpless." He shook his head. "You did your thing, and now that's gone. I feel better, but I didn't even realize I was feeling bad, let alone that a demon was messing with my head."

"Demons are tricky, but I'm glad you're feeling better. Now you know what you're facing, and you'll be stronger. Those are really good things." I emphasized the positive, hoping that he'd focus on it instead of how creepy it was to know something was actively highjacking your thoughts.

I turned to the last guy. He was going to be a problem.

"Can you make him shift back?" I asked Dastien. "I really don't want to fight anything with claws and fangs."

"Sure. Someone go grab a set of clothes from one of the SUVs," Dastien said as he tugged off his shirt. He held out a hand toward the wolf, and I saw power ripple through the pack bonds. The bond connecting this guy and Dastien was thinner than any of the others, likely because they weren't in the same pack. Maybe Max would be mad I hadn't asked him to do it, but I knew Dastien better and I knew he could do it.

The bond flashed bright and then pulsed. A second later the wolf shifted. It was slower than the normal shift. Usually it was so quick I couldn't track it. But this time, it looked painful.

I had to look away, and by the time he was human again, he was panting and moaning.

Dastien tossed his shirt on the guy so he was at least covered.

I noticed Phoenix watching me and I raised my brows in question.

"I'm cool, but that was a lot."

I shrugged. "Werewolves are drama."

"Hey!" Tessa said. "Not all of us."

I gave her a wink. "Eh. We're all drama sometimes." I found a shady spot under a tree—with no demons in the shadows—and sat. I leaned back against the trunk and closed my eyes. "Let me know when he's decent." I was going to take this moment to prepare, pray, and breathe.

Inside that house was something really, truly bad. Whatever killed the wolves wouldn't be here—I didn't think—but the portal itself was bad. By definition, any portal to Hell was bad.

A long time ago, I'd faced a similarly sized portal. It was what had caused Hunter to freak out and say some awful things to me. I know now that he'd been afraid, and I was the easy target for all the fear that turned into anger and hatred. I was sure the anger and hatred probably died off after a bit, but the fear that experience instilled in him likely stuck around for a while.

It stuck with me, too. But I didn't get to run away. It was a necessary part of my job to go in and close the portal, even when I was scared.

I just had to do it right this time. No collapsing buildings.

A few minutes later, I heard the sound of running feet. "Here. I got the clothes."

Another minute and someone tapped on my shoulder. I opened my eyes to see Phoenix squatting in front of me. "He's ready." He studied my face for a moment. "You okay to do this?"

I nodded. "Yep. It's what I do." Phoenix rose and took a step back so that I could get up from the ground.

As soon as I took a step forward, the werewolf started writhing. The only thing that stopped him from attacking me were Dastien and Max's hands pinning him to the ground.

I studied him for a moment. I'd been so focused on finding the portal and taking care of evil that I hadn't really *looked* at anyone of the pack while I worked. But now it was so obvious I couldn't believe I hadn't noticed it.

If I let something like this slip by me, then saving Van had really taken more out of me than I'd realized. That was a little terrifying. Not to mention dangerous.

I was going to have to do better.

I looked at Tessa and tapped my hand—our signal to watch the demon-ridden wolf—because I had a feeling he might need more than just Dastien and Max restraining him.

Her bond with Dastien lit up, and I trusted them to take care of the rest.

I moved to stand to the side of the pinned werewolf. I didn't want to kneel in front of him yet—not until I had to—because werewolves moved really fast. If I got too caught up in what I was doing, I might forget what this man was capable of, which could get me into trouble.

He was tall, muscular—because all werewolves were beefy—and blond, but I didn't think he was one of Meredith's brothers. His hair wasn't quite white-blond enough to be one of the Molloney guys. His eyes stared at me with anger. Anger that hadn't been there a second ago. Then, they flashed from a bright blue to amber. Usually werewolves eyes just brightened with spiritual light when the wolf got close. It was the first time I'd seen the color actually change like that. I wanted to ask questions, but now wasn't the time.

I held my hand over him, feeling for a tie between him and the demon because I couldn't *see* any red strings. But honestly, there were so many pack ties when dealing with their kind that it was like trying to find one specific noodle in a vat of spaghetti soup.

After a minute of searching, I found it. "Ah-ha. Got you." The demon tie was fresh. New. And I needed to cut it before it rooted deep into his soul. I held the tie tightly in my fist. "What's your name?"

"Stephen," he half-growled his name.

Fun times.

Dastien pressed fully with his hands, making sure that Stephen stayed down. He gave me a nod. He wasn't going to let anything happen to me, and I trusted him to keep his word.

I nodded thanks, then focused back on Stephen. "Full name, please." I tried not to sound annoyed, but I kind of was. I needed to let that go.

"Stephen Alexander Davidson." His leg kicked out, and I jumped away.

"Garrett," Dastien said, and Garrett moved in, grabbing his legs.

Another wolf came to help Garrett. He looked up at me, and I would've bet that he was wondering what the heck was going on. If I were him, I'd be wondering the same thing.

"Can I see what you're doing?" Tessa asked. "Because Phoenix already can, right?"

I nearly jumped at how close she was. "What?" She wanted to *see*. Right *now*?

Stephen started growling, but not like a wolf's growl. It was a demon growl.

"Dastien did fine with it, and it's not like I'm new to seeing strange things," Tessa continued.

"I'm kind of in the middle of something right now."

"Please."

I thought quickly. Tessa was used to having visions. She saw things from the past and future, but she'd never *seen* the spiritual realm.

Tessa was a werewolf, a hereditary witch, and her mate had done okay with it. The chance that she'd lose it was slim to nil, and Dastien would help her on the off chance that she didn't react well to it.

"Fine." I closed my eyes, resigned to the fact that this could mess everything up. I held out my arm. "Touch my skin and you'll see what I see for about the next thirty minutes. Maybe couple hours. That depends on you." I felt her touch my arm, and then gasp, but I was focused on the demon.

The evil thing was tucked mostly under Stephen's back, with its long, thin fingers wrapped around his head and its chin dug into the crook of Stephen's neck, hiding its face.

Stephen might think he didn't want my help, but yeah, he needed it.

I gave the demon a smile. "In the name of Jesus, I withdraw your hold over His servant, Stephen Alexander Davidson."

He roared.

"You have no power in this realm." I shoved my own power into the thin, red, glowing tie that snaked from the demon on Stephen's back and wrapped around him until it disappeared inside his heart. I watched tie turned from red to pink.

"In the name of Jesus, I cast you out." I yanked hard, then shoved a little more power down it, burning the tie to ash.

The demon launched itself at me, but I was ready, my feet braced.

Phoenix was yelling something, but I dropped to the ground and the demon flew over my head. I sprang up, running after it, tackling it to the ground. Pinning it with my knee on its chest.

"You have no power here." The demon's spindly arms and legs tried to shove me away, but in this position, the demon was weak. *"You are weak, worthless, mortal."*

"Goes to show what you know," I answered him in demonic. I regretted it instantly.

"It's you!"

"Oh for fox sake." I was tired. That was my only defense for doing something so stupid.

I punched it in the face. *"Aperta!"* I opened a portal next to us and rolled off the demon, kicking its side.

I screamed, *"Claudere!"* But as the portal closed, I heard the demon screaming the name I didn't want it to scream.

"Astaroth!"

I sat on the ground for a second. *"Shitaki mushrooms.* I'm a *forking idiot."* Responding in demonic. What was I? New?

Sorry, God. I know those technically weren't curses, but they felt like them. I could use a little help.

I popped up and ran to the door of the house and started pounding on it. "Hello! I need to talk to somone right now!"

"What just happened?" Dastien asked, but I didn't have time to answer. I could feel them pacing the lawn behind me, but I was too angry at myself to look back.

Tessa was trying to tell him, but she wasn't sure.

"Sam. Talk to me. What happened?" Dastien yelled from behind me.

"I gave away my hand. The demon called my father as I pushed it through the portal." I banged on the door again. "I need inside. I have to close the portal before my father gets here." I banged again. "Hello! Open up!"

"Move," Dastien said.

I wasn't sure when he'd gotten to the front door—it was like he wasn't there one second, and the next, he was picking me up and moving me away from the door.

Dastien kicked the flat of his foot into the door.

Bang.

The door flew off its hinges, crashing into the wall beyond.

Dastien turned to me. "Do your thing, but use words." He motioned to the doorway. "You have to communicate so that I can help."

"Right. I'll try."

The house was dark and it reeked of mold and dirt and death. I took a few steps inside, and to my left, spotted a living room. There were children's toys strewn over the carpet and—

Wait. *Toys*?

Toys meant *kids*.

That just blew all. I hated it when kids were involved.

Demons messing with kids was so much worse than when they messed with adults. They did so much damage to the innocent. Demons didn't care about things in the mortal realm—like sleeping, bathing, or eating. Kids weakened really fast when they didn't eat. From what I heard about how long this had been going on, I was scared about what kind of state a child who lived in this would be in.

And that meant I needed to speed this up. I had no idea where the people who lived here were, but there was a solid chance that they were in big trouble.

If they were still alive.

I hoped they were still alive.

"I'm heading to the room over the garage." That was where I'd seen the most demons leaving. "Search the rest of the house. Restrain any mortals. Don't engage. Don't hurt them. No matter what they say or do. Just restrain. I'll need to see them when I'm done with the portal."

I turned to scan the werewolves, and they all nodded. From my quick count, we were already down two—the guy who I'd just helped, plus probably someone who'd stayed back to help him while he recovered.

Fine. It was still way more backup than I was used to having. Even when I was with the pack.

"Phoenix, Tessa, and Dastien can stay with me. The rest can search the house. I need a little space to do my thing." I walked past the living room to the back of the house. I didn't mind an audience exactly, but I didn't really want a big one either.

I ignored everything that I was seeing—the demons, the ghosts, the mess and trash and gore on the floor in one of the hallways—and headed to the right.

Formal dining room. The table was turned on its side. The chairs were toppled over, two of them smashed to bits. Another was missing a leg. There was food and trash and rotting things everywhere. And something written on the walls.

I wasn't going to look too closely at that. It was fully creeping me out.

"Man, this reminds me of that apartment," Phoenix said. "The smell..."

"Yeah," I said. "But this one is worse."

"Yeah, because I can see everything from the start."

"Actually, there were more demons that time, I think." I wasn't sure on that. Maybe it just felt like more because the apartment was smaller. "But this one feels darker. It's the portal. From everything I'm feeling and seeing, it's probably been open for a while." I turned and found the kitchen.

The pressure was getting thicker with every step I took. This was the side of the house with the garage, which made sense.

There had to be a stairwell that led to the room over the garage somewhere…

Sure enough, just past a little built-in dining nook, I found a back set of stairs.

As soon as my foot hit the bottom stair, I heard the screams. The demonic tongue. Felt the heat. Smelled the sulfur.

It seeped dark and heavy and helpless emotions, and I knew what I was walking into.

I really, *really* didn't want to fall through that portal.

God. Give me strength.

I started up the stairs.

CHAPTER EIGHTEEN

SAMANTHA

I MOVED up the stairs slowly, carefully, when all I wanted to do was run up them. But that was the wrong move.

The enemy loved to rush people. Rushing meant mistakes. No time to think. Speaking and moving on emotion rather than thoughtful words and steps. But man, did I want to rush. I hated staircases.

Demons loved in-betweens, like stairs, and this one was no exception. They were *everywhere.*

I ignored the ones hanging from the ceiling, tugging on my hair, screaming in my face, telling me I was dumb, worthless, ugly. I didn't think so highly of myself that I didn't have my own doubts every once in a while. That was normal insecurity. But the vile things the demons were saying? Those were lies.

Demons loved to tear people down. They lived on drama—anger, fear, anxiety, violence—that was their food. The best way to fight them—other than prayer—was by shutting down all those anxious thoughts. To let go of fear. To control your actions and anger.

So, I shut it down. I tuned it out. I pretended there was a

shield around my body and that the words would bounce off, never touching me. Never hurting me. And I kept moving.

I stepped over demons in my way, and—

Tessa screamed.

Dastien spoke in low tones. I wasn't sure what was wrong back there, but one glance back told me Tessa, Phoenix, and Dastien were struggling to keep up. I knew there wasn't anything on this plane that could hurt them, so I kept moving up the stairs.

A demon grabbed my arm. I wrenched it free, twisted its arm, and flung it behind me.

Tessa cussed, and there was a crash.

"Sorry!" Even though I trusted that they were fine, I looked back.

Tessa was hunkered down on one of the stairs, trying to be as small as she could be, while Dastien spoke softly to her.

Right. Tessa could *see* right now, but she didn't understand that she couldn't interact with the spiritual realm like I could. A demon swiped at her face, and she threw herself into Dastien.

Dastien held onto the stair railing, trying to keep his mate from falling. Not that falling would really injure her—or if it did, she'd heal fast—but it would still *hurt*.

Phoenix was doing better, watching the demons but making slow, steady progress despite them.

Alright. Tessa needed a little help, or this was going to take forever. "They can't touch you," I said. "You can see them, but they're not strong enough to do anything to you. Those rules don't apply to me because I straddle realms. They can touch me, but for you, they're ghosts. They're not on the realm that you live on. Just ignore them. Walk through them. The more attention you give them the more power they have over you. So. Cut. It. Out."

"Easy for you to say," Tessa said. "I can *see* that thing, and I definitely don't want it touching me." Tessa shouted her last few words into the face of the demon, and then she punched it.

Or tried to.

Instead, she'd punched her way through a wall.

Bits of drywall exploded around her, and the cackles of the demons echoed through the house, raising every hair on my body.

I wasn't afraid. Not of these demons. Lessers were weak.

But there was something I *was* very afraid of.

That demon I'd tossed to Hell had yelled for my father.

There was a very real chance he could be rushing toward the portal right now, and *that* was something I wanted to avoid.

We had to hurry. "Seriously, Tess. Ignore them or leave the house. I mean it." I looked at Dastien, who gave me a nod. He'd get her out of here if she kept freaking out. "Don't give them fuel. Don't give them your fear or anger or anxiety. That just gives them more power, and they don't need any more power. Do you understand?"

Tessa's wide, wolf-bright eyes looked at me. "Yes."

"Good. They're not corporeal right now, but the more attention you give them, the more they can interact with this realm. I know it's hard, but you have to ignore them." It was one of the many reasons I didn't like sharing my sight. I understood demons. They were monsters. Legit monsters. They were made to be scary, but that didn't mean you had to be afraid of them.

"How come we could fight the ones that came through before?" Dastien asked.

He was talking about the battle in the church in Santa Fe. A battle they'd fought before they met me. I wasn't there so I didn't know exactly what had happened, but it made international news. "Probably because my father lent them the juice to fully cross over. The ones you fought then were in *this* realm, but these aren't. I doubt he'll ever make that mistake again. It cost him years to rebuild his strength." And I was pretty sure that nice little lull I got was over now. "Just...please. Ignore them and move on. We have bigger things to worry about."

Tessa closed her eyes. "You're right. I'm sorry. I've fought demons before—seen ones just like this—but I was able to hit them. It freaks me out that I don't have any control over this right now."

"Yeah. I get that. But they're winning the battle with you right now. So, suck it up and fight."

There was a roll of power that went through Tessa. A ripple of fur ran over her body—there and gone so fast that I almost thought I imagined it. But then she looked up. "I'm better now. Sorry." Her eyes were even brighter now. I assumed she took some power from her wolf to give her confidence, but it didn't matter how she'd done it. Just that she was better.

My gaze went to Phoenix, who gave me a nod. He was fine.

I studied him for a second to be sure, but he truly did seem okay. He always seemed to go with the flow, more than any person I knew. He was more okay with all of this than Tessa, which honestly, I shouldn't have been surprised by, but I was.

Alright. I turned to continue up to the attic. "Let's be quick. My father—"

A demon reached down from where he was hanging on the ceiling and grabbed my hair, tugging so hard my head snapped back. I grabbed its hand, twisting it and tugging until it slammed into the stairs at my feet. I leaned down. "Don't do that again." I threw power into my voice, and as it started to shrink in size, I knew it saw the flames in my eyes.

I let it go, and it scampered up the side wall. It's tiny spider-like legs scratched against the wall as it moved around us and down the stairs, disappearing into the house.

I watched it go, and then Tessa caught my gaze and gasped.

Dang it. I hated when people saw the flames. Now she was going to be afraid of me.

No. I couldn't think that way. I was good. She was my friend. She'd seen far worse. Everything was fine.

But it wouldn't be if I kept getting distracted.

Holy foxing sticks. That was the whole point, and I fell for it.

Enough. I needed this done.

I took the rest of the stairs two at a time.

I got to the room above the garage and paused.

It was dark, but enough light flickered behind the shades of the one window in the room that I could see. There were demons everywhere.

"We need to get the lights," Tessa said.

"No," I said. "It's easier to see them in the dark."

"I'm not sure I want to see them better," Tessa said, and then she muttered something in French I couldn't make out.

Dastien let out a small laugh at whatever she'd said, then he spoke to her softly, making her laugh. It was a good sign that Tessa was laughing now. That was really good. It meant there was less for the demons to pull from.

I studied the room, the demons, the portal, and then wanted to let out my own curse. At times like this, I wished I could let a few good ones out, but I'd already cussed outside. That was more than enough for today.

Think, Sam. Think.

Okay. Demons were fine. There weren't any that I needed to be worried about. None with power. None that should give me any trouble.

There weren't any other monsters in here aside from the demons, so that was also fine.

But the floor was marked with Satanic symbols, lining the portal, marking the boundary between Earth and Hell. The symbols glowed red with dark power, fueled by whatever sacrifice was made to forge the portal.

Well, at least now I knew why the portal was still open.

Usually portals collapsed on themselves after a few hours. Every once in a while, someone made a spell big enough to keep one open, but it was rare. This was one of those rare times.

This was going to be a royal pain to close, and it would take time.

I studied the symbols, trying to find a way to undo what had been done here, but I couldn't get my eyes to focus on it. I kept looking into the portal.

Heat and screams and the scent of sulfur came from it, bringing up all kinds of pain, fear, and trauma that I didn't want to think about. Not now. It was way too soon.

I felt myself stepping closer to the portal, drawn to it. My breaths started to come faster. My heart raced. I saw the demons scrambling below, and a drop of sweat dripped down my face. A scream ripped through the portal—one of pain and fear and desperation—and suddenly, I felt like I was back there.

Memories flashed through my mind of my father chasing me through Hell, of my skin burning in the fires, of the terror and the fear and—

Someone warm and kind wrapped their arms around me, and my back pressed hard into his chest. "Don't take one more step, Sam. Please," he whispered in my ear.

Phoenix.

I blinked and looked down. I was right on the line, about to cross over the spells. One more step, and I would've fallen through.

He pulled me back a few steps. "Do you want to call for Eli?" he whispered.

"He's busy or he'd be here already." The last time we saw him, he'd been in his full armor. It meant that he was in on something really big. Much bigger than this.

Every move had consequences, and I didn't know what pulling him away from battle would do. It'd been a few days, but that was nothing to angels. Their fights could last a millennia.

I couldn't afford to distract Eli. So, no. I couldn't call him. He couldn't close a portal like this anyway. I had to do this myself.

I took a breath to steady my nerves. "It's just a lot. Breaking the spell on the floor is going to take so much energy, and if I don't do it right, then it could backfire on us and…" I closed my eyes, feeling along the tie to my father.

It was pulsing rhythmically. "He's coming. I can feel him pulling power from me. That's why I got so close to the edge of the portal. Honestly, I don't understand how he isn't already here, but maybe I'm having a little luck today. If I weren't already tired—"

"Let's wait," Dastien said. "Let's get you some food and rest tonight. Come back tomorrow at peak sunlight."

No. I felt a hard pass on that with every fiber of my being. "Can't. Legit can *not*. Every hour, minute, second this thing stays open makes it worse. We still don't know what's killing the wolves. We leave this thing open with my father and his power and he comes through..." My mind started to spiral though all the ways this could go wrong. "No. Absolutely not. I have to close it *right now*. And then the clean up—"

"We have the care team, and your mom can put us in touch with any priests that need to do anything else. Just focus on closing the portal," Dastien said.

He was right, and it was always better to focus on the problem right in front of me.

"Man." I scanned the markings on the floor. "This is a mess." I gave myself another second of leaning back into Phoenix. "I'm not complaining. Just tired. This is going to drain me big time."

"You can do this, and I'll be here to catch you when you crash." He squeezed me tighter, and I wanted to stay in his arms forever. The guy gave the best hugs. "We can get milkshakes or cookies or whatever you want as soon as you're done. Okay?"

"Okay."

He pulled away from me just enough to spin me in his arms and duck down, leveling his gaze with mine. "Close the portal. And then we'll deal with all the rest." He brushed a quick kiss on my lips, and when I gasped, he deepened it. I felt myself sinking into it, into the feeling of him, and the way he made my heart race. It was as if he were feeding me his energy and strength and will through our tie and suddenly, I could breathe again.

He pulled away enough to rest his forehead against mine. "You got this."

"Right. Okay. I can do this." With one kiss, he'd shoved away all the exhaustion, spiraling thoughts of all the ways it could go wrong, and the feeling that I was in a Sisyphean battle against evil until it felt like it was in another realm.

I focused only on what I needed to do.

Close the portal, Sam.

It wasn't a portal that I'd opened, which meant I needed to be a little careful with how I closed it.

Portals wanted to stay closed. They were an aberration. Most opened and then closed again within hours or a day. No more. Someone had to continuously feed the portal to keep it open.

This one had been open for days, or maybe a week, or it could've been even longer. That was why the situation in the city was getting worse and how something that could kill werewolves had found its way through it.

I didn't know everything about Satanism, but I knew enough to know that the symbols used in this spell were powerful. There were some basic ones, and some that I'd never seen before. Those were the ones that worried me the most.

I bent down to get a closer look. On the mortal realm, they were just paint—or what I really, truly wanted to believe was paint—but in the spiritual realm, they glowed. Some of them black, some red, but all made me feel panicked the closer I got to them.

That was the idea. No one with any intuition would ever set foot in this house. They wouldn't know why they rushed past the house or turned around when they approached, but it was because of these symbols.

They were protecting the portal.

They were fueling the portal.

And the way they swirled and linked together with streaming lines of power, I knew something truly evil had been done to open this portal.

If I was reading it correctly, the spell had to be canceled out first. If I tried to close it first, not only would it stay open, but by trying, an alarm would sound, signaling every evil thing in the area to come fight me for my power. And *that* was something I definitely didn't have the energy for.

Demons back to Hell, yes.

Closing portals, sure.

Battling all the things that go bump in the night in this realm? Hard no.

I unzipped my belt bag and grabbed out the plastic bag of salt. It wasn't a big one—I silently thought about going back to the car for more—but screw it. A little would be enough. If it wasn't, I'd send a wolf to find my backpack.

I walked around the symbols on the floor, sprinkling salt on them as I quietly prayed. Asking for strength. For cleansing. For the power to do *good.*

When I was done, I put away the empty baggie and did the same thing as I walked around the room spraying holy water on the symbols.

I used the prayers that Frank taught me. The ones to bring forth angels and send demons back where they belonged, but it was slow moving. The prayers took time, energy, power, but slowly the light in the symbols started to dim. First, just a little. Just barely enough that I was tempted to focus on one symbol until it was gone, but that wouldn't work with the way they were linked. It was almost like the time I'd put all my jewelry in one travel pouch. All the necklaces got completely tangled in the most impossible way. This was so much worse. I was uncoiling a complicated, tangled knot of horrific power.

I had to work a little at a time, going back to previous parts as I moved along the circle, and even as I made progress, I felt the clock ticking. Every second that I took felt like an eternity, until I was forcing myself not to grind my teeth.

My father pulled at the tie between us as I worked. Tugging at my power. Draining me bit by bit. He was raging—so, so angry. I could hear his voice whispering my name and the revenge he was going to take on me for getting away. His footsteps were in time with my heartbeat, which amped up my anxiety, and I thought about running away while I still had time.

I gasped as he tugged hard, nearly losing my balance.

"Whoa." Phoenix gripped my elbow. "You okay?"

"No." He was draining me. Quicker and quicker.

I couldn't think about that now. I squatted down on the floor to get closer to the symbol I was working on.

Sweat trickled down my back in little rivulets.

No. I looked up at Phoenix. "He's coming."

There was a *thud,* and the walls shook.

"Samantha?" Tessa asked.

I glanced at her. She was huddled next to Dastien, his arm protectively around her as she watched me.

My father *roared.*

"Samantha!" Tessa yelled, stepping away from Dastien. "You have to finish this. Astaroth is almost here."

"I know. But the power here is—"

And then I heard *his* voice. *"Samantha. My darling. If you wanted to play, all you had to do was call my name."* He kept talking, but I knew what he was doing. He was trying to distract me with fear and intimidation, but I was on this side of the realm. And he was on *the other side*. For now.

Move, Samantha. Fucking hurry. I thought the words, yelling them at myself.

I jumped over to the last symbol. It was a horned devil with flames coming out of its mouth. The flames flickered in the spiritual realm as I sprayed the symbol with holy water until they gutted out. I said the prayer one more time, and then—

Something hit me in my stomach, and I flew through the air.

Oh, shit.

CHAPTER NINETEEN

SAMANTHA

I WAS FLYING through the air, eyes closed, braced to crash, ready for pain and—

Someone caught me. Strong arms around my waist.

I looked down and met Phoenix's eyes.

"How can we help make this go faster?" he asked.

"I don't know." I took a breath. "Just don't let me fall through that portal. He pulled me so hard, and I can't go back there. Not again. Not in my body."

He gave me a small smile. "I haven't let you fall through one completely yet. I don't plan on it now."

The walls shook so hard, it felt as if the room was going to be torn apart. "The portal isn't stable."

"What does that mean?" Tessa's eyes were wide, and I knew she'd been through some bad things. But this could get worse than she'd seen.

"If I don't do it right, the portal could implode."

"That would mean it would close, right? Is that a bad thing?"

"Yes. It would close, but the last time I saw that happen, it destroyed a massive apartment building. This…" I looked at the portal. It was bigger than that apartment building portal. So much more powerful. "It could take out the whole block. Maybe more. The people here…"

Phoenix set me on my feet. "Better get it closed the right way, then."

"Yeah." I stepped away from him and turned to look down into the portal. "Shit. Shit. *Shit.*"

Before, there had been demons running everywhere, climbing on top of each other, but now they'd stopped moving. At some point while I'd been working, they'd stopped and dropped down to their knees.

Now, they were making a keening noise, and I knew what that meant.

Astaroth was close.

I shoved everything back into my belt bag and pulled out my cross. I raised it in the air.

I was out of time. The symbols on the spell still gloweda little, but I couldn't wait. I couldn't spend another second trying to untangle the spell. This had to be good enough. I had to end this.

God, help me! Give me the power to fix this. I can't do it on my own. I need your help.

"*Claudere!*" I yelled, throwing everything I had in me at the portal. I used all of the power I had, the prayers running through my head, the might of the sacred relic stored in the cross that I held out, focusing everything through it.

Dark power flowed up through the portal, knocking me back a few steps.

No. This wasn't happening. "Claudere!" I pushed hard. My power felt like fire rushing through my veins. I hated the feeling, but I would use it.

I would use it.

The portal started shrinking—bit by bit.

"You're doing it!" Tessa said. "Keep going. Keep—"

But it swelled open again, and the power came pushing back at me. If I thought my power felt uncomfortable before, now it wasn't just fire in my veins. It was acid running through me, eating me from the inside. The pain forced me to my knees, and I screamed as I reached my hand over the now dull and dead symbols.

But the portal wasn't closing.

Why wasn't it closing?

My father's laughter rang in my ears. My heart raced and I felt like I was going to throw up from the pain and the exhaustion and the fear.

"Please!" I wasn't sure who I was begging to make it stop, but I needed something more than just me. *"Claudere!"* I groaned under the strain of fighting my father's pull. The tie between us burned bright and thick, and I could see my power leaving me, flowing down the tie, powering him.

It felt helpless, but I kept pushing, pushing, *pushing*.

Hot tears rolled down my face, but I couldn't feel myself crying. I just kept screaming under the pressure of it all.

If I'd the wherewithal, I would've cut the tie to my father, but I couldn't cut the tie *and* close the portal. I had to pick.

I screamed as I shoved more power at the portal, and it finally started to close again.

"Don't give up." Phoenix put his hand on my back. "You're doing it. I know it's hard. I can see that you're hurting."

I leaned back into his hand and felt something warm and good flow through me. It countered the fire and acid feeling that made me want to crawl out of my skin. It started from his hand and spread like a balm through my body.

His arm wrapped around my waist, and I fell back into his lap.

I was so close. *Please.*

Please.

Please.

"He's almost here. I can see him down there, but the portal is almost closed. It's so small now. You can do this."

For some stupid reason, I believed him, and I shoved what

little power I had left at the portal, screaming with a force that I shoved through the spiritual realm. I took a breath.

Lord, help me do this. One more time. Please. "Claudere!"

The house shook.

Demons screeched as they were sucked through the closing portal.

A crash came from downstairs.

Oh God. I hoped the house could withstand this.

Because there were more coming. I could feel them, hear them, smell them all barreling toward the portal as it called them back to where they belonged.

But it didn't matter. I just needed this over. How much longer could the portal last?

Just a second longer. Just one more second.

One more second of pushing my power to force the portal fully closed.

One more second of fighting my father.

One more second and this would be over.

The portal that used to be eight feet wide was now a foot across. Maybe less.

I was so close, but it wouldn't slam closed like I wanted it to.

I gritted against the strain of it.

I could do this.

I would do this. I didn't have another choice.

And then I yelled, *"Claudere! Aboleo!"* I pushed what little I had left into the words, forcing my will through them.

The symbols on the floor burned with spiritual fire until they turned to ash.

With them, the connection to my father weakened to a low-level hum, and I knew I had it.

I was winning.

The portal was finally, truly, closing. With every breath, it closed another inch.

Yes. *Yes!*

I leaned back against Phoenix, my breaths coming in pants, my arms shaking as I held the cross over the portal. But it was enough.

It was tiny now. Two inches across. If that. Just enough to let heat and screams and the scent of sulfur through, but not big enough to let a demon through.

It would close.

Thank you, God. Thank—

"Samantha!" A voice yelled at me through the tiny portal. *"Help me!"*

Everything in me froze.

Oh no.

Oh shit.

Gabe!

"Gabe! Hurry!" Before I could think, I lunged for the portal, but I couldn't get there. Phoenix's arm kept me pinned tightly against him, but I needed to get to Gabe.

I wasn't sure I could reverse what I'd done. I'd put everything I had into forcing it closed. Trying to bring all that power back would be impossible.

But I screamed as I tried.

My head swam, and my head lolled back against Phoenix's shoulder. His arm pulled tighter, and his hand covered my mouth. "Don't. *Please,* Sam. Don't say the words. You can't open it again. You don't have the energy. You go get him now, you're not coming back. You have to stay with me. You have to let go. Let the portal close."

I struggled to get free, elbowing Phoenix in the stomach. He let out a grunt, but he held me tighter, keeping me pressed against him. Not matter how hard I tried, he wouldn't let go.

Phoenix cushioned us as we fell to the floor in my struggle to get free.

I screamed behind his hand, hot tears running down my face, because I'd failed. I'd failed my best friend again. What kind of person leaves the one who saved them to suffer in Hell?

I had to do something.

If Gabe was this close, I had to do *something*.

I tugged at Phoenix's hand, and he moved to away from my mouth.

I knew it didn't matter. It was too late, but I couldn't help it. *"Gabe!"* I yelled through the spiritual realm. *"Hurry!"*

"Sama—"

The portal snapped closed. And with it, the little bit of hope that Gabe would make it out was gone.

But all the demons in the house were gone, too.

From what I could feel, none of the demons in the neighborhood had survived the portal closing. All of them were back in Hell.

I hadn't seen anything that could've killed the werewolves fall through it though. Something was still out there.

I closed my eyes.

Gabe hadn't made it out. He couldn't fight against the push of the portal closing like that. No demon could. Not even my father.

I sagged against Phoenix. "Fuck. *Fuck!*" I couldn't help the curse from flying out of my mouth. Or the tears that came faster. Or the feeling of worthlessness that weighed down my heart.

"You don't know that it was him," Phoenix whispered in my ear. "You couldn't keep the portal open with your father that close. It wasn't safe and—"

"I know." I twisted in his arms so that I could bury my face in the crook of his neck.

I knew he'd been right to stop me, and for whatever reason, he was the only thing making me feel better. I tucked my face into his neck, trying to get my tears and breathing under control. "I know that. I do. But even if it was just a chance of it being him—"

"But didn't you say most demons can mimic other voices? Even your father?" Tessa asked.

He could. I knew he could.

"I know you want to find your friend, that you feel responsible for the danger that he's in now, but isn't it more likely that it was your father manipulating you? He wanted the portal open. He was almost here. We know that. We heard his voice. The way the walls shook. It was just like when you went to save Van. He would've come through, and then—" Tessa's voice broke. "We got lucky the first time, but I don't think I could beat him a second time."

Phoenix rubbed one hand up and down my back, while the other held my head against him. "You just did some major work here, and you have to be exhausted. Just breathe. Don't worry about anything. Just focus on my breathing." He took slow, measured breaths, and mine eventually followed his.

There was a tingling weightless feeling in my body that I knew was exhaustion. I'd just spent what little strength I'd rebuilt since I saved Van. Which was frustrating because I hadn't found whatever killed the werewolves. And still, I was sad.

Gabe had been close.

But had he? Was that really him?

I let the feeling of Phoenix rubbing my back, holding me, anchor me to what was real, and my head started to clear a little. I was lying on top of Phoenix on the attic floor, and I remembered it was gross up here, but I couldn't get up. Not yet.

Tessa was right about how my father could change his voice. She'd fought him. She knew what he was capable of.

I did, too, but the sound of Gabe's voice screaming my name through Hell…it haunted me.

If that wasn't Gabe, then my father had known exactly what button to push. But it didn't change the fact that for a second, I thought it was my best friend. I'd *wanted* it to be him.

"I know that it probably wasn't Gabe, but it felt like him. The hope…" I swallowed down the shame I felt at leaving Gabe behind. Again.

I needed to get out of here. "The house is fine." I didn't blow up a city block closing the portal either, so that was a good thing. "There shouldn't be any demons in the neighborhood anymore. We still don't know what was killing your werewolves, but this was the start of fixing it. I have to get out of here. I need the sun and a safe, clean space, and I don't know what else. But I have to get out of here."

I rose up a little bit, and Phoenix ran his hand over my hair, brushing it away from my face. "Okay." He sat up, pushing me up with him, and moved me off to the side as he rose. "You look wiped."

I groaned. "That's code for looking like trash."

"Never." He leaned down and lifted me up, wrapping his arms under me to hold me in place.

I wrapped my arms around his neck, my legs around his waist, letting my face fall in the crook of his neck again.

I let myself melt into him as he walked us down the stairs. This time, there were no demons pulling at my hair. No one yelling horrible things at me. Nothing but the smell of Phoenix's cologne. It was nice. Calming. Masculine. Earthy. The feel of him carrying me made me feel treasured.

Maybe he didn't think that, but it felt nice to be carried this way. Comforting. "Thanks," I whispered to him.

"You don't need to thank me. This is exactly where I want to be," he whispered as he moved through the house. "Hey, Dastien," he said a little louder. "Can we get the cars over here? I have no idea where we left them."

"Yeah. I heard the guys downstairs. The two we left outside already went to get them. No one else was in the house. No normies. No supernaturals. Nothing but the demons."

Good. Because I didn't have much left in me.

Phoenix carried me outside, into the sunlight, and then knelt down, easing me to sit on the ground. I kept my eyes closed and let myself collapse back onto the front lawn of the house. The feeling of the sun on my face washed away the darkness of guilt and shame at having left my friend caged in Hell.

Phoenix squatted beside me, running his hand over my forehead again. "What can I do?"

I shook my head. "Nothing. Just tired. I'll be fine in a second."

Probably more like a few days, but we didn't have time for me to be down that long.

"Food? Water?"

I took a breath. I wanted neither, but… "Yeah. I probably need both."

"Good. We'll make sure to get you both."

"What's happening?" Max said from my other side.

I rolled my head to look at him, blinking my eyes open.

Max's brows drew down as he scanned my face. "What's wrong? I've never seen you like this."

I didn't know how to answer that.

"Are you okay?" Max started to press his hand to my forehead, as if checking for a fever, but Phoenix stopped him.

That wasn't what was wrong with me anyway. Not even remotely. "Peachy."

His eyes flashed wolf bright as he studied me. "You look pale. Usually, you come out of stuff like this jazzed."

"Not today." I probably looked like a zombie. No wonder Phoenix was worried about me. "Closing a portal to Hell when my father and some really nasty magic are trying to keep it open takes it out of me."

"Your father?" It was his tone more than the question that had me closing my eyes and taking a breath.

Not everyone knew why I could do the things that I did. Just my closest inner circle—which didn't include Max.

Way to make it awkward. I'd said too much because I was tired.

The sun was too bright, even for my closed eyes, so I put my hand over them.

Maybe I was more tired than I thought. "I need food and rest before we go looking for whatever has been going after your pack members."

"You think you can still do it?" Max asked. From his tone, clearly he didn't think so.

"Yep." I had to.

Then there was a bright light—bright enough that I could see it through my closed lids and hand. It was different from sunlight. It was a white, cleaning, healing light.

"Just what in the high Heavens do you think you're doing?"

I winced. "Eli..."

"I told you to stay put. To call me if anything came up. You disobeyed me why?" I knew that tone. It might've sounded like he was bored, but it meant the opposite.

Fantastic.

I was in so much trouble.

CHAPTER TWENTY

PHOENIX

ELI LOOKED AT ME, and I stood. He wasn't in the full gear I'd seen him wearing the other night—no helmet, just gold bracers and a chest plate. He held a flaming sword in his hand, and his gray-tipped, white wings were stretched wide. I couldn't tell if he was on the mortal plane or the spiritual plane. I thought he was likely on the mortal one, but I wasn't good enough at this stuff yet to tell the difference.

Wait. I could figure this out. Max was staring up at Eli with wide eyes. Tessa and Dastien hung back on the yellow house's porch stairs. They were sitting together with Tessa tucked tight against Dastien's side. She shook as she clung to him.

From what I could tell, Dastien had handled seeing the spiritual realm when he'd had the sight at the Sanctuary, but that might not be a fair comparison. The only demon he'd seen was Gabe, who was supposedly an ally. Tessa had walked into a fully infested house and looked extremely pale. I knew she had visions, so it was possible she'd had one and seen something bad. Or who knew what had happened? I'd been so focused on Sam that I hadn't paid attention to anything else in the attic.

Some of the other wolves were hanging around the front yard, some still wandered through the house, and others were driving up with the SUVs.

I was ready to get the heck out of here, but I wasn't sure Sam was ready to move yet. I opened my mouth, but Eli answered my question before I could even speak it.

"She's not," Eli said.

He was reading my mind again. Like that wasn't creepy at all. "I figured."

I knew he was an angel or whatever, but I didn't like the way he stared down at Samantha like she'd done something wrong.

"She did," Eli said without looking at me.

Man, I truly hated that he could read my mind.

"Tough." He bit the word out, *still* not looking at me.

I swallowed down the shitty retort I wanted to sling at him because Eli was an angel. He stood there, seemingly annoyed, like we'd interrupted something, and I wasn't stupid. I knew I couldn't pick a fight with him. I'd lose—*big time*. But man, if he was angry at Sam, he was dead wrong for it.

I'd seen what Samantha had done, what she'd fought against, what it had cost her. I didn't know how it happened, but I knew exactly when she'd gotten weak. Just like I knew that my touch would help, even though I had no logical reason for knowing it or any explanation for why it should.

It had to be something with our bond, but I hadn't talked to Sam about what might be possible with it. I wanted to say that we hadn't had time, but that was bullshit. We could've talked about it at some point in the last few days, but I'd wanted to ease into this thing with her. I wanted to date her without rushing and pushing her to tell me things she wasn't ready to talk about. Now, I was regretting that move.

Could I have helped her more if we'd had those conversations? Maybe. Because—as I watched her lying on the grass—I knew she was totally, fully, completely spent. And yet, if someone asked her for help right now, she'd haul herself up and do the hard thing. *Again.*

And he was mad at her for it?

Eli shot me a look that said I should stay out of it, but I wasn't going to do that.

"What did she do wrong?" From my end, it seemed like she'd done everything she was supposed to.

That house had been infested with an open portal, and now it was clear of evil and the portal was shut and gone. She'd also cleared the demons from the neighborhood—because I searched, and I didn't see any—and from the werewolves that we came to help.

No one died.

No souls lost.

It was all good.

"Correct." Eli flicked his wrist, and his sword, wings, and the little bit of armor he was wearing totally disappeared. Instead, he wore a white button-down shirt and ripped, light wash jeans. But there was no mistaking he was otherworldly, no matter what he wore. His shoulder-length blond hair waved in a nonexistent breeze, and he still glowed, with a white aura surrounding him. Though maybe only those with spiritual sight could see his aura.

Eli moved to stand on the other side of Sam. Max got up, backed away from the angel, and sat next to Tessa on the porch stairs.

Eli gave me a smirk, and I was pretty sure he thought it was funny how quickly Max ran away from him.

He gave me a nod.

Right. Same.

It wasn't that I didn't know how powerful Eli was. I just didn't think he'd hurt me.

"That remains to be seen," Eli said in an ominous voice, but I wasn't buying it.

No, he wouldn't hurt me. Sam would kill him if he did.

"Maybe. And speaking of Sam…" Eli crossed his arms and he

stared down at her. "She did a good job, but in her current state, she knows better than to take on too much." His feet were bare on the grass. I hadn't noticed until he knelt next to her.

"She was supposed to call for me if she needed to do *anything* other than rest, heal, and *slowly* resume training." He flicked her forehead. "There was nothing slow about what was done here." He flicked her again.

Sam swatted at Eli's hand, trying to bat it away, but her eyes were closed. She missed him completely. "Come on, Eli. You knew that wasn't how this was going to go." Samantha blinked her eyes open and then shielded them with her hand again. "Can you turn down the light effects a bit? My head is hurting, and it's *super* annoying right now."

Eli flared brighter for a second, and then he grumbled something under his breath. I was glad I couldn't hear it. Eli was getting on my bad side.

"That doesn't bother me, Phoenix. The important thing to remember is that you don't want to be on *my* bad side." The light aura around him dimmed, but it wasn't gone-*gone*. He'd just toned everything down for Sam. Which was decent of him.

I didn't want to be disrespectful—I knew Sam and Eli had a unique relationship—but I wasn't about to let him beat Samantha down when she was literally already down.

I sat on the ground next to her, making sure to block the angle of the setting sun so that she didn't have to hold her hand up.

"Thanks," she said.

I brushed my hand across her forehead. She still felt a little clammy and was a little pale, but otherwise, she seemed fine. But something nagged at me, just beyond my perception. I had no idea what it was, but I knew I couldn't leave her alone. "You okay?"

She turned her head to look at me and gave me a smile. I could still see what she saw—the lines around the werewolves—their bonds. I could feel evil lingering, even if I couldn't see any demons around us anymore. And when I looked into her eyes, I saw the flames in them. I was sure only someone who could see into the spiritual realm could see them because no one had ever mentioned them before. I knew that sometimes people could see the fire around her—like when she'd that nightmare—but I had a feeling not many people had seen her like this.

"Correct," Eli confirmed. "On all of your assumptions."

At least I wasn't completely off base with what I was thinking. If I had to guess, the look in her eyes, the power she had, and the things she fought were what scared her ex away.

I raised a brow in question to Eli.

"See? You understand more than you think you do." Eli gave me a sly look, and I wasn't sure what to say to him. Instead, I looked down at Sam.

She was still watching me, and I wished I knew what she was thinking. The flames in her eyes didn't bother me. They didn't make her evil. She worked hard, sacrificing her safety, well-being, and risking her life to save people over and over and over again. So, no. The eyes were just a part of what made her special, but there was something else that caught my attention.

The silver threads—hers and mine—twisted together, running from the light in her soul to mine.

She'd described it before, but I'd never been able to see it. She'd never let me in like this, and I was glad she had. I wanted to be in this with her, but the only way that I could do that was if she let me *see*.

And now that I could see, I couldn't help myself. I reached out to touch the threads, but my hand went right through them.

Sam laughed. "Found them, huh?" She reached up, hooked her pointer finger around them, and gave them a sharp tug. A tug that made me feel like the ground was falling out from under me.

I lost my balance, but I managed to catch myself before I fell on top of her.

Sam stared deep into my eyes, and it was more than just a stare. With the flames in her eyes, it felt as if she was seeing into me, and I didn't know what to say.

"Are you okay?" she asked.

Wait. She was asking me?

Yeah. I was. On every level. "I'm great, but you don't need to worry about me," I said seriously, hoping she got my meaning. I wasn't talking about the tie she'd tugged on or the fact that I'd almost fallen on top of her.

I meant that I was fine with everything that had happened in there.

Everything I'd seen.

Everything that she was.

There would be no name calling from me. No telling her she was evil. And definitely no running from her.

She continued looking at me, searching me, as if trying to discern if I was telling the truth.

I was. She might not believe me now, but trust took time, especially when she was still dealing with what whatever her ex said to her when he bailed on her.

"Wait," Eli said. "Has she told you what he said? Because she refuses to tell me."

Right. He couldn't read Sam's mind, and he was just an angel —meaning definitely not all-knowing. "No. But whatever it was, it clearly devastated her."

"Can we *not* do this right now?" Sam groaned. "It's really not the time to delve into the past. We have things to deal with. Like what is killing—"

"Fine. You don't want to talk about it, then back to me now." Eli leaned down, getting in her face. "Why did you not call out to me?"

Sam rolled her eyes and pushed him away. "You were supposed to be watching me. Plus, the last time I called you, it seemed like you were in a massive battle. I didn't want to pull you away from that again. I assumed if you weren't here, then you were too busy to come. I would've called you if I really, actually *needed* you."

"If you called me *before* you *needed* me, then maybe you

wouldn't keep getting in over your head." He shook his head. "Stubborn. That's what you are."

"No. I'm determined and persistent. Those are good qualities." Samantha closed her eyes. "Besides, you can't close portals. That's why you need me. So, what good could you have really done?"

That was an interesting bit of information. I thought he could do anything, but apparently, I was wrong.

"You're annoying me," Eli said to me.

"Don't pick on Phoenix," Sam said. "Go back to whatever important battle you were fighting."

"No. I'm not going anywhere yet, especially since you've proven yourself untrustworthy, angel."

"*Don't* call me that," Sam snapped at him. But her voice was gaining strength from fighting with Eli, so I wasn't about to step between whatever was going on with them.

"It's accurate," Eli said. "You are an angel, of sorts."

"No, it's really *not* accurate." She tried to sit up, but her arms shook, and she fell back onto the grass.

I grabbed her hands and pulled her up to sit. "Better?"

"Yeah." She took a breath. "Thanks."

We were going to need to get her some food, but she could probably do with some water right now. "Anyone got water in one of those SUVs?"

"Yeah," a voice called out. A second later, one of the wolves—I hadn't gotten all of their names—handed me a water and a packet of peanut butter crackers

"Perfect. Thanks." I snagged both, and opened the water for Sam.

The werewolf gave me a nod and then went around handing out snacks to everyone else, but I was focused on making sure Sam had hers.

Her hands shook as tried take a sip, so I snagged it back from her and tipped it for her.

"Sorry," she said when she was done taking a sip. "I hate that I'm this weak." She looked down and away. I knew what it was like to fight so hard to be strong for everyone else. I'd done it for my family, but never on this level.

"Sam will be fine," Eli said as he sat back on his heels. "She just has to be patient and *ask for help*." There was a bit of an edge to his words that I didn't like.

I bit my tongue to keep myself from telling him to lay off. Sam was exhausted, and I wasn't going to be able to sit here silently much longer if he was going to criticize her. I refused.

"That only works when the other person can't read minds."

I ripped open the package of crackers and handed one to Sam. "Well, maybe you should learn that it's rude for you to constantly be in my head. And talking down to someone who just did a good thing at great cost to herself? That's pretty shitty."

Samantha muttered something too softly for me to hear, but all the werewolves started laughing.

Eli shook his head. "I thought we were over the adolescent phase."

"Apparently not," Sam said.

I was about to ask what she'd said, but Eli shot her a look. "You will not repeat that."

She rolled her eyes. "Can we go somewhere else? I need to recover before we go patrolling tonight. And I want away from this house."

I wasn't sure what the werewolves were doing. My focus was on Sam, but I hoped they could wrap up whatever it was so we could leave soon.

I looked over to Tessa and Dastien, who were getting up from their spot on the porch stairs. A group of werewolves stood by the SUVs that were all now parked in front of the yellow house.

Max said something to the ones by the SUVs and some got in the cars, but four stayed where they were.

Dastien and Tessa stopped by Sam.

"Four of the Wayfarers are going to stick around here," Dastien said. "They'll work the cleanup and start tracking down the people who live here, but we don't need to stay for that."

"Great. Because I'm so ready to go." Sam wasn't as bad as she'd been after she went into Hell, but she was far from okay. Food and hydration, then a nap. If she wanted to go patrolling tonight, she was going to have to do all of it or we were going to have words.

"We totally can do that, but you have options, depending on what you need," Dastien said to Sam.

Sam nodded. "Okay. What are they?"

"We can go to the big house the Wayfarers are renting here. It's a new build, outside of the city, so potentially okay enough for you. Not a guarantee that it'll be totally spiritually clean, but it's very likely fine. I had a priest come bless it while we were flying here just in case you liked that option. But the rest of the pack members who didn't come out during the day are all there resting. So, it's not the most private."

"Right," Sam said, and her shoulders hunched just a little bit.

"If you want more privacy, we can go to the hotel and start checking rooms to see if any are clear enough for you to stay in, but you might need to actually do some clearing before you can rest. Which—given what you've just done—I'm not sure you have the bandwidth for."

"Yeah. No. That sounds like a bad idea," Sam said, which I was relieved to hear.

From what I was feeling from her, I could tell she was on the verge of of collapsing.

I held out the water for her again, and she took another sip. "Thanks," she said, and then looked at Dastien. "Any other options?" She took the cracker I held out, giving me a small smile.

The look made me feel a lot better. There wasn't much color in her cheeks, but there was some. It was a start.

"Or we can go to a restaurant and get you food. See if that gives you enough energy to clear a hotel, but the house still might be the better option."

I liked the food thing. She needed more protein. "We should definitely get her some real food. This snack isn't going to cut it." I knew he wasn't talking to me, but food had to be a priority. Sam was exhausted, and she had to keep her strength up. Somehow I knew she wasn't going to pick food, even if she needed it. "She needs to refuel."

"Agreed. I saw what she did in there. I *saw* everything." Tessa's voice shook a little as she spoke. "What she did and what they were saying and my flashbacks of what has happened before when Sam…" She cleared her throat. "I'm exhausted just witnessing that."

I wanted to ask questions about the flashbacks, but the way Tessa was wringing her fingers together, I wasn't sure I should. I didn't want to make her explain more when she was clearly still processing it all.

Tessa took a breath, and Dastien turned to her. I saw their bright, golden bond light up and a bead of light travel down his line to hers.

Huh. I guessed that was how they mentally communicated. I wondered if I could do that on our bond. Ours was silver, so maybe not. But did the color really matter? Why were theirs gold and ours silver?

"If it were me," Tessa started, drawing my attention back to her. "I'd want some quiet. She's not going to get that at a restaurant. She doesn't like fast food. So, it'd have to be a sit-down restaurant, which means people and all the chaos that brings for her. She has to make a choice."

"Fair point." If the kitchen at the Wayfarer house was stocked, I could just make her something. It might be faster. Or we could pick something up. I looked at Sam. I hated to make her decide, but I didn't know enough about her yet to make the decision for her. "What do you want to do?"

I glanced at Eli to see if he had any thoughts on it, but he just shrugged.

Fine. I had no idea how their relationship worked on these types of things, so I stayed out of it and let Sam decide.

Sam crumbled the rest of the cracker in her hand as she

thought, then shook the bits onto the grass. I wasn't sure she'd even taken a bite of it. Not great.

"Let's try the Wayfarer house first," she said. "If it's safe, and I can find a room to crash in—great. And if we could get some kind of carry out or delivery or something, that would be perfect. I don't care what it is. Just not fast food. Not a restaurant with people." She looked at me, her eyes filled with an apology. "I can't handle that right now. I don't want to be around people, especially in this city. I need a second before I go out searching for other things and—"

"You don't have to explain." She didn't need to justify anything. I was here to help her in any way that I could. "Let's head to the house, but you need to eat before you crash. Okay?"

"Yeah. That works." She made a face, like she really didn't want to ask for the next thing. "Also…"

"I know that look," Tessa said. "You really must be not feeling great if you're actually asking for a vitamin IV."

"I'm not that bad…" Sam winced, as if she knew she was lying to herself and to us. "I just know that I need to be ready for whatever happens tonight, and so, yeah. As much as I'm sick of them right now, I'll take any boost I can get. I might not need a full IV, but maybe a shot of vitamins. You think you can talk to the pack doc for me?"

Tessa turned to Dastien, and that little ball of light bounced back and forth as Dastien pulled out his phone. "On it," he said.

I rose from the ground. "You want me to carry you?"

"Not really." Her cheeks pinked a little bit. "It's kind of humiliating to be carted around like a kid."

"Not when you just battled against part of something that's been killing our wolves," Max said. "Nothing wrong with getting a little help now and then."

Sam looked at Eli. "Can't you just—" She waved her hand in the air. "—make me feel better."

"One time, angel. I broke the rules *one* time, and you won't let me forget it. No way. Maybe I would have if you'd called for me…" The angel shrugged, and I wondered if he really wasn't going to help Sam.

"You're punishing me? Seriously?"

He was really getting on my shit list.

Eli dropped the arrogant smirk. "No. That was meant to be a joke. I'm not punishing you. That time when I healed you? That was life or death, and you were a child." When he spoke like this, he sounded older than he looked. Much, much older. The whole cadence of his words changed. "I crossed a line, and if you'll remember, I wasn't allowed to come help you for three years. *Three. Years*. Do you remember what happened while I was kept away from you?" The light around him flashed once and then it was gone. "We don't have time for that. Not now. Things are getting dangerous in the heavenly places, forces are moving against the Kingdom, and I need to be able to come to you when the time arises." The arrogance returned with a raised brow. "Assuming you won't continue being a stubborn moron."

Sam blew out a breath. "Fine. I guess I'll just do it the hard way."

"Builds character." He poked her side, and she jerked, slapping his hand away.

"I think I have enough character." She looked up at me, a plea in her eyes.

She didn't need to ask. I reached down, and she put her hands in mine. I tugged her to her feet and walked with an arm around her to make sure she didn't pass out on the way to the SUV.

I remembered she'd crashed hard at my house, and I really didn't want a repeat. She wasn't going to pass out and hit her head on the ground. Not while I was here to help her.

Garrett opened the car door and folded back the seats. "Why don't the two of you rest in the way back. Gives her room to stretch out."

"Thanks, man."

"Not a problem."

I helped Sam get back there, and as soon as I slid in, she spread out, placing her head in my lap.

"This okay?" she asked.

"Yep." I ran my fingers through her hair. "Feel free to close your eyes."

"It'll be a forty-five-minute drive to get to our base here," Garrett said from the driver's seat. "We like to stay a ways out from the city. Give our pack a little room and privacy to run in wolf form. Just waiting on a couple more people, and then we'll get on our way."

"Fab," Sam said. "I'm just going to take a nap." Her eyes were already closed.

I thought I'd have to fight her to get her to nap, but within seconds, her breathing evened out.

We'd made it through the first battle today—closing the portal.

I wasn't sure what would come next. I hoped the fight wasn't as bad as what I'd just seen.

But as I leaned back in the seat, I knew there wasn't a chance of that. The pictures I'd seen on the plane were horrific, and if I thought about it too much, I'd take her straight to the airport. Get her as far away from here as I could.

She'd hate me for it, so I restrained myself. For now.

I brushed my fingers through her hair again, watching her as she slept. Even if I was scared for her and what might happen tonight, I was grateful I was here, helping her.

I couldn't imagine any place I'd rather be.

CHAPTER TWENTY-ONE

PHOENIX

IT TOOK a few minutes to load everyone up. While we waited, Eli slid into the row in front of us, on the opposite side of the car from me. He twisted in his seat so that he could stare at me full-on. "You're doing a good job," he said softly.

I pointed to myself because that seemed odd. I hadn't really done anything, aside from yell frustrated thoughts at him in my head.

"She was going to jump into the portal. You knew it. You kept her grounded and here. That's what you're supposed to do. That's your job as her anchor."

"How did you know?"

Eli tilted his head. "I got information from everyone's heads while we were out on that lawn. I'm fully caught up."

"Right." I'd thought he was doing that, but now I knew for sure.

I had stopped her from falling into the portal, but it'd been instinctive. I didn't think that warranted any kind of praise.

"Instinctive actions are still actions, and it shows that the bond you have is working correctly."

I leaned forward as much as I could, lowering my voice. "What can this bond do exactly?"

Eli tilted his head and gave me a sly smile. "That's for you to find out."

That was supremely unhelpful.

Eli shrugged, and I knew he didn't care that I was annoyed with his inability to be anything other than cryptic. "How are you doing with it?"

"Good, I think." I wasn't sure what he meant exactly, but I thought everything was going okay. At least from my perspective. "Why?"

His gaze lowered to Sam's face. She was curled up in a tight ball with her head on my lap. One of my hands was on her shoulder, and she'd raised her hand in her sleep to link her fingers with mine, as if she wanted to make sure I wasn't going to disappear on her.

"She seems comfortable with you," Eli said after a moment, and he actually sounded happy about it.

"I hope so." I didn't think I'd given her any reason not to be, but I knew I'd make mistakes. I just hoped she gave me a chance to fix them whenever I did.

The front passenger door opened, and Max got into the seat.

Tessa and Dastien got in a moment later, sliding into the middle bench seat with Eli.

The angel stayed with his back against the door, watching me and his charge.

"Alright, everyone. We'll be there in a bit. Let me know if anyone needs a pit stop anywhere," Garret said. "Otherwise, we'll be on the road for about forty-five minutes."

Clicks filled the car as everyone buckled, and I did the same. I couldn't put one on Sam, but I wasn't worried about it. Garrett would drive safely. I hoped.

As soon as the car started moving, loud dings filled the car. Everyone looked at Eli, who rolled his eyes, and then stared at the front of the car. The dinging immediately stopped. "I don't care about mortal rules."

Tessa started to laugh but covered it with a cough.

"Nice try," I whispered to her, which made her fully laugh.

I liked Sam's friends. They were all different, but pretty great.

"Not to interrupt the love fest going on in your head, but what's the plan here?" Eli asked, and the only way I knew it was directed at me was the tone. It sounded like a command or interrogation, but the question was so vague that I wasn't sure what he meant.

Was he always this vague? "In Charleston?"

"No. With *her*."

Now he thought I was a moron. Perfect.

Even with all the werewolves quietly listening in, I answered him. "I'm doing my best not to rush things." It would be great if Eli could get on board with that plan.

"I don't really get on board with things. I'm too old for that." He looked at Sam as she stirred in her sleep. "She's the closest thing I have to family. I take care of her. She's *important*."

He didn't have to tell me that. She was important to me, too. "Understood."

"I can only stay here for a little bit, and then I have to get back. I was in the middle of..." His eyes got a distant look in them. "Anyway. Things are happening. The next few weeks should be interesting. And the coming months are very much up in the air. I'm going to be close in case she needs me, but make her call out to me before things get this bad again. If she's doing something dangerous, I need to know. She can't take crazy risks."

"Got it. I can try, but I'm not going to make her do anything she doesn't want to do." I refused to manipulate her.

"Good." He looked at me for a minute, and I held his gaze. "You're not disturbed by what you saw?"

I stared at him. "Do I seem disturbed?"

"No." He studied me for a second, and I knew he was likely rummaging through my mind.

The idea severely creeped me out, but I didn't have anything to hide. He could search for whatever he was looking for because clearly I wasn't giving him the answers he wanted.

But while he was searched, he could answer my questions. "Can you make *seeing* permanent? So I can see like her all the time?"

His brows rose. "Really? That's something you'd want?"

"Yes. I can't help her if I can't see, and she feels…torn." I didn't like to pressure her, but I needed to be able to see what she was seeing. "I know she feels a lot of anxiety about making that call."

"If you're sure, I could make that happen."

"What about strength?" Dastien chimed in. "Could you give him other extras?"

Wow. Okay. That wasn't something I'd thought about, but it would be helpful. I didn't want to have to rely on werewolves to help her do her thing.

Yeah. I could be really good with that.

Eli leaned back against the door and crossed his arms. His eyes were glowing bright, and there was something in his tilted smile that I didn't trust. "I could."

"Wait. You can do that?" Tessa was squished between Eli and Dastien, but she managed to turn a bit to look at Eli.

"Well, not me exactly. But I could put in a word with the one in charge, and I'm sure he'd be amenable. Favor has been given to certain humans since the beginning of time." He said it like it was obvious, and we were dumb to not realize it. "Samson is a good one remember in that sense. It's in the Bible. You've read it, right?" He sounded both outraged and confused.

"The guy that was the amazing warrior, right?" Garret said from the front. "Given favor by God. His hair was his kryptonite, though."

Eli let out a small breath and rolled his eyes, which was an odd look for the angel. "That's the one." He looked at me. "His hair wasn't exactly his kryptonite. Losing it was. It was the source of his power." He was quiet for a moment, as if he were letting that sink in. "Would you want that? Knowing that if I did ask for favor to be shown, you would truly tie yourself to her."

I started to say that we'd already done that. I was tied to her. I couldn't touch the tie like she could, but I could see it now. When she let me borrow her sight, I could see everything she could. I couldn't interact with it like her, but it still felt real to me. Especially the shimmery silver threads that literally tied our souls together.

"Yes, you did do that," Eli said, answering me before I said a word. "But this would be more complicated. It would be conditional. With the strength, sight, and the anchor tie, if something happens to her, if she died...well, you'd go with her. You'd be more like them." He motioned to Tessa and Dastien.

I could see their bond. The thick, glowing, and golden cord ran from Dastien to Tessa. It was completely different than the one I had with Sam. Ours looked like two thin silver threads twisted together and seemed weaker.

"It is weaker and different because their bond is more vital than the one you have with Sam. To be clear, if one of them dies, the other will, too. Their lives are linked. Yours are linked, too. I'm not forgetting that. But if something happened to you, she'd be okay. Or if something happened to her, you'd also be fine. That would change." He pointed to my tie. "See how it's translucent. It's there, but it doesn't feel like you can grab it exactly."

"Sam can."

"Yes, well, Sam is Sam." He gave me a smile. "But theirs...it's thick. Strong. Indestructible. It holds power." He reached out and tugged on the golden rope.

Dastien growled—deep, rumbling, just like his wolf—and reached out, smacking Eli's hand away.

"My apologies." Eli gave them a smile that was all teeth and no apology.

"Don't do that again." His words were growled, more wolf than human. I couldn't see his eyes from where I was sitting, but

I'd learned enough about werewolves to know they must be that bright, glowing golden color of his wolf.

I'd noticed Tessa and Dastien's bond before. They talked to each other through it, and when they did, a little flash of light seemed to zoom back and forth across the golden cord. Sam said she could feel a hum in the air when they talked through it, and that it sometimes rubbed her the wrong way while she was working.

I didn't hear the hum like she did, even when she let me borrow her sight. From what I could tell, the sight she passed along to whoever touched her was a watered-down version. I wanted more. I wanted to be in on everything. But I knew she needed more time. Which was fair. Completely and totally fair. I was being selfish and greedy for wanting everything, but that didn't change the need burning inside of me.

That need had struck like a flash of lightning when I first saw her, and I knew that she would change me. I didn't know how, but I knew. The flash brightened that night on the stairs, changing everything about me and my worldview in one night. For a while, I thought that she'd come into my life to change who I was, and that I'd never see her again. But I couldn't forget about her.

I never forgot her.

I'd had serious girlfriends, but I'd never had the kind of connection I had with Sam. On bad nights, I'd wonder if Sam had gotten married young and had a kid. If she was happily living her life while I was living mine and feeling a little empty, wondering about all the could've, should've, would've's. And I dreamed about what I would do if I managed to find her again.

But I'd felt crazy for thinking that way. It was insane. So, I dated. And when it came time to make a real commitment to the woman I'd been dating for years or let her get on with her life, I bought a ring. But I never proposed because the ring wasn't hers.

When I closed my eyes, I didn't see the ring on my girlfriend's finger. It was on Sam's. It was her face in my head, my heart, my soul. So, I'd broken up with my girlfriend, not even knowing if I'd ever see Sam again.

My *abuela* had been right. When you know, you know. And I *knew* deep in the fabric of my being that—even if it was insane and no one would understand—Sam was it for me.

One week, one hundred weeks. It didn't matter to me how long we'd been together. Sam would always be it for me, and I wanted Eli to do whatever he could to make our bond stronger. I didn't *need* time to think about it.

I didn't need time, but Sam did.

She was slow to trust for good reason, and I wasn't about to force her to do anything she didn't want to do. Not again. I know everyone said that this anchor tie wouldn't have worked if she didn't want it, but the guilt still lingered. I didn't want to do anything without talking to her first. But I wasn't worried about us not lasting, and I knew she felt for me what I felt for her. Even if she hadn't wrapped her mind around it yet.

"So?" Eli said, pulling me out of my thoughts. "What do you say? I need it verbally."

Yes. That was my answer. But I swallowed down the urge to scream—*yes, do it now!*—and instead, said something much more sane. "Sam and I have to talk to about it. I can't decide something like that without discussing it with her first."

"Good answer," Eli said.

The way he said it rubbed me the wrong way. "I didn't realize I was being tested."

"Everything in life is a test. Literally everything."

Right. I knew that, but it was different when an angel said it. He might have toned it down, but I was still able to see the spiritual realm. I knew it would wear off soon, but for now, Eli had this glow around him that seemed to glitter. When he wasn't toned down, it was overwhelming.

"Can I ask you a question?" I said.

"You're going to think it anyway, so why not just ask it?"

"Because I have manners, and you're an angel. Which means

you carry some authority with God. I don't want to overstep. No matter how much you look like a stoner surfer dude, I know you're not."

"No. I'm really not. But I like to think this look makes me more approachable. Which means people lie to me less. Which is the point. Lying is abhorrent." Something about his face changed, grew serious—his eyes hardened, and I knew that I was looking at the older version of Eli. The one that could be terrifying if he wanted to be. "Go ahead." His words resounded inside me, and I felt their power.

"When you saw me in that apartment—you know the one I mean?"

"I do."

"You said you saw great things for me. A warrior for the light. That wasn't soccer stuff you were talking about, right?"

One side of his mouth quirked up. "Do you think it was soccer stuff?"

"I used to think so. Especially because of the great things. And I thought maybe my work ethic and example for others would be the light in the dark. But now…I hope it's not anything to do with soccer. I don't want my soccer career to be my defining characteristic. Not that I didn't have fun playing, but I'm hoping you meant something else."

"You play soccer?" Garrett asked from the front.

For a few minutes, it'd been easy to ignore everyone except for Eli, but we weren't alone. Somehow, the angel's powerful gaze made me forget that Garret was up there, driving the car. And worse—that Max was listening to this whole conversation.

I didn't mind Tessa and Dastien. Tessa and Sam were especially tight, and I liked Dastien. He was a good guy. But Max.

Shit. I'd told them on the plane I managed my investments for a living, but not how I'd gotten the money. "Yeah. I played soccer."

"Like for fun?"

He sounded so confused that I almost laughed. "No. Like for a job."

"Were you any good?" Max asked, his tone made me want to punch him.

That wasn't good. Or smart. I wasn't sure what to say without being an asshole back to him. I didn't want to brag or make a thing of it, but—

"He's Phoenix-*freaking*-Herrera." Sam's sleep-thickened voice came from my lap.

I glanced down to see her eyes open.

"Arguably the best soccer player in the world." Sam spoke with her eyes still closed.

I smiled down at her and squeezed her fingers that were still linked with mine.

We'd talked about how she followed my career, but her saying that meant more to me than when anyone else said it. "Hey." I brushed her hair back from her face with my free hand. "I thought you were asleep."

"Drifting, I think. In and out, but not fully asleep." Her voice was soft, and she sounded like she was seconds away from sleep, but I guessed she hadn't been able to fully relax. Which I got. She was in an SUV full of supernaturals. It might be normal for her, but there'd been some tension between her and Max. And she'd only just met Garrett. So, letting down her guard to sleep might be hard until we got her fully settled in somewhere.

"How are you feeling?" I asked.

"Fine. Hating that I'm still weak, and annoyed that I'm mad about it. Because of course I am." She sighed. "You sure you won't fix me up, Eli?"

"Yes, angel. I cannot afford the price this time."

"But you can give him powers?"

Her question confirmed that she had been listening this whole time. I wondered why she hadn't spoken up sooner. Maybe because she wanted time to think about what Eli was offering? Or maybe she just needed time to breathe?

A ball of light bounced back and forth between Tessa and Dastien. In the times I'd spent with them, I'd noticed how in sync they were with each other. Their personalities complemented each other so well, and they always seemed to know what the other needed—whether it was a touch or a smile or food or whatever. I hoped that one day it would be like that for me and Sam.

"You're not fully mortal—" Eli's words drew me back to their conversation. "—and you have a role to play right now. If I do anything to alter your path, it would be bad for *everyone*. So, I have to be very careful where you're concerned, angel. But it's not because I don't want to help you or that I think you should suffer."

She sucked in a breath and rolled to face the seat.

"Oh, angel. I didn't mean to hit a nerve." Eli leaned over the back of his seat. All the joking was gone. He looked softer, kinder, and I could see how he loved her as reached out to her.

She shied away from his touch. "I'm fine," she said, but it was muffled with her face to the seat.

I grabbed her chin gently and turned her face so that I could see her. A tear was rolled down her cheek, but she brushed it away before I could. Something Eli said had set her off, and I wished I could ask her through our bond what it was. I wanted to fix it. To yell at Eli for saying whatever it was that hurt her. But I had no clue what it was that hurt her. "What's wrong?"

She shook her head, her eyes still squeezed shut. "I'm just tired. It makes me emotional, and I'm just so sick of fighting." She sighed. "How long have I been doing this Eli? Battling evil." Her back was still to everyone, but I knew everyone in the car had heard her.

Eli looked down and a pained look crossed his face. "You've always seen things and cleared rooms. Since before you could talk. When you were a toddler, it was more instinctive than anything. But truly battling evil? Since you were four or five, I think. The years blur." He rubbed his forehead. "How old are you now?"

"Twenty-four." She finally blinked her eyes open and met my gaze. "I'm just tired. Honestly. Sometimes it feels endless and hopeless. Like I'll never actually win. Like I'm meant to suffer through it all, over and over again, until one day I can't do it anymore. And I'll lose."

There it was. *Suffer*. That was the word that hurt her.

"I'm sorry for the fight you have ahead of you. Of all the ones that have come before. I know it's hard, angel, but there's only each battle. One at a time." Eli reached a hand to her, resting it on her back even as she squirmed away from him, leaving it when she stilled. "The war will never be over until Armageddon begins, and we're not there yet. The best we can do is beat evil back for as long as we can."

"I just don't know how much more I have in me."

The hopelessness in her voice scared me. "You don't have a choice. You have to keep going."

"I know I do. I *will* keep going. I'm not giving up. I'm just having a moment." She was quiet for a second. "I don't think I was ready to fight again." Her words were so soft that I barely made them out, but from Max's gasp, I knew everyone had heard her.

Eli cleared his throat.

"You were right. I should've called you. I'm sorry. I—"

"Ah. I see it. Now, this I can do something about." He looked up at the front seat. "Keep driving steady, Garrett. This might be a little startling."

"What are you—"

I didn't get to finish the question before a blast of power hit me, slamming my back into the seat, and all I could see was white light.

CHAPTER TWENTY-TWO

PHOENIX

THE CAR SWERVED and my head hit the side window. I held onto Sam. Eli's light was so bright, I couldn't see, but Sam wasn't wearing a seatbelt. I couldn't let her get hurt.

I blinked a few times, and when I could finally see again, Eli was leaning fully over the seat. White light flowed from Eli's hand on Sam's back onto her, spilling over her and bathing her in a pool of his power.

She let out a shuttering breath, and another tear rolled down her cheek.

I brushed it away.

"Better?" Eli asked after a moment.

She twisted enough to see him over her shoulder.

He must've seen something in her eyes that I couldn't because he sighed. "Ah. Yes. Okay. Here. One more. Don't swerve this time, Garrett."

"No, sir. I didn't know what you meant before."

"Now you do."

I held onto Sam, bracing my feet on the seat in front of us in case Garrett swerved again.

Another blast of power and light hit us, but it didn't feel as surprising as it had a second ago. And thankfully, Garrett didn't swerve this time either.

"There we are," Eli's voice cut through the light.

When I could see again, I wasn't sure what he'd done because I didn't see much of a change. Sam was still crying.

"That was it. Much better. There's nothing a moment of Heaven's Peace can't fix. Right, angel?" Eli looked at me. "Always remember what you're fighting. It's a spiritual battle, and there are many kinds of forces at work. Some of them demonic. Some of them much more subtle. If either of you or anyone working with her during something like this starts to feel down immediately after a battle, then the battle isn't over yet. You can't always see the forces at play. Go back to the basics. Put on the full armor."

Full armor? Was that like a literal thing or some kind of metaphor?

Eli grunted. "What's the full armor, angel?"

"*Buckle* of Truth. *Breastplate* of Righteousness. *Feet fitted* with the Readiness of the Gospel of Peace. *Shield* of Faith to Extinguish the Flaming Arrows of the Evil One. *Helmet* of Salvation. *Sword* of the Spirit. Be alert. Always praying."

I looked from Sam to Eli and back again.

"Ephesians six. There are more words to it, but those are the basics of battling spiritual warfare." She answered my question before I could ask it. "He made me memorize it when I was a kid." She rolled over, and Eli pulled his hand back, settling against the door again.

"Thanks," Sam said. "I got lost in the dark for a second."

"Because I spoke of your suffering," Eli said. "It's your soft spot, and the Prince of the Air took advantage of that moment and pulled you right into the darkness."

Her lip trembled for a second. "I just wish it wasn't always so hard. I'm *tired*, Eli."

"I know you are, but it's not the end yet. So, focus on the

good," Eli said. "Think of seven good things that have happened today. Hold on to them. Gratitude will get you through."

Her gaze immediately shot to me, and she gave me a sheepish smile. "Sorry."

She didn't have anything to be sorry for or ashamed of. "What for?"

"It takes a toll sometimes. I'm left feeling a little raw, and things sometimes slip in. With everything…I got lost for a second. But I'll be okay now."

A light shone down on Eli, and he turned his head up to the sky. He was quiet for a moment. "I'll be back. Call for me. Seven things, Samantha." He tapped Sam's forehead and disappeared.

"Does he do that a lot?" Tessa twisted in her seat to look at Sam.

"You mean coming and going like that?"

"Yeah. I never know when he's going to show up." Tessa was still a little pale, but she looked better than she had on the porch stairs of the yellow house.

"He's juggling a lot, and while I'm his only charge, he's often busy," Sam said. "It's why I didn't call on him. But he was right. I wouldn't have been okay if he hadn't come, stayed with me, and did his thing just now."

"What did he do exactly?" Dastien asked.

"We all saw his light," Tessa said. "But I don't know what it was exactly. And I didn't see anything wrong with you. No darkness. No demons. Nothing."

"I didn't see anything either," I said. Which felt worse because I was her anchor. I should've known if something was wrong with her. Shouldn't I?

Sam was quiet for a second. "Satan has many names. The Devil, the Morning Star, the Light Bringer. But in this realm, he's the Prince of the Air. He's not omniscient, but he's old enough to know humans really, really well. He can predict what people are thinking based on his knowledge and the frequencies of the emotions a person gives off. Which means he can manipulate literally anyone. It takes a lot of discernment to recognize what he's doing, and a lot of strength to combat it. But he's everywhere. Like the air. Weaving in and out of everything on this plane. And he can whisper in your ear without you knowing it. His thoughts can sound like your own thoughts in your head. He can flip logic until up is down and wrong is right, twisting your thoughts and guiding your actions to his ends. It's…incredibly deceptive."

"I don't like the sound of that," Max said from the front. "I don't like that at all." There were sounds of agreements from everyone in the car.

"That was the problem. The enemy doesn't like me or what I do, and when I do my thing, it's like I put a spotlight on myself for him to see. Like—*here I am. Come get me.*" She shrugged. "By doing what I do, I make him notice me. There's a cost to everything, in every way, for everyone. Physical, spiritual, and emotional. Even if you don't know it. I pay the cost for what I do—which is an extreme version of what I'm telling you—because it's worth it, but sometimes my guard isn't fully up for any number of reasons, and then I go to a dark place."

"So, you're saying we left that house that you cleared, with no demons around, and you were still under attack? And none of us noticed." The shock made my stomach turn and my heart ache. I'd thought she was just tired and emotional because of the exhaustion. It never crossed my mind that she was being spiritually attacked. Especially since I could *see* the spiritual realm.

"To be fair, I didn't even notice. Eli just knows me well enough to look for the signs. Tears are the big one. I'm not a big crier. I guess I have been lately because of the whole PTSD thing and my nightmares. But yeah. I don't usually cry because of something that Eli says. So, that was a dead giveaway. As for what Eli did? That light was Heavenly Peace. He bestowed a few moments of pure peace on me, leading me out of my dark thoughts so that I could think clearly again."

"And if he hadn't come? What would've happened?" Tessa looked as sick about it as I felt.

"I would've gotten really, truly depressed. Enough so that I wouldn't have been able to do my job tonight. Which was kind of the point." She wiped her hands down her face. Her eyes were rimmed in red, but she'd stopped crying.

That was better, but I didn't like what she'd said.

She rolled onto her back, looking up at me with her head still in my lap."It's possible that I would've shaken it off. It's also possible that I wouldn't have. That I would've gotten weaker, more tired, more hopeless, and that would've led to me making a big mistake—potentially a fatal one."

Her words sent terror rolling through every bit of my soul.

I was going to have to be careful with her. Much more observant. The learning curve here was real, but I had to get over it quickly or I could lose her. Which wasn't an option. "It must be hard to keep your guard up all the time." I brushed my hand along her cheek, letting my fingers wipe away the last of her tears.

"It's exhausting, but like you said earlier—I don't have a choice." She gave me a smile, but it was forced.

She didn't have to smile to make me feel better. I didn't want forced smiles. I wanted to earn real ones. "But you have someone to help you now." Me. I meant *me.*

"I guess I do."

I studied her and she seemed to be studying me. I'd been searching for what my next thing would be. The day I crumpled on the field in Spain, I knew I was done with soccer, but I also knew that I needed something. I was too young to be purposeless.

The last few months really felt like I was waiting for something. I didn't know for what, just *something*. I didn't need a job because I had more money than I could spend in one lifetime. But I'd felt a little lost until I saw Sam again.

Then, I watched her fight to help my sister.

Then, I saw how she struggled to save Van.

And today, something just felt right. Even in that attic, it felt like I was supposed to be there. To help her. To fight beside her. It was better and more important than anything else I'd ever done.

If I looked back at everything that had happened in my life—the hard times, the good times, soccer, the night I met Sam and had a crash course on the spiritual realm, the money that would allow for freedom to do all kinds of things, finding martial arts again, the endurance I'd gained from having a pro athlete life, the nutrition, even the way my *abuela* taught me to cook. It felt like everything before this—big and small, good and bad—had prepared me for what I'd do next.

This was it. Fighting by her side, battling evil, that was going to be my thing. "I'll be there to help you."

"I'm hoping you will—"

"No." She misunderstood me completely, and I wanted to be sure she got what I was saying. "You thought that was a question, but it wasn't. I *will* be the one by your side, fighting with you, guarding your back."

"Sure of yourself."

"Confidence is sexy." I gave her a wink.

That got a bigger laugh from her, and a scoff from the front seat.

I wished we were having this conversation with a little more privacy, but I didn't care. As long as I was with her and she was mine, everything else would work out.

"Right," she said.

I ran my thumb over her cheek. "Your color is better."

"I'll recover quickly. You're catching me at a bad time. My father has been busy, and he drains me. He's really freaking pissed at me right now. So, he's pulling at me hard. Harder than he ever has before. I'm not sure what to do about it. If there is anything to do… And I'm wondering where all this will lead. It feels endless, hopeless, and just flat-out exhausting, but—"

I had to stop her there. "Don't think about it all at once. One day at a time. One battle at a time." I looked up to find Dastien watching us. "What's the status on food? What she did back there was a lot."

He gave me a nod. "It's always shocking what she can do. It

took a group of us, plus Eli, plus some of Sam's blood to get a portal like that closed. She has to be starving."

"I'm fine, you guys. Really."

She kept saying that, but I knew she needed food. I'd seen her do the zombie-like eating thing before, and lunch had been a long time ago. "I'm assuming with the way you guys eat, the house is fully stocked?" Werewolves ate more than I'd seen anyone eat, and I'd been a professional athlete. We ate a ton.

"Yes," Garrett said from the front. "We have anything you might want."

"Great." I looked down at her again. "What do you think you want? We can pick something up on the way, but I'd like to get you settled somewhere if you're this tired."

"Honestly, I don't care. I'm too tired to have an opinion."

I got that. I really did. "Do you want to try to nap?"

"No. I don't know that I can sleep right now."

"Okay." But she didn't make a move to sit up. She just watched me, studying me. For what? I didn't know. Maybe in a few years I'd be able to read her well enough to know what she was thinking, but right now, I didn't have a clue. Not yet.

"What do you think could be taking out the wolves?" Dastien asked, changing the subject. Which was a solid distraction for Sam.

"It could be anything, really," Sam said. "I don't know how long that portal was open, but it felt like it'd been there for a while. And I have no idea what happened to the person who did the spell. Which could be a bad sign. Anyone that can work magic like that needs to be handled, one way or another."

"I didn't recognize the symbols exactly, but that was an active spell on the floor, right?" Tessa seemed much better as she leaned into her mate.

"Yep. A really good, complicated one. Definitely still active. It fought me as I tried to close it. Well, that and my father."

"We all felt it." Dastien had a bit of a rough edge to his voice. "I didn't want anything to do with him again. Once was enough.

Then, after what he did to Van, to you, and...what will it take to kill him for good?"

That was a really good question.

"I don't know. Sometimes I think he can't be killed. That's why he's trapped where he is."

"But he's gotten out before?" Max sounded worried, and I didn't blame him.

I didn't like the sound of Astaroth getting free at all.

"I don't think what Tessa and Dastien fought was him fully out. I wasn't there, so I can't say for sure, but I think what you fought was a part of him. His real essence will stay trapped in Hell until Armageddon. This is hard to explain, but sometimes he can kind of make a part of him escape. He's twisting the rules by not fully leaving. It's not fully him. It's like a surrogate monster-type thing, but when he makes that happen, the monster can fight and interact with the mortal realm."

"Man, I hope I'm not here for it if that happens again," Garret said from the front.

"Same," I said.

"Can you still *see*?" Sam asked me, drawing my attention back to her.

"Yeah."

Her brows scrunched up as she studied me. "Are you okay with that?"

I couldn't help but smile. I knew she'd been hurt so many times, but I wasn't going to hurt her. She could ask me as many times as she needed to. "I'm okay. I promise."

"Are you afraid of—"

"No." She didn't need to spill all her worries about us to the entire car. "I'm not afraid of you or what I saw you do or anything else. I promise."

I saw what I thought was hope in her eyes, and I wanted to tell her that everything would be okay, but I didn't think she'd truly hear me. Not yet anyway.

I brushed my fingers across her forehead, down her cheek. I

liked the way her eyes fluttered closed and the way she leaned into my touch.

There was something we needed to talk about, but I didn't want to do it in a car full of werewolves. And yet, if Eli was paying attention right now—and I was pretty sure he was—and if he could make this happen before we went out patrolling, then I had to talk to her now. While she was still awake. "I'm thinking about what Eli said, and I want to do it."

Her eyes opened. "You mean strengthening the anchor tie to make you stronger?"

"Yeah. I don't want to push you into something you're not ready for, but I want to be able to help you more. Watching from the sidelines is really hard for me. I know you can handle yourself, but I'd feel better if there was something more I could actually *do*, other than carrying you out of bad places. Which I feel like I'm proving to be really solid at."

She laughed. "You are an excellent carrier of me, and an amazing puller-out-of-portals guy."

"Maybe it's time for a promotion." I gave her a wink.

"You don't want to think about it for a while?"

"Nope." I didn't need to.

"Okay. If you're sure..."

"I am." *Eli, if you can hear me, make it happen.*

I glanced up at the front. "How long until we get to the house?" I asked Garrett.

His gaze flicked to the rearview mirror, meeting mine. "We've hit some traffic. Twenty more minutes, give or take."

"Cool." I looked down at Sam, who'd closed her eyes. Her head had never left my lap, and I was glad that I could be here for her today.

I wanted to be here for her every day.

I'd have to talk to her about that when we got back to Texas. Maybe I'd talk to Frank and Ana first. Get their blessing for what I wanted next.

I wasn't one to hold back my thoughts, and neither was Sam.

Which I liked. Both of us were open and honest and real, but I couldn't tell her the other thing I wanted to right now. Not just because we had so many people listening in, and what I wanted to tell her was private, but also because the timing didn't feel right. She wasn't ready to hear it yet, but she would be soon.

Holding back the things I wanted to say didn't sit well with me, but I would be patient.

I had to wait.

Because when I looked at Sam, I saw my future.

CHAPTER TWENTY-THREE

SAMANTHA

I WOKE to the sound of a bell.

A deep, rolling, tolling bell. One that went through my soul, dragging me awake.

I sat up on the bed, gasping for air, panicked, terrified, heart racing, but nothing was happening. Not that I could feel or hear. Not that I could *see.* Nothing at all.

And yet, the bell meant something was happening in the spiritual realm. It was a toll sent directly from the Heavens. A wake-up-right-now-and-get-to-work alarm.

Right. Okay. Work. I could do that.

I sat up in the bed and realized I had no clue where I was.

It was a nice room, but it wasn't familiar at all. There were no knickknacks or anything like that. It was basic with no personality—no color, no pictures, no books—but still, the furniture seemed high-end hotel nice. But it wasn't a hotel. Even in the darkness of the room, I could see that the layout meant house. The bed faced a door—an interior door, not a hotel room door. The bathroom looked too cookie-cutter residential with its white penny tile floor, basic vanity, and shower-tub combo.

It smelled clean, like the sheets and blankets covering me had been freshly laundered. I could see my bag in the corner of the room, along with my backpack and my belt bag.

The curtains on the wall next to the bed were closed, and there was no light streaming in through the cracks. It was dark out, but I knew it wasn't that late. At least it didn't feel like it was.

My phone was on the bedside table. I snagged it. 10:43 PM.

Wow. Okay. I was wrong. I'd slept a lot later than I'd thought.

The last thing I remembered, we were on the way to the pack house. So, I assumed this was it, which meant I was outside of the city, and everything should be five by five. But that bell didn't toll for nothing.

Only one way to figure out what was going on.

I threw the covers off and got up. I was still dressed in my clothes from earlier, but my shoes were missing. I didn't see them the floor anywhere. Weird.

I shoved my phone in my pocket and spent about a second looking for my shoes before deciding I didn't need them. My socks would keep me warm enough. I wasn't planning on going anywhere. I just needed to find Phoenix and the werewolves, preferably Tessa or Dastien, but honestly, any of them would be fine. Someone would know what was going on and why I'd been woken up.

I snagged my belt bag—just in case—tossing it over my head and across my body as I left the room.

I heard voices, but I couldn't make out their words. From their tone, they were having fun. Which meant there should be nothing to worry about.

Except, I still felt the bell toll echoing through my soul, urging me to get up, get ready, fight.

It'd never been wrong before.

I moved down the hallway, following the sounds of the voices, until I reached the top of a set of stairs.

I thought about texting, but I could hear Phoenix's voice. He was saying something, and someone—Tessa—laughed.

The doorbell rang, and I froze.

Everything in me screamed for me to run, which made no sense. It was just a stupid doorbell.

Except I'd been woken up by someone who wanted me ready to fight.

Oh, no.

"I'll get it," Max said, and something inside me raged.

Oh, *no.* I had a feeling I knew what was about to happen, but it was early for them. Which made no sense. But I knew better than most that evil didn't always play by the rules.

Footsteps grew louder, moving toward the door.

"No," I whispered, and I started running down the stairs. "*No*," I yelled, finally finding my full voice. "No one open that door!"

The stairs had a landing and turned a corner, ending in the entryway. Off to the left was a formal dining room with a big table. A bunch of the pack surrounded the table, which was covered in maps.

A few of the werewolves turned to me, and then I saw Phoenix. He opened his mouth to say something, but the doorbell rang again.

Max was already reaching out with his hand on the knob.

"Stop, Max! Don't open it! Those are demons!" I jumped down the last four steps, and my feet slid on the hardwood floor as I landed, and I crashed into Max.

He hit the door, which was a good thing. He couldn't open it now.

Max shot a look over his shoulder like I'd lost my mind. "No, it's not. They're just a couple of kids, Sam." He stepped back, forcing to move back, too. "They must be lost. I have to help them."

I went around Max and shoved my way between him and the door. "No. We're not opening the door."

"Have you lost your mind, Samantha?" He was nose to nose with me, eyes flashing bright. "Move."

"No." I turned, putting my back to him.

The top half of the door had frosted glass panels, and I could see two, short beings on the other side of the door. One a little taller than the other. Even though I couldn't see the faces, I knew if he answered it, there was going to be a big fight.

I didn't want to fight those things. Not again.

"What the hell, Samantha?" Max started to pick me up, but a force of power rolled through the house.

"Don't touch her." Dastien's command rolled through the pack bonds.

Max let go instantly.

"Hello?" a high-pitched voice said as it slammed its hand on the door. It sounded like a little girl, maybe four or five. She was crying, sobbing. But it was a lie.

"We need help." The doorknob jiggled. "Please, ma'am. We're so lost. Do you know where my mommy is?"

"We need help," said the little boy, who started banging on the door, too. "Will you please let us in? I need to find my mommy."

"Everyone can hear them just as well as I can," Max said. "What is your problem?"

I turned, spreading my arms wide. "Absolutely not. I do not invite demons into any houses. Ever." I glanced to the room full of werewolves. Everyone seemed to be confused, watching us with horror.

"Are you nuts? Those aren't demons. Those are *helpless children*." Max started for me.

"Stop." I held up my hand. "Don't you dare come at me again." Challenging an alpha when he was already on edge was stupid, but he had no clue how stupid he was being.

Dang it. I hated when I looked like the crazy person. I looked at Phoenix. "Help me." My gaze went to Dastien. "Someone help me *now*. I can't fight Max and the demons on the other side of this door. Get Max away from me so I can focus."

Phoenix snapped out of it first, and then Dastien. Each of them grabbed an arm and pulled Max away.

I studied the werewolves. "You guys asked me to come here for a reason. You have to trust me to do my job." I turned to the door and locked the deadbolt. "Absolutely no one is to open this door for any reason."

I faced them again, and they were still looking at me like I was insane. Well, not Phoenix, Dastien or Tessa. But everyone else.

I was getting really annoyed. The demons were begging for help and crying and banging on the door now, and the werewolves were *still* looking at me like I was the bad guy here. "Stop looking at me like I'm the bad guy. They're not kids. They're *demons.*"

I got a bunch of blank looks.

Oh, for the *love*. "I know it's hard to ignore what you're seeing, but you have to trust me. Stop thinking the worst of me when you already know you're in over your head here. I'm trying to *help you.*" Most of the werewolves still looked like they were taking their cue from Max, which made sense. Even if it was getting under my skin.

Time to prove it. Again.

I faced the door and looked at the demons through the glass. "We're not doing this your way. *Show yourselves.*" I pushed the words through both the mortal and the spiritual realm.

"Only those with eyes that see will know who we are." Their words hissed along both realms.

"I have eyes that see and ears that hear," I said along both realms. I could feel the room silent and still behind me. *"In the name of Jesus Christ, Son of the Living God, who is my King, reveal yourselves now."*

I took a step away from the door.

The figures stepped back and hissed. Even though I couldn't make out their faces through the frosted glass, I knew what I'd see. Solid, inky black eyes—the kind of darkness that breeds only death and terror.

The demon children started banging on the door and

screaming all kinds of awful things through both realms. Things that didn't need to be repeated. *Ever.*

"What the hell is happening? This doesn't make sense. Those were kids. They're kids." Max muttered under his breath. He tried to break free from from Dastien and Phoenix to get closer.

I held out my hand to stop him from trying. "Listen, guys. I told you they were demons. By definition, demons are deceptive." I turned to Max. "You asked me to come, risk my life when I'm already not fully recovered from my last fight, and then you won't listen to me? I'm wondering why I'm here." I scanned the room again.

A few of them looked away. Some looked confused. But I needed them all to understand that if they didn't get it, I couldn't work with them.

"I don't want to have to prove myself to you when we go on patrol tonight. You didn't believe me outside of the yellow house. You saw one of your own being controlled by a demon, and I saw your faces. Some of you still didn't believe me until it was over. It's nighttime now. We're going to go out there and patrol soon, so I need this to be the last time I have to show you what's really there for you to listen to me. I can't always take the time. When I say something is demonic, you have to trust me and do what I say, and even if what you're seeing or hearing doesn't make sense with what I'm saying."

"I'm sorry. I..." Max looked down, not meeting my gaze.

"I get it. I'm different. I can see things you can't. That's why I'm here. But seriously, Max. I don't want anyone patrolling with me who doesn't get this. If I can't count on you to listen to me in the safety of this house, then I really can't trust you out there."

I looked at Dastien, and he gave me a nod. "I'm sorry," he said. "I should've acted faster. This is on me. I'm the Alpha here, and I know you. I trust you with everything I have. I will make sure that everyone with you is on the same page."

"Thanks." I tried to reel in my anger because so many of the guys here were new to me, but Max wasn't. And he was the one that had fought me the most.

"For the record, for anyone new to working with me, you don't invite evil inside. Even if it's not your home. Sometimes the invitation to come inside sticks with you, not the location. You don't want one of those demons following you home." I took a breath. Something niggled in the back of my brain. Something I was forgetting. I had to—

"Wait." I glanced at my watch. "It's early for them. I don't get how..."

I needed to talk to them.

I took off running through the house.

CHAPTER TWENTY-FOUR

SAMANTHA

I SHOVED THROUGH THE WEREWOLVES, forcing them apart to let me through. I needed a back door. A side door. Some way out of this place other than the front door.

And I needed to get there before the Black-Eyed Children left.

To the right was a formal living room with two couches facing each other, some arm chairs, and a fireplace.

Beyond that, through a doorway, I could see a hallway and steps up to a kitchen and what might be a great room.

"Where are you going?" Phoenix asked as he kept pace beside me. "Talk to me."

"It can't be a coincidence they're here at this house tonight when I'm here and fighting evil. They're early. They never come before witching hour. It's not their pattern. Which means they have to want something from me in particular."

Beyond the informal living room were French doors to the backyard.

Bingo.

I flipped the lock. "Last person out closes this door. No one outside who doesn't have my back. Those are my rules."

I stepped into the backyard, and my socks were instantly damp. I hated the feeling of wet socks. It must've rained while I slept. Whatever. Soggy socks weren't going to hurt me.

Phoenix walked beside me. "What are those things?"

"Evil. One sec," I whispered. "I'll explain more, but I want to catch them before they run." I moved around the side of the house, and found a gate in the fence leading to the front yard. That was a relief. I could climb a fence, but I wasn't very graceful at it.

I rounded the house and slowed down to a walk. They were still banging on the door, trying to terrorize the people still in the house. The Black-Eyed Children fed on fear. But I wasn't afraid of them.

I stopped ten feet shy of them. "You're early today," I said.

They turned to me in unison, dropping the whole screaming vulgarities act. "We have a message for you, daughter of Astaroth," the girl said, her voice was reedy and haunting.

That was new. The last time I ran into some Black-Eyed Children, I'd spent weeks chasing them around the city. I'd expected them to run, but a message from a Black-Eyed Child? That had never happened before.

They had my full attention. "Do you?"

"We do," the boy said.

I could sense everyone gathering behind me, waiting, watching to see if I needed help, but I wouldn't. They might try to leap at me, but if they did, I'd open a portal and close it. They'd get sucked down, and that would be that. I just had to maintain distance between us. "Alright. What is it that you want to tell me?" I crossed my arms as I stared down at the demons.

They took a step forward. "Gabe sent us to you."

I dropped my arms to my sides, and my heart fell through the floor.

A flash of him yelling for me rang through my mind and his voice commanding me to run.

I blinked, pushing the memory away. I swallowed down the

fear and guilt. That was what they wanted from me, and I was giving it to them. I had to stop.

They both grinned, revealing tiny, pointy teeth, and the fact that they could taste the wave of fear and shame that had just coursed through me.

I didn't like it, but there wasn't anything I could do about that. "What does Gabe want me to know?" I asked, while taking a step back.

"He says that you need not look for him. He will come when he is able." The girl stepped closer to me. "But we'd love it if you'd try." Her voice dipped deeper with that, and I wasn't sure I wanted to know more.

"That's it?"

"He also said to tell you that you're about to be in a very dangerous spot. Your past is catching up to you."

My past? What part of it? Did he mean my father?

The boy laughed. "You can trust us. We're very good. If you let us in the house, we'll protect you from *him*."

Nope. I wasn't an idiot. I wasn't sure if *him* meant my father, Gabe, or something else, and I wasn't going to let them in so I could find out.

"Are you sure Gabe sent them?" Dastien asked from somewhere behind me.

"No." I'd heard Gabe yelling for me today when I was closing the portal, but that could've been my father. Or really any other demon that could mimic voices. Demons lied like it was their life. There was no way I'd trust any demon, aside from Gabe. "But Gabe's sent a demon with a message before. A long time ago. Just not this kind. Usually it's a lesser demon." And if Gabe sent them, there would be some sort of proof.

"How do I know Gabe sent you?"

They took another step toward me. "He said if you asked, to tell you that he's not in a cage anymore."

"That's not proof of anything. Try again." I was sure everyone in Hell knew Gabe had been in the cage. The demons loved to torment the caged souls.

"He said to say that when he found you the first time, you were in the house, hiding in a nook in your father's *play* room."

Play room?

Oh. Right. They meant his *torture* chamber.

That was accurate. That was exactly where I met Gabe for the first time. What I didn't know was if my father knew that, too. He pretty much knew everything that happened in his realm, so I wasn't sure this proved anything either.

"He said to tell you to watch for the hag. She's the key. You have to find your past and that will lead you to where you must go. But be careful. Danger lies where even you cannot see it." These words were said only along the spiritual plane, and I wasn't sure I believed them either.

I wasn't even sure what they meant.

What the heck was a hag?

Could I trust anything they said?

They'd only said it along the spiritual realm, which meant they didn't want the werewolves to hear it. But why?

Wait a second. If this was really from Gabe, then they'd know our code word. "What's the password?"

They shared a look, and I knew they didn't have one.

This conversation was officially over, and whatever warning they said along spiritual plane about a hag and my past was garbage. I didn't know what they really wanted, but I was done with them.

I started to pull power, but they leaped, slamming me into the ground.

"Stay back!" I yelled at the werewolves as I kicked them off me. "You can see them, but you can't fight them. They're not of this realm." The wolves would only make it harder for me to find a window to open a portal.

I had to push them back and away from me so that I didn't accidentally get caught in the portal with them. Which they knew.

Every time I'd push one back, the other would attack.

Nails scraped my arm, but I ignored the pain. I had to focus.

I heard Dastien yelling advice to me, but I wasn't focusing on the words. I knew what I was doing. Mostly. I'd been trained, but positioning them so I could send them to Hell was proving to be harder than I expected.

Which, of course, it was. I hadn't been training. My limbs felt heavier than usual, and I was slow. So freaking slow.

The boy punched my side, and something inside me gave way.

Son of a mother. That was going to bruise.

The girl's nails swiped too close to my face, and I dropped to the ground.

The girl pounced on me before I could roll away from her. She punched through my stomach.

The side hit and the stomach punch were spiritual hits. I saw the red lines linking us together. Demonic ties. That was why it felt like something gave way inside me.

A wave of pain and sorrow hit me so hard that for a moment, I couldn't move.

"Get *up*, Sam." Phoenix's voice cut through everything else. "Break the ties."

I knew I needed to do that, but everything hurt, and my soul was screaming, and—

Wait. I could use this.

I could use the ties.

I kipped up and gripped the demonic ties in my hands, twisting them until I had the demons under my control.

"Don't let me fall, Nix!" I yelled, reaching a hand back behind me, trusting Phoenix to keep me safe.

"*Aperta*!" I opened a portal under the girl, and she fell, screaming, grabbing onto the robes of the boy.

He screamed awful things at me, gripping the tie between us, dragging me with him.

I started to lose my balance.

I saw the demons below. The fire. The hordes. Everything.

I was too close. Way too close to the edge.

The tie jerked hard, and I fell. "Oh shi—"

A hand gripped mine, hard, and then an arm wrapped around my waist, tugging me back. "Burn the ties, Sam," Phoenix said in my ear. "Now."

I sent a burst of power, and the ties snapped.

The Black-Eyed Boy fell, screaming down the whole way, following where its fellow demon went.

Phoenix tugged me up against him. "Close it."

"*Claudere*!" I blew out a breath and crumpled against him for a moment. "Well, that sucked, and this is why I never miss a day with Chris. Even if I'm weak. Fuck that was closer than it should've been." I winced. "Dang it. I cussed." Man, that meant I was still tired, which made sense since my breaths were still coming fast.

Phoenix laughed. "Don't worry about the curse. You're fine." He squeezed me tighter. "You got it done, and that's the important part."

I leaned back so that I could peek up at him because I remembered one important thing. "Wait. You could see their ties. You can still see everything?"

He nodded. "Yeah. I was going to ask you about that. I have a question when…" He motioned with his chin to all the werewolves watching us.

Right. He didn't want an audience.

Interesting that it stuck around, though. I was going to *try* to not pick things apart, but it should've faded by now. I'd have to wait to talk to him about it when there weren't so many people watching us.

I stepped away from Phoenix just enough that I could turn and look at him. "Thank you."

"No problem." He studied me, searching me to see if I was hurt, but I didn't think I was.

"I'm fine."

He gave me a nod. "I think you are, but babe, you're shortening my life every time you almost fall through a portal."

"I don't do it on purpose."

He raised a brow, as if to say that he didn't think that was a thing. "You have a good nap?"

I took a breath, giving myself time to assess. "Yeah. I guess I did."

"Excuse me, but what the fuck was that?" Max stepped through the wolves, his eyes wolf-bright blue.

I wasn't going to apologize for saving his butt. "Those were Black-Eyed Children, who get their name from their soulless, inky-black-as-night eyes. They always come looking like children, but the story for why they need help can change—they've been in an accident or the house burned down or they're lost or their parents left them alone—they'll say whatever it takes to get someone to open the door. It's always dead of night, that was how I knew something was up. It's not witching hour yet."

"What would've happened if I opened the door?"

I shrugged. "They either would've killed everyone in the house, or tortured and then killed us all. Sometimes they hide in houses, tormenting the inhabitants, making them crazy, afraid, getting them to fight amongst themselves before they kill them, but that's rare. Chris, Cosette, and I spent weeks chasing a group of them down a year ago, and it was a mess."

I scanned the wolves. "Any other questions?"

No one spoke up, and as I stood there, I realized there were *a lot* more wolves here than had been with us at the yellow house.

And now it was time to get back to work. Wait—why were there so many wolves here? I scanned them, and it looked like *all* the Wayfarers were here. "Did you guys call in *everyone* to patrol, or what?"

"Not quite." Tessa wore black leggings, a black hoodie, and black running shoes—her ready-to-fight outfit. "We still have more on standby, but Dastien and I talked while you were sleeping, and we agreed. You can't get hurt. We called in everyone we could and are patrolling as a pack tonight. No splitting up."

Okay. That was fine by me. "When do you want to leave?" I needed a few minutes, but I could be ready pretty quick.

"That depends on you. We have some time before the most active part of the night."

I glanced at my watch. She was right. We had two or three hours before the veil was fully thin.

"You did your usual sleep-eating thing, but you slept for a little while after that." She studied me, and I wasn't sure what she saw. I hadn't looked in the mirror. "We didn't want to wake you up, but now that you're up, are you hungry?"

I thought about it. "I could eat."

"Great," Dastien said. "The pack should eat anyhow. Safer for everyone." Dastien had a point. Nobody wanted to be around a hungry werewolf. "We eat a late meal, and then we start patrolling the streets. We can do that on foot or in the car, but I think car is better so we can cover more ground. If you see anything, we pull over. Take care of it. What do you think?"

That was smart. "Sounds good. A meal out is fine, as long as we can have some sort of private room somewhere. There are a lot of us, and it makes it easier for me."

"And protein heavy," Tessa added.

Garrett was local. He might know a place that would fit those needs. I spotted him in the crowd. "You think you know a spot that would work?"

He thought for a second. "You know what, if this place I'm thinking of is still around, then yes. I do. Otherwise, I can figure something out." He pulled his phone out of his pocket and started typing.

"Great." My stomach growled. "Apparently, I'm hungry." I paused. Now that I was thinking about a plan, I had another idea. "Patrolling works for now, but I need to find the root of the problem, and our best bet is finding whoever was living in that house.

The one with the portal." I looked at Dastien. "Did you ever find them?"

"We've been working on that," Dastien said. "We know the name of the owners—a young couple and their four-year-old son—but we haven't been able to find them, yet. The mom is from here. The most likely place to look for them would be her parent's house, but there's no record of her parents owning a house here. It's possible that my assumption is wrong and the family is staying with someone else or maybe they've left the area entirely. We have numbers for them, but they're not answering any of their phones when we call. I could track their phones, but that would break a few laws. So, I'm hoping we can save that as a last resort type of deal."

I didn't want to break any laws at all, so yeah, that was fine with me. "So, it's a dead end."

"Not necessarily. My guy's still digging around. It could be that her parents are renting or they moved or maybe they bought a house under a trust. We found out where they work, but it's after hours. Asking coworkers for information will have to wait until the morning."

"What about social media?"

"Either they're super locked down or they're anti social media." Tessa shrugged. "We're hitting dead ends, but we're not giving up. We'll find them. For now, all we have is patrolling."

I pressed my hand to my stomach. I had a bad feeling about those people. They couldn't have just disappeared, unless they were dead. Or worse. Possessed.

But I kept thinking about the toys on that living room floor—scattered about, well-loved, but now abandoned.

There was a little kid somewhere who needed my help.

Kids—younger ones especially—could be really susceptible to demonic attacks.Their souls were still too transitory, not fully enmeshed in the mortal realm.

I hoped he was okay, but there was nothing I could do until we found them. "Well, then, patrolling is what we'll do. With a portal that size open for who knows how long, it should be a pretty active witching hour. I'll take care of anything we find as we go, but I'm hoping we don't run into whatever is killing your wolves until we find whoever opened that portal. I can't send the monster back to Hell only to have that person open another portal to bring the monster back through. But angrier. And focused on revenge."

A few of the werewolves made noises at that. I knew they just wanted me to find whatever it was and kill it, but I had to prepare them for the fact that it might not be that easy.

I didn't have anything else to say, so I started for the back door again.

As soon as I stepped onto the wood floor, I could feel how incredibly wet my socks were. I pulled them off and moved through the house. "I'll be right back."

I needed new socks. Shoes. And to refill my belt bag.

Actually, I should bring my whole backpack.

I started prepping as soon as I got to the room. I made sure everything in my belt bag was restocked, then I moved things around in my backpack so that I could reach whatever I needed quickly. I'd almost finished zipping up my bags when I changed my mind.

I dug through the backpack, pulling out a small glass jar filled with my own invention of salt, selenite powder, sage dust, and falling ash from a priests' incense thurible. The dust burned demons as if they were glowing bits of embers, and if things got dicy, it was an effective way to make demons scatter. One microscopic grain on them and *poof,* they were gone.

When I finished, I went to my suitcase, which was still sitting by the door to my room. I knocked it onto its back and knelt down to dig through it without destroying my neat packing job.

Someone knocked on the open door. "Hey," I said to Phoenix.

"Hey." He held out my shoes. "I brought you these. I put them by the door but figured you'd need them."

"Thanks." I reached up, taking them from him. "With all the

drama I didn't have to a chance to make sure everything was okay while I slept?"

"Yeah. The guys are all really nice. Good group. A bunch more of the pack showed up. I guess the stuff in the yellow house has some of them on edge." He leaned on the door jamb while he looked down at me. "The pack doc gave you an IV, but you didn't wake up for it. That kind of worried me, but your mom said it was fine."

"You called my mom?" I winced. Man. She was going to be so mad at me. I definitely should've called her when we landed, and probably after the whole portal thing. But calling—or even texting—hadn't crossed my mind.

"Yeah. Sorry," he said, but he didn't look or sound too sorry. "She wants a call back."

Okay. I could do that. But I knew she was going to rip into me for not keeping her updated on how I was doing.

I sat back on my heels. "I'm sorry I worried you. My mom gives me IVs while I sleep all the time. It's fine. I think I'm just used to it now."

"Got it." He blew out a breath, and from the way he was standing, I could tell he was worried about something.

He stepped into the room and closed the door behind him. "I heard what those demons said," he whispered softly. "Something about a hag and your past, but you didn't tell anyone else. I only heard it because I still have your *sight.*"

"Right," I whispered back. "I mean, I guess I should tell them, but I just don't know that it's going to turn out to be anything. I don't want to give them hope at finding some clue. They've lost family this week, and giving false hope feels cruel."

"So, you think they were lying?"

"I don't know. Honestly. But if it turns out to be something, I'll tell them right away. I'm not ruling it out, I'm just taking it with a massive grain of salt."

"Got it. I'll try to keep an eye out for anything hag-like, too."

"Sounds good."

There was a look on his face that I couldn't read, but it worried me. "What else is wrong?"

"Nothing's wrong," he said, still whispering. "But I was wondering if you thought Eli already made me able to see the spiritual realm permanently?"

It was possible, but Eli hadn't told me he was going to do that. But that didn't mean anything. Eli did a ton of things without asking or giving me all—or sometimes any—of the information. I hoped this wasn't one of those times, but it could be. It definitely could be.

My stomach dropped as I realized why he might be asking about this. Did he want it gone? And if he did, what did that mean for us?

I was going to be sick. "I don't know. I guess it's possible." I looked away because I couldn't afford to lose it when he asked me to fix it for him. I didn't want to cry. "If you want, I could call Eli down to see if he could take it away, but I'm not sure—"

"No." He squatted down in front of me and reached for my hand. "You're misunderstanding me or I'm not being clear, but don't panic on me." He gave me a tilted smile and just a little peek of his dimple. "I told him I wanted it, but I—"

"Just because you thought you wanted it doesn't mean you can't change your mind, and I can—"

"Stop. Absolutely not." He gave my hand three quick squeezes. "Take a breath."

I shook my head. "But if you—"

"I'm not him. I'm Phoenix. The guy that has dreamed of you for years, that is amazed at what you do. The guy who pulls you out of portals and will continue to do so. Although, maybe if you could be more careful, that would save my heart. For real."

"I'm so confused right now."

"That's because you're used to people lashing out at you and freaking out. Even your best friend freaked out about it earlier today. Tessa was a disaster in the attic. So, I get why you're worried. But I'm not going to freak out. I'm not changing my mind. But you need time to see that I'm different, so I'm not hurt or upset by your assumption that I want anything fixed." His voice was even and calm and it made everything in me settle. "I like being able to see what you see. I just wondered if it was possible that Eli made it permanent already. And if not, if we could make it permanent. If you'd be okay with that."

"Are you sure?" I was so in for permanent with him, but a part of me clearly kept waiting for him to bail. I had to stop thinking that way.

He was right. I was used to everyone freaking out when they saw what I saw. Or sometimes, just freaking out because I said I could see what I saw. So, this felt so weird.

And yet, it was everything I'd ever wanted.

"I'm not going anywhere. I thought maybe you'd be upset that you're stuck with me, but judging from your panic attack right now, you're as just afraid of me leaving as I am of you wanting me gone."

I laughed. "I'm the worst. I'm sorry. I keep expecting you to bail, and that's not fair."

"Maybe not, but you have a really traumatic past, and we're going to work through that. So, we're good. But maybe the next time Eli comes, we ask him to make it permanent. And maybe we can also ask about those extras. I know we talked about it in the car, but I just want to confirm now that you're a little more rested. Is that still okay with you?"

"I mean…yeah. But are you really sure that's what you want?"

"Absolutely." He leaned into me, and his lips brushed against mine. Softly. Briefly. And then he stood and took a step back from me. "I'll be downstairs. The temperature has dropped a bit. You were shivering out there, so don't forget your coat." He opened the door and tapped a hand on the door jamb before turning and walking away.

I stood there frozen. In shock. "Okay," I said, but he was already gone.

What in God's green Earth just happened?

I… I really thought he was asking me to get rid of it, and it was extremely disorienting to have him say the exact opposite thing.

When had I become so distrusting of people? Sure, I had good reasons, but I'd half-expected Phoenix to bail on me after this week. More than half-expected it. *Fully* expected it. Even though he kept telling me over and over that he was staying.

Man. I was such a moron.

I fully loved the guy. Why hadn't I told him that?

And more importantly, why hadn't I kissed him back?

CHAPTER TWENTY-FIVE

PHOENIX

I WALKED down the stairs of the rental house. I didn't have to look at the faces staring at me to know they'd heard Sam and I talking upstairs. I didn't think they'd overheard about what the Black-Eyed Children had said because no one questioned me, and Tessa and Dastien weren't asking for more intel.

Unfortunately, their awkward glances told me they'd heard the part about how I could still see everything and how Sam wanted to know if I wanted out.

The latter was what annoyed me. Not because she'd asked. I understood why. But I'd tried to keep the conversation short because I didn't want to expose all of Sam's insecurities to everyone. And yet, when she took everything the absolute worst way, I had to tell her what I was really asking.

Still, I'd said more than I planned. I hoped she wouldn't be upset when she came downstairs and realized how much they heard. Although, this was her world. She might already be fully aware.

I hit the last stair and gave the silent werewolves a nod.

Tessa broke off from the group surrounding the dining table to approach me. "How is she?"

"She's going to be fine." I'd make sure of it. "I think she's weaker than she wants us to know, but the sleep did her a lot of good. Her color is back. She'll get it done for you guys."

"I wasn't worried about that part. Somehow she always does, even when the cost is impossibly high. I worry about her, though." She studied me for a second. "How are you?"

Oh, no. I wasn't answering that with so many people listening. "Good. What's going on over there?" I motioned to the group huddled around the dining room table.

Tessa looked at Dastien, who was standing with Max at the head of the table. A map laid across the table. Circles in brightly colored marker flowing across the map with no real pattern that I could discern.

"They're finalizing the plan for patrolling," Tessa said. "There was some debate about whether to add this incident to the map, but we decided it only happened because Sam is here. So, at least we agree on that much. And Garrett is finding a restaurant that has a private room that's willing to stay open late." She motioned to Garrett, who was currently pacing in the living room while talking to someone on his cell.

"Cool. Sam's gathering her things. I think she'll be ready in a few."

"Got it. I'll go hurry them along." She spun without waiting for any kind of reply, and I was left at the foot of the stairs, not knowing what to do next.

I rubbed my hand over my hair. I'd cut it short a few weeks ago, and it was getting longer. Time was passing, and I was left feeling like the ground was a little shaky under my feet.

A group of werewolves on the living room couches were all staring at me. They seemed to want something from me or they were waiting to see if I would say anything, but I didn't have anything for them. No reassurances. Nothing. I was used to people looking to me for direction on the field, but this felt different. Heavier. Probably due to the danger factor.

I was a little out of my depth, so I took the easiest out I could think of. "I'm going to go grab a water." I pointed to the kitchen, mostly so that I could break this awkward silent stare-off.

The rental's kitchen was smaller than the one in my Austin house but bigger than the one at the Sanctuary. It was all white and cream tones, with very little color and zero personality. Not my thing, but It was at least clean and well-stocked with pans and utensils.

The werewolves had packed the giant fridge full of food—both ready-made and things to cook meals. I noticed there wasn't any alcohol in there, not that I wanted any—I wasn't big on that—but it surprised me with so many guys here. Not a single beer. But when I'd asked, they said their bodies burned through alcohol so fast they couldn't feel the effects. It was a waste of money.

Which made sense. But, as I leaned on the island, one beer would be nice right now. Maybe not as good for me as the water I'd grabbed from the fridge, but something to settle me down wouldn't be a bad thing.

There was an antsy feeling in my stomach that I didn't like. I wasn't sure why it was there. I took a drink of water and closed my eyes.

It wasn't that she hadn't kissed me back. I knew I'd shocked and surprised her, but we were taking it slow. I didn't want to rush her at all, and at the same time, I wasn't backing down. Ever.

But I was feeling things she wasn't ready for. I wanted to sprint to the finish line—ring, wedding, everything.

Holy shit, Phoenix. Get a grip. I had no chill when it came to her.

It'd been no time at all, and yet, because of the extreme situations, I already knew what kind of person she was. She knew who I was. And life was short. I didn't want to wait.

I would because that was the logical thing to do, but everything in me screamed to hold on to her, lock her in with a ring, and never let her go.

My phone buzzed in my pocket, and I checked it.

I was a text from Win. *I have big news. Stop sending me to voicemail. When can you talk?*

I wanted to text back *never*, but that would've been rude. She'd done a lot for me and my career, and she deserved better than that.

I thought about it for a second. I could call her now, but I truly didn't want to. Not with everyone listening, and I wasn't sure how long I'd have to talk anyhow. *I'll call you in a few days. I'm still taking some time off.*

Okay, but the deal I've got for you is good. They're not going to wait around for an answer forever. We have to talk soon.

Her pushing me to answer wasn't going to work on me. *If you ask me right now, I don't want any deal.*

You can't be serious, Nix. This is insane. You're being crazy right now, and you're going to regret it. You won't be able to come back from this.

She stopped texting, and that was a good thing. I was mostly ignoring all texts and calls. My phone was on do not disturb at all times, but Win's texts came through, as did all of my mom and sisters, and Ana and Frank's, too. I'd added them to my favorites, as well as Sam. Although, I hadn't ever texted Sam.

Maybe that should change. I wondered what she'd do if I started flirting with her via text. That sounded like fun.

I tapped a new message and started typing her name, but my phone buzzed in my hand.

Win's name flashed on the screen, and I blew out a breath. Procrastinating on this wasn't working. I had to face Win or she'd never stop bugging me about this. "Yeah?" I said.

"Is that any way to answer the phone?"

She was right. Even though I told her I didn't want to speak right now, being rude wasn't okay. "Sorry, Win. What's up?" I looked at my watch, wondering how long Sam was going to hide in her room.

Maybe a coffee would draw her out. I'd seen that they had her essentials already stocked, which Tessa had told me was standard when she came on trips with them. Apparently, there was a list that Ana sent around with all of the things Sam might need when traveling. Whatever pack was hosting her always made sure they stocked what she needed. Tessa offered to add anything I wanted on this list if I planned to join Sam regularly. Which was really nice of Tessa.

If we were staying up late, a coffee wasn't a bad idea. Sam might really need the caffeine boost.

I searched the cabinets for a to-go cup.

"Are you listening to me?" Win asked.

"No. I was zoning. Sorry. It's not a great time but tell me what you have for me."

"You have a very generous offer. Three years. Twenty mil Euros a year. You agree to play, I think there's room to go a little up on that."

The top cabinets were all a bust. Maybe they'd be in the bottom ones, but that was so not where I'd put them. It wasn't my house, though. Worth checking.

"Are you listening to me, Nix? We're talking over sixty million in US dollars for three years of playing."

That was a lot of money, but I didn't need it. Who wanted to pay me that much after an injury? "For?"

"Madrid."

She was right. It was a good deal. Their team was awesome, and it was a generous offer. "I don't know, Win." I honestly didn't need the money. Was that more than my last contract? A little, but not that much. And I hadn't really spent any of that money. I wasn't lying to the werewolves when I told them I was just managing my investment accounts now.

"What's not to know?"

I searched the island and found a cabinet on one side that had storage containers and insulated cups.

Jackpot.

"Nix!"

"Sorry. I'm in the middle of something." Maybe she wouldn't consider it important, but I liked doing nice things for Sam. "I don't know if I want to play again."

Her sigh echoed in my ear. "Listen. I talked to your mom and your physical therapist. They say your knee is fine."

"It is." I filled the cup with ice. "*Mostly*. I'm still babying it a little. I'm wearing my brace when I train and doing some stretches, but it's fine." Was it as good as before? Probably not. Did it matter? Again, probably not. I was still faster and better than almost every professional player out there.

I tucked the phone between my shoulder and poured in the coconut-almond milk, then the cold brew—her favorite brand. I added two stevias.

Spoon. I need a spoon. Which drawer was the silverware in?

"Are you even listening to me?"

Ah-ha. Found a spoon. "Not really." I wasn't trying to be rude, and I knew she really cared about me. Well, also about making money from my deals. So, she wasn't completely altruistic.

She made a little screech in my ear, and I laughed. "Sorry. I'm not trying to be difficult. It's a no for me. I'm done playing."

"Why? You are amazing to watch." She'd never said that before, but I didn't think she was buttering me up. She sounded genuine and more than a little flabbergasted. "You might think I say that to all my clients, but I mean it with you. I don't get it. What's happened to you? How can you walk away from everything you worked your ass off to achieve?"

I'd told her no so many times now, but she wasn't taking no for an answer. It was time to lay it all out for her. That didn't mean she'd accept it, but this was how it was going to be. "You know what I felt when my knee blew?" I put the lid on the cup for Sam.

"What?"

"Relief." I set the cup aside and leaned back against the counter. I snagged the phone from the crook of my neck, stretching out a cramp that had started there. "I mean—sure, pain. But relief so strong it shocked me. I didn't realize I was burning out, but I was. I am. I'm tired of all the travel, and the grueling pace and the fans. You have one off day, play with a cold or when you're tired or are anything other than perfect, and they're just vicious. Throwing things at my car. Yelling at me when I'm trying to do anything around the city. I don't need that shit. It's just *work,* you know? I'm too old for this, Win. There's tons of young kids ready and dying for a chance to take my spot. Find the next great player. Give them the spotlight."

"Damn it, Nix." Her voice was resigned, and I was relieved she was finally getting it.

Suddenly, I was glad I'd answered the call. She needed to hear me. "I'm sorry. My heart just isn't in it anymore."

"This is because of the demon girl." I didn't appreciate her tone or her calling Sam a *demon girl,* but I got it. She'd been talking to my mom, and I was turning down a huge paycheck. It didn't make sense to her.

"I wish I could say this was all because of Samantha, but it's not." Was it? "I mean—maybe I could've been convinced before I ran into her again, mostly because I was bored. But…" I laughed, thinking back to what happened over the last week. "I'm definitely not bored anymore."

"So, what? You're going to be a househusband now? Go all domestic?"

She meant for it to be emasculating, but it wasn't. In this context, it actually sounded great. "Why is that a bad thing?"

"For someone with your talent? Are you joking? It's *criminal.*"

I pulled the phone away from my ear until she stopped yelling at me.

"Okay. Fine. You don't want to play. I've got every major network begging to have you as a commentator. Especially since you're trilingual."

I could actually speak five languages, but I wasn't about to remind her. "That's still a lot of travel, Win. I'm over it."

"What if we got the schedule down? You could record from a studio and not actually be at all the games. If you move back to

LA, I can get this sorted no problem. Zero travel. Zero practices. You'd just be working a handful of days a month. How many games do you think you could commit to per year?"

I leaned back against the counter and shook my head. She was going to hate my answer. "None."

I winced at her cussing, and I spotted Tessa peeking around the corner. I gave her a wink. I wasn't sure how long she'd been listening to the conversation, but she was Sam's best friend. I didn't mind her hearing.

It was a good thing she couldn't hear Win's side of the conversation, though.

"You've only known her for like a week, and you're giving up everything for her." The shock—and maybe beginnings of outrage—was peeking through Win's voice.

I didn't expect her to get it, but she was going to have to respect my decision.

Or not. "Yep. That's exactly what I'm doing." Max came around the corner to stare at me. It didn't take a genius to read the disappointment and jealousy on his face. The guy clearly had a thing for Sam, but she was absolutely clueless. I had a feeling she was going to leave a trail of broken hearts when the wolves realized she was taken for good.

"No hesitation?" Win asked.

More werewolves filed into the kitchen.

Oh shit. Could they hear both sides of the conversation?

Damn it.

They were intimidating as they lined up on the other side of the island to stare at me, not hiding that they'd apparently been listening in the whole time.

"Sixty million?" Max whisper-shouted to me.

I shrugged. "One sec, Win." I put the phone on mute for a second. "It was a little more before, but I'm injured now. Add in my sponsorships, and money isn't a problem." I turned off the mute button and put the phone to my ear. "Sorry, Win. I'm not alone right now. What was your question?"

"Hesitations? You're giving up a lot, Nix. And I want to be sure you know what you're doing. What if this thing with demon girl doesn't work out? I wouldn't want you to do anything you'd regret."

"Her name is Samantha."

"Fine. Whatever."

I shoved down the frustration, trying to keep calm even though I knew Win was trying to piss me off. "No, Win. No hesitations or doubts. This is it for me. I know it might not make sense to you, but I'm fully aware of what I'm giving up. And I'm okay with it. I don't need more money or fame or any of it. I've had it all. Now, I want a life with Sam."

I studied the werewolves gathered around the island. They were a protective bunch. I liked that for Sam, but I wasn't going to be intimidated. Not by my agent, and certainly not by them.

"Damn it, Nix. You love her, don't you?" She sounded surprised, but I wasn't. Sam was easy to love. Literally the easiest thing I'd ever done in my life.

"Yes." I looked at Tessa. Her eyes were so wide I almost started to laugh. The only thing that stopped me was that she might tell Sam. Which could not happen.

I shook my head at Tessa and then at all of them. "Don't you dare tell her," I whispered as softly as I could, knowing that they'd hear me.

Tessa shook her head, and mimed zipping her lips shut, locking them, and tossing the key.

A wave of power came from her as she whispered something I couldn't hear. The power ran like lightning through the pack ties—thick and thin, but all glowing—and the werewolves bent their heads in submission.

Tessa gave me a wink and a thumbs up, and I knew she'd made it so that they wouldn't tell Sam either.

"Your mom doesn't like her. Didn't you tell me that was a dealbreaker for you? It was an issue with the girl you dated before Mel."

I sighed, staring at the ground. The rest of the wolves didn't need to hear this. I waved a hand to make them go away, but they didn't budge.

Fine. Just fine. I didn't need fake privacy. They'd hear me no matter where I was.

"It's not a dealbreaker. Not for Sam. It would be nice, but my mom doesn't understand what Samantha went through. She just remembers the crazy, dangerous neighbor girl fresh out of a psych ward and who almost got me arrested a few weeks later. Mom loves to hold a grudge, but she doesn't believe me about what really happened that night, and trust me, Sam isn't crazy. Not even a little bit. And she's not after my money, so don't even try that one."

Win was quiet for so long that I pulled the phone away from my face to make sure the call hadn't dropped, but she was still there.

"Look, Win. I appreciate everything you've done for me, but I think I'm done with the game. I've got some other things that I'm interested in, and I'm going to pursue that."

"Her. You mean her."

"Yeah." I was trying to be vague.

"If it doesn't work out with her, if you change your mind, you get bored, call me. We can get you a job commentating. If you don't like that, we get you coaching somewhere amazing. You want to go into movies or reality TV or whatever, I've got connections there, too. Everyone wants a piece of you."

Maybe that was true, maybe she was exaggerating, but either way, I didn't care. The only person who was going to get a piece of me was Samantha.

Win didn't get it. No one would, but the good thing was that no one else needed to understand. I was the only one who needed to. It was my life, and I was firm in my decision.

"Thanks, Win. I appreciate your support, but I'm going to be okay."

"One more thing before you go. I'm putting down the agent persona for now. On a more personal level."

I couldn't imagine what else she wanted. It felt like we'd covered everything, "What's that?"

"Mel."

Oh, just fucking perfect. With all the wolves listening. "No. I'm not doing this."

"She doesn't get what went wrong or why you broke up."

Max crossed his arms, and I knew this was going to come back to bite me in the butt.

I stared at the ground, wishing they'd at least give me the illusion of privacy, but whatever. "I tried to explain it, but Mel didn't get it. Trust me, there's no window left open there. If you want to be a good friend to her, then tell her to move on."

She blew out a breath. "Look, Nix. I'm worried about you. You're shutting out everything in your life. Your family, your fiancé—"

The wolves all leaned in, and Tessa let out a high-pitched, "What?"

I rolled my eyes at her. I'd never seen people listening in so blatantly to an obviously private conversation. "That's not true. She wasn't my fiancé. I never asked her to marry—"

"Fine. Whatever. You had the ring. She found it. What the hell is up with that, Nix?"

I winced because I didn't know she'd seen it, and I was sorry I hadn't hidden it well enough.

"That screams intent to propose," Win continued. "You're walking away from everything. For what? I'm honestly worried about you. Are you mentally okay?"

I looked around the room and shook my head, hoping they'd keep what I said next between us. I wanted to wave my hands at them to get them to leave, but if they hadn't left by now, I didn't think they would. It was actually better this way. They weren't being sneaky about listening in. It was very overt.

"I'm sorry that Melissa found the ring and misread the situation. I bought it because I saw it and I had to buy it, but it was never intended for her. Not even for a second. If she dug through my shit, then that's on her. I never asked her to marry me. I never hinted that I was going that direction. We hadn't even talked marriage yet. I was focused on my career, and she was focused on hers."

"Who did you buy it for? Were you cheating on her?"

Oh, for fuck's sake. "No. I would hope you know me better than that. I'm not a cheater. Never have been, never will be." It was insulting. "I don't owe you any explanation, but you're her best friend. So, I'll tell you. It's up to you if you want to tell Melissa. It might hurt her more, which is why I never told her. But…" I took a breath. I couldn't believe I was explaining myself in front of everyone, but there wasn't any way around this. I couldn't leave Melissa with any hope. That would be unkind after everything we shared.

"Kiran asked me to go ring shopping with him for Lyla. It was like the fourth shop we hit, and I looked into the case, and I had this flash of this person. And it made me smile, made me *feel*—" I cut myself off. They didn't get to hear everything, and neither did Win. That was too much. "The ring is a one of a kind antique, and I knew if I didn't grab it right then—even if it made no sense since because I hadn't had *any* contact whatsoever with this person in *years*—I'd never find a ring like it again. The words *I'll take it* were out of my mouth before I could stop them, and now, the beautiful, antique ring that was never going to be Melissa's is sitting in my safe at home."

"This person is Samantha. The girl you're with now. Right? That's what you're not saying."

I'd planned on leaving that part out, but I wasn't going to lie, either. "Yes." Tessa let out a squeal, and I ignored it.

"This will crush my best friend."

"Then, don't tell her. But I've moved on. I'm not going to come back to her, so please make that clear. It wasn't anything she did. It just wasn't meant to be. I'm sorry, but it's over."

"But you're walking away like it was nothing—from her and your career—and it wasn't. All because your grandmother died and you hurt your knee. Are you sure you won't regret giving up Melissa and your soccer career once you're done grieving?"

At that moment, Samantha walked into the room. The werewolves parted, and I could see that she'd changed into leggings, a long sweater, and a leather jacket. Her hair was braided away from her face, and she wore running shoes, so I knew she was ready for a fight. She was wearing her backpack, and the belt bag was slung across her body.

Samantha tugged nervously on the belt bag's strap, and her gaze darted from me to the wolves and back again. She had no idea how beautiful she was. How strong. How *good.* She continually threw herself into fights to help others, without about the cost to herself.

She stopped next to Tessa. "What's going on? Who is Nix talking to?" she asked loud enough for me to hear.

"His agent. Everyone is being obviously nosy," Tessa said, and she gave them all a zip-it look. "I've never seen a bigger bunch of mama hens in my life."

Samantha shook her head and looked at me. "Sorry." She didn't have a damned thing to apologize for. "They do that. But at least they don't hide when they're listening in. That would be considered rude."

A surprised laugh slipped free. It was all a little rude, but I couldn't be mad when they were looking out for her.

"Nix. Are you going to answer me?" Win's voice was full of frustration, which was understandable. I wasn't agreeing to anything she wanted.

I crooked my finger to Sam. "No, Win. I'm not going to regret a thing. I need to go."

"Are you really sure? I need you to be super sure before I start turning down these offers. Do you want to at least sleep on it?" Win asked.

Sam stopped in front of me, and I tilted the phone away. I

snagged the to-go cup and handed it to her. Sam's brows scrunched as she looked into the cup but the lid was opaque. "What is it?" she whispered, which was fair. Her mom pushed electrolytes on her like it was going out of style, and when it wasn't electrolytes or water, it was vitamin and protein-packed smoothies.

Sam could have treats. I'd slip them to her whenever I could, even if it pissed Ana off. "Take a sip and find out."

She rolled her eyes and took a sip. The moan she let out after was everything. She looked up at me with her big gray eyes. "You made me coffee," she said with awe in her voice, like I'd done her some big favor. But it was just coffee.

I brushed a kiss on her forehead. "You're welcome."

I was finally getting what Eli meant about this anchor gig, and I was more than good with it.

I put the phone back to my ear, and Win was still ranting about what I was giving up—my career, Melissa, and everything else. I'd had enough. "Listen, Win. I'm sure of what I'm doing. I'm done with all of it." No more giving explanations for my choices. I was a grown man, and I'd live my life as I wanted. "Be good." I hung up before she could argue with me and slid my phone into my back pocket.

All the werewolves had left the room, but I knew they were still listening. Not ideal, but I wasn't going to let it stop me from flirting with Sam. "How is it?"

"Perfect. Because it's you. Obviously." She shook her head. "Can you do something not perfectly? It's incredibly intimidating at this point."

"I sometimes leave my shoes and socks scattered on the floor. I hate wearing them." I waggled my eyebrows at her, and she laughed.

"Oooh. That's bad," she said, playing along.

"Sometimes, I don't do the dishes right away." I took the spoon I'd used to stir her coffee and tossed it in the sink. "I just leave them there." I held out my hands. "Until *much* later."

"That's disgusting." But she didn't look grossed out at all. She was smiling.

I nodded. "When I get sick, I'm a big whiner. Huge baby."

"*Ugh*. Now I have *the ick*. Majorly turned off." She made a face. "I'm never going to look at you the same. It's definitely over."

I grabbed her free hand, took her cup, and set it aside. "I get super into taking care of people that mean a lot to me." I pulled her against me. "I might even be a little bossy and overbearing."

"Oh man. And I thought alpha werewolves were overbearing." The words were muffled against my chest, but I could hear them all the same.

I leaned down so I could rest my chin on her head, wrapping my arms around her.

She took a deep breath and relaxed fully into me. This was why I wouldn't leave. Win would never understand, but she didn't have to. "You haven't seen anything yet. Don't worry. It's coming. I'm not a very big rule follower, either. And overly honest. That's gotten me into trouble. I don't hold a lot back. I tend to overshare."

"Since you mentioned that…" She squeezed me tighter for a second before pulling away. "Who was on the phone?"

I didn't want to tell her, especially about the offer. She wouldn't understand why I was turning down the money, but I wasn't going to keep things from her. "My agent." I put my hands on the counter behind me, leaning into it to keep from grabbing her again. She wanted space, then she'd have space.

"What did she want?"

"Me to play soccer. She had an offer from Madrid. And if not that, she had offers for me to be a commentator."

"Oh." She grabbed her coffee, staring into it. "Are you going to leave then?"

I could've dragged it out, but not with something like this. "Not a chance. You can't get rid of me that easily."

Her gaze shot up to me. "But you have to—"

"No. I don't *have* to do anything. I won't lie and say it's not because of you. It is incredibly easy for me to say no to Win—that's my agent, Winnifred—when I have you. But I know exactly what I'm saying no to, and trust me, when I said I was relieved to be done, I meant it. I'm almost thirty. That's ancient in pro sports. The knee blowing out would've just been the first of my injuries."

Someone cleared their throat. Tessa and Dastien came into the kitchen with Max and Garrett trailing behind.

Dastien laid the map on the island. "Alright, Sam. This is the place we're going. The red circles are places where we've lost wolves. Green ones are mortal casualties. We're thinking this area over here, by the water, is likely where we should start. Do you have other thoughts?"

Sam looked at them and shrugged. "I have no idea. I don't work like that." She waved her fingers over the map. "You know that."

"I know you don't, but there's so much area to cover and we don't want to split up if we don't have to."

"Did you try to have a vision?" Sam asked Tessa.

"Whatever this is doesn't want me to see anything helpful. I hear a kid screaming. I feel fear. I know I'm in a backyard fighting something and that a wolf is getting hurt. But…" She gave a small shrug. "None of that is helpful."

"That would be too easy." Sam reached her hand out to squeeze Tessa's arm. "Don't worry about it. I'll figure it out, but I don't know about this." She waved a hand at the map again. "Drive me around wherever you think, and when I see something, we'll pull over, and figure out what's what."

"You'll be more communicative though, right?" Dastien asked, his tone low and pleading.

Tessa looked at me. "She has a habit of wandering off." She turned to Sam and pointed a finger. "Don't do that. It scares us."

Sam gave a cute little half-smile. "I'll try?"

Tessa pointed at her again. "Did you hear how she said that? With the way it went up at the end. It was a question. Not a statement."

"Sorry?"

"She did it again!" Tessa snatched the marker from her mate's hand and tossed it at Sam.

Sam laughed and batted it away. "Okay, okay. No need to get violent." She looked at Dastien. "Did you stock the SUVs?"

"I did. As always. We're good to go."

"Great. Thanks. Did you happen to put some chalk in it?"

Dastien gave her a long look as if that request threw him. "No. That's a new ask from you."

She let out a breath. "I didn't bring any either. That's what took me so long to come down here. I took apart my whole backpack. It's not in there."

"We can stop somewhere," Tessa said. "Garrett—what's open that would have sidewalk chalk?"

He shrugged. "I'm sure a drug store or grocery store would have some. One sec. I'll have one of the SUVs drive ahead. Any particular kind of chalk? Requirements?"

"Thick is better. Like sidewalk chalk, not the kind for blackboards. Any color is fine, but white is best. Just not pink or red. Cool?"

"You got it. Anything else?"

Sam shook her head. "No. Sorry for the trouble."

"Not a problem. One sec." Garrett left for a minute and then came back. "Alright. I sent one of the cars ahead. They'll get it taken care of and meet us at the restaurant. Speaking of the restaurant, it's around this area." He pointed to a spot on the map. "I know it's not as secluded as you'd like. It's pretty central to the city, but this late? That's the best I could do. It's an Irish pub. Their kitchen closes at midnight, so we're good there. And we'll be close if something happens. We're going to have a car out patrolling while we eat, just in case there's a call that needs tending to."

"Sounds good," Sam said. "It's a private room?"

"Yeah."

She shrugged. "Okay. I'll deal."

Tessa turned to me. "You watch her. She *will* wander off."

"Yes, ma'am. I can do that." I gave Sam the smile that always made her blush.

She rolled her eyes at me. "You're such a jerk. You did that on purpose." She grabbed her coffee from the counter, holding it close to her body as if to guard it from anyone who might take it away from her. "I'm ready when you are."

Everyone started for the door, but I waited so I could snag Sam's hand.

Win might think I was making a mistake, but as we loaded into the SUVs, I knew this was it.

So, after I buckled up, I opened my cell and typed a message. *Hey there.*

Sam's phone buzzed in her belt bag, and she pulled it out. *Who is this?*

Me. I poked my finger into her side. *Did you know that the pack are super nosy?*

She laughed. *I did. They're the worst, and they love to gossip.*

We texted the whole way to the restaurant, and I didn't care one bit if we were being rude to everyone else.

It was nice—essential even—to have some time to ourselves. If it couldn't be a date, then we could at least have a private conversation. It didn't have to be about anything big. Just a connection.

Because that was what everyone wanted in life. Connection. Community. Unconditional love.

Samantha had found a lovely family for herself that gave her everything she needed, except for romantic love. She'd been on a quest for someone. From what Frank had said, it was an astronomical number of first dates that she'd been on the last couple of years.

There would be no more first dates. This was it. For both of us. I would fight hard for her, and I wasn't going to let anything—or anyone—ruin what we had.

Not tonight.

Not next week.
Not ever.

CHAPTER TWENTY-SIX

PHOENIX

WE ENDED up in the backroom of a pub. I'd literally never seen so much meat ordered, but the wolves just kept adding more and more food until the poor waiter looked a little stricken. It took a while for the kitchen to fill the orders, but there was a ton of conversation while we waited.

The pub was dark and moody, but the room we were in was a little better-lit. It held two long banquet tables with thickly cushioned chairs. Sam faced out, looking into the main area of the pub, and I sat next to her.

For some reason, Max sat on the other side of me. The man hated me—or maybe not hated but there was a lot of jealousy there. It didn't take a genius to see it. The man was devastated I was here with Sam, and he wasn't hiding his hurt or disappointment. At all.

Tessa was seated on the other side of Sam, and I leaned toward the two of them, while Max stayed quiet. If he wanted to talk to me, I was happy to clear the air, but I wasn't going to wait around for him to break the awkward tension between us.

Eventually, a few waiters came into the room carrying plates piled high with food. It took a while for everything to get handed out and arranged. Just as I was taking my first bite, Max finally spoke.

"I'm glad she has you." He said the words softly and so evenly that it took a second to register that they were directed at me.

I turned a little toward him. That was completely unexpected given how he'd been since the plane. "Thank you." I wasn't sure what else to say.

"I apologize for my behavior. I'd thought…" He shook his head as he looked away. "Being a werewolf is difficult in some ways. There aren't a lot of females born, and the laws around turning someone are very strict. But if you marry a human, they eventually die. It's…it can be lonely at times."

Wait a second. I didn't know much, but I knew Tessa was bitten. And I was pretty sure that Chris' father or grandfather was bitten—I couldn't remember which. "But you could turn someone, right? I know it happens sometimes because Tessa was turned."

"Sure, but Dastien almost lost his life for that move. He broke a lot of rules to gain his mate, but it worked out in the end. She forgave him, as did the council who used to rule the packs."

This was the most he'd said to me, so I stayed quiet, letting him finish.

"I've been rude to you. That's not how I usually behave, and while I cannot help that my wolf had chosen her, I know that she did not choose either of us." He leaned back in his chair. "I met Sam a few years ago, and she made a huge impact on me. Her power and beauty and courage. It's captivating. I tried to flirt with her, but she didn't seem to pick up on it at all. So, I told myself it was because of our age difference—" He gave me a look. "I'm much, much older than you."

"I didn't realize."

"It's hard to tell among werewolves, but…" He went back to staring straight ahead as he spoke to me. "I decided that maybe Sam needed time to grow up, live a bit, before settling down.

Something I wished my sister, Meredith, had. But she found her mate young and…anyway, I thought in a year or two, I'd formally court her. We've worked together a few times since then, and I always tried to show her that I was interested, but she never picked up on it. Ever. Which, in retrospect, is pretty humbling. So, imagine my surprise when she shows up with you. And she lets you touch her, lets you talk to her, lets you carry her when she needs it. You should know that she never does that with anyone."

"She doesn't? What happens when she passes out?"

"Tessa helps her or her mother or Eli. Once, Chris carried her, but she was totally passed out. Otherwise, I'm pretty sure she would've objected."

"Really?"

"Truly. It seems I might have lost my window with her."

There was no *seems* here. He'd absolutely lost his window. "She's mine." I said it without a challenge in my tone. I didn't want to fight with him. It was just a clear, direct statement of fact.

"I get that now. Just know, she's special to me. You've been given a gift, and if anything happens to her, if she's hurt, if she's upset, I'll blame you." When he looked at me, his eyes were glowing bright blue. "And I won't hesitate to rip out your throat." He said the last part so quietly that I barely heard him.

A hand slammed into the table, rattling all the glasses. "Max." Tessa's voice rang out. "*Enough*."

"What did I just miss?" Sam asked.

"Nothing." I reached under the table and put my hand on her leg. "Everything's okay." I knew Max meant that literally. He wouldn't hesitate to kill me if I let something happen to her, but if something…if Sam died, I was sure I'd let him. I didn't want to live in a world without her.

Sam's gaze searched mine. "Are you sure everything is okay?" She leaned in closer, whispering into my ear. "You don't look okay. What's wrong?"

Tessa started to say something, but I cut her off.

"*Nothing*. I promise." I leaned away so she could see my face and believe my words. "Don't worry about a thing." I leaned forward so I could raise a brow at Tessa, hoping she'd let this go.

Tessa rolled her eyes and muttered something that had a few of the pack members laughing.

Max didn't say another word, but what he'd said sank in. This —what Sam and I had—was unusual for her. It was more intense than anything I'd ever had before, and I knew she was it for me. Somehow, Max's words solidified that in my mind. They shouldn't have, but they did. It wasn't just the bond. It was more than that. If she'd needed someone other than me, she would've picked any number of supernaturals. I saw how they looked at her. I saw how they followed her as she moved. She was captivating to all of them, but it was me that she picked. Me that she let in.

Something inside me uncoiled with that thought. I hadn't forced her. She *wanted* me. Eli told me that, and I believed him. But not fully. Now, as I took in Max's words, it hit me that I had been there in that bathroom for a reason. It was destiny.

Destined. Meant to be. Ordained by God.

That was why it felt so right and easy to turn down Win's offer. To walk away from everything. Because this was my true purpose—to fight evil beside Samantha.

I sat there in the noisy room with conversations flowing every which way, but my mind wasn't there. Instead, my life was flashing before my eyes. Every choice. Every step. Every path led me straight to Samantha. It felt like it was orchestrated by the Divine Mastermind.

I was going to need to snag that ring from my safe.

I'd have to deal with my mother, too. That was going to be trickier. But if my sisters helped…

As everyone ate their meals, the pack members asked Sam more and more questions, some of them about demons, others more personal. She tried to answer them the best she could and even made jokes about the things that seemed completely off the wall, poking fun at herself. She talked with her hands a lot. It was adorable.

She was adorable.

When I was done with my food, I pushed back from the table to stretch my knee.

Tessa pushed her chair back and leaned close behind Sam's chair so that I could hear her."Sam's pretty amazing," Tessa said softly.

I glanced at Sam to see if she could hear us, but she was leaning forward, telling one of the other guys a story. She was an introvert and a little shy, but when they asked her about the spiritual realm or about things they'd heard she did, that shy part of her seemed to dissolve. I was pretty sure she wasn't even aware of it, but she had the whole room riveted, and even a few of the people beyond it were taking peeks at her.

"Agreed," I said to Tessa, and then as my gaze drifted back to Sam, I saw her plate. Oh, hell no. She'd spent too much time talking and not enough time eating her dinner. I nudged her. "Hey, babe. Don't forget to eat. Okay?"

"I've been eating." She looked down at her plate and winced. "Okay. Right. I should be eating more." She stabbed a bite of roast and chewed.

"Better." I looked at Tessa, who was smiling at me. "What?"

"You're good for her."

"Thank you. I'm hoping I will be. I'm pretty new to this, and *dude,* talk about a learning curve. But I'm catching on."

She considered me for a second. "You know, I keep forgetting you're a total outsider. You just slid right into our lives at the Sanctuary so easily and naturally that I forget you probably don't know much about us."

Easily and naturally? I took that as an amazing compliment. "That's okay. I'm just picking things up as we go. I really try to just go with the flow in life."

"That's good and all, but I'll try to fill you in a little better from here on. I was the outsider once, and it was really…unsettling."

Dastien reached over, running a hand down her back. I saw their bond light up, and knew they were having one of their silent conversations.

Sam leaned across me to tell Max something. I took the opportunity to reach out and run my hand down her braid and give it a gentle tug because I couldn't be near her and not touch her.

Her gaze drifted to mine, and she gave me a soft, questioning smile.

"Everything is still fine." I brushed my hand down her cheek.

She let out a small breath. "You sure?"

"Absolutely."

I waited until Sam went back to answering another question before looking at Tessa again. "So, how do we go about patrolling tonight? This is my first time doing this, and I want to make sure I'm able to protect her in any way I can. I'm not sure how I should prepare for this."

"The bad news is there's no way to really prepare. Especially on this one. We're just going to wing it and let her take the lead. Just know that none of us want her hurt. Sometimes demons come through the portals, and I can see them. We—" She motioned to herself and the rest of the wolves. "—can fight those kinds of demons. So, we'll jump in front and take the lead there. No problem." Tessa paused. "Well, not exactly *no problem*, but we get it done. Sometimes it can get dicey, though."

"I saw the news footage." Before that, there were some rumors that of supernaturals existed, but the cameras caught everything the day Tessa, Dastien, and the rest of Sam's friends fought demons in a chapel in Santa Fe. It woke everyone up to the fact that normal humans weren't the only advanced creatures on Earth. There were way more out there, and things went a little crazy for a while.

"I guess most people saw that footage, huh?"

"Yep." I was sure no soul alive had missed it.

Dastien muttered to Tessa in French about how he hoped to

never face a situation like that again, and Tessa answered back in French, telling him not to worry.

Cute. These two were cute. I liked them as a couple. Usually, I liked only one of the people in the couple. It was rare that I liked both. But the more time I spent with them, the more I appreciated the family Samantha had found for herself.

The room slowly went quiet, and I noticed Sam wasn't talking anymore. She wasn't eating either. Instead, she was staring off into the restaurant's main dining room. All the werewolves' eyes were bright.

"Phoenix? Can you still see the spiritual realm?" Max asked.

"Yeah."

"What's she seeing that we can't see? She didn't answer when we asked. She's too in the zone. If she's found something, I'm scared to snap her out of it and have her lose a trail."

I searched the room, trying to find what Sam was focused on. The spiritual realm was a mess, and I wasn't sure how to process any of what I was seeing. That was going to take some major time to figure out. But as I focused, I didn't see anything unusual. Just a bunch of people having dinner or drinks. One group was getting up from their table. Another group was laughing by the bar. A few dudes were playing darts. Nothing seemed weird.

But when I peeked another look at Sam, she was clearly looking at something in the dining room, tracking it with her eyes as it moved.

"What is it?" Tessa asked.

"I don't know." I could still *see* what Sam could see. It was like a transparent haze over everything, but the main dining room seemed full of regular people. Some of them glowed. Some of them were shadowed. Some were just…nothing. Normal, I guess? Did the glow or shadow mean that they were some sort of supernatural? Or was that from their aura? From sin? Or what? I didn't know, and now wasn't the time to ask.

"Samantha," I said. "What should I be looking for?"

She didn't answer. Just kept staring, narrowing her gaze a little and tilting her head to the side as she watched whatever it was.

She said sometimes things on the spiritual realm were tricky and they took all of her focus. It was why she sometimes disappeared without saying anything. This was definitely one of those times.

I went back to looking at the bigger room. I tilted my head the way she had, but nothing screamed unusual to me. But what the hell did I know?

The couple at the table directly in her eye-line had a little thread linking them, and I figured they must be married. They were older than me, maybe about ten years or so, and likely out for a date night.

There was a bigger table beyond it with a large, rowdy group who were—

The scrape of a chair being pushed along the floor echoed in our now silent room. Sam grabbed her belt bag that was hanging over the chair and walked out of the room, quickly weaving through the pub.

I rose from my seat. "That's not the exit. Where's she going?"

"The bathroom is down that way," Garrett said. "But there's a door that leads to the kitchens, too. There might be a back exit."

"I don't think she's going to the bathroom. I'm following her." Tessa rose from her seat and moved through the room.

Screw that. "I'm going, too." If she was in the bathroom, then I'd just have to play the overbearing, overprotective boyfriend card. But I didn't think that was where Sam was going, either. Even if I couldn't figure out what she had seen exactly, I knew something was wrong.

I tried to stay calm as I wove through the tables, but the main restaurant was packed with people and waiters with trays and I didn't want to cause a scene.

Tessa was smaller than me, sliding around people, and I lost her when she rounded the corner.

Damn it. I turned the corner just seconds behind her, but the hallway was empty. There were three doors—men's and women's restrooms and a door that led to the kitchens.

I cracked the ladies' door just in case. "Samantha? Tessa?" I shouted through the crack.

No one answered.

I checked the men's just in case, but it was empty.

I went to the kitchen door. I ignored the shouts and the heat and the chaos and kept moving back until I found another door. One that led to an alley.

There was a parking garage behind the building, and I could smell the trash in the dumpster behind the kitchen. And off in the distance, Tessa ran around the corner of the parking garage.

I took off, sprinting to catch up, feeling grateful that my knee was healed.

CHAPTER TWENTY-SEVEN

PHOENIX

WITHIN SECONDS, I was next to Tessa, so I slowed. "What's going on?" I whispered as we hung back about twenty feet from Samantha.

"I don't know. She asked me to stay back and be quiet," she whispered.

What? Why? "Does she do this a lot?"

"I honestly never know what I'm going to get with Sam. I've never met anyone quite like her, and her skill is completely unique. I usually feel pretty good about myself if I can follow half of what she's doing."

That wasn't going to work for me. I needed to know what to do to help her.

Sam stopped ahead of us, then waved us over to join her. "Do you see that?" Sam asked me.

I tried to figure out what she meant, but I didn't see anything off. "What?"

"Her." She made a little noise of frustration. "The lady walking through the park. The one in the long, black puffer coat. She's trailing behind that other lady. They've stopped now and are talking by the fountain." She glanced at me for the first time since she left the restaurant. "Can you still *see*?"

"Yeah, baby. I can. I'm just not used to it. I'm not sure what I'm supposed to be focusing on." I looked over, trying to figure out what to looking for, but it just looked like a lady. Maybe my ability to *see* was wearing off? But I could still see all the ties around us.

"It's subtle at first. Just look at her. Her face. Not her clothes. I can only see it for a second when she turns toward me a little. Just a there-and-gone flash."

I nodded and waited, and then the lady turned. For a second, as she turned, it was as if the skin on her face was transparent. Under it, I could see muscles and sinew. It was disgusting.

I sucked in a breath.

"What do you see?" Sam asked.

"One time, my mom dragged us kids to the museum in LA," I said. "The Human Body. There was this part of the exhibit where they had a replica of the inside of a human. Muscles, bones, tendons. No skin. That's what she looks like. The skin isn't really there. But how? What is that?"

Sam exhaled hard. "Oh, thank God. I thought I was going nuts. Those two were eating dinner together, and I kept getting glimpses of it, but I wasn't sure. Not until they got up to leave. I've never seen anything like it." She looked at me. "What *is* it?"

If she didn't know what it was, there was no way I'd know. But she was right, there was something wrong there. It was unsettling for sure, especially with the way the skin seemed to disappear as the lady moved.

"One second," Tessa said, and her bond lit up. "Asking Dastien to ask Garrett. He's a local. Maybe there's some lore here that he knows about. It could be something local, like what we saw in Utah."

"Good call. I can't keep track of everything. I try, but I don't need to dig up every evil thing in the world. I have enough images in my head to fuel my nightmares for multiple lifetimes."

Tessa's phone rang, and she handed it to Samantha. "It's Garrett. You answer it. I can hear him fine when he's talking to you."

Sam answered. "Hello?" She said and she waved me closer, holding it away from her ear so that I could lean in and hear, too.

"Hey, Sam. It's Garrett. I think what you're seeing is called a boo hag. It's a local legend." He let out a low laugh. "I can't believe there's truth to any of this. It feels insane, but I hear that's your jam, so here we go. A boo hag—as far as I know—is used as a way to keep teenagers from staying out all night."

"A boo *hag*?" Sam asked, and she looked at me.

That was weird. Maybe the Black-Eyed Children had been telling the truth.

"Yeah. That's what it's called. But I honestly don't know if it's a real thing. It's just local mythology."

Sam was quiet for a second, and I wished I knew what she was thinking.

"You still there, Sam?" Garrett asked.

"Yeah. Sorry. I'm just putting some pieces together in my mind," Sam said. "There's often a layer of truth in legends and lore. Tell me everything you know about this boo hag creature. Don't hold anything back, even if you think it's stupid. It's not like I'm going to judge you if you're wrong."

There was a rush of breath through the phone, and then Garrett started to speak. "The legend says there's a demon, witch, or whatever—it's not clear what it is exactly—that acts as a succubus. It steals the life from someone, and when it's done, when the person's soul—and thus their body—is dead, it takes their skin and wears it."

Wears it? That was disgusting, but having see that thing, it felt like that was what we were looking at.

"During the day, the boo hag lives in its latest victims skin, living out that person's life, but in the middle of the night, it leaves the skin behind and wanders the streets, looking for its next victim. Without the skin, you can't see it. And if you're not careful, the boo hag will follow you home at night, and you'll be its next victim." Garrett let out a nervous half-laugh. "But it's just something moms say to keep their kids from staying out all night."

"No, it's not," I said. "Because I'm staring at something that looks like it's wearing someone else's skin. And if I'm understanding you correctly, the skin she's wearing is a person that's already dead?" I wanted to make sure I was following this correctly.

"If the legend is right, then, yes, I think so," Garrett said. "If you wait, if we track her, then she'll lead us to her home. You're supposed to wait for the boo hag to leave again, get into her house, destroy the skin, and then..." He huffed. "This is where it just feels dumb. I don't know that this next part is accurate."

"Don't worry about that. Just finish telling me what you know," Sam said patiently coaxing words from Garrett.

"Fine. Okay. Well, legend says if you want to kill the boo hag, you have to leave something outside of where her skin is—like on her doorstep—for her to count. While she's gone, you destroy the skin. When she comes back, she'll stop to count, and if you leave enough of whatever it is—beads, grains of sand, whatever—she'll get caught in the daylight without her skin and die. Which sounds nuts, but apparently this thing has a counting compulsion? My great-grandma used to keep a bowl of sand on her doorstep, just in case."

One detail bumped for me. "You keep calling it a her."

"I guess I do. I don't know if that's part of the story I was told or if I'm just making it that way because a hag is usually a mean word for an ugly lady. But I don't know. I think I might be making that up."

"Thanks, Garrett," Sam said. "This demon thing is disgusting looking. I've never seen anything quite like it." She paused and looked at me. "This is what the Black-Eyed Children were talking about. They told me the *hag* would lead me to what I was looking for."

That was what I was realizing, too. "I think it might be exactly what they were talking about."

"Wait. The Black-Eyed Children told you something?"

"Yeah. Only on the spiritual realm, though. I wasn't sure I should believe them, and honestly, this could be a trap. So, I decided not to fill you in. I'm sorry. I didn't want to get anyone's hopes up. Trusting a demon…well, it's not usually smart."

"Okay. I can understand that," Tessa said. "What did it say exactly?"

"I don't remember the exact words, but it said that the hag would lead me to my past which would help me get to where I wanted to go. But then they said that there was a danger I couldn't see. Which might be the invisible monster that's killing the wolves or it could be something else entirely."

"It sounds like this has potential, but you don't sound convinced," Tessa said.

"I'm not. They said the message was from Gabe, but they couldn't give me the code word we use. So, if anything, it feels like a trap."

"But this the thing could lead us to whatever is killing the wolves?" Tessa asked.

"Potentially. Yes."

"How do you want to handle this?" Tessa.

Sam stood quietly for a second, watching the two ladies as she thought. "I mean we could do exactly what Garrett said and follow it. See where it leads us. Wait for it to shed its skin and leave its home. Then, break in. Burn the skin, and…" She was quiet for a second, and I knew that wasn't going to be the plan. The boo hag was walking with another lady, and maybe she was just a friend of the boo hag. But there was a chance it was the next victim.

I didn't know Sam that well, but I knew her well enough to know she wasn't about to leave a potential victim alone with a demon. That wasn't how she worked.

"Sorry. I can't do that. We're going to have to do this another way." She held the phone out to Tessa. "I just need a second to wrap my head around this. I feel like I'm missing something…"

Tessa took the phone. "Thanks, Garrett. I'll keep you posted with what we end up doing, but Dastien can find me if you guys want to catch up." Tessa hung up, and her bond lit again. As soon as I saw it brighten, I realized I had more werewolf questions. How far would a bond like that reach? I'd assumed they needed to be in the same room for it to work, but Dastien wasn't anywhere near us.

I wondered if Sam and I could talk through our bond like the werewolves could. That would be incredibly handy.

I filed that thought away for later. I'd ask Samantha, but something told me Eli would be better at answering that question.

And now that I thought of Eli, I wondered if I should tell Sam to ask him for help. Was that overstepping? Did I care if it meant keeping her safe?

She paced up and down the sidewalk as she thought, her eyes never fully leaving the boo hag. I glanced at Tessa, who shrugged —she didn't know what to do either.

Okay. So, we'd wait.

Sam stopped pacing. "Did someone end up getting chalk for me?"

"Yeah," Tessa said. "One of the SUVs left before dinner. It's in one of the trunks."

"Good. That's good," she said, but she sounded distracted. "Don't know why I feel like I'm going to need it soon, but…"

She was struggling, and the only person who could really give her sound advice was Eli. I still didn't want to overstep, but it turned out that I cared more about her peace of mind than overstepping. "Do you want to call Eli?"

She chewed on her lip. "Not really, but…" She rolled her eyes. "Yeah. I guess I might as well. If this thing is what's killing the werewolves, then we'll need help. And if it's just connected in some way, then still, he might have some advice. He was pretty annoyed with me earlier." She sighed. "Screw it. *Eli?*" Her voice wasn't that loud, but something about it resonated through my soul, almost like an electrical current running through my body.

I rubbed a hand on my chest. "What was that?"

Her eyes widened at my comment. "Sorry. I didn't know I'd hit you with it, too. I called him through the spiritual plane. I can project my voice along it, and I boosted it with a little extra power. Sometimes that's the only way he can hear me."

"Don't worry about it. I'm okay. Next time, I'll know what to expect." It hadn't hurt, exactly. It'd been more of a surprise than anything else.

A second later, the angel was standing in front of us. He was in his plain clothes. No wings or armor or flaming sword. Which was a relief, especially since we were standing on a public sidewalk. Well, that and he was much more intimidating when he came showing every bit of his angelic form. "You rang?"

"Best way to get rid of that." Sam motioned to the lady behind Eli with a head nod.

Eli turned, and then gave a gruff *huh*. "It's been a long time since I've seen one of those." He turned back to us. "Follow it to its lair. Break any remaining ties it's hidden. Burn her skin. Portal her to Hell. But you can't skip the following her part. It's linked and has ties. It will just come back until those are ash. You'll have to follow it to wherever it lives."

"Why wait?" Sam crossed her arms as she stared up at the angel. "Can't I just portal it to Hell now with its skin on? Wouldn't that be much easier and take care of everything? You always taught me that one step is better than two."

Eli smiled, as if Sam just said something that made him really happy.

He gave me a nod confirming that, and then focused on Sam again. "You could, but there might be some lingering demonic attachment to the family. This type of demon sometimes attaches to a single person, but more often, also with a spouse or a family or a *home*. Those ties are—"

"Tricky to find. Right."

"Why are they tricky?" I asked.

"The boo hag has a special tie where it keeps its skin. It acts like a portal of sorts, but more like a door. If it's closed, Sam can't see it. She won't be able to find it until the demon comes through it again. And only for an instant. It's why these little pests have lasted in the mortal realm for so long. They're a nightmare to kill."

"Right. So, we follow it," Sam said.

"Exactly. If you don't break the tie first, then you're leaving a door open for the demon to come back. Except its skin will be gone. So, it'll take whoever is on the other end of the tie—meaning an innocent family member or whoever moved into the house. The best way to take care of this demon is to follow it home, and then wait for it to leave without its skin. Get into the house, burn the skin, break any remaining demonic ties. Which eliminates the need for a fight. Only once you're sure all the ties are gone can you send it to Hell. Don't worry, the hag will know. It'll come for you. And you'll know you've done it well."

Forget two steps. That seemed way more complicated.

Sam let out a groan and muttered softly to herself.

Tessa laughed, and I turned to her. I raised a brow when she didn't say anything.

"Oh. She wants to know why everything has to be done the hard way."

Oh. Yeah, that was fair. Nothing in life was ever easy.

"What about the lady it's with? I can't just leave it with a victim. That would be *wrong*." Sam was frustrated, and I got it. It would've been much easier to not have to worry about all the connections, but I had no doubt that Sam would.

"It can't do anything while wearing the skin. It will get rid of it before it starts draining its next victim," Eli said.

"What if it goes home with that other lady, sheds it there, and then kills the new lady?" Sam asked.

"It won't. It won't shed its skin anywhere but its designated safe place." Eli was quiet. "They're not roommates. The other lady is thinking about calling a car service and waking up her husband when she gets home. The rest of her thoughts are pretty inappropriate. The hag is trying to convince the woman to hit a club instead. Trust me, angel. The demon will go home before attacking anyone. It will make sure its skin is in the safest place it can be. Then, it will hunt."

Samantha glanced at her watch. "It's after midnight now. How do I know this isn't a trap? I ran into some Black-Eyed Children—

"You what?" Eli's tone was thick with ice.

"Stop," Sam said. "It happened fast. They knocked on the door, and I had to deal with them. Woke me up from a dead sleep with a stupid bell."

"Ah. Alright." Eli huffed. "If I needed to know, He would've told me. Fine. What did they say?"

Samantha quickly filled him in on what happened, and then Eli was quiet.

"We need to patrol for whatever's killing the wolves, but according to the Black-Eyed Children, this is tied in some way. Do you know how?"

"I don't. No demon should be able to open a portal, but it's wearing another's skin. It could be a loophole. If it is, I've never seen it done before. But that demon can't kill werewolves. It's tied to the mortal in such a way that it doesn't have the supernatural strength of a wolf."

"So, you don't think this is connected?" I asked Eli.

"I honestly don't know. It could be or it could be a trap or it could be both."

Sam groaned. "I don't have time to fall into some demonic trap. I need to find what's actually killing the wolves."

"Then, leave the hag." He gave Sam an arrogant smirk. "This thing can't kill werewolves. If you've got better things to do..." His words dripped with sarcasm and judgment in a way that made me want to hit him.

Eli waved a hand, as if to usher her along.

That wasn't necessary.

He narrowed his gaze at me, but whatever. *Don't talk to her like that.* I thought the words at him.

Eli gave me a smile, one that seemed part-amused, part-evil.

"You're a jerk sometimes," Sam said before either Eli or I could say anything.

"But a lovable one." Eli's grin changed to be more cherubic. He might've been an angel, but I was starting to see a bit of a gray area with him. The grin was all wicked.

"I'm an *archon*. Not exactly an angel," Eli said, as if that cleared everything up.

"Stop it, Eli." She looked at me and Tessa. "So, now what? I have to follow her around until she goes home?"

"DCan you think of another way?" Eli made a smug face that was kind of annoying. "What did I just tell you about these demons?"

He shot me a look, but I really didn't care that he heard I thought his face was smug and his tone was annoying. I thought a lot of things all day long. As long as I didn't say them aloud, they didn't really count.

"Fair enough," he said.

"Oh. Dang," Sam said. "I see it now, and man, I'm really off my game. That's going to be much easier. So many less steps and less waiting around."

"Do you need more help?" Eli asked.

"NO. I got it. I don't think I need help with this, but maybe later if you're not busy? I'm still not sure what's killing the wolves or how the hag is connected."

Eli gave her a look, and she interpreted it. "Stop. Man, you're in a mood today. Fine—how busy are you right now? You're not in armor."

"*Exceedingly.*"

"Don't worry. We have her back," Dastien said as he crossed the street to us. The rest of the werewolves were trailing behind him. "We won't let anything happen to her."

"I'll hold you to that." Eli looked at me. "You'll stay by her side."

Of course I would. We could technically split up because I could *see*, but I wasn't going to do that. "No place else I want to be."

"Good," Eli said. "I'll try to come back if I'm able, but it might not be for a bit. Just know that the boo hag very well might be some sort of wild goose chase. Or it could be part of a trap. Or the Black-Eyed Children could've been telling the truth—that it will lead you to the monster you're searching for. But demons don't tell the truth unless it serves their end. So, if they told you the truth, they might want you to find the monster. Which would be a whole other kind of a trap. Be very careful, my angel."

"I will be." Sam studied him for a second. "Are you okay? You've been off lately. You're starting to worry me."

"If I wasn't okay, there would be nothing you could do to help it. Don't worry about me. There are battles happening, but nothing for you to concern yourself with. At least, not yet. For now, just focus on getting your job done." He gave Sam a snarky smile. "You're welcome, angel." The way he said it—with that sarcastic, arrogant tone—grated on me, but I knew he said it that way to tease Samantha.

I was starting to understand their relationship, and I knew what she was going to say.

"I'm *not* an *angel*." She whispered-shouted the words at him as predicted, and I had to swallow down my laugh.

"Thanks, though," Sam said. "Go back to whatever you were doing." She lifted a hand to wave at him, but he was already gone.

The entire Wayfarer pack was around us now, waiting to find out our next step. Sam seemed to take it all in, and I could almost see the wheels turning.

"What's the plan?" Dastien asked. "Put us to work."

She nodded, looking from the ladies, to something in the spiritual realm—I wasn't sure what—to the group, and back again.

"If a couple of you could stay and watch her, that would be good." She started slowly, as if she was working it through as she spoke. "I don't want her catching up to me. That seems like it could turn into a fight, and I'd rather not have that happen. We need to save up energy for the big bad."

There were some scattered agreements.

"The rest of you maybe can bring the cars to us so we can patrol once I have this sorted? If I trusted the Black-Eyed Children —which I'm not sure I do—the boo hag could lead us to whatever has been killing members of the pack. Or this could be some kind of a trap. It's really fifty-fifty. So, I'm thinking I take care of this, and then we'll likely need to move fast once I know more. Which I guess is all kind of vague but just be ready. I don't know what the boo hag is going to do when I burn its ties. So, I need eyes on it. For now."

"We're always ready for a fight, and we will absolutely have a team on her," Dastien said, while looking at Max.

Max nodded and pointed to five guys, who started out on foot, following the two ladies as they slowly made their way through the park. If Eli was right, they were on their way to whatever club they were going to hit.

Dastien focused on Sam again. "Where are we going?"

"I don't know where it's going to end up, but I'm following a trail." She pointed off to the right and behind her a little. "I'm going that way. The trail is super dim, so it's going to take all of my focus to stay on track. If someone wants to coordinate with the group, that's fine by me. I just can't. I'll be quiet while I focus."

"No problem," Max said. "Coordinating this bunch is my job." He turned to Dastien. "Do you and Tessa want to go with her? You can pick other wolves if you want more—"

"No," Sam cut in. "I'd like to keep it a small group. Too many will draw attention, and again—this isn't the patrolling portion of the evening yet. We still might hit that depending on how much information I gain after dealing with the hag and—"

"You don't need to explain," Max said. "We'll get it taken care of."

"And I want the chalk."

Max nodded to a few of his guys who took off jogging. "They're bringing the cars around. I'll get it to you, no problem."

Sam took off without another word.

"Can you show me the line that we're following?" I asked, keeping pace beside her.

"It's a light pinkish red. Really thin. This little line below my finger right here." She ran her finger above something, and it took me a second to see it through all the other visual noise in the spiritual realm. But once I did, I saw the fine, dim red string. "It's tying her to somewhere or someone. That's her hold on this world. I'm going to follow that to the source—her lair."

"I just want to make sure I understand. We follow this tie to where it ends, cut it and close any doorways. Hopefully, the hag will come running, and you portal it—skin and all—to Hell."

"Exactly." She stopped for a second, focusing on the dim tie again before following it. "Eli had a bunch more steps in it at first, but he's not one to follow some stupid instructions like that. It's not how he taught me to do it either. Which is why I tried to call him out on it, and why he was so snarky with me."

"Got it."

"The tie is the big thing, and I'm guessing there'll be some sort of doorway where it stashes the skin in its room. Maybe a closet or a basement or something. That way if something happens, it can come back through the doorway. But following the tie will lead us there. And if the Black-Eyed Children were right, then this will lead us to where we really need to go. So, hopefully we can get this done quickly with little to no drama. Then, move on to the bigger problem."

"That sounds easy enough."

She shot me a look eerily similar to Eli's oh-you-mere-mortal look, and I almost laughed.

"You've jinxed us now. We're *screwed*." She shook her head.

Now, I did laugh. "What?" I didn't jinx us.

"You said it would be easy. Now, it's going to be your fault when it's an absolute pain in the tush. Don't worry. Someone always ends up saying it." She looked over her shoulder. "I want full acknowledgement that it wasn't me this time."

Someone laughed behind us, and I turned to find Dastien and Tessa. They'd moved so quietly, I hadn't heard them catch up.

"Every time someone says it's going to be easy, it turns into a disaster," Tessa said. "Epic. Disaster."

"Well, shit." Now, I kind of wanted to take it back.

All three of them laughed, but I didn't mind being the newbie.

My life before Samantha had felt tedious. It might have seemed cool or fancy or whatever from the outside, but on the inside, it was a lot of hotels, a lot of travel, a lot of working out, and a lot of attention that didn't always feel good. I'd known I needed a change, but at the time, I had no idea what.

Everything I was seeing, feeling, and doing with Sam felt the opposite. She made me feel alive and filled with purpose. Maybe I shouldn't feel that way. I was just following her around and mostly useless, but I was learning.

I would learn.

And in that house earlier, I hadn't been useless.

I'd seen when she was taking it too far, and I'd stopped her. Now, she could save this family.

Would it be enough for me?

I wasn't sure. I was going to have to see where I landed, and if I needed to be able to do more. *Be* more. I didn't know what that meant or where it would lead me. But I knew whatever it was, I'd be by Sam's side. For as long as she'd have me.

CHAPTER TWENTY-EIGHT

SAMANTHA

I FELT like I was leading everyone on a wild fey hunt, except I was with werewolves, not fey. And we were hunting demons, not mortals. Whatever. It felt similar as we wove our way through the streets of Charleston. I lost the demon tie a few times. It was stretched thin and weak and if I wasn't paying close attention, it would disappear into the noise of the rest of the spiritual realm.

After a while, I noticed that one of the SUVs was trailing behind us, so I stopped long enough to get in. I wanted to drive, but I didn't trust myself not to wreck. I was barely able to follow the tie as it was. Add in driving, and yeah, no. That was a bad idea. So, once again, I found myself being driven around Charleston while I called out random course corrections.

It was hard because ties didn't live in the mortal realm. They could take the shortest distance—as the crows fly—but the car couldn't drive through buildings or houses. I had to try and figure out where it was going, backtrack, circle around. It was a slow, frustrating process.

"There," I said finally. I was just thankful I wasn't in the back-seat for this drive. It was a lot of sudden turns and stops and all kinds of things. I would've barfed from motion sickness ages ago. "Stop. Right up there." I pointed to a house where the red string disappeared inside it. I knew this was the one because the tie had grown brighter and more solid, not so elusive. This had to be it. "The gray one with the navy door. Third on the left."

"I see it," a familiar voice said beside me.

I turned to see Phoenix. "Wait. Have you been driving this whole time?" I honestly was so singularly focused, I hadn't heard or seen anything else since getting in the car. I'd just been barking orders while leaning as close to the front windshield as my seatbelt would let me.

He gave me a smile, his dimple popping. "Yeah, babe. I have."

Oh man. Had I been rude?

Phoenix found a spot to parallel park, and I looked away, trying to rethink the drive.

I seriously hadn't been paying attention to what I was saying or how I was saying it. All of my focus had been on not losing sight of that demon tie. It was so faint and hidden and covered by layers of the ties of everyone who lived here. If I looked away at all, it would've been gone—totally indistinguishable from all the other ties in the city. There were too many distractions. Ties zipped and zagged all over the place. Humans were loosely bound to their relatives, friends, and—to the surprise of most people—sexual partners.

I always found it funny when I mentioned that as I cleared ties from people. They always responded with a mix of horror and shock, but sex wasn't ever just a physical act. We aren't just physical beings. The spiritual realm was always involved. Most didn't realize—or like knowing—that they were leaving bits of their souls all across town.

Phoenix cleared his throat. "You okay?"

"Kind of." I sighed. "I just was trying to think if I'd been rude to you when—"

He gripped my arm gently, and I turned to him. "Stop inventing things to worry about. I'm not offended. You were focused. I was driving. We're here now. Simple as that. It's all good."

"Okay." I hoped he wasn't just being nice.

I looked behind me, truly seeing the world around me for the first time, not just the spiritual realm. Tessa and Dastien were in the second row, with Garrett and Max in the way back. They must've been the ones following us in the car.

I wasn't sure where all the other Wayfarers were, but it didn't matter right now.

First things first.

I opened the door. "Be right back."

"Wait," Tessa said, and she turned to the back. "You have the chalk?"

Garrett nodded. "Yeah. One sec." He leaned over the third row, into the trunk, and snagged a bag. "Here." He passed it to Tessa, who passed it up to me.

I opened the bag. "Perfect. Thanks." I pulled out the package, picking a thick, white piece of sidewalk chalk. I broke it in half so it would fit in my belt bag, and tucked it away in one of the pockets. As soon as I zipped it up, a feeling of peace washed over me.

It was like I knew everything was going to be okay.

It made no sense, but that was why it was important. Something—some*one*—whispered in my head, and I knew what I needed to do to win this fight. All I had to do was listen to His voice and be ready to do what I was called to do.

"I'm ready. For real this time." I jumped down from the SUV.

"Wait. I'm coming with you," Phoenix said.

"Okay, but just you. There's a light on inside. Someone's home. You guys will scare whoever this is without even trying."

"It's not like I'd show them my sharp teeth, Sam. You know I don't do that," Tessa said.

"Except that one time..." I teased her.

"Oh, shut up," Tessa snapped, but she was laughing.

I hopped down from the car and waited for Phoenix come around the other side. Dastien got out and leaned against the car, leaving the door open. "Shout if you need help. We'll be listening."

"Will do."

I paused on the sidewalk to take in the house. Sometimes it was hard to tell what was going on inside. Sometimes it was glaringly obvious. But aside from the tie that clearly ended here, the house seemed fine. There wasn't any demonic activity around it. No evil aura urging me to run the other way. No dark halo. No sign of a portal. Nothing out of the ordinary at all.

Huh. Weird.

But the tie definitely ended in here. I couldn't see the end of the tie exactly. I knew that it was stronger here, which usually happened at the other end of a tie.

This had to be it. I was sure of it.

And if I was wrong, I'd apologize for ringing someone's doorbell in the middle of the night.

I walked up to the door with Phoenix a step behind me and pushed the doorbell.

I waited a second, but no one came.

I pressed the doorbell again.

Waited.

"Maybe no one is home?" Phoenix said.

"They could be asleep. It's really late." But the light was on. I banged on the door harder. "Hello!" I yelled through the door. "I'm sorry to bother you, but I need to speak to whoever lives here. It's a matter of life and death. *Please.*"

I hit it one more time, and sure enough, a moment later, the door opened.

The man in front of me started to ask a question and then froze. Exactly how I'd frozen as soon as the door opened.

He was wearing black sweatpants and a black T-shirt with a print of a knight in armor holding a flaming sword in his hand. The knight was white, but the flames on the sword were yellow and orange and red. Under it, it were the words *Ephesians 6. Know it. Live it.*

I laughed when I got to the end. "Great shirt." He always had the best shirts. *Dang it.*

He leaned against the door jamb. "Thanks."

"You never gave me the website for where you got them."

I could almost feel Phoenix holding his breath. I didn't know how, but I could.

"Yeah. I didn't want to give up all my secrets. If it was the one reason you thought I was cool, I couldn't afford to give that up."

He'd intentionally kept them from me? That was annoying. "I had no secrets from you."

He looked down, and the regret on his face was impossible to miss. "Yeah. I know." He cleared his throat and looked at me again. This time all the shock and humor were gone from his face. "What brings you to my doorstep in the middle of the night, Sammie?"

"How do you know him?" Phoenix asked softly.

I dropped my chin to my chest and closed my eyes. "My past. This is my past. This is what the Black-Eyed Children were talking about."

Car doors slammed behind me, and I didn't have to look back to know that everyone was out of the car now.

"Eli must think he's really funny right now," I said softly. There was no way he didn't know where the tie led. And he just let me come here and ring the doorbell completely unprepared, like a moron.

No wonder he'd used that cocky, arrogant tone with me. I thought he'd been trying to annoy me—as usual—but nope. This was why.

I was going to have to talk to him about that. "Look, Hunter. I didn't know this was your house."

He crossed his arms and stared at me. "You didn't?" He sounded as confused as I felt—maybe even a little disbelieving.

That was frustrating, but if he wanted to think I waited years to track him down…and then, on top of that, waited until the middle of the night to talk to him…

No. I wasn't going to even try to address that. It wasn't worth the time. "I'm here on a work trip with the Wayfarer Pack." I motioned behind me without looking back. "Earlier tonight, I ran into a particular demon. I was given advice to follow a demonic tie to its source, and it led me here."

The smile slowly melted and the color drained from his face. "What?"

"There's a demonic tie on your soul." I pointed to his chest. "Do you live alone?"

He was quiet for a beat, and then yelled, "What?!"

"It's not your fault. I know you're a good guy. I'm not saying anything—"

"I don't get it." He waved a hand when I tried to defend what I said. "No. Stop. I'm not saying you're wrong. I know what you can do. I just…*how*? I'm so careful."

This was the tricky part. If the tie was in him, then someone in his house was the boo hag. "Are you married? Dating someone? Or do you have a roommate or…" I needed to find the end of the tie.

"Why are you asking me that?" His gaze went behind me. "I was sleeping, so maybe I'm being slow, but this is…" He scrunched his brows. "Am I having some sort of nightmare?" He looked at me again. "This is a nightmare, right?"

"Great. Now seeing me is his nightmare," I said under my breath. "Again. That feels…*special*." That was one of the things he'd said to me when he left. I was a nightmare. His worst nightmare.

Phoenix's hand came to my shoulder, and he leaned close. "Don't let him bother you like that, but to be fair, I don't think he meant it that way."

"Who are you?" Hunter asked, and not very nicely.

This was so not going how I'd planned.

Actually, I hadn't gotten as far as planning this part of it, but this sucked. "I…um…" I looked at Phoenix, whose brows rose, as if to tell me it was up to me what I said.

Great. I sucked at this kind of thing. "This is my…" Dang it. What was I supposed to call him? "…Phoenix."

"*Your* Phoenix?" Hunter sounded shocked.

I was messing this up.

I looked back at Phoenix, who gave me the smile that I was pretty sure he absolutely knew made me melt. It was the dimple. It wasn't fair he had that.

"*Help,*" I mouthed. I didn't know what I was supposed to call him. We were grown-ups. Boyfriend felt so…adolescent. And temporary. What we had was more than that but calling him my anchor sounded so bizarre. No one on God's green Earth would understand what that meant, especially when I wasn't even sure I understood the full implications of it.

Phoenix stepped around me and held out his hand. "Hi. I'm Phoenix. Samantha's *boyfriend*." He tipped his head down to look at me as he said the last word.

My heart picked up at that, and he winked at me.

"Anyway." My voice was way too high, and my cheeks were flaming. "Sorry." I cleared my throat. "Man, I'm messing this up." But this was not what I'd been expecting at all.

I heard Tessa laugh from the sidewalk and then try to stifle it. I sneaked a peek, and sure enough, she was shaking her head. "Shut up," I whispered as softly as I could, knowing she could hear me just fine. But that just made her laugh even harder.

Okay. Fine. This was awkward, but I was well and fully shocked.

And son of a biscuit eater. Frank mentioned something about Hunter moving to South Carolina, but he hadn't said where. And even if he had, how big was Charleston? What were the chances that I would knock on the door of the only person I knew here?

No. Wait. This was a God thing. Only He could set things up like this.

I'd been thinking of Hunter and expecting Phoenix to behave similarly, so He made sure our paths crossed.

I looked up at the night sky. *You have some sense of humor.*

It was too late to back out now. I came here to rid someone of a demonic tie. That it turned out to be Hunter didn't matter all that much. "Phoenix, this is Hunter. My ex." I looked at Hunter. "Can we come in?"

He looked past me. "Those guys with you, too? Are they coming in?"

I glanced back at the SUV. Everyone was out of the car and waiting on the sidewalk, ready for me to wave them forward. "They're with me, but we'll leave them outside for now." I looked at Hunter. "I don't want to overwhelm you."

He stepped back from the doorway. "Alright. Come in."

"Thanks." I stepped into his house. "Sorry to show up here and barge in unannounced. I know it's a little late."

"It's fine." He looked beyond us to the street, and then his gaze slid to mine. "You said they were pack? Like werewolves?"

"Yes. I'm the resident demonologist for the Sanctuary pack. I took the job a while back, but I travel around with other packs that need help as part of my job. Today, that job is in Charleston."

"Got it. And Phoenix is…"

I shrugged. "Just Phoenix." He wasn't a werewolf if that was what Hunter was asking.

Hunter's eyes grew wide. "Like an actual bird that goes up in flames?"

Phoenix stepped into the house. "Nah, man. I'm not a supernatural. That's just my name. Thanks to my hippie mother."

"Got it." He studied Phoenix for a second. "You look familiar."

"Yeah. I get that a lot." He didn't say anything else—no confirming or denying—just left it out there. I'd noticed that he never told anyone what he did or who he was, even if they sort of recognized him. He didn't seem to mind attention, but he didn't go looking for the spotlight.

When Phoenix didn't say anything about why he might look familiar, Hunter closed the door and showed us to his living room. There was a big TV, a small couch and two love seats on either end making a U-shape. There was a black and white patterned rug and a marble-topped coffee table. He didn't have a ton of knickknacks, and I didn't see too many signs of a lady living here.

"What's this really about? There's no way I have a demonic tie," he said, and I realized I'd been scrutinizing his living room. Not my best look.

I sat on one of the loveseats and stared at him. The faint red tie disappeared into his soul, and man, this wasn't going to be fun. "Have you ever heard of a boo hag?"

He looked at Phoenix for a second, who was standing next to the loveseat. Hunter seemed to decide something and sat on his couch. I had no idea what just ran through his head, but he focused back on me. "Yeah. Yeah, I have."

At least I didn't have to explain that part. "There's really no easy way to say this, and I'm sorry. I know it's going to absolutely suck coming from me. But tonight I saw a boo hag at a restaurant. I followed its tie to its lair. It led me here."

"Give me a break." He rolled his eyes. "You had me going there for a second, but I'm not a boo hag, Sammie."

I swallowed down my frustration with him. He didn't need that. "I'm not saying you are. You don't look like one to me."

"Great. Then, we cleared this up, and you and your *boyfriend* can go so that I can go back to bed." He started to get up.

"No. I need to get rid of the tie. It's important, but the boo hag lives here. Do you have a roommate or a girlfriend or—"

"No. There's *no one,* Samantha. I don't have a girlfriend who lives with me. I'm not married or anything. Are you satisfied now? Knowing that I regret what happened?"

Oh, boy. "That's not what this is about. I'm sorry you have regrets about the way things ended." I shoved down all the awful things he screamed at me the last time I saw him. That wasn't important right now.

Someone had to live here. Otherwise, what on earth was he doing with the boo hag's demon tie? "The boo hag that I saw had curly, strawberry blonde hair. Thin, not too tall. She was wearing a long, black puffer coat. Does someone live here who looks like that?"

"My sister. Sophia. You never met her. She was the one going to college in the UK." He paused, and a look of fear crossed his face. "She has curly, strawberry blonde hair, but she doesn't technically live here. Her job…there was a problem. The family she nannied for was going through something, and she was fired. She moved in a few weeks ago. It's just temporary." He closed his eyes. "You can't honestly think she's been taken by a boo hag." His face hardened. "You're wrong."

"I'm so sorry, Hunter. I wish I was wrong."

"You're *wrong*." His face was turning red, and I knew this was about to get ugly.

"I wish I was wrong," I said softly, calmly, but there was no easy way to say this. Nothing I could do that would help. "But I'm not. I'm so sorry to be the one to tell you this. I really, truly am."

"No, you're not. You're enjoying this."

I leaned back. He really thought the worst of me if he could say that. "No, I'm really not. This is awful. For everyone. You especially, I know." I took a breath. "Has your sister been acting off at all? Anything—"

"No!" He left no room for convincing. "You're wrong. You have the wrong house. My sister is *fine*." He got up and started pacing. "You always do this, Sam. *Always*." He waved his arms as he said the worst things about me. About how I caused so many problems. That evil was drawn to anyone who dared to spend any time with me. It wasn't as bad as it had been years ago, but none of this was exactly fun or nice or anything remotely pleasant.

I leaned against the seat and looked up at Phoenix.

He raised a brow and then motioned with his chin. "Don't listen to what he says," he whispered to me while Hunter continued his rant. "He's hurting—"

Hunter said something super inappropriate that I wasn't about to repeat.

"Scratch that. He went too far with that one. Want me to beat him up?" He gave me a wink to let me know he was joking.

This moment was why I was here. This.

Phoenix had noticed something off with his sister so he tracked down Frank, even though he didn't know what his sister was into. He just knew something was wrong. When I told him to run from his sister, he didn't argue. He trusted me.

Hunter always fought with me. I'd forgotten that part. I remembered all the fun times and brushed off all the times he questioned what I *saw* or how I did things. I'd been so glad for a friend that I never minded explaining myself. But I'd forgotten it was never just an explanation. It was an argument. An argument that sometimes got a little ugly.

Phoenix was different. He believed me. He wasn't holding back, and yet, I was. I kept waiting for him to be like Hunter. But he never would be.

Hunter was still ranting, and I knew it wasn't going to get any better. I had to just fix this and leave him to grieve. Me being here wasn't helping him at all.

I rose from my seat and reached out to Hunter as he paced by, grabbing a hold of the tie. I closed my eyes and let my power rise, relaxing enough so that I felt the fire in my veins.

And then I poured it into the tie.

Hunter gasped and stumbled back, falling onto the couch.

"There. The tie is gone," I said, trying to keep my frustration out of my voice. "I'm so incredibly sorry about Sophia. I know you don't want me to stick around, so I'm going to try to get out of your way. I just broke the tie it has to you. The boo hag will be racing back here now. I'll take care of that, too. I just have to check the house for one more thing, and then I'll wait outside to deal with the hag. It seems the best thing for you is for me to leave. I hope you know that if you need anything, you can call me." I started to walk away, but Hunter let out a little helpless noise.

"Shit, Sammie. I'm sorry." He swallowed and bent down over

his legs. "What do I do when my sister comes back? What do I tell my parents? I can't..."

I didn't have any way to make this easier. Not really. "Again, I'm so sorry, Hunter," I said it softer this time. "I have some friends who will help you with what happens after. Counseling and getting proper death certificates and all the details that comes with a loss like this. They'll also help you decide what to tell the rest of your family and friends. But I want to make sure I get the last demonic tie. I'm going to look for a doorway in the house so that it can't come back and hurt you. Is that okay?"

Hunter didn't answer, so I took that as a yes.

"Will you wait with him?" I asked Phoenix.

"I can. You'll yell if you need me?"

"Yeah. Thanks." Hunter was crying, but I knew he didn't want me to comfort him. I was probably the last person he wanted around him right now.

I needed to get this done so I could hand him off to the experts. They'd take care of him, and he'd be more open to accepting their help.

I made my way through the house. There was a small office off the dining room. A guest room. A bathroom. And then I hit the jackpot. It looked like it had been a guest room, but this had to be her room. There were clothes on the floor.

I stepped over them and made my way to the closet. I could feel the doorway's pull.

I opened the closet door, and a light came on. I moved the shoes on the floor, trying to see if it was there, but there was nothing.

I searched the back wall. Nothing.

I shoved the clothes along the right railing to see the wall, and that was when I saw it. The spell, written in red. It felt like the portal, but different. Less. More subtle, but also less complicated.

And there was a hook. Where I guessed she kept her skin.

Gross.

I unzipped my belt bag, and sprayed water on the metaphysical door. It hissed and steamed, and I said a quick prayer of cleansing.

When I finished, the words faded and that tugging feeling in my soul was gone.

The house was cleared. Easy enough.

I made my way back through the house and into the living room. Hunter was still crying on the couch, and Phoenix was leaning against the wall.

"How's he doing?" I asked.

"He's not talking, but he's devastated, Sam. This is really awful."

"I know." Despite everything that happened between us, I never wanted Hunter to hurt like this. I moved to sit next to him. "I took care of the portal. I'm so sorry, Hunter. If there's something I can do or anything—"

The front door swung open, and Hunter's sister walked in.

Wait. Not his sister. The boo hag.

Thanks so much for the warning, Tessa. I wanted to yell at her, but it was too late now.

I rose from the couch, ready for a fight.

So much for doing this the easy way.

CHAPTER TWENTY-NINE

SAMANTHA

CLOSE UP IT was easier to tell that the boo hag was a demon. Much easier. Its skin looked like gauze stretched over muscle.

Sophia scanned the room, settling on Hunter. "Hey, Hunt. You having a party without me? There's a bunch of people outside." It smiled at us, until it saw me standing there, watching it.

The facade faded, and it was almost as if, for a split second, the skin it wore faded to nothing. "*You.*"

"Me." It might not know who I was, but it knew *what* I was. I hadn't shoved my power back inside me. It was on display for anyone who could see the spiritual realm.

It scanned the room, then turned and sprinted through the house. I assumed it was heading for a back door.

"Dang it."

"On it," Phoenix said. "She's running out the back," Phoenix yelled as he ran through the house, knowing the werewolves would hear him. "Don't let her get away."

I turned to follow Phoenix, but Hunter grabbed my elbow. I stared at his hand, and was so thankful I was wearing a sweater and a jacket. I shoved down my power just in case he went for my skin. He knew how this worked, and there was no way I wanted him to touch my skin while I was open to the spiritual realm.

Never again.

"Show me."

Everything in me froze.

Did he really just demand that from me?

No. I'd misheard him. There was no way he actually wanted what he was asking for.

I narrowed my gaze. "What is it that you want me to show you exactly?"

"*Please*. I need to know my sister is gone." His grip tightened on my jacket. "I *have* to know. I can't let you kill her if that's really her."

I closed my eyes. Man. I went years—*years*—never showing anyone what I could see, and now, I was apparently letting anyone see? What was wrong with me? This wasn't how I worked.

Bad things happened when I showed people what I could do.

"I know I didn't do well last time—"

My eyes opened, and a surprised, humorless laugh slipped free before I could stop it. "*Didn't do well*?" I took a breath because anger and bitterness would do no good to me here.

Wait. I had to say something. "You lost your ever-loving mind. Ranted at me about how I was *evil*. You said some of the worst things anyone has ever said to me, and then you stormed out. I haven't heard from you in *years*." I looked up as I tried to rein in my temper. "God, you really have an unfunny sense of humor sometimes."

I took a second to shove the anger back down, but man, Hunter fired me up with that one ask.

There was no way he'd do okay with it. We'd just told him some really bad news. Epically bad. That wasn't going to help him accept what he would see.

"I'm sorry, Samantha. Truly." For the first time tonight, Hunter didn't sound aggressive with me. His voice softened to the

Hunter I'd known when we first met. "I know what I said. I know what I did, and I know that I probably hurt you. But you just told me that my sister is dead. That some monster is wearing her skin. If I can't…" His voice trailed off. "If I can't *see* it for myself, I'll always wonder if…" He paused. "Please, Sam. It's about closure for me and my sister."

I got that. I did. I understood the need for closure. Which he might not get. Not unless he could see.

Instead, he'd blame me for his sister's death. He would think I was the evil one who sent her to Hell. Especially since he'd *seen* before. He would need to see the truth for himself more than anyone else I worked with. He couldn't take it on faith or trust. Not anymore.

"If I do this, it might make it worse for you," I said.

"*Please.*"

Now he was begging?

I couldn't believe I was doing this. "I will show you again, but would you like to call a friend over? Someone to sit with you until it wears off? It will last a little while, and if you don't…"

"One of us can sit with him until a friend comes or it wears off," Max said as he walked through the door. "We have the boo hag. Where would you like to do this?"

"Is it in the backyard?"

"Yes." Max shrugged. "We probably should've stopped it from coming in, but we thought it might exacerbate what was happening in here. Sorry if that was the wrong call. We were standing just outside the door, waiting to see what it would do."

Ah. Now, it made more sense why no one gave me a warning. "Got it. Don't worry about it."

Max studied me, then his gaze went to Hunter and flashed wolf-bright.

Oh boy. Now, Hunter had the wolves mad at him. Because of course they'd heard every word. "Alright, Hunter. I'm going to show you what you've been living with for the last little while, and then I'm going to send it where it needs to go."

I looked at Max. "Where are the others?"

"We've got a good-sized group here now, but one group went on patrol. They'll stay mobile in case we catch a lead here. They're hanging closer to the water, in the neighborhood where the yellow house is. I have a feeling that if this is all connected, we'll end up back there. But I might be wrong."

That was actually smart. "No. I have a feeling that'll turn out to be a really good call. Can you tell them to wait for me before they engage in any kind of fight?"

"Sure. I can do that." He turned to Hunter. "There's a lock on the gate? We can all jump it, but it would be helpful to just open it. It draws less attention."

"0-8-2-7." His voice was soft and unsure as he answered.

Hunter couldn't have surprised me more with that code.

"Got it." Max went outside, and I just stood there with my jaw gaping open like a moron.

"You're kidding with that. It's some kind of sick joke." August twenty-seventh was the day we started dating.

"It was easy to remember, and no one else would know it." His shoulders crumpled. "This is turning out to be the absolute worst day."

He was right. He was a victim here. His sister was dead, and I didn't need to pile on more. But why would he choose that date of all the codes for his gate?

Let it go, Samantha. This was the final sign that I needed to just let everything that happened with Hunter go. I wasn't going to be bound to past mistakes or hurts. Not anymore. "I'm sorry for your loss. Truly. Are you ready?"

"No. I'm not. But I need to see."

"Okay." I let my power well up inside me as I walked to him and held out my hand. "Whenever you're ready."

He stared at my hand for what felt like a long time, and then his breath rushed out of him, and he gripped my hand, hard. It was almost as if he didn't think he'd do it if he didn't go all in.

Fine. It was done. I closed my eyes, relaxing everything fully to make sure passed on what I saw.

I heard footsteps behind me.

"Whoa," Hunter said. "Why do you glow so much?"

I didn't have to look to know who he meant, but I did because he made me happy. I smiled over my shoulder at Phoenix. "He glows like that because he's a really, *really* good guy." And I needed to realize that I was worthy of him.

I wasn't sure how it was possible, but I needed to work on just being grateful he was mine.

Phoenix smiled at me. "You okay?"

I nodded. "Better now."

His smile deepened, giving me the dimple, and I rolled my eyes. He was too much.

"Okay. I'm ready," Hunter said, and he dropped my hand.

I wiggled my fingers to get feeling back in them. "Let's go." I waved him forward. "After you."

Phoenix and I followed Hunter through his house to the back door that opened onto a deck. The railing around the deck was strung with Christmas lights. There was a grill and a small table and chairs—enough to seat four people. Beyond the deck was grass, and I could see a garden off to the right.

I knew it couldn't have been Hunters. One of the things we had in common was our complete black thumb.

"That was Sophia's," he said, answering my unspoken question. "She didn't have room for a garden at her place, so she asked to use my backyard. Before she moved in."

"I'm sorry. I wish I had better news."

The wolves held her as she writhed on the ground. No one was hurting her, just keeping her pinned until I got there.

Hunter started forward, but I held up a hand. "Just look from the porch. *See* the truth of what is here on the ground."

I watched him. His face was already pale, but when he saw her as I could, his legs crumpled.

Phoenix came behind him, easing him down into a sitting position on the deck.

"Do you know how long she's been like that?" Hunter asked.

"I don't know. I just saw her. She was eating at the same restaurant we were, and I followed the tie here." I still wasn't sure how this connected to the bigger bad that was killing wolves, but I knew it would come. "How long ago did your sister move in?"

"A few weeks, maybe? Her roommate disappeared, and then she lost her job. She needed a place to land, so of course, I helped her."

Lost her job. He'd said that before. "Where did she work again?"

"She was a nanny for a family."

There it was. The connection I'd been looking for. I wasn't sure it meant I could trust those Black-Eyed Children, and I didn't know if Gabe had really sent them, but I couldn't deny there was something here. "Do you know if the family she nannied for lived in a yellow house?"

"Yes. Why?"

"I closed a portal there earlier today. Do you know where that family moved to?"

"I don't know for sure, but the wife's parents live a few blocks away. Really close to the water." He rattled off an address. "I'd check there first if you're looking for them. They're good people, and I wasn't sure why they fired Sophia, but I guess I know now."

I looked at Dastien, but he moved away as he pulled out his phone. He'd heard. "Don't engage without me," I said.

Dastien held up a hand to signal that he heard me.

I sat next to Hunter. "I'm so incredibly sorry for your loss. I wish there was something more I could do."

"Are you sure there's no way to bring her back? Not like an exorcism you can perform or something? Anything?"

I wished I could give him a hopeful answer, but there wasn't one. "That thing over there isn't your sister. I need you to understand what you're seeing. That is a demon who has already murdered your sister and is now wearing her skin. Your sister's soul isn't there any longer. Only the shell." I didn't want to leave any room for him to misunderstand what I was saying. Otherwise, in time, he might twist what he saw. He might think she could've been saved. That I murdered his sister, not sent a demon to Hell.

Seeing it up close could be more hurtful, and he was already grieving. "I didn't want to make this harder, but if you want to get a closer look, we can."

"I think I have to. I don't want to leave any question in my mind."

"Okay." I got up and motioned for him to stand up. "Come on. Let's go see it."

He rose slowly, and I turned, walking toward the demon pinned to the ground.

As I approached it, the demon started saying things. Awful things. Things I didn't think his sister would ever say. Or I hoped she wouldn't have ever said.

Hunter took her in. Took me in. The wolves. Phoenix. And then looked back to his sister, staring at her for a good long while.

"That's not her," he said as silent tears ran down his face.

Two wrongs never made a right. No matter what he'd done to me, I never wanted to see him in pain like this. "No. I'm so sorry, Hunter. It's not her. She's gone."

"Can you show her to me?"

I pressed my lips together. He knew the answer, but he was asking anyway. It would be easy for me to be frustrated, but instead, I tried to show patience and kindness. I'd already snapped at him a couple of times, but I wasn't going to do it again. I needed to finish strong. The way that I knew would make my mother proud.

"You know I can't do that, but I want you to remember you're a man of faith. You know where she is, okay? You'll see her again. It's not forever. It's just goodbye in this realm." He didn't look at me. His gaze stayed focused on the monster that had taken his sister's skin as silent tears kept rolling down his face.

"Okay." He took a few steps back. "Do it. I can't…" He paused. "I can't look at this anymore. This is—" His voice broke. "This is awful. My sister didn't deserve this. What good can come from this?"

I grabbed him before he could go. "I know you're upset, but I want you to remember this world is broken. And evil can flourish. Bad things happen to good people all the time, but the demon did this. I don't know what good will come from it, but I know she *will* be redeemed. She will not be forgotten. I'm going to end this because it's what I can do to help, but please, think about talking to someone. Don't lose faith because of what a monster did to your sister."

"I know you're right, but my heart is too broken right now to hear your words. I'm sorry, Sammie. I'm sorry I was awful to you."

That was what I was worried about. "This wasn't because of that. You're not being punished. That's not how God works."

"I know. But you being here makes it feel like it was my fault." He spun and walked back to the porch. My gaze caught Phoenix's, and he gave me a nod, following Hunter to sit with him.

I was making it worse for him. I hated that. Which meant I needed to finish this and get out of here. Fast.

"Alright, everyone," I said. "I'm going to open a portal right under her. I don't want to fight her, and I don't want anyone falling in. On the count of three, you let her go and jump as far away from her as you can. You won't be able to see it, so you gotta go with me on this. I say three, you move. Werewolf fast. Got it?"

There was a chorus of yeses, and I started to count. "One."

"Two."

"Three."

The wolves jumped away, and I said, "*Aperta*," quickly, sending my power along the spiritual realm.

Sophia tried to get up, but the portal opened up below her, and she screamed as she fell, disappearing into Hell.

"*Claudere.*" The portal shut. "Well, that was easier than it could've been." It was somewhat anti-climactic after all the battles I'd fought lately, and then I winced.

I just jinxed it.

Something really bad was going to happen. I could feel it.

Oh well. Too late now.

I looked back at Hunter. Phoenix sat with him as Hunter silently cried.

This sucked. I didn't feel like I'd done any good here. It wasn't my fault he was weeping on his back porch, but in a way, I felt like I caused it.

Which I knew was as wrong as Hunter feeling like he caused it. But I understood the feeling. Truly.

I walked up to the porch, stopping just a few steps away.

"What do I tell my parents?" Hunter asked.

Man. I had no idea. "Whatever makes you feel comfortable. The pack has a team that can help with that."

I motioned Max over. "Can you set him up with your care team?"

"I can absolutely do that. They're on standby, but I'll get them here now that he's approved it." Max pulled out his phone to get it rolling.

"Thank you." I looked back at Hunter.

Was I supposed to stay? I didn't want to. I wanted to leave. Right away.

Phoenix looked up at me and raised a brow. The silent question on his face. He didn't know what to do either. It felt like we were intruding on something private.

"Can I call someone for you? Do anything?"

"No. I texted my friend. He's coming."

I nodded. "Max will have someone stay with you, but would you like me to stay until your friend gets here?"

"No." He looked up at me. "I…I had things I wanted to say to you if I ever saw you again, but I…I can't do that now. I need you to go. Now. Please."

"Sure. You have my deepest condolences." Was there something I was forgetting? "My personal email hasn't changed. Let me know if there's ever anything I can do to help you."

A howl ripped through the night, and I spun to see Max had shifted.

"What?"

Another wolf shifted and a chorus of howls broke through the night.

"What's happening?"

"One of the Wayfarer wolves is injured. Close to dying." Dastien's eyes flashed a bright golden color, and he reached out, grabbing Tessa's hand—I wasn't sure if he was gaining strength from her or vice versa.

I knew all pack members were connected through their bonds, and packs were also loosely connected. I didn't know how much of the attack these wolves felt, but even the werewolves who hadn't shifted to wolves were struggling to hold their human forms.

"We sent the team that was out patrolling to the house Hunter mentioned. It's not going well," Tessa said.

Dang it. "They should've waited for me."

We had to go. Now.

I looked at the werewolves who hadn't shifted. "Someone stay with Hunter. Finish what Max started. Stay until the care team arrives, and then come find us. The rest are with me. Get in the cars."

God, help us. I hoped I wouldn't be too late, but I had a feeling I already was.

I ran through the yard, following Dastien and Tessa through the gate, around the house, and sprinting for the SUV. I'd never been so glad to have a reason to leave a place. Even if it was for a fight.

I didn't want to linger in the past, and I certainly didn't want to sit around comforting Hunter. I knew the care team would help. They were trained for this exact situation—they'd secure a death certificate for Sophia and handle the procedures and paperwork that would get Hunter in a place where he could grieve, and eventually, heal.

I was trained to help the grieving process, but Hunter didn't want to hear it from me. There was too much history between us. Someone else would be much more effective for him.

So, I let everything happened at Hunter's house go as reached the SUV.

"I'm driving," Dastien said. "I have it in my phone already. Garrett—you get in the way back with Max. We can't have him losing it if your wolf dies."

"Got it," Garrett's words were more growl than anything else.

Dastien slipped into the driver's seat, and Tessa rode shotgun.

The SUV behind us the seats all folded down, and the wolves who had shifted were leaping into it from the trunk.

When Garrett and Max were settled in the way back, Phoenix flipped the seat back in place and motioned me to get in. I slid down the bench, and he got in, closing the door. "We're set," Phoenix said to Dastien.

Howls ripped through the night, and Max answered it. I covered my ears with my hands, and Tessa glanced back at me.

Sometimes it was easy to forget that she was a werewolf. Because she'd been bitten, she was short and not as muscular as the typical female werewolf. But with her eyes glowing like the moon, there was no mistaking what she was.

"He's dead." She turned to Dastien. "*Drive.*" Her alpha power rippled around her, and I knew she was itching for battle.

This was it.

This was what I'd come to Charleston for.

We'd lost another wolf, but I wasn't going to let another one die.

This had to end.

I would end it.

CHAPTER THIRTY

SAMANTHA

DASTIEN SPED through traffic like it was his job. He was usually really safe, but my heart raced as he wove between cars.

"Don't worry," Tessa said. "I can smell your fear, but werewolves have really good reflexes. He won't wreck."

"Easy for you to say," I said, teasing her. "Fast healing werewolves are super annoying sometimes."

Tessa huffed, and the tension in the car went down a notch or two.

"Is your life always like this?" Phoenix asked as Dastien ran another red light. There was barely any traffic, but still, I wasn't enjoying this car ride. At all.

"No," I said, almost automatically, but Tessa shot me a look. "Come on, Tess. It isn't always this bad. At least not for me." I shrugged. "The pack usually calls me out on something every month or so. Sometimes not for a couple months, and then we have a heavy month with two or three calls. But for the most part, it's an exorcism they need me to perform."

"There was that demon in New York," Tessa said from the front. "And the one that we hunted in Mexico."

"Right." Way to be super helpful, Tessa. "I mean, okay. Yeah. There are exceptions, but at least seventy-five percent of my calls with the pack are simple exorcisms. Which is more like what I did in the apartment. Not like what I did with your sister. That was different. That was an excellently planned and executed plot from my father. Same with Van. Usually, these things have nothing to do with me." I looked at Tessa. "Right?"

"That's fair. Dastien and I travel quite a bit investigating all kinds of things, and the FBI has asked for our help a few times. This kind of danger is more our speed. I think there have been only a handful of actual monsters that we've needed Sam's help with."

Max howled and started to go wild in the back. Garrett let out a string of curses.

"*Stop,*" Dastien's power rolled through the car, nearly stealing my breath, but the scuffle in the backseat stopped instantly.

"You okay back there?" Dastien asked, his voice sounded deeper, rougher, more growly than I'd heard before.

"Yeah. Yeah. I'm good," Garrett said. "*Damn it,* but I'm holding on."

Tessa twisted to look at us. "Another Wayfarer just died."

Damn it. I was supposed to be helping them, and I'd done nothing. "I'm so sorry. I told them to wait for us, but I should've made that an order. I knew that group was ready to fight whatever was killing their pack, and now—"

"It's not your fault," Garrett said with a grow in his voice. "Those guys wouldn't have been able to back down. They knew they weren't supposed to engage, but their wolves were in control, pushing them to check the house. We're getting close. Who's going wolf?"

"You and I are," Dastien said to Garrett. "Tessa stays human to do any talking and coordinating."

"Good. I can't hold this shape for long. My wolf wants free."

"The other SUVs are right behind us. Whatever this is, it ends tonight." Dastien's gaze caught mine in the rearview mirror. "You point us at it, we fight it. You need to open a portal, you tell us where, we move. I don't want you getting hurt. That helps no one. Got it?"

I nodded. "Got it." I wasn't sure that was how it'd go, but I appreciated the sentiment.

Dastien pulled to a stop in front of a house. It looked to be in the same neighborhood as the other house. "Hunter said it was close to the yellow house, but this feels really close." We'd driven around a lot, but this felt familiar.

"Yes. We're maybe a minute's drive."

We might've even walked past the house. "Okay." Maybe I hadn't noticed it because the other portal had been too close by? Because there was definitely an aura here. Smaller, but noticeable in the wee hours.

We all got out of the SUV, and Dastien and Garrett immediately started stripping off their clothes.

The other SUVs parked and the rest started doing the same, while the wolves that had changed already raced to the house.

"Whoa," Phoenix said. "What are they doing?"

I kept my eyes turned away from the guys. They didn't care. From what I knew, werewolves didn't have a hint of...wait. No. It wasn't that they weren't modest. It was more that switching forms meant getting naked. No one stared or got creepy about it. They put clothes back on as soon as they shifted back to human. That was just part of being what they were, who they were.

But I didn't need to see all that. "They're going to shift. Can't do that with their clothes on."

"Well, they could," Tessa said. "But it gets tricky. You can get caught in the clothes. That isn't something you want when you're going into a fight."

I went around the other side of the SUV, letting my power roll through me, and studied the front of the house.

Demons were everywhere. All kinds. All sizes. It was a *cluster*. But none of them should've been able to kill a wolf.

Everything went silent for a moment, and then there was a howl.

Followed by more howls.

The wolves raced off around the side of the house to help their pack members.

Wolves were fast. There was no way a human could keep up with them, even Phoenix. Instead, we ran behind them with Tessa hanging back to protect us.

"Do you know anything?" I asked Tessa. "Is Dastien telling you anything?"

"No. Not yet."

"Can you still see?" I asked Phoenix.

"Yes," he said.

Weird. I wondered if Eli had done something to Phoenix, but that was for another day.

"Can you Tessa?"

"No. It was gone hours ago."

That was more typical. Something was going on with Phoenix, but I couldn't worry about that right now.

"There are so many demons climbing out of the house." Phoenix sounded worried. "Are they drawn to the fight or…"

"Could be that, but there's another portal open in there." No wonder I had to wander around the neighborhood so much. I'd been so confused by why it'd taken so long to find it, but now it made complete sense. There had been two portals the whole time. This one was just smaller, so I hadn't noticed it. I fixed the bigger one, and thought I was done.

Exhaustion was my only excuse. I'd been so wiped when I finished with the first one, and it was so big and complicated with layered spellwork, that I'd thought it was the source of everything.

I was wrong, and wolves were dying tonight because of my mistake.

There were howls and growls and snaps of breaking branches around the back of the house. I slowed to a walk as we slid through a hole of broken bushes the wolves had made on the side of the house.

The wolves were fighting, but there wasn't anything to see.

Where was the monster?

A wolf was lifted into the air and flung at the house. He crashed through a window, and I hoped he was okay.

It was just glass. He had to be fine.

But based on the movement of the wolves, they were fighting blind, too. Which wasn't easy.

"I don't see anything," Phoenix said. "Did it go away?"

"Neither do I." Why couldn't I see it? Dark magic? A curse? I wasn't sure, but I could feel magic pushing along my skin, making it itch and crawl like ten thousand spiders were swarming every inch of my body.

I couldn't fight what I couldn't see. "Maybe I can change that." I held my hands up in the air. *"The Lord gave me eyes to see and ears to hear, and in His name, with the power of the Holy Spirit, and Jesus, the son of God, Who came into the world to save us, I command you to show yourself."*

There was a roar and a ripple, and my heart picked up.

I knew that roar.

I knew it.

It plagued my nightmares.

"Eli! I need you!" I screamed through all the realms.

I gripped the bond I shared with my father and started knotting it furiously. One. Another. A third. *Please, God. Let this be enough.* If Astaroth started draining me through our tie, I wouldn't make it through this fight.

The roar came again, then a laugh.

That was the sign.

He knew I was here now.

He felt me.

"What the hell was that?" Phoenix asked, his eyes wide.

I couldn't say the words. I couldn't answer him. I didn't want to say it. I didn't want it to be true.

"Please tell me that isn't what I think it is." Tessa sounded scared, and she had good reason to be terrified.

"Don't follow me." My voice sounded hollow and airy. "Get as far away from me as you can. I'll lead him away, and then…" And then, I wasn't sure.

There was only one other thing that was important. "*Run*."

I turned and started sprinting down the side of the house, knowing that he would chase me. He wouldn't let me go now.

There were shouts around me, but I threw myself into the front yard as if the hounds of Hell were chasing me.

Because that was as good as the truth.

Tessa and Phoenix called for me to stop as I sprinted down the street, but I couldn't stop.

I was so beyond screwed.

I hit the street, and the pavement rolled like a wave under my feet. I nearly tripped, but I caught myself.

My father was powerful. His influence—spiritual, mental, physical—could be felt in every realm. He wasn't visible to mortal eyes, but he could interact with the mortal realm more than any other demon. A person would have to be an oblivious, brain-dead moron to not feel his presence.

This demon was one of his creations. It wasn't him exactly. This monster held a fragment of him in it. A big enough fragment to do a lot of damage and *kill*.

I was stupid. I'd taken it as good luck that my father hadn't found the portal in the yellow house, but now I was wondering if he'd influenced whoever opened it.

And worse—it never occurred to me that he was already through it.

Or at least, that one of his forms was here.

Phoenix sprinted next to me. I knew he could run faster than me, especially since I hadn't been training, but he kept pace with me.

"You have to get away from me."

"No. I really don't. Why isn't Eli here yet?" The jerk didn't even sound winded.

"I have no idea. He must be busy." He'd said he was busy, but he usually came when I was in this much danger.

Footsteps crashed after me. Right behind me.

My father was fast, and I wasn't much faster. But I did have a head start. I couldn't let that slip away.

I slid as I turned down another street—not slowing down. I didn't dare slow down.

Thud.

Dirt and gravel rained down on me, but I didn't stop. I didn't hesitate. I kept sprinting as fast as my legs would carry me, cursing myself for letting Mom, Chris, Cosette, everyone talk me out of training. I shouldn't have taken any days off.

If I made it out of this alive, I promised myself I would work out every day, no matter what. Wait. No. Two times a day. More. Anything to get me back to where I'd been. To get me better than that.

I needed a plan. Something. I didn't know what, but Phoenix was in danger.

I glanced to the side. He was still running right next to me. We were sprinting down the middle of the street, passing houses of sleeping people, blissfully oblivious to the evil running behind us.

I glanced at my watch. It was closing in on three in the morning. Astaroth's peak power.

Panic swelled inside me, making it harder to breathe, and my pace slowed just a little. "I don't know what to do." I knew I had to do something. I couldn't keep this up.

"Then, we keep running. I can do this until dawn. I can carry you if I need to and still keep it up."

"I…" I wasn't sure if he was joking on that last part or not, but I didn't think we'd have time to test that out.

My father was going to catch me.

My legs were already burning, and there was no way I could—

Something slammed into my back, and I hit the pavement hard.

"Samantha!" Phoenix yelled and then grunted as my father batted him away as if he were nothing.

"Phoenix!" The scent of blood hit me. My blood. I hadn't felt it at first, but my face burned with pain, and I knew I was screwed.

Worse—I didn't know if Phoenix was okay.

Panic started to take over.

My breaths came in short gasps.

A claw dug into my ankle, and it popped painfully as my father's beast started dragging me across the pavement.

I blinked away the pain-induced spots in my eyes and tried to look back. I searched the street for Phoenix and spotted him. He was crumpled on the ground. *"Phoenix! Wake up!"*

Where were the wolves?

Where was Tessa?

Maybe this was better. I told them not to follow me. If they were here, they'd just get hurt.

But where the hell was Eli? He should be here by now. *"Eli! I need you right now! I'm not kidding around!"*

Steam rolled off my father's monster as he coalesced into a black, evil-looking beast. His eyes glowed red, and his mouth was like my father's—too wide, with too many sharp teeth, grinning in a way that liquified my insides with fear. His massive paws scorched the ground with every step, dragging me back toward the house.

Back to the portal.

This couldn't happen. I had to fight.

Get your butt moving, Sam.

I groaned in pain as I forced myself up a little just enough to twist my torso and keep my face from scraping along the pavement.

Better. Now, do something.

I needed to make him let me go. That was step one.

I kicked my good foot at the claw gripping my other ankle.

The claw tightened, and I gasped trying to breathe through the pain.

No. This wasn't happening. I couldn't let this happen.

I twisted my body a little, trying to find something to grasp, but there was only rough concrete. My nails cracked, and I screamed as I tried to get free.

This was useless. I needed something—anything—to slow him down, but there was nothing for me to grab. Nothing to stop him.

My fingers bled and my face ached. Frustration and fear tangled frantically together as I tried to get free because I knew where he was heading.

Back to the house.

Back to the portal.

Back to Hell.

I couldn't let that happen. I'd rather die now.

Even if I went through the portal alive and somehow found my way back, I couldn't survive it again. Mentally or physically. Years ago, the first time my father took me to Hell, my body had been a mess. Wrecked. So sure, they weren't wrong about not training too hard too soon, but he caught me so fast when I wasn't training.

Too fast.

Living-nightmare fast.

I wasn't ready for this. It was too soon. I'd just saved Van. I couldn't go back. I really, truly couldn't. I wouldn't survive it.

Panic thickened the air, and it was nearly impossible to get a full breath in.

I didn't have super strength, and I couldn't heal fast. I wasn't fully Nephilim. My father hadn't given me any extra abilities that would help in a situation like this. All I could do was see, interact with, and control the spiritual plane.

My only hope was to find some way to make him let go and to run faster this time.

I had to get free.

And I had to close the portal, but I couldn't do it with him breathing down my neck. Not if it was anything like the portal that had been in the yellow house. I needed time.

"Stop thinking stupid things," my father's monster half-spoke, half-growled at me.

He couldn't read my mind, but he knew me. He was letting me know he knew exactly what I was going to try to do, if I could just figure out how to do it.

He gave my ankle a jerk, and my hip bounced on the pavement.

I screamed from pain, but I heard a clang.

My bag. I was still wearing my belt bag. *Thank you, God.* I'd never taken it off.

I wasn't used to having it. I rarely needed it, but for this trip, I had it. But what was in it?

Think, Sam. Think.

What made that clinking sound?

The jar. The *jar.*

It had my own mixture of salt-selenite-sage dust and falling ash from a priest's incense thurible. It existed on the mortal plane but held supernatural powers. It was one of the few things in my arsenal that could cross into the spiritual realm. A few grains of it and lesser demons lost their hold on this world, sending them back to Hell.

I wasn't sure it would work on someone as high-ranking as my father—even if this was just his stand-in monster. It might just really, really piss him off. And he was already pretty mad…

Screw it. I needed him to let go of my ankle. I had to be able to run.

I unzipped the bag and reached in. My hand hit the cool glass.

Thank you, God. It's here. I can do this.

I needed the dust to cover him. If I opened the jar and threw it, the dust would just land on me or the ground or something else. I could blow it onto him, but not while he was dragging me like this. I had to change my position. I had to sit up.

I dumped the powder into my palm and closed my fist, dropping the empty jar with a *clang*.

My father's monster looked back at me. Its massive inky-black body rose above me and its twisting black horns blocked everything else from view. "What are you doing?" A glob of it's black spit dripped onto me, burning my cheek.

No time left. I screamed as I forced my already aching body to sit up. I laid my palm flat and blew the dust at him.

The grains hit his face and turned to embers, burning him.

He dropped my ankle, and it hit the ground. Hard.

My father's monster roared with anger and pain as he swatted at the embers, trying to put them out, but I was frozen. Watching him.

This was it.

This was my chance.

Run.

I had to run.

Move, Sam.

I scrambled up. Pain ricocheted from my ankle up my leg, but I gritted my teeth and kept moving. I couldn't let it slow me down.

Fear and adrenaline quickly numbed the pain, and I ran—hobbling but still moving fast.

Wait. No. I was dumb. I was going the wrong freaking way. I was trying to lead it away from where Phoenix was, but I needed to get back to the house. I couldn't risk trying to open a new portal. He'd pull on my power. He'd drain me. He'd drag me through.

Or if I got him through it, managed to stay on the mortal side, and closed it—he'd just come right back through the portal in the house.

I had to get back to the house.

And I needed time in the house before he got there.

If I could beat him back to the house and close the portal, every demon in a two-to-three-mile radius would get sucked back through. Including my father's monster. Because he didn't have dominion in this realm. He wasn't supposed to be able to come through the portal. He wasn't supposed to be here.

I knew there was something weird about the way the portal had fought me in the yellow house. This had to be it. There was a spell on it, and I bet my life my father had been keeping it open.

I had to get rid of this one the same way.

Close it, and I'd get rid of him.

It was the only way to end this.

My father roared through the monster behind me, and I knew I couldn't outrun him. Not like this. Not with my ankle totally wrecked.

I'd used the one trick in my bag with the powder. I needed something else to buy time. I needed to—

Oh, wait. My bag.

Wow.

A crazy, hopeful, *dear-God-please-let-this-work* idea formed, and oh wow.

Wow.

Chills broke across my skin.

This was it. This was why I needed it.

Thank you, God! I sent the praise up to Him because I wouldn't have asked for it if He hadn't seeded that knowledge in my head.

I hit the end of the block and turned the corner. There was a tiny spot in between two cars parked on the street. I dropped to the ground, pulling the chalk from my bag.

Thank you, God. You knew. You always know.

I drew a circle around me, drew four Orthodox crosses around it, and said a quick prayer. It'd been forever since I'd done this, so hopefully I didn't forget a step.

Whatever. It had to be good enough.

I wasn't sure where Eli was or if he was coming or even if God was listening to my prayers. But I wouldn't stop trying.

"Please, hear me, God," I screamed across the realms. *"There are*

people in danger. My father freed one of his monsters into the mortal realm. I need help. Send Elilaios or whoever. But now. Please!"

Astral projecting like this wasn't the best idea. It left my body vulnerable to being injured, a demon taking it over, or any number of things, but it was all I had.

Being separated from my body wore me out when I kept my spirit visible on the mortal plane. I couldn't stay this way for more than a few minutes at a time without growing weak, which wasn't ideal in the middle of a fight with my father when I was already weak.

But if this took longer than a few minutes, there was a good chance my father would win either way.

I couldn't think like that.

Circle done, protection symbols drawn and working. It was the best I could do right now.

I closed my eyes and slipped from my body.

My spirit-form darted across the street. *"Hey, Astaroth! You're going the wrong way!"* I rarely ever used his real name, but this time I wanted his full attention on my spirit.

He roared, part of his horned bear-like face still red and smoking from the embers, as he ran across the street. He didn't care about how his body dented every parked car, how each step took melted the asphalt, or how every bit of him destroyed anything he touched.

I was much faster in this form. I wasn't inhibited by the confines of my mortal trappings. I could think *go to the end of the street* and be there.

My father was recovering from the dust, and I hoped he wasn't seeing clearly or he was too angry to realize I was moving faster than I could in the mortal realm.

If he did, I'd figure out what to do next, but I wasn't giving up.

I pictured the end of the block and told my body to go there.

Too quick for my eyes to register, I flew down the block.

My father roared and picked up his pace.

I visualized the house on the next block, and my spirit-form flew there.

I didn't want to risk jumping way too much or I'd risk giving myself away. So, instead, I ran. And ran. And I forced myself to go slower even though I wanted to push my body to go as fast as I could.

My power wasn't endless. I needed to make sure I didn't drain myself too quickly, just in case my father figured out what I was doing. I needed to seem real enough to lead him far away from the house. Then, I could snap back to my body, get to the house before him, and close the portal.

Wait. Why was it so quiet?

There were no more stomping feet behind me. No more roaring. No more crashing of cars. Hissing of melting asphalt. No more anything.

I glanced over my shoulder, but he wasn't there.

He was gone.

I stopped running and turned in a circle.

Where did he go?

Maybe Eli showed up and took care of him and I didn't notice?

That seemed highly unlikely.

But he was gone. He wasn't following me.

I didn't know where he'd gone to, but it was pointless to tire myself out.

My heart raced, my breathing was heavy, and I knew my physical body was laboring and starting to struggle. I must've been weaker than I thought.

I closed my eyes and felt the pull toward my body. The tug was there, and I couldn't ignore it. The air rushed around my soul as I flew toward my body.

I opened my eyes, but instead of feeling at home in my body, I really, truly couldn't breathe.

A clawed hand tightened around my neck.

Motherfucking shitballs.

I'd messed something up. The circle hadn't held.

He found me.

CHAPTER THIRTY-ONE

SAMANTHA

I TRIED to pull the claws from my neck so I could get in some air.

"You can't out-trick a trickster." My father's voice was confident, deep, and laced with anger.

Oh God. Help me. There was no way I could get away from him now.

"I'm older," he said.

And he was. My father was, but this wasn't really my father. It was just a piece of him he used to power one of his monsters.

Wolf howls broke through the night and I knew help was coming, but they were too far away.

I looked into the monster's red eyes, and I wanted to beg, but I bit my tongue, tasting blood.

I wouldn't beg. Not him. Not ever. He wasn't a merciful being. If I begged for my life, he'd give it to me, but the cost would be…

No.

I would never beg. Never make a deal. Not with him.

He lifted me slowly, not snapping my neck, even though he held it painfully tight.

"I'm wiser. And infinitely more powerful than you."

I knew that. I *knew* it. Especially now, with his hand wrapped around my neck. Hot tears ran down my face, and I knew this was it.

"And as your father, it's my right to end your life."

No.

No.

Oh God, please. Send Eli or any angel. Please.

I sucked in a shaky, shallow breath.

The wolf howls grew louder, but they were going to be too late.

I pried at his claws again, trying to pull them away from my neck.

My feet dangled above the ground, and every time I kicked them, his fingers tightened.

I couldn't breathe.

Couldn't get any air.

It was over.

My vision narrowed and filled with black dots.

Suddenly, the monster let go. I sucked in a breath as the clawed hand dropped me, and I slammed into something painfully hard. I blinked my eyes open, and I was on the ground. Light filled the night. A light so pure and bright that, for a second, I couldn't see anything.

I scooted on my back away from the light. From my father roaring. From my death.

My neck throbbed and ached. I tried to turn it to see what was happening, but a sharp pain rolled down my back.

So, I stayed down, staring into the night sky, but there was light. So much light.

And sounds of a fight.

And the snarls of the wolves.

And my shallow, reedy, gasping breaths, but I was alive. So far.

I knew I should be doing something, but I couldn't get up. So, I turned my head to see the fight.

At first I thought it was Eli. The glow. The flaming sword. All of it.

But no.

It was Phoenix.

Phoenix was fighting the monster.

What was happening? *How…*

Phoenix moved so gracefully, so fast, with his sword on fire. His movements flowed, reminding me of Cosette and Van the one time I'd seen them sword fight. But they'd trained for so long. How was he this good?

It didn't make any sense.

He swiped his sword at my father's monster, but it leaped out of the way. Somehow, the monster had gotten bigger since he'd chased me. I wasn't sure how, but the wolves were here now and—

A wolf dove into the fight, its jaws clamping down onto the monster's arm. The beast roared, flinging the wolf off him, and then I realized why none of the wolves had followed us.

The monster had split his form into two so it could run after me. They hadn't abandoned the fight. They'd been fighting him, too.

But now he was back together, and there was no way any of us stood a chance.

The wolves prowled around Phoenix, but every time they tried to make contact with the monster, they either missed or he swatted them away with his power.

I watched in awe for a moment before I remembered what I had to do.

I didn't want to leave. I didn't want to move. I wanted to watch Phoenix fight, but I had to go. I had to end this.

A wolf came beside me, licking my face. It whined, and I looked into its eyes. I knew this wolf.

"Tessa?" My voice sounded scratchy.

The wolf whimpered.

I closed my eyes. Just for a second. Just to gather myself. "Don't draw attention to me. Stay here. Keep it distracted. Buy me some time so I can end this." I whispered the words hoping she'd do what I said.

Everything in my body protested as I struggled to get up. Pain rolled through every fiber of my being, but I gritted my teeth and forced myself to move. Up and off the ground. Stumbling on my wrecked ankle, I moved behind my father's monster and edged my way backward, sneaking back to the house.

Only when I was sure no one was watching did I turn and take off in a hobbling run. I kept my jaw clenched as I forced myself to keep moving. My body was bruised all over, and my ankle screamed at me. Every step was excruciating. But pain meant I was still alive.

So, I kept moving as fast as my body would take me.

Two houses.

One.

Here. *Here.*

I climbed the porch steps and tried the door.

It was locked. *Damn it.*

I couldn't kick it down like Dastien could, even if I wasn't hurt.

But the back window had shattered when the wolf was thrown through it. I could get in that way for sure.

I went around the house to the shattered window and climbed in, screaming through my gritted teeth as I landed on my bad ankle. Tears ran down my face, and I wanted to stop. To quit. Give up because I felt so beyond done. But I couldn't. I could still hear the fight outside, and I wouldn't abandon them.

I shoved the pain and fear and despair away and focused. I had to focus.

One breath. Just like Chris always told me. One breath to calm myself and focus on what needed to be done.

As soon as I took that breath, I felt the portal.

It was small.

Smaller than the other one. A lot smaller.

That was good. It meant I could close it faster. It was the little shred of hope I needed to keep going.

I screamed with every step as I moved through the house, up the stairs, into the attic. My ankle was trashed. It was terror and sheer stubbornness that kept me going.

And there it was.

Another attic. Another portal. Just like the other one.

Damn it.

I was right. This one was smaller, less symbols, less complex spells, but I couldn't believe I didn't sense it before.

I couldn't beat myself up about it. I'd done what I could, and there was no changing the past. I just had to fix it.

I unzipped my belt bag as I approached the portal. This time, I sped through the prayers, dumping salt on the whole circle and all the symbols around it as I spoke the words, countering the spell that kept this portal open as fast as I could. I didn't have time to untangle it. I had to force it shut despite all the mess around it. But if I could weaken the elements, that would be make it a little easier. So, I kept at it and—

The whole house rattled.

My time was up.

He knew.

My father's monster knew what I was doing and where I was.

His roar hit my soul, filling me with dread.

He was coming for me.

No time to freak out.

Faster. I had to go *faster*.

I dug into my belt bag, pulling out the bottle of holy water.

Almost done. Just keep moving.

I quickly circled the portal one more time with the holy water.

The house continued to shake—rattling on both the spiritual

and mortal planes, making it hard to stay on my feet—and I knew it was getting closer.

His roars grew louder, but I shut them out.

I shut everything out.

But just as I finished countering the spell on the floor and felt it flicker into nothing, something picked me up and tossed me across the room.

I slammed into the wall so hard my vision went black for a second. And then I hit the floor, bouncing twice, before lying in a motionless heap.

I couldn't move.

It was over.

I'd lost.

"*Get up.*" My father roared, his breath hot on my face.

But I couldn't move.

I couldn't speak.

I couldn't yell.

My head was still dazed from slamming into the wall, and I was pretty sure I had a concussion. There was nothing I could do now. I couldn't get my limbs to work. I had no fight left in me.

A hand wrapped around my wrist, yanking me toward the portal.

Panic and adrenaline forced everything into focus.

"Let her go!" A deep voice yelled.

Light filled the attic. So much light that it hurt my eyes. I blinked a few times, and then I saw the most beautiful thing ever.

Phoenix.

He was bathed in gold light. His aura had expanded, and he seemed bigger, taller, stronger. He didn't have any armor, just the flaming sword, but he didn't need anything else.

He darted around monster's claws, moving faster than I'd ever seen him move. His dance-like moves flowed as he dodged the monster's swiping claws.

He dropped low and stabbed the flaming sword into the monster's side.

It roared and dropped my wrist.

That was all I needed. That one distraction.

"Claudare!" I tried to speak the word, but my throat ached, and it didn't come out right. The portal wasn't closing.

So, I focused my mind. *Claudare!* I thought the word, forcing what power I had left into it, and I hoped it was enough.

It had to be enough. This was all I had left.

The portal started to close, and my father's monster raged. I pressed myself into the floor, crying, because I was so spent and done.

Demons screamed as they were pulled into the portal from every direction.

The monster tried to pull himself free of the vortex, but Phoenix kept fighting it, even as it was diminishing—in size and power.

Phoenix swiped his sword across the monster's arm, and it turned to ash before it hit the attic floor.

The monster stumbled back a step.

"Bye, asshole," Phoenix screamed as he kicked the monster in the stomach, sending it toppling down through the portal.

Thank you, God. I didn't know how Phoenix had gotten the sword or the glowing power, but I knew who had given it to him.

I relaxed into the floor with tears rolling down my face as I watched the demons disappear into the portal. The light around Phoenix seemed brighter as he moved to stand over me. His sword was pointed at the floor. He scanned the room, protecting me, making sure no demons came anywhere near me.

I watched him, breathing hard, my heart beating so fast my chest ached, adrenaline making my body feel like it was shivering. But all of that meant that I was alive. *Thank you, God.*

The fight had been way too close. Too hard. Once again, I felt completely unmatched by my father. This was too many times. All together, it felt like a lot. More than a lot.

Tears coated my face. But it was okay because Phoenix was

alive and freaking amazing. He stood over me until the last demon was gone and the portal was closed.

When it was finally shut, the house was so quiet. Phoenix took a deep breath and looked down at me.

"Help!" he yelled. "Sam is hurt! We need help!" He held the sword away and dropped to kneel next to me. "What hurts? I don't know what to do. How do I help you?"

I shook my head. Everything hurt, but I couldn't think about that. I couldn't focus on it, or I'd scream. "How…" My voice was raspy from where the monster had strangled me. "What—" I pointed to the flaming sword in his hand.

"I don't know. I saw you get tossed, and I couldn't do a damned thing. I think I was knocked out cold for a second, but when I woke up, I couldn't find you. So, I called out to Eli, but he didn't come. I heard you call for him while we were running, but he never came. So, I called out for God to help me. I begged Him to help *me* help *you*. You couldn't do it alone and—"

Eli appeared in the room—glowing, armor, no sword, and too late to do any good in this fight. As usual. "He did well. I was watching, but I had to give him the room he needed to ask God for help if he wanted the power to help you. If I came, he wouldn't have asked." Eli watched Phoenix. "He's worthy of the gift, I think." Eli gave me a smug smile, and I knew—*I knew*—he planned this whole thing. He helped put the dominos in place so Phoenix would show up at the right time. He gave Phoenix hints in the car earlier and set everything up, and he definitely knew what God would do if Phoenix asked.

Phoenix's soul had always glowed brighter than anyone else's I'd ever known, but now it was just *more*. If Eli knew this all those years ago. If he saw the potential in Phoenix's soul. If he'd put Phoenix on a path to help me and even somehow led Mom to that apartment all those years ago…

I wouldn't put it past him. Eli was a master of the long game.

"You're such a manipulator." My voice was a broken whisper, but I knew he could hear me just fine.

"Oh, come on, angel. It was fate, and there was free will involved. He could've made any number of choices. I just gave him some hints, a nudge here and there, opened up doors. I can't control a mortal's actions. Just...*guide*."

I closed my eyes for a second before looking up at Phoenix. "He played you." I swallowed, trying to wet my aching throat. "He wanted you for me. Like this." Tears flowed again, but for a different reason.

"*Shhh*." He brushed the hair that had fallen out of my braid away from my face. "Everything is okay."

"*Okay*?" I whisper shouted. I couldn't believe Phoenix wasn't mad. He deserved better than a life of chasing literal demons and saving my butt.

"What does it matter if he manipulated me a little bit when this is what *I* truly wanted?"

Eli spread his arms wide as if he'd performed a massive magic trick that had just paid off. "You see? Everything always works out. Just as it is meant to." He sighed. "I tried to tell you that day in the apartment, but you didn't listen. I knew as soon as I saw him that he was going to be what you needed, but the timing wasn't right. Now, it is."

"When did you see him?" How long had Eli been planning this?

"I saw him when I saw him. The details aren't important."

The details were everything, but I didn't have enough voice in me to argue with him. "You gave him extras?" My voice cracked at the end.

"Oh, no. You know I can't do that. I might bend the Law, but I won't break it outright. The Lord is the only one who can give power like that. But I did ask if He was willing to bestow a gift on a special spiritual warrior. And when Phoenix asked, the Lord did as He wanted."

I was flat on my back, exhausted, emotional, ready for bed or food or I didn't know what, but Phoenix lowered his forehead to mine. "Don't freak out about this. Please. This feels right to me."

"Are you sure?" I didn't want him to regret the choices he'd made. It would destroy us—destroy *me*—and I wanted this. Someone to stand by me. Someone to feel alive with. Someone to fight beside me . Someone to love. And I desperately wanted to have all of that with Phoenix.

He rose up enough to brush a kiss on my forehead, then he looked in my eyes. "I'm absolutely sure. More than anything in my life ever. I promise. Being with you, doing this, feels like coming home. And I can't be anything but grateful for the ability to help you." He gave me the grin that I loved so much. The one with his dimple. "I didn't like standing to the side while that monster beat the crap out of you."

I croaked a laugh. "I don't really like getting beaten up either."

Phoenix looked up at Eli. "How do I sheath the sword?"

"Picture it gone and move your wrist like this." He demonstrated.

"And to bring it back?"

"Do the opposite," Eli said it as if it was the most obvious thing in the world.

Phoenix rose and gave it a try, vanishing the fiery sword, then reappearing it—here, gone, here, gone—until he looked comfortable. "Cool." He squatted down beside me. "How hurt are you? Can you get up?"

"I don't know. Bad. Everything hurts. My ankle might be messed up." It throbbed, and I wasn't even putting any pressure on it. I looked at Eli. "My throat hurts. My face is killing me. I blacked out when I hit the wall, and I have the worst headache."

"Concussion for sure, then." Phoenix knelt beside me, brushed a hand against my forehead, and leaned forward. His face was serious as he studied mine. "But your pupils are okay. Even." He leaned back. "So, that's something."

My gaze slid to Eli. "Come on. Just this once?"

"No." His voice was soft and kind but firm as he knelt on the other side of me. "I start saying yes, and I'll keep saying yes until I cross a line. I can't start now. I won't be able to stop. And I can't afford to lose the ability to come when you need me. *Buuuut* have you figured out all the things your bond can do?"

"What does that mean?" Phoenix asked.

"What do you think it means?" Eli's tone was beyond grating.

This was my most-hated of Eli's moods. The know-it-all, smug, answering-a-question-with-a-question form of Eli was the *worst*. "Shut up. We'll figure it out ourselves." My voice was little more than a croak, which took some of the bite out of my words.

"Do you always end up this hurt?" Phoenix gave me a once over, then sighed. "I want to hold you, but you hit the floor so hard. I feel like if I try, I might hurt you."

"It's unfortunate that she always ends up hurt, but she's not being abandoned in her fight," Eli said. "He is watching, and I'm helping line up everything she needs as the battles intensify." He bent to me, gazing into my eyes. "We always knew your road was going to be hard. Didn't we?" He said the words softly, and even if they were true, they made my heart ache.

"We did." Eli had been coming to me for as long as I could remember, and he'd told me it would get harder and harder. I just didn't think it would get this bad, this often.

Eli rose. "There were battles laid out for her, and though she is fearful and discouraged from time to time, Samantha knows this is the path for her. That the reward at the end will be great, and in the meantime…" He looked at Phoenix. "I trust you'll figure out what to do. After all, your bloodline is holy, and that is what allowed Him to bestow a gift."

Phoenix looked confused. "What do you mean?"

"That's why he glows?" I asked. "I feel like an idiot."

Eli looked down at me and smiled. "Indeed. You, of all people, should've known."

I looked at Phoenix, and the way he glowed with that heavenly aura wasn't new. It was more intense now, but it wasn't new. He was like that when we first met. It was why I was so drawn to him.

"You're welcome, Samantha." For an archon, Eli could give the most devilish smile. "Maybe I was manipulative to set this up, but it's what you needed. It's what he needed, too."

I didn't know what to say, but I suddenly wanted to be anywhere but here. "Okay. I better see how the ankle is."

I whimpered as Phoenix pulled me gently to my feet, and I let out a gasp as I put weight on it. Everything started to go black.

Phoenix swept me up in his arms. "I better just carry you for now, okay?"

"Yeah." I didn't like to be carried, but I guessed I needed to get over that. "My ankle's definitely toast."

"We'll get it x-rayed and then see what's what. It could just be a bad sprain." He gave me a small smile. "For now, I'll carry you. It's kind of romantic, right?" He winked.

I huffed. "I don't know, Nix. I'm a mess right now. That might be a stretch."

"I know what I know. You like it when I carry you."

I rolled my eyes because I didn't, and yet…I kind of loved it.

"Also, the raspy voice is really sexy."

"See," Eli said. "This is working out just right."

I couldn't believe I was laughing right now, but I was. "Shut up." I was going to hit Eli. Not right now, but the next chance I had, I was definitely hitting him.

"Samantha?" Tessa called up to us. "Phoenix said to wait down here, but I wanted to know if everything was okay. The pack doc is working on someone right now, but he'll—"

"She needs medical attention, but she's stable for now. I think," Phoenix answered her before I could attempt to shout back. "The portal is closed. The monster is back where it should be. I haven't looked around, but the house should be pretty clear. We're going to need to get her to a hospital. I'm not sure how bad she's hurt. The doc needs to look at her."

"Ummm…" Tessa said, and a knot formed in my stomach. That was her code for when she needed help but didn't want to ask for it. "I'll check on the doc. We had some gravely hurt wolves, so if it's not urgent, he needs a few to finish. And in the meantime, I have something I need her to see. If she can."

I wasn't sure I could take much more, but I'd figure it out. "What is it?" I couldn't shout, but I didn't need to.

"It might be able to wait for later, but I'm not sure," Dastien called out from below us. "If you could check it out, that would help."

I leaned my head back against Phoenix's shoulder. "I'm so spent. I just want to go home."

"You can always say no, angel." Eli looked at me with sad eyes, and I knew he regretted not being able to fix me.

"Can I?" I wasn't so sure—I wasn't sure God would forgive me if I left an innocent to suffer. I wasn't sure *I* could forgive myself either.

"There are always choices, angel." A light covered him, and he sighed. "I'm being called away. I have to go. I'll check on you in a bit."

With Eli gone, I felt sad. I had no reason to feel sad just because he left, but I did.

He frustrated and annoyed me sometimes, but I loved him. I wished he didn't always have to go.

"You okay?" Phoenix whispered to me.

"No. But let's go see what they need and how urgent it is."

"Okay." Phoenix started for the stairs, still cradling me in his arms.

Tessa met us at the bottom of the stairs. "Whoa. You said she was hurt, but she looks really bad. Is she okay? Should I call an ambulance?" Tessa turned to Dastien, and their bond lit up.

Dastien studied me for a second. "I'm going to get an ETA on the doc." I was sure he was going to say something, but then he turned and ran through the house.

Tessa stared at me with sad eyes, and I hated that look. I'd seen it before, and I knew she felt bad that I'd been hurt. Again. "I'm okay."

Tessa winced at the sound of my voice. "No. You're not. We'll fix you up again, but I hate this."

"I'll be fine, Tessa. Everything in the area should truly be gone now that I closed this portal." I looked around the house to make sure I wasn't just assuming that, but I didn't see anything. "If it's all the same to you, I'd like to fly home soon. I need my own bed."

"We'll have to see about that," Dastien said as he came back. He looked at me with sad eyes. "The doc is setting a bone. If he stops now, he'll have to re-break it. We heal too fast, but he'll be up in a minute. He'll check you out and see if you need the hospital. If not, and you're cleared to travel, I'll call the pilot. I'd love to take you home, but I have to make sure traveling won't do you more harm."

I couldn't help the groan that slipped free. "Fine. Let's got see what you need me to check out. No promises, though. I don't have much left, you guys."

"Just a quick assessment," Tessa said. "If it can wait, then it can wait. Maybe we can even find a local priest to take care of it. But there's a family living in the frog that needs your help, and I think—"

I knew those were words, but what Tessa said didn't make any sense. "I'm sorry, a frog? They're living *in a frog*?" I must've hit my head harder than I thought.

"No." Tessa busted up with laughter, then slapped her hand over her mouth as she tried to stop. "Lord. No." She wiped her eyes. "I'm sorry. I guess I needed the laugh because it's not that funny…but no. Not the animal. It's an acronym for finished-room-over-garage. F-R-O-G."

"Right. Okay." That made so much more sense, and if I was right, this was the family we'd been looking for. "Let's go see what they need from me." I looked up at Phoenix. "Are you going to be able to carry me for much longer? Maybe one of the werewolves could—"

"Not a chance. I've got you, and I'm not letting you go until we get the ankle checked out and see about the concussion."

"Concussion?!" Tessa yelled.

"I'm going to go hurry the doc up," Dastien said before rushing off.

"You had to tell them about that?" I asked him with as much whine as my raspy voice could allow.

"Yes. They need to know how hurt you are." Phoenix looked at Tessa. "Lead the way."

CHAPTER THIRTY-TWO

SAMANTHA

PHOENIX CARRIED me across the house, and up another set of stairs. An open door led to a small apartment. Apparently a frog. Tessa moved away from the doorway to let us through.

The apartment was clean and bright, but there was a dreariness, a heaviness in the air that made it feel thick. I immediately wanted to leave, which was how I knew I couldn't. Not until I made that feeling go away.

The common room had a kitchenette, a small table that seated four people, a small couch and a TV. Everything was clean and tidy, neutral-colored, and currently occupied by a family of three. A couple and a small boy—maybe three or four years old.

Toys were strewn about the room, and the TV played a popular cartoon about a dog family, but my eyes were stuck on the boy. His cheeks were pale, dark circles under his eyes, and his skin had a little green tinge to it. He was sick, fading, and from the looks on the parents' faces, they knew something was very wrong with their son. I'd bet good money they had no idea a small demon had its arms around the boy's neck and a thick, strong, red tie was attached to the boy's soul.

Cheese and crackers.

The demon wouldn't have gone when the portal closed because of the tie.

I was exhausted and everything hurt, but I shoved all of it aside as soon as I saw the suffering little boy.

The mom and dad stood at one end of the couch, eyes darting between me and the boy.

Tessa stayed off to the side, and I knew she was there in case I needed anything. I didn't think I would.

This wasn't going to take long, but if this was the family from the yellow house, I wanted to make sure none of them had helped Sophia. It was concerning that the boo hag had opened up a second portal. I wasn't sure how it was possible, but I didn't know much about that kind of demon. I'd never seen anything like it before tonight.

"Hi, I'm Samantha." I looked up at Phoenix. "Put me on my feet."

Phoenix gave me a look that said everything about how much he hated that idea.

"Please."

He sighed and gently set me on my feet. I stayed leaning against his side, afraid to put any weight on my bad ankle.

The dad cleared his throat. "We saw the commotion outside, and we stayed in here. But we were watching, and...well...when they came into the apartment to check on us, they said..." He pressed his lips together. "We're hoping that you might be able to help our son. We're *desperate*."

I bet they were. Based on the coloring of the little boy, he didn't have much time left. "I'd like to ask a few questions before I start. Can you tell me what's been going on?" My voice was hoarse, and Dastien came through the door and handed something to Tessa.

I spared her a glance as she dumped a packet of powder into a water bottle. Electrolytes. For me.

She crossed the room and handed me the water bottle.

"Thank you," I mouthed to her.

Her brow scrunched as she nodded to me. I knew my best friend. She was torn between wanting me to get looked over and wanting me to help this kid. She waved a finger in a circle. *Hurry.*

I got it. Both would happen. The little guy was first, though.

"It all started when we heard noises in our house. Not this house. Ours. This is my in-law's house. We don't live here. They're out of town, and it's..." The man blew out a breath and looked at his wife.

She gave him a nod, but I could see how hard she was gripping his hand. She was shaking, and I wasn't sure if it was fear or exhaustion or the same desperation her husband had.

"I'm sorry," the man said. "It's been a long few weeks, and I have no idea how to start. Or how to tell you any of this without sounding crazy. I've questioned my sanity more times than I can count in the last few days."

I started to hobble over to sit on the armchair next to them, but Phoenix picked me up again, placing me in the chair.

I looked up at him. "I'm okay."

"You're not." He crossed his arms. "Take care of this, and then we're going to the ER. And you're not going to fight me on that."

He wasn't wrong to insist on it. I probably needed an x-ray of my ankle. I really hoped it wasn't broken. That would seriously mess with my ability to get back in shape. "Fine. Go over there, though." I waved to where Dastien and Tessa were standing. "I'm just going to chat with them for a second."

He bent down, placing a kiss on the top of my head. "I'll be right there if you need me. Don't try to get up without my help."

I gave him a smile and turned to the couple.

They were scared, huddled together, and the demon was hissing at me. It could hiss all it wanted to. I was going to ignore it. For now.

"Sorry about that. He's protective of me." I smiled at them. "And I hurt my ankle—among other things—in the commotion outside." And I was feeling every bit of it. My face burned more and more by the second and talking made it worse. From the looks on my friends' faces, I was sure I was a mess.

Oh well. Nothing I could do now, but power through.

"Your son is going to be okay. I'm going to help him in a few minutes, once I understand what happened. When I do help him, he'll be tired and hungry, but he'll be himself again. You might want to take him to get some IV fluids, but he'll be fine." I reached out to the mom, touching her arm, careful not to brush against her skin. "I *promise* this will be okay." She took a shuddering breath, and tears welled in her eyes. "You don't know me, but I wouldn't say that if I didn't know it to be absolutely true." I pulled my hand away as she started to sob.

"Oh, God." Her voice cracked.

I took a big sip of the ice-cold water. It was salty and sweet and tasted vaguely of watermelon. I usually complained about that, but not today. "It looks—" My voice broke. "Sorry." I took another sip. "It looks like you've had a really hard time lately. Can you tell me about it?" I wanted to know if it was the boo hag who opened the portal, or if there was something else I needed to worry about here. I had to make sure whatever opened these portals was gone for good.

"It's been horrible. I've been so scared and hopeless. I…" She swiped at her tears. "It…I guess it started with noises. Footsteps in the hallways when nothing was there. It was creepy, and honestly, freaked me out. I started to sleep with a nightlight on, and eventually, my son stopped sleeping at night entirely. We're exhausted—we've been exhausted for what feels like forever, but there was this feeling at night that just…I don't know how else to say it, but it wasn't good. So, I understood why he wasn't sleeping. I didn't force him or fight with him about it. All of us felt it, so we kept the TV on, trying to distract us from that feeling."

"Not sleeping will weaken you so fast." Physically, emotionally, and especially, spiritually.

"It does," the dad said. He had bags under his eyes, and I

knew he was probably much younger than he looked right now. Stress did terrible things to a person.

"What happened next?" I didn't want them to relive their trauma, but I wasn't going to save this boy just to have another demon come for him.

"Laughing. The laughing started."

I sat up straighter. I was pretty sure I knew what laugh she was talking about. "What kind of laughing?"

"Whenever our son would get scared, there was this deep laughing that made every hair on my body stand on end," the dad said. "And I knew we were being watched. We searched for cameras in the house. I even let our housekeeper go. We threw out the baby monitors." He huffed. "It wasn't like we needed any of that. We were all sleeping in one bed at night. I turned off the WiFi in the house at night in case there was something happening there. Like a hacker or something. I tried every rational explanation. Nothing helped."

Nothing *rational* would explain it when it was supernatural. "Okay. What was the housekeeper's name?"

"Ana María Castillo."

I turned to Dastien and gave him the signal to look her up. Just in case.

He nodded and started typing on his phone.

"What made you leave your house and move in here?" I asked them.

The man let out a relieved breath, as if he'd been waiting for me to tell him he'd been imagining it all. But I wasn't going to do that, and I saw the hope light in his eyes. "A bunch of things started happening." His voice was stronger and more confident now. "It felt like it was escalating. Stuff started moving around the house. Doors slamming. All kinds of things, but then Braden—sorry. I didn't say that before. We didn't introduce ourselves." He rubbed his hand along his brow. "My son's name is Braden. I'm Timothy McDaniel. This is my wife, Jessica."

I gave him a reassuring smile. "I'm Samantha Lopez. Over

there are Dastien and Tessa Laurent. And the man who insists on carrying me everywhere is Phoenix, my boyfriend." I glanced at him in time to see his smile. I left off his last name just in case they were soccer fans. "We're all here to help you." I gave Timothy a nod. "We know this has been really traumatic, but the spooky stuff is my jam. I came here from Texas to help with what we fought outside. I'm really good at my job. I just want to make sure when I fix Braden, I'm fixing him for good. Okay?"

Big, fat tears rolled down Jessica's face. "Okay. Yes. Whatever you need." She looked at Timothy.

"He got sick—he wasn't eating," Timothy said. "He was throwing up and crying in pain. Except the doctors couldn't find anything wrong with him. He was just slowly wasting away, and with the stress of trying to figure out what was going on, and the house…we ended up moving in here with Jessica's parents. We just needed a break."

"And you usually live in a two-story yellow house? Nice porch. White accents. Pretty flowers in the front and a big tree just a few minutes from here."

Jessica narrowed her gaze and looked at Timothy before turning to me again. "We do. How could you possibly know that?"

"I'll get back to that. I need a few more answers so I can connect some dots in my mind, and then I'll help your son. Okay?"

Timothy gripped her hand and nodded. "Anything. Anything you need to know. I just want answers. Something that makes sense."

That might not happen. "I'm not sure it'll make sense in a normal way. You're dealing with the supernatural here, but I know what's going on for sure. I'm just wondering what started it." I took a sip of water as my voice started to give out. "Did you have someone in your house regularly aside from the housekeeper that you fired? A nanny? Babysitter? A friend that visited a lot? Anyone who spent time in the house could've done what I saw there. I have to make sure I find the right person and keep them from doing it again." Keeping a portal open like that was hard to do. It would've taken preparation. And whoever had created that portal also opened the smaller one here.

It wasn't the parents. I had zero doubts about that. They were way too freaked out by this whole thing, not to mention upset about how sick their son was.

But if boo hag Sophia had worked with someone else, I needed to know. Maybe it was the housekeeper, but it could've been someone else. Or it could've just been Sophia.

"A nanny. Braden has a nanny, Sophia. Or he had one. We finally fired her this week."

That meant the nanny had been in *both* houses.

"Did your housekeeper or anyone that regularly visited your house come to this house?"

Jessica shook her head. "No. Just Sophia. And she only came here a few times."

That was a relief. I didn't have to worry about tracking down anyone else. Which simplified things. It had to be the boo hag. "Did Sophia change recently? Did you notice anything different?" I took a sip of water. All this talking was hard on my throat, but I had to push through it.

"Yes. Her roommate disappeared and was declared dead. Sophia got…weird is the best way I can describe it. At first, we blamed her weirdness on the grief. It can do strange things to people, but then we were so distracted by everything in the house we just let her stay. When we moved here, we didn't need her as much. And then we started to notice things were worse after she was here. So, we fired her. Even if we felt crazy for it. We didn't have a legitimate reason to fire her, but she just…wasn't right anymore."

"You made a very good call. You should always trust your gut, even if it doesn't always make immediate sense. The Spirit works in us that way. Just a feeling or a thought guiding you. So, don't feel bad at all about listening to that voice in your soul."

"Wait. She really was the problem? Did we make a mistake by letting her stay?" Timothy's gaze darted around all of us.

"You didn't make a mistake. This isn't your fault. Sophia changed and opened a doorway into the supernatural. The thing plaguing your son is supernatural," I said to Timothy and Jessica. "I'm going to tell you plainly what it is, and if you have questions, you can ask at any time."

They both nodded their agreement.

"Sophia opened a portal in your attic and another smaller one in this house."

"A what?" Jessica's mouth dropped open. "What does that even mean? A portal to *where*?"

"To Hell."

Her reaction—a gasp, paling skin, open mouth—confirmed my assumption that it wasn't them. There was no way they'd done anything supernatural, let alone Satanic, in their house. They didn't help Sophia, either.

"Do you know what a boo hag is?" I asked.

Jessica laughed. "You have to be kidding. That's not a real thi…" She trailed off when she noticed I wasn't laughing. "You're not joking?"

"No. I'm not joking, but it won't be bothering you again. At some point, Sophia was taken over by a boo hag, who opened portals to Hell that let demons into your yellow house, and another portal that let demons into this house." Their eyes grew wide. "I closed both portals, but there's a lingering demon." I handed my water to Tessa, then focused on Braden. "And it's time to send it back where it belongs."

"Wait." Timothy scooted forward on the couch. "You're saying my son is what? Possessed?"

"That's exactly what I'm saying."

"Do we need a priest or what?" Jessica asked.

"Nope. I'm going to fix it for you. Can I have your son's full name?" My voice was getting raspier by the second, but this wouldn't take long. I was almost done, and then I could rest.

"Braden Michael McDaniel," Timothy answered without hesitation.

I gave Jessica a smile. "Good, solid name."

She laughed softly. "Yeah. I guess. Will you please help my baby?"

"I'd be happy to." I limped over to the couch—waving Phoenix away when he came after me—and I grasped the bright red tie, ignoring the demon that hissed at me. It was a lesser one, and now that I'd closed the portal, it was weak.

If this had only been going on a couple of weeks, it hadn't gained enough strength to withstand the pull of the portal without paying a steep cost. I wasn't sure if it had been bigger before this, but now it was just the size of a kitten.

I burned the tie to nothing. "In the name of Jesus—" The demon started to scream as I spoke. "I cast you out and away from His servant, Braden Michael McDaniel. The door to his soul is closed, and you will never return." I pointed to the floor. "*Aperta*."

The demon screamed louder now, but I refused to even acknowledge it. I gripped its hands, pulled it, and then threw it at the portal. "*Claudare*."

Braden gasped and started crying, calling for his mom, climbing onto her lap like a little monkey. She cuddled him, rocking back and forth on the couch, patting his back, whispering that everything was okay, and from the glimpse I got of his face, Braden's color was back.

She wasn't wrong. Everything was going to be very okay for Braden.

Good. This was really, truly *good*.

I wished I'd gotten a power boost from that, but it was a tiny demon, and I was so hurt. If I felt a lift, I couldn't tell. I was left with almost no energy, so I spit the rest out as quickly as I could. "Braden will be fine now, and all the portals are closed. Your house and this one have been cleared of all the demons that were haunting it. If you want, you can have it blessed by a priest or a pastor. However, it does look like the boo hag did some damage to your house. It's a bit of a mess. But it should be okay to live in again, as long as you feel comfortable with it."

"I don't know if we can go back there. I..." Timothy swallowed as he stared at me with wide eyes. "This is almost too crazy to believe. It feels so surreal, except it happened."

"You can sell your house and leave this awful chapter of your life closed. I wouldn't blame you, and the house is clear. So, don't worry about whoever moves in there next."

"And Braden is fine? The demon that had him won't come back?" Jessica cuddled her son to her, running her hand up and down his back even as his crying lessened.

"It won't come back. Braden's fine. He'll need to eat. Build up his strength. As I said before, an IV might not be a bad idea if he hasn't been keeping fluids down, but that's between you and your doctor." I studied the exhausted parents. "Think about going to church, okay? It'll help all of you. The supernatural realm is real, and you need to strengthen your spiritual armor. Especially now that you've had this experience. You'll be sensitive to the other realm."

They nodded. "Anything," Jessica said. "We'll do anything."

She said that now, but she might change her mind. That was up to her. "I'll have Tessa give you my card. If you have questions or something comes up, call me. I'm happy to talk to you or give advice. And if anything starts happening again, definitely call me right away. Okay?"

"Thank you," Jessica said. "We are so thankful you were here. That you came. I can't—" Her voice broke, but she didn't need to say more.

"Don't worry. It's what I do." I looked back at my friends. "It's what we do." I tugged on my ear, and Tessa nudged Phoenix.

I was grateful as he took the few steps to close the distance and swept me into his arms. There was no way I could get up again. Now that this was done, I was *done.*

"We'll let you guys get some rest," Phoenix said as he turned toward the door.

"We have a care team to help if that would be of use." Tessa kept talking, but the world was graying out.

I rested my head back against Phoenix's arms. "Passing out, now," I whispered to Phoenix as my eyelids grew heavy. "I want to go home, please."

"Okay, babe." I felt us going downstairs. "Dastien told me the doc is waiting with the SUV. Just rest. I got you."

I let the darkness slowly take me, knowing I was safe.

Everyone was safe.

I'd done a good job, and now I just wanted to sleep.

And go home. To my own bed. My new bed with its mountain of pillows and my lovely new butter soft, warm duvet.

I needed the Sanctuary.

And Phoenix.

"You got me, babe. I'm not going anywhere."

"That's good." I could feel his warmth and the sound of his heart, and I fell into a blissful sleep.

CHAPTER THIRTY-THREE

PHOENIX

I PACED THE HOSPITAL ROOM. It was a plain, very basic room. Just one bed, though. Which was good. We didn't have to worry about filtering our conversations because she was sharing a room with another patient.

The bed took up most of the room, but there was a big window and a recliner chair. I'd sat in it for a while, but when I called Sam's mom to walk her through everything that had happened, I'd gotten up to pace.

Ten steps to one end of the room. Five down the length. Ten to the head of Sam's bed. And then I started over again.

"This sounds like quite a trip," Ana said when I finished telling her about what had happened. "The tests all sound like she'll be okay. Has she had fluids?"

"Yes. We've given her two bags so far, but she's still asleep."

"Has she eaten?" Ana asked. Her voice was calm, but I knew she had to be worried.

I was still worried, and I'd talked to a team of doctors who swore to me she'd be okay.

"Not since dinner." I glanced at my watch. The sun had risen on our way to the hospital, but we didn't have to wait in the ER. The pack doc had privileges at the hospital and got her admitted quickly. "She's been mostly out of it. She slept through the CT, but the concussion is mild, or else we'd be stuck here for at least a few days. She can go home whenever she wants, which will be when she wakes up. One of the last things she said to me before she fell asleep was that she wanted to go home."

"She always wants to go home. She needs to feel safe, and this is her safe place."

"I get that." What else was I forgetting to tell Ana? "Doc said she'll need to go screen-free for a bit while her brain heals, but…"

"She's been through worse, Phoenix. She's tough. She'll be okay." Ana was trying to comfort me, and I appreciated it, but I wasn't sure I could be comforted. Not until Sam was awake and she could tell me herself how she was feeling.

"I just…" I paused my pacing to stand over Samantha. "She scared me."

"I get that. I do. I've been there so many times."

My eyes burned, and I cleared my throat, trying to shove the feelings away. "But, um…I have someone on standby at a place with really good *migas* for her. I have a coffee ready to go in a cold cup. I was kind of a jerk about it. I made one of the guys here FaceTime me while he made it then bring it to me."

Ana laughed softly.

I started pacing again. "And she's had enough fluids that I'm not going to hesitate to give it to her." I wasn't going to fight with Ana about that. She could be unhappy with me, but if Sam wanted her coffee, I was giving her the coffee.

"Already taking her side, huh?" There was a smile in her voice.

"Yeah." I leaned against the wall by the window and closed my eyes. "I've never been so scared in my life. That monster had her and…" I swallowed. "I don't know how she's okay, Ana. She hit the pavement hard, and then her head hit the wall in the attic, she bounced when she hit the floor…it was bad. Her whole side and back are seriously bruised, and I was worried there was some internal bleeding or that her back was broken, but everything came back clear. Just bruised."

"Not going to lie, Nix. That sounds really bad. Where was Eli?"

"He…it's complicated. But he didn't show until the fight was over."

Ana made a frustrated sound. "She's okay, though. Right? There isn't something you're forgetting to tell me?" Her voice was a little more high-pitched than normal, finally showing her nerves. "You sound pretty upset for someone who keeps saying everything is okay."

Somehow hearing the worry in Ana's voice made feel like I wasn't totally unhinged for freaking out. "It's just me. I can't settle down. The pack doc and the team here all agree that she's mostly fine. Just beat up. Her ankle is sprained but not broken. He gave us a brace for it, and the doc said it should be fully healed in a week or two."

Ana grunted. "She's not going to like that."

"Nope. She's got some bruises around her neck from where the monster strangled her, but those will fade. When she was awake, she said her throat was sore, but the docs said that was normal for strangulation victims." I swallowed down the waves of fear and anger and helplessness that made me want to throw up. "She has some cuts on her face, so I had them call in a plastic surgeon to look at it. He gave us some special creams, but said it shouldn't scar. She looks bad, though." I rubbed my forehead, trying to stop the headache that was building there from the stress of seeing her hurt. "But they said she's fine." I knew I'd said it over and over again, but mostly I was saying it so I could believe it. "She can go home when she wakes up, and unless she changes her mind, that's what we'll do."

She gave a little *mmm-hmm.* "And how are you, Nix? Have you eaten?"

Was she kidding? "No. Every time I think about it, I want to throw up." I was still shaking. I knew it'd stop sometime, but it felt like I'd been having a panic attack since we got here, and they started talking about scans and brain damage and concern over why she wasn't able to stay awake.

But everything had come back okay, and still, I couldn't settle.

If they'd said she couldn't travel, I was going to ask Dastien to send a plane for Ana. I just…I'd never had to advocate for someone in a hospital setting before. I didn't know if I was making the right calls. The pack doc was great, but was he the best? I had no clue.

But she could travel. Thank God. Once she was rested, we'd go straight home.

"Nix. You have to calm down. You have to breathe. Like this." She took an audible breath and let it out slowly. She did it again and again, and I breathed with her, even though I felt like I was suffocating the first couple times.

"That sounds a little better. Can I give you some advice?"

"Yeah. Anything." She'd been doing this for a lot longer than I had, and I trusted her. Probably even more than I trusted my own mother. I looked at Sam in the bed.

Her chest moved steadily up and down as she breathed. She was fine. Sleeping soundly.

"Get in bed with her."

"Ana," I whisper-shouted at the phone. What the shit was this? "I'm not taking advantage—"

"*Woooow*, Nix. You must be really far gone if you think I meant *that*."

I squeezed my eyes closed. Oh my fucking god. I was an idiot, and beyond embarrassed. "Sorry. My brain isn't working and—"

"Nix. Hear my words. You have to calm down. You have to regulate your own nervous system, or you won't be able to help her. The thing that I found worked for me was physically feeling that she was okay. I would get into the hospital bed with her, and wrap my body around hers. Feeling her warmth, her breathing, her being alive, helped me calm down. She used to think I did that for her comfort, but it was always for mine. I needed it way more than she did. So, get in the hospital bed next to her and close your eyes. Feel her warmth. Feel her breathing. I bet you twenty bucks it'll help calm you down."

"What if she wakes up when I get in the bed?" Sam needed to rest. She was healing while her body slept.

"Then, give her the coffee you just ranted about. She'll call you her savior and be even more in love with you than she already is."

Hearing her mom say that calmed me down a lot. We hadn't said those words to each other. It was too soon, and yet, it wasn't. It really wasn't.

I laughed because this was just too much. I was getting ahead of myself again. "Okay."

"You're doing a great job."

All the air rushed from my lungs and my eyes burned. "You think so?" My voice was way too hight. I cleared my throat. "Truly? You're not just saying that?"

"I know so. I know you love my daughter and are doing the very best for her. Calling in the plastic surgeon to consult about her face was a good call. Demanding a full scan to check for internal bleeding was also great." She paused. "You're doing great. You just need to calm down now."

Right. She said that like it was easy. I pressed a fist to my heart, willing it to slow down as I took measured breaths. My heart didn't even race like this when I was in the middle of a championship game.

"Get in bed with her. Try to rest. You've been up for over twenty-four hours now, and that's not helping your anxiety."

I'd never had trouble with anxiety before, but apparently, seeing Sam getting beaten up by a monster was enough to set me off. That was my limit.

"I'll call Frank and let him know she's okay."

Oh. Right. I hadn't even thought about Frank. "Appreciate it."

"Call me when she wakes up."

"Will do. Talk soon. Bye."

"Bye," Ana said.

I hung up and took the two steps to the hospital bed. Sam was sleeping deeply, and I was really glad for that.

Maybe Ana had a point. It was worth a shot.

I'd showered while Tessa watched over Sam. They'd brought me some of the sweats that they always seemed to have stashed everywhere. Now, I knew why. Werewolves often ended up naked and needed clothes quickly.

But at least I was clean. Which made me feel a little better about climbing into bed with her.

Tessa and Dastien had gone to get food, shower, settle some stuff with the Wayfarers, and most importantly, grab our bags from the house. They'd be back any minute now, and when they got here, we'd wait for Sam to wake up, then fly home. All I had to do was wait, and Ana might be right. Waiting in her bed—and getting some rest, too—might help.

I toed off my shoes and slid onto the bed next to her, laying on my side so I could watch her sleep. I wanted to hold her hand, but I was scared it would wake her up. Instead, I closed my eyes and listened to the sound of her breathing. It was so soft I had to really concentrate to hear it.

I could still *see* the supernatural realm, but while I'd waited for her to get out of her scans, I'd figured out that if I focused hard enough, I could make it go away. It'd been essential here because Sam wasn't kidding, there was too much spiritual noise in the hospital. It was oppressive. But it'd also been helpful.

I'd gone through the hospital and looked into empty rooms until I found the only one that wasn't full of spiritual awfulness. The pack doc made sure that one was her room, and I was grateful.

Her friends in the pack were actually really amazing. I hadn't been around such a genuinely good group of people before. Even Max had grown on me.

Max was the one waiting to order food for Sam as soon as she woke up. He was thankful Sam saved him from losing more pack members. I felt bad for him, but I think he was getting over the realization that Sam wasn't free anymore.

Max and his Wayfarers were planning to stay in Charleston to make sure everything was truly okay before heading to their home base in Colorado. He wanted to do something nice for her before she left, and food was an easy way to do that. A thank you and an apology was what he called it, but I didn't think Sam needed either of those. She wasn't someone to hold a grudge or require a thank you for something she considered her calling.

After a few minutes of lying next to Sam, I realized Ana was right. My heart didn't feel like it was pumping so fast it was going to explode anymore. The tumbling knot in my stomach was slowing and settling. The feeling that I was going to lose her was fading.

I focused on that feeling, and then loosened my vision, letting the spiritual realm fill it again, so that I could stare at the bond between us.

Anchor. That was what he called me. An anchor so her soul never got lost. But Eli had implied more in the attic. She'd asked him to heal her, but he refused. But then he'd asked if we'd found out everything our bond could do, which made me think that the two were connected.

I'd seen the werewolf mates talk to each other through their bonds, but I wondered if maybe I could send strength through ours. Or healing. Or something that could help her.

Wait. I remembered something.

When she was closing the portal in the yellow house, I touched her and wanted to give her some strength, and it seemed to work. I thought I was imagining it or just wanted it to be true, but what if it was? What if I'd done that?

Could I do it again?

There wasn't any harm in trying.

I closed my eyes and thought about the bond. I pictured it in my mind, and then I pictured a white light flowing from my side to her. I pictured her brain healing, the bruises fading, the road rash on her face disappearing, the swelling of her ankle going down, and every other little injury the doctors had cataloged going away.

It was instinctive, and I grew warmer as I focused on that bond.

There was a gasp, and my eyes opened.

Sam stared at me with wide eyes. "Phoenix…"

Whoa. Did that really just work? "Hi, Sam."

"What did you just do?" she whispered.

I studied her face and saw that it was healed. No scrapes. No bruising.

Holy shit. Eli was right. He gave me the key to help her. To truly be the one to help her do what only she could do. This was the biggest gift I could imagine, and I was beyond grateful.

And suddenly I was starving. For food, for her, for the life we'd build together.

I brushed a kiss on her forehead. "My job. I did my job." I leaned forward, and I kissed her.

But it wasn't just a kiss.

It was everything. I poured the strength into it, and when her mouth opened in a gasp, I deepened the kiss until both of us were gasping and pulling at each other and—

Someone knocked on the door, and I realized I was hovering over her on my forearms. "Yep. That's it. I can't keep it in anymore. I love you." I pressed my forehead to hers. "And I'm sorry, but we're just going to have to get married now."

Sam gasped, and her eyes widened, but before she could say anything, the door swung open, slamming into the wall.

"What did you just say?!" Tessa yelled.

Sam and I both started laughing. I was pretty sure Sam thought I was joking, but I wasn't.

I definitely wasn't.

But if she needed time to get used to the idea, that was okay. I could wait.

I moved back to my spot beside her, and Dastien caught my gaze.

He gave me a nod, and I knew what he meant.

The same thing had happened to him when he kissed Tessa. His wolf had chosen for him, and that was it. He would've married her the second he met her. He'd told me that much earlier.

I didn't have a wolf to blame or a bite to give, but I was just as serious.

This was forever.

This wasn't our last battle against evil. God had given me this power—given it to me so that I could guard and protect Samantha—and I would to take my role very, very seriously.

I didn't know when the next battle would come or what tomorrow would bring. It wasn't going to be easy. I knew that much. And we had hurdles to face—like my mother—who was going to have to get over it. Because Sam was it for me.

She was everything.

Whatever life brought us, from here on out, we'd face it together.

TO MY READERS

I hope you enjoyed Book Two of the Days of Iron and Clay!

And if the ending didn't give it away, the romance is going to finally heat up in Book Three. Phoenix is the best, and the way he shows up for Sam? It's going to be epic.

Look for Book Three of Days of Iron and Clay in the Fall/Winter of 2025. I'll have a clearer date for you in a couple months, so stay tuned to my Instagram and Facebook for updates.

Until then, if you haven't yet, check out the Samantha story in the anthology - *Two More Days*.

Join the Ink Monster newsletter for updates, and keep in touch via my Instagram - @aileenerin. That's where you can find me the easiest. I'm usually pretty quick on DMs. 🩶

xoxo

Aileen

ACKNOWLEDGMENTS

Y'all. Y'ALL! The spiritual warfare that I hit while working on this one was legit. Like whoa. But I'm so glad with how it turned out, and I'm hoping you're enjoying the journey that Sam and Phoenix are on.

A special shout out to my editors - Kime Heller-Neal for developmental editing. And Cheri Patton and Kristi Latcham for copy editing!

It's funny that you learn some things about yourself later in life. At least, that's been my experience. Almost two years ago, we found out that Isabella was dyslexic. My mind was blown. How was that possible? The daughter of an author and a film producer? All we do is read and tell stories. But the more I learned about dyslexia, the more I realized that she got it from me. I remembered all the failed spelling tests, the way I struggled in 3rd and 4th grade, and suddenly, it all made sense.

It turns out that being dyslexic is my super power, and I know that it'll be Isabella's, too. She's so dang creative, already writing screenplays and stories. Because it's what fuels our creativity. But it's also why Kime, Cheri, and Kristi have to work so hard to catch all of my million typos.

It takes a team, and I'm so incredibly grateful for their help.

Kime has worked with me for a long time. She helps me bounce ideas around and is always down to chat through any story problems. We go through a few rounds of developmental edits as I hone the story. I don't know how I'd do it without her help and guidance.

Cheri isn't just my copy editor. She also designed the cover of this book and helps me do all the things. I'm fully convinced she can literally do anything she puts her mind to, and SLAY it.

Kristi isn't just my copy editor, either. She's my mother-in-law. She's the best kind of mother-in-law. Because she's like a dear friend, a second mom, and quite possibly the best grandmother in the history of grandmothers. I'm truly blessed.

My daughter is eight—almost nine—and she's begging me to read my books. She even put it in her letter to Santa this year (2024). But she's scared of Harry Potter, soooo, yeah. That's not happening yet. But one day, she'll read this note at the end of this book and know that I couldn't wait to share this with her. Because she's the BEST KID EVER.

My loving, patient husband now expects a call where I tell him I'm going to delete the whole book, burn it to the ground, quit writing forever in the back half of the second act. Why is that part always so hard to write? If any of you can find a way to get around that, let me know. Because seventeen books later, and I still hit that moment in every time. But he's the best, and always so encouraging. If he hadn't pushed me to write, to get my MFA at Seton Hill, to keep going, then I wouldn't be living my dream right now. He showed up for me. So, when you wonder where I got the inspiration for Phoenix, it's Jeremy. He's the ultimate master of go with the flow. ;)

And if you've made it this far, then, thank you, my dear reader. You've made my day by reading my book. Reach out any time. I'd love to hear from you.

Xoxo,

Aileen

Aileen Erin is half-Irish, half-Mexican, and 100% nerd—from Star Wars (prequels don't count) to Star Trek (TNG FTW), she geeks out on Tolkien's linguistics, and has a severe fascination with the supernatural. Aileen has a BS in Radio-TV-Film from the University of Texas at Austin, and an MFA in Writing Popular Fiction from Seton Hill University. She lives with her husband and daughter in Texas, and spends her days doing her favorite things: reading books, creating worlds, and kicking ass.

For more information and updates about Aileen and her books, go to: www.aileenerin.com

Or check her out on:

facebook.com/aelatcham
x.com/aileen_erin
instagram.com/aileenerin
bookbub.com/authors/aileen-erin